Pierce Roberts is a practicing companion animal veterinarian who, in his initial novel, weaves modern day science with the terror of a past century Nazi Death Camp physician.

When he is not practicing his profession, he enjoys family time, grandkid time, fishing, reading and the outdoors.

Dedication

To my wife Kathy, the love of my life

Pierce Roberts

DEATH BY DNA

AUSTIN MACAULEY PUBLISHERS™

LONDON • CAMBRIDGE • NEW YORK • SHARJAH

A CIP catalogue record for this title is available from the British Library.

ISBN 9781787107540 (Paperback)
ISBN 9781787107557 (E-Book)
www.austinmacauley.com

First Published (2017)
Austin Macauley Publishers Ltd.
25 Canada Square
Canary Wharf
London
E14 5LQ

Acknowledgements

Thanks to Andrea Doherty who provided the initial formatting, editing and story advice that helped develop an idea into a publishable book.

Also thanks to my long-time friend Marty, whose extraordinary sense of humor is reflected in the characters' interactions. Irish humor at its best.

Thanks to Austin Macauley's team for all their hard work and guidance.

Chapter 1
Rural Northwest Wisconsin

April 11

The odor from the cow's retained placenta was so foul that just the act of placing a protected, well-gloved arm vaginally into the animal gave even the most seasoned veterinarian's gag reflex a solid test. The best you could hope for was a good breeze to blow away the putrid odor while you held your breath, trying not to inhale the smell of rot and pus. Freeing the decaying placenta from the uterine wall would allow the cow to continue to cleanse herself by contraction of her womb.

A cow's life revolved around eating, drinking and reproducing so she could continue producing milk, and this was a valuable Holstein, an exceptional producer of milk with a high butterfat percentage. She was a sturdy cow with a large black and white frame, but hadn't been able to freely deliver her big bull calf. A farmer assisted mechanical 'pulling' of the calf resulted in a life on the ground, but a stubborn placenta still attached to the uterine wall. A diseased uterus could cause infertility, which was a death sentence on most dairies.

This cow was Tom's second patient of the day, and he knew he would probably have to eat lunch in his truck because he would reek of rot before the morning was over. The good news was at least he wasn't working on pigs which all smelled bad to him.

Tom O'Dell's life as a large animal veterinarian was starting to wear him down. The relentless daily travel—twenty-four hours a day, if needed — to the local dairy farms, which were his primary focus, along with the physically demanding work of wrestling reluctant or recumbent patients, was starting to cost him his good nature and quite possibly his health. He worked long, hard days and despite all that effort, he had only scraped by financially since his divorce, although money wasn't a huge factor for him. He felt his efforts made a real difference in the lives of his patients and the families who worked much harder than he did. He hated complainers and whiners, so he sucked it up and did his job with a quiet, proud dedication.

Today was his thirty-eighth birthday and he had kept it quiet. Despite a call from his mom early in the morning, it was like any other day. But this day marked another year gone so much of his travel time was spent thinking about his life and wondering if he needed to focus more on himself. Here he was in his late thirties, a failed marriage, childless and working as a solo practitioner — a rarity in this modern age. He questioned how long it would take before he was injured on the job, and then resigned to a future of aches, pains or disability. A physical injury was the reality of working with thousand-pound animals. Just a swift kick to the gonads could have him singing soprano, or the sudden turn of a boney head that was poorly restrained by a farmer could render him unconscious, fracture his jaw or skull, or damage his eyes. Hell, he knew a lot of colleagues who had been injured or died when their mobile-clinic trucks crashed on icy roads. One friend had simply fallen on a muck-slicked floor in a milking parlor, which had left him permanently confined to a wheel chair.

Tonight, though, he planned on being totally unavailable while relaxing with a great medium rare steak off the grill and a couple of ice-cold beers. A night dedicated to only himself — no calls, no running out, and no problems.

Tomorrow he would start over again, like some rodent on an exercise wheel.

Chapter 2

Tom O'Dell was a physically strong, albeit worn out, veterinarian. His Irish heritage, which had given him jet-black hair, blue green eyes and a tall muscular frame, also fueled a stubborn work ethic, which had sustained him through ten years of college at the University of Wisconsin. Although he wasn't from a rural background, Tom had always felt more akin to animals than to humans. Growing up, his family had raised and competed in field trials with some of the best black Labs in the country. Anyone could reliably find a lab in his truck or at his side.

As a small child he had raised rabbits and homing pigeons, but what he loved the most was to be in the woods deer hunting, at a trout stream fishing, or in his waders at a frosty marsh waiting on ducks. He had developed outdoor survival skills, which along with his natural self-reliance and determination, gave him the confidence that no matter what he faced each day, he could get through it.

Tom's goal when he entered the University of Wisconsin was not to become a veterinarian. He originally planned to study chemistry and become a teacher like his mom. His father sold insurance for a living, but lived to raise black Labs, not yellow or chocolate, which the family felt were socially inferior and therefore not real Labs. Tom, it turned out, had absolutely no interest with insurance sales, but plenty of interest in the dogs.

In college it took only one introductory class in Animal Science to direct his attention to farm animals. That first class led to others in dairy, beef, and horse production. Those classes then led to others in nutrition and meat science. Rapidly, he found himself craving all sorts of agricultural classes such as agronomy, agriculture economics and sociology. After those first four years, he graduated without the chemistry degree, but as the proud recipient of a Bachelor's in Animal Science.

He pondered whether or not he should pursue a teaching certificate and go work in a rural school system or enter post-graduate school for an advanced degree. Shortly after his May graduation, everything changed when he accepted an invitation to ride on farm calls with a local veterinarian who often visited his parent's kennel. That one ride turned into a summer job. After few weeks, he realized he wanted to practice veterinary medicine.

Tom returned to UW that same fall to start the prerequisite courses needed to apply for admission to the Vet School. He carried heavy class loads and, by midwinter of his second post graduate year, he started the application process with all the required testing and interviews. By late that May, he had a provisional acceptance as a first alternate pending completion of his spring classes, and when a female applicant turned down her acceptance in order to go to Med School, he was admitted to the last available spot in the fall class.

Veterinary School was a four-year intensive study marathon that honed skills to diagnose and treat all species of animals. Classes in internal medicine broken down into body systems such as neurology, cardiology, gastroenterology and ophthalmology developed his diagnostic and treatment skills. Anatomy and physiology prepared students for their surgery cases. Those long days and nights of hard study conditioned Tom for the difficult cases and the physical trials he would face as a future veterinarian.

At the start of his third year, Tom looked forward more and more to a career as a large animal practitioner, especially working on his first love, dairy cows. There was something about the smell and nature of a cow that appealed to him and he focused all his elective study on bovines. He felt confident and at home working on them.

He graduated fifteenth in a class of ninety-two and, after passing his state and national board exams, he accepted an associate position in the Racine area and was basically tossed into the fire with little or no direct oversight. He struggled each day, never made a serious error and gradually learned the art of veterinary practice, which he found more difficult than the science.

Those two years as an associate was enough and he searched out a good area to start his own dairy practice in northwestern Wisconsin. It seemed the perfect spot to build a good practice and have plenty of personal time to enjoy the outdoors. That was his plan, but as it turned out, his work, which was his passion, gradually consumed his life and with it, his happiness.

Chapter 3

Now ten years later, he had enjoyed his birthday steak, but not without feeling guilty for ignoring the persistent ringing of his phone.

"It's my birthday dammit, leave me alone," he mumbled to no one.

Tom had recently started to feel more and more like he was being watched, under a microscope like one of his test samples. He questioned whether coming home each day with only Jed as company was isolating him intellectually and causing a bit of paranoia to surface.

Maybe that was it! There had been no one to complain to or receive sympathy from since Sara had left him three years ago. He really didn't blame her for the divorce. Who wanted a worn-out, stinky husband who was rarely home and had no quality time for her? She wanted to live; Tom lived to work.

Already he was on his fourth beer and starting to feel more and more sorry for himself. Drifting into a gentle alcohol-induced snooze he was rattled awake by a loud pounding on his back porch door and Jed's defensive barking.

"Darn you, Jed, you're giving us away!" he said not too loudly, and reluctantly pushed his way out of his leather easy chair, walked over to the mirror, ran his fingers through his thick hair and mumbled, "What the hell?"

Through the screen he was relieved to see his good friend and former classmate, Brad Upton, a USDA veterinarian, at the door reaching over to greet Jed.

"Watch out, you varmint, that dog will have you for a snack!" Tom yelled out.

"You call that a dog?" Brad retorted.

That got them both laughing heartily and Jed decided it was a good time to do an enthusiastic tail wagging, drool-laden Lab dance to signal his approval of Brad's visit.

"Happy birthday, you old SOB!" Brad announced, handing over a six-pack of PBR to his longtime friend. "Surprised I remembered? Well, I didn't, but Ellen did. Had to come over to talk to you on official business anyway, so I figured I'd kill two birds and chance you'd be home. Didn't figure to find you half in the bag!"

"Wait just a minute, I'm not close to that and if you can remember, I was always able to drink you under the table with one kidney tied behind my back." Tom answered. "So what is so "official" about the official business you're here on?"

"Well, it's a pretty complicated situation, but after we have a cold one or two, I'll go over it and see what you think."

Chapter 4

"There has been some unusual mass die-offs of unique animal species around the world over the last nine months," Brad started to explain. "You probably heard about the more publicized ones like the flock of over 100,000 blackbirds that dropped like feathered hail on Kansas City, the fur seal deaths on Hudson Bay, bottlenose dolphins off the Outer Banks of North Carolina, and the millions of monarch butterflies that fell from the sky while migrating through Mexico. All these deaths were acute with no anatomical, physical or pathological reason determined as the cause. Mysterious, but the world's leading biologist and naturalists reasoned that these incidents were not out of the ordinary and could be expected from time to time. Unfortunately, they were wrong. Dead wrong!

"It turns out these highly publicized incidents were just the tip of the ecological iceberg. On every continent, there were smaller-scale die-offs of single species ranging from fewer than fifty, up to tens of thousands in each event. In every case we know of, the government in the affected countries arranged complete clinical pathology of those animals. Some testing was done in prestigious health protection facilities such as our CDC, France's Pasteur Institute, Britain's Center for Public Health, or the Russian Institute of Bio pathology, confirming field results which essentially report no disease process or lesions noted. The World Health Organization reviewed all the field data generated from the testing and recorded it in a common databank.

"There didn't seem to be any universal link that could wipe out only an individual specie of animal at a time, and we are talking about everything from a small invertebrate to the largest vertebrates on the planet. The only common thing we found was the deaths were sudden, almost like throwing a light switch, and that in these identified kill zones, no other animal was affected, even if they were a closely related species. For example, mule deer and elk grazing in the same field and only the elk die. The same thing in Brazil. A rain forest full of birds and only the blue and gold macaws die. It's unbelievably scary!

"I've been with the USDA for all but two years since we graduated UW and I can tell you there is a real sense of panic in the ranks. You understand our mission at the USDA since you deal with us on a daily basis in everything you do, whether it is always obvious or not. We are to protect public health by assuring quality in all aspects of agricultural production. The mission lines have become a little blurred as we are now a huge bureaucracy, so we seem to get involved in a lot more than just federal safety regulations. This die-off problem has now been placed squarely on the agency's lap and when it did, it fell like a giant turd.

"So far as we know, there have been no reports of domesticated animal deaths. However, if only one or two died here or there and no competent necropsies were performed or reported, we would never know. Any animal that dies without an identifiable disease or pathology should now be suspect. The real question is: suspect of what?"

Tom could sense that Brad, a normally easy-going, roll-with-the-punches kind of guy was giving him some serious information. The question was *why*?

"So," Brad continued, "the crap is about to hit the fan and we, as veterinarians, are standing right in front of it. Every one of us in the field needs to thoroughly investigate animal deaths and perform standardized necropsy and tissue sampling procedures on each animal or group of animals that die suspect. Your regular duties will come second as this is considered a national security threat, so essentially as a sworn public health officer, you and every other veterinarian in the country has been drafted into the service of the country. This could be a short-lived nothing or challenge the survival of every species on the planet, including Homo sapiens.

"The current plan is that each state, based on size and agriculture economy, would be divided into one to four monitoring zones. Each zone would have a regional USDA vet in charge and one veterinary field captain directing over site and coordinating the rest of the field teams. Refusal to serve on a team would result in loss of USDA accreditation so, in essence, anyone refusing would be put out of business.

"As regional veterinarian in charge, I am setting up my districts and I want you to lead Wisconsin Zone 4, which would include all your current coverage and four additional counties, so an area of about 50 by 110 miles."

Tom looked hard at Brad and instead of asking *why me*, he quietly got up and walked over to his vintage GE refrigerator, leaned in and pulled two PBRs out, wiping the damp bottles with an old dish towel. Turning to Brad he announced, "These are mine, you want some, you can get your own.

"So, if I understand correctly, I must accept this 'honor' and work on this project or you will shut me down—no choice. What the hell happens to my practice while I'm screwing around helping the USDA?"

"You and the three other Wisconsin area captains will be flying to Atlanta for three weeks of clinical pathology training including toxicology and all the other 'ologies.' While you are gone, we will contract a relief practitioner to cover your practice needs. When you return, you will basically be on call to handle all the investigations in your region and be responsible for training the other vets in your area in forensic necropsy. This has to be a no-mistake, no-error effort. Anyone of us could discover information that provides the breakthrough we need.

"Just think of it as a three-week CE course where you will come out better in clinical pathology, and be part of a very important program to protect the nation from a potentially new form of terror. You will be compensated for your time and your practice should be just fine in your absence.

"Think Atlanta in the spring, sharing time with colleagues and receiving training that will make you a better vet. So good that maybe you could win a Nobel Prize in Science. Now, pass me a damn beer!"

Chapter 5
Atlanta, Georgia

Brad only stayed until ten p.m., understanding that Tom had a lot to think about, organize and complete in less than a week. Tomorrow, Tom's relief vet would come in at dinner time and he would have to spend the next several days going over the cases, familiarizing him with the territory, and learning the practice philosophy. Tom would have to call his vendors and authorize the new vet's purchases of supplies and drugs, and he would need to travel to his parent's home to put Jed in their care, maybe the toughest thing of all.

His innate survival instincts were rapidly kicking in, and he found himself on virtual mental autopilot as he completed each task. Soon he was packing to leave, a little apprehensive, a bit nervous, but also excited about the new challenging role he was about to take on.

His Delta shuttle service jet landed at Hartsfield-Jackson Atlanta International Airport late on Saturday afternoon. He was surprised to see on the landing approach, the difference between early spring in Georgia with all the flowering trees and shrubs compared to the patchy snow-covered landscape he had just left in Wisconsin. By the time he returned home in three weeks, he was afraid he would have missed that transition from barren to beautiful as spring broke winter's icy grip. He would have to forego the start of trout and walleye fishing (although, anymore, he rarely had time to go). The one thing he would miss the most was traveling on his rounds to visit his patients on the greenest of green pastures. Plus, it was comforting to see the new calves that initiated lactation, which everyone in the area relied on. Three weeks in spring would be a long time to be away from his own slice of heaven—and Jed.

As Tom worked his way down to the baggage claim area, he was surprised at the enormity of the airport. Most everyone was rushing, appeared stressed and a little disoriented. As he weaved his way through the amorphous crowd, he found himself self-consciously sniffing at his shirt, an old habit making sure the aromas of his profession weren't his aftershave — Eau de Ewe, Bovine #9, or Pigsty Guy. Today, thankfully, the light sent of Old Spice on his collar reassured him.

The baggage claim area held a surprise as he saw Brad's familiar tall, bald, husky shape and wide smile greeting him.

"I thought you might need a lift to the flea bag hotel we are staying at," Brad joked. "That only seems appropriate, putting vets in a buggy place."

"I'm not worried about fleas, but maybe all the other stuff you government types might drag along," Tom retorted, extending his hand, feeling the strength of their friendship.

"Grab your bags, Tom, and we'll go jump in my company car and get something to eat before you check into the Bates Motel. There are a lot of us staying there, but they are putting us all over the city since we have about 350 attendees. That's a bunch of brainpower. They hope we can make a real difference!"

Their ride to the Nelson's Place Diner only took fifteen minutes and they could see the new Residence Inn Extended Stay Hotel from their table. Brad noticed Tom's visible relief when he saw the new, modern building, their home for the next three weeks.

Realizing now how hungry he was, Tom ordered the chicken and waffles, and Brad followed with a big order of corned beef hash, eggs and grits. A real southern start to their big adventure.

After their meal, Brad dropped Tom at the hotel before heading back to the airport to pick up another incoming veterinarian.

"I'll pick you up at noon tomorrow for lunch, unless you plan on going to church to repent of your sins. I thought then we could take in a Braves game. I have meetings in the early morning, so you might want to walk around the area and take in the big city—give you a chance to stretch your legs. There is a great park about four blocks east of here with lots of hiking trails and paths."

"So, basically you're telling me to go fly a kite."

"Just like I've been telling you for years."

Chapter 6

The next morning, Tom woke automatically at his normal start time of five a.m. When he remembered that he wasn't in bed at home, he groaned and rolled over several times before deciding to get up anyway.

Tom's room was a super clean and comfortable rental suite. It was nicely set up so he could reheat in the microwave and keep food and beverages in the small refrigerator. Best of all, the AC allowed him to keep the room just the way he liked it — only slightly warmer than the refrigerator. *So far, so good*, he thought as he cranked up the Mr. Coffee.

He called Enterprise Car Rental and arranged a small, compact car to be dropped the next morning before he left for orientation at the CDC. He really didn't want to rely on Brad to taxi him back and forth, especially if they ended up on different schedules.

He parted his curtains and saw the sun was up, bright and inviting, so he decided a walk in the fresh air down to that park Brad had mentioned might be a good idea. Besides, he most likely would be sitting on his butt a lot in the next several weeks, something he never did for more than a few hours so any physical activity would be welcomed.

As he left the hotel, the early morning sun was warm on his face, but he could feel the heaviness of the humid air as he started walking at a brisk pace. The streets were fairly quiet, mostly vacant and he reasoned most of the locals were getting ready for church services or just plain weren't up yet. After several minutes, he removed his light jacket having underestimated the warming of the early spring day. The morning birds were carrying on big time as they foraged for food or looked for their mates. That noisy racket brought a smile to his face as he was thinking that, just like the birds, the early vet gets the worm.

He found the park Brad had described and started slowly walking on one of the trails that led into a wooded area. About fifteen minutes into the walk, he came to a beautiful natural stone formation being warmed in the Georgia sun. It seemed a good place to rest for a few minutes.

Tom picked out a nice group of larger rocks and climbed up to seat himself, and as he found a comfortable position, he felt something squish under his hand. Startled, he jerked his hand away to find a dead gecko flattened to the rock. Feeling badly, he brushed the tiny carcass away and wiped his hand on his jeans. He moved to a secondary spot and, while surveying that area, found two more dead geckos. He stood on the rock shading his eyes and saw another dozen or so dead remains, a few of which the birds had been working on.

He knew this couldn't be normal and remembered why he was in Georgia — could this be similar to the die-offs of the other animals? He climbed down and walked over to a picnic area, found a covered garbage can and pulled a McDonald's cup and lid out. Tom took it to a nearby drinking fountain and rinsed it thoroughly. Returning to the rocks, he pulled out his phone and recorded the scene before carefully picking up six of the dead lizards and placing them in the cup. He then started back to the hotel.

No ballgame today, he thought as he left Brad a voicemail.

Chapter 7

Tom stopped at a 7 Eleven on the way back and purchased pint-sized Ziploc bags, a Diet Coke, Lysol spray, and some antibacterial hand soap. When he entered his room, he immediately washed his hands and his pant leg where he had wiped after smashing the first lizard. Then he sprayed himself down with the Lysol. Feeling better that he wasn't immediately about to die, he gently slid each specimen from the cup in an individual bag and wrapped the bags in a plastic grocery sack. He placed them into the mini refrigerator and called Brad again, this time with a message reflecting a sense of urgency.

Brad called back in a few minutes apologizing and listened without comment as Tom explained in detail what had transpired that morning in the park.

"See, I told you it was a nice park," he began, "but I'm stunned that maybe we have something happening here right under our noses. You stay put while I make some phone calls and I'll pick you up in twenty minutes or so. We'll go to the park and do some investigating."

"So, no ball game today?"

"Not a chance, but maybe you just hit a home run!"

Tom ended the call and mumbled to himself, "more like a foul ball or bean ball!"

That twenty-minute promise turned into more like forty-five and when Tom opened his door, Brad was pouring sweat and looked really stressed. Tom had never seen Brad break a sweat in all the years he had known him.

"Sorry it took so long, but I had to jump through a bunch of hoops to get some basic protective gear and sampling equipment. Did get a real cool Geiger counter. Damn bureaucrats!"

"So, this is like an end-of-the-world investigation?"

"Maybe for those geckos in your ice box and those folks trying to save 15% on their car insurance!"

That was more like the normal Brad, the jokester. Tom laughed, but felt like spraying himself again with the Lysol. He resisted the urge, reasoning that he was always in muck and working with diseased animals and carcasses so he must have immunity to all types of weird pathogens. Plus, he ate all kinds of fast foods, so if that hadn't killed him, it wasn't likely some damn out-of-this-world disease would stand a chance.

Brad's big Ford Explorer peeled out on the hot parking lot asphalt as they left the hotel. Neither spoke as they made their way to the park.

Chapter 8

By the time they arrived at the park, there was bright yellow CDC Restricted Entrance tape draping the park's main entrance. Two Atlanta Metro Parks vehicles and two white CDC vans were parked close by with their lights flashing brightly.

So much for a quiet Sunday's walk in the park, Tom thought.

Brad pulled up behind the CDC vans and scanned the area for a familiar face. Everyone looked very business-like and a little out of sorts except one woman who was obviously in charge, directing the others. She turned out to be Brad's very good friend, Dr. Kate Vensky, a USDA colleague and somewhat of a veterinary genius. She was talking intently with the two uniformed Metro Rangers, a short black woman in scrubs, and two men wearing bright yellow t-shirts with CDC prominently displayed on the fronts and backs. Brad motioned to Tom to follow him, and they made their way over to the assembled group.

As they approached, Kate looked up and smiled warmly as she greeted Brad. She wore an olive, fitted t-shirt and khaki shorts, and her hair was pulled back to fend off the Atlanta heat.

"Looks like this investigation has taken a sudden turn downhill. How the heck are you, Brad?"

"I'm better now that I see you are here! I didn't realize you were going to be here also. I thought it was just us peons that needed a trip to re-education camp."

"I was put in charge of the entire project just yesterday. Aren't you lucky? I'll make sure you get the special treatment you deserve!"

"Kate, this is my friend and colleague Dr. Tom O'Dell. He's the one who found the geckos. But I have to warn you, Tom is in dairy practice so be careful, he's used to recognizing bullshit!"

Kate smiled and extended her hand to Tom, "Pleasure to meet you, Tom, but any friend of Brad's probably should have his head examined."

"He did have it examined, but they couldn't find anything," Brad chuckled.

"Leaping lizards, great to meet you also, Kate!" Tom laughed.

Brad met Kate at his first USDA orientation meeting he attended after joining the animal health service ten years before. She was a regional supervisor even though she was five years younger than him, primarily because she was a hard-working, extremely intelligent person, who was able to finish her course work in a compressed fashion, receiving multiple degrees in less time than it took most individuals just to get through Vet School. She was one of three people in the world holding a Ph.D. in Forensic Veterinary Medicine that had been sponsored by the Department of a Homeland Security. To top all that, Kate was a stunning brunette with the build of a beach volleyball player.

Brad scanned her left hand for a ring and thought, *'She's still single, but what man could keep up with her anyway?'* He knew because he had tried a long time ago.

Kate started the introductions. "I'll try to get everyone introduced before we get started."

"These two gentlemen are my colleagues with the USDA, Drs. Brad Upton and Tom O'Dell from Wisconsin; Dr. Susan Moore with technicians, Bill Thomas and Ted Smith of the CDC; and Greater Atlanta Metro Park rangers, Nick Wysinski and Mary Broen. This park is about 200 acres and contains two miles of trails. There are three designated entrances, but the rangers feel that you could enter almost anywhere, as there are deer and kid trails in and out all over. So the plan right now is to clear the public out and bring in some tracker beagles to see if the gecko problem extends beyond the area where Tom found the originals. And remember, when the media shows up, the cover story is that we are looking for a possible rabid fox that was spotted this morning. That should keep the foot traffic down for a few days and depending on what we find, allow us to keep the park closed. If there are no questions or comments, we will have Dr. O'Dell lead us to the primary location. Ranger Broen, will you please point out any unique features of this park, and any other possible areas that we could investigate? Tom, I'll let you take it from here."

They started up the path leading away from the main park entrance and Tom started to describe what happened that morning.

"I got here shortly after seven and started on a brisk pace up this far trail through the pine grove and picnic area. About five hundred yards in or so I came to a beautiful large stone formation that was in the full morning sun and decided to climb up and take in some of that sunshine."

Ranger Broen pointed ahead to the rocky area.

"That is Armistead Rocks. Most all the prominent park features are named after confederate war heroes. That natural granite formation covers about two acres and is full of green anoles, which I think is what you are calling geckos. Also hiding in those rocks are copperheads, rattlesnakes — at least two species — as well as all kinds of small mammals, coons, skunks and possums. Any dead vertebrates would most likely be consumed in short order by residents of the rocks or scavenging birds."

"Isn't that just peachy," Brad complained.

Tom continued, "So I climbed up over there went to sit down and crushed a lizard under my left hand as I was swinging myself up on one of those big rocks. I first thought I had killed it, but when I moved, I saw that there were more along the top of many of the rocks. Pretty much everywhere. I picked up a half dozen which I have in my hotel room refrigerator because I was afraid they would degrade in the heat or be eaten by scavengers."

As they got closer, Kate took over and gave her instructions.

"We will do a walk or climb through of the area just to survey it, so be careful. Watch out for any creature, alive or dead, including invertebrates. Don't touch or pick up anything, but use your phone's camera to record things you feel might be important. We will head east to west first about ten yards apart, if possible. Be careful on those rocks and shout if you see anything dead or alive and what it is."

They lined up and started into the rocks, and since it was the warmest time of the day, Tom figured there would be a lot of creatures sunning themselves.

Barely a minute had passed when the shout-outs began.

"One dead anole here!"

"Another one here... and another!"

"Damn, a very large copperhead here, alive and he looks pissed!"

There were also skeletal remains of snakes, birds and either a raccoon or opossum. The only freshly dead were the small lizards and they had counted over forty.

Brad had out his pocket Geiger counter and tested around the tiny carcasses, but only registered small amounts of background radiation, which most likely was coming from the large rocks themselves. Kate yelled and motioned for them to assemble.

"Well, that was interesting. I think this is a true idiopathic die-off — unique to this lizard only, and there will need to be a full investigation with complete testing of the animals and area. I'll order in more investigators so this park will stay closed until we feel we can't gain any more information by keeping out the public. Those tracker beagles should narrow our search area to specific points, so will the rangers cordon off any area they hit on? I'll give each of you a specific task to move this investigation forward till then."

"And God help us," Tom muttered under his breath.

Chapter 9
CDC Conference Center for Forensic Investigation

Next Day

"Okay, it's time to get started. Would everyone take his or her seats, please? The longer we take to get started, the longer we will be here today. And we have a lot to cover," Kate announced from the stage podium.

There was some audible groaning and the usual suspects feinting deafness as they shuffled to their assigned seating. The newly built auditorium was a state-of-the-art multimedia classroom with comfortable individual workstations that allowed the participants easy interaction with the presentations. The room smelled of fresh paint and new carpet.

At the back of the six-hundred-seat auditorium was the presenter's platform, which was flanked on either side by a jumbo curved screen 'E', or Exceptional Hi-Def multimedia video screens. Much like sports venue screens, these were state-of-the-art, with the sharpest picture available from any seat in the house. Each participant's workstation housed a Dell Science and Research limited edition laptop costing in excess of five thousand dollars each. They basically performed like a computer Maserati. A participant's name was engraved on each unit and a government property warning label with a serial number was affixed below that. All data in and out of these computers was either encrypted or unencrypted automatically. Tom eyed his unit suspiciously wondering if it was also equipped with a self-destruct feature.

"I am Dr. Kate Vensky, Southeast Regional Director for the USDA, and on behalf of our assembled panel and the citizens of the United States of America, I would like to warmly welcome you to this discovery and training effort to diagnose and hopefully prevent further specie die-offs. Part of this effort will be creating standardized protocols to more effectively investigate and report these incidents. There is a lot more going on around the globe than most of you are aware of, and our panel assembled on this stage will fill you in on how widespread these attacks on life have been. I now have the pleasure to introduce our esteemed panel. To my immediate left is Dr. Ted Johnston,

Director of Emerging Diseases at the CDC, and next to him is Dr. Jules LeClerc of the Pasteur Institute in Paris. On my right is Dr. Alicia Boskoff of the Russian Federation's Institute of Bio pathology, and finally Dr. Bruce Bentley of Britain's Center for Public Health. Please welcome your leadership panel."

Kate stepped back, gestured for the panel to stand, and applauded as the assembled participants rose to their feet to welcome them with enthusiastic clapping and cheers. As they returned to their seats, Kate continued.

"We also have representatives from other national health services including Canada, Mexico, Germany, Japan and China. For our international participants, if there is any need for translation or clarification, please see the concierge at the conference help desk. Also, as a reminder, there is a shuttle bus service and you will find the routes and schedules in your welcome package. It's also critical you remember to wear your biometric ID badges and use them in conjunction with the fingerprint scanners to enter or leave these facilities. You will not get in without that badge or your fingers."

"You all know, in general, what has been happening from the news reports and your interactions with other colleagues here. What you don't know is the enormity of the number of incidents and what we know about these events and the common etiology. Your leadership panel has been actively involved in this investigation and each will give the perspective from their national agencies.

"I will now turn the discussion over to Dr. Johnston who will give the American experience overview. Because of the enormity of what we are covering today, I ask that you please write down any questions you have. When we return after the ten o'clock break, we'll go over the laptops and you can then enter your questions, which will be electronically collated as to common content so we aren't wasting time answering the same question multiple times. Dr. Johnston."

"Thanks, Kate. Welcome, everyone, to the CDC. We appreciate the sacrifices you are making to help us prepare a response to this mystery. I will be going over some non-publicized incidents from the Americas. Again, please save your questions for later as we do have a lot to cover."

The large screens sporting the government logo of the CDC faded from view, and a bright woodland pasture viewed from a distance gave way to a field of devastation with hundreds of animals that appeared to be reindeer laying recumbent in death.

"I will work from north to south so these first images were taken in early November of last year in Canada's Northwest Territory and represent 342 deceased woodland caribou found by a fur trapper. As you can see by the photo documentation, these beautiful large ruminants resemble animals after being struck by lightning, still in full rigor despite our forensic analysis indicating that they were seventy-two hours deceased. The carcasses were also not frozen due to an unusual mild weather spell and had barely started decomposition. Another interesting finding was that major predators and scavengers did not consume the caribou remains and, in fact, looked like they consistently avoided the area by about 100 yards. They were curious, but avoided getting too close.

"In December of last year, there were two events on the eastern shore of Maryland involving avians. The first was a die-off of overwintering snow geese numbering approximately two thousand. They were found in their customary head-in-wing sleep position on the banks of a tidal estuary. Many of the carcasses were lost to a rising tide, but we were able to do full necropsies on a good sampling here at the CDC, unfortunately, with no determination as to cause of death. The other occurred on the same day as two poultry transport trucks coming from opposite directions, arrived at a commercial poultry processor in Salisbury with one hundred percent of their loads DOA."

The screen then switched from the photo of a clustered pile of dead white chickens to an image of a green anole. Johnston continued.

"Yesterday, here in Atlanta at General's Park, one of our attendees happened to find a small population of dead Green Anoles that might also be part of the problem we are investigating. Very suspicious, but way too early to call. If it is an idiopathic die-off, then it seems almost deliberately directed at us.

"In the interest of time, I'm only going to do two more examples. One is from the Amazon River basin where a large colony of Army ants dropped dead in total on an observed migration that was being documented and filmed by the National Geographic Society."

The screen morphed again to show thousands of red-brown ants consuming and defoliating a jungle forest. Falling shards of leaf waste fell like rain as the overhead canopy was destroyed. Then out of nowhere, ants started falling from the trees like an insectivore snowstorm. Eventually, the ground was covered with inches of dead ants. There was a mumbled, yet audible, tone of astonishment as the assembly viewed the footage.

"Thanks to NatGeo and the Smithsonian for sharing that with us. That was the first public viewing of what they captured on video.

"My last example involves migrating schooled Bluefin tuna off of Costa Rica that probably involved over five hundred 150- to 200-pound prime sushi grade Toro. The actual number killed is hard to determine because of ocean current dispersal, but sport fishermen in the vicinity reported a sudden 'boiling up' of dead fish, and without any pathology found on necropsy, leads us to believe this also was a die-off. Potentially over a million dollars of dead fish.

"So, in summary, I think you can see that no specie seems immune from this unknown killer. What specie is next? Perhaps it will be us!"

Chapter 10

After a mid-morning break, an IT technician reviewed the function of the computers they had been issued and provided tips on maximizing their performance. State of the art was an understatement—more like Star Wars. Tom pondered his unit and then glanced over to Brad who motioned like he was playing a game of video solitaire. Here were two guys who couldn't use all the features of their smartphones, but now had access to many times more computing power than it took to land men on the moon. Tom particularly hated the idea of using fingerprint recognition security to open the server, and was creeped out when it greeted him verbally in a cool female voice, "Good morning, Dr. O'Dell. What can I do for you?"

As the session was to begin, Kate excused herself from the small group she was with and walked to the podium. As she passed Tom's workstation, he noticed she stole a glance at him with a look of unease on her face. *What was that about?* he thought to himself. It unnerved him, but then Kate wasn't the type of woman Tom was typically in contact with — beautiful, confident, intelligent... single. His mind started to race over the potential reasons for her glance.

"It must be my dashing looks and quick wit," he quietly joked to himself.

"Are you talking to yourself or the computer?" Brad quipped. "Because if you think that computer voice is sexy, we definitely need to find you a woman!"

Tom laughed at Brad's banter as Kate addressed the group with confidence. Her command of the room was no accident. She worked her entire professional career at establishing a credibility that preceded her work in the field. With no time for love, Kate focused on her career, and a successful career she has had. But now she felt like something was missing.

"I hope you will find the computers easy to operate and a valuable tool for use here and as you go into the field. They give you access to all the notes from these proceedings and limited access to many other government data bases listed in the App area. And no, you won't have access to information on Area 51, Bigfoot or the Kennedy assassination."

Kate moved away from the podium as she tucked a loose strand of hair behind her ear, "At this time you can enter your questions for our discussion after lunch. Just remember to click Submit to send them over.

"Now I would like to have Dr. Jules LeClerc on behalf of the world-famous Pasteur Institute to share their experience with you. Jules…" Kate prompted as she moved to a seat at the front of the room.

Jules LeClerc stood from a group in the middle of the room and made his way to the podium. He was a man in his early fifties who looked as though he never worked a day of manual labor in his life. He wore a crisp, white button-up shirt with the sleeves rolled neatly to the middle of his forearms, tailored slacks and a brown leather belt that was the perfect match to his leather boots. His dark, short-cropped hair was tousled in a way that made Tom think he drove a sporty little convertible to the conference.

"Bonjour et merci, Kate. Good morning to all. We are all here looking to solve a mystery, many questions need answers, but to this point we have none. We, at the Pasteur, are basically a non-governmental disease analysis and research facility. We work on health concerns from around the globe and are involved in vaccine development, treatment innovations and health personnel training and education. Often, we find the seemingly easy problems stump us and the more complex are resolved effectively. As you say in America, such is life. Sometimes the answer is right under your nose, but you cannot see it. That is why you are here — more noses and eyes."

He continued in near perfect English. Dr. LeClerc had a somewhat lackadaisical demeanor that was a stark contrast to the importance of the conference. He, too, had command of a particular group of the audience — the women couldn't look away from his good looks. The accent probably didn't hurt either.

"Our facility was presented with a number of specimens from incidents in France and Africa. We looked at honeybees from the lavender fields of Provence and flamingos from the Congo, among others. The bees were very interesting in that in the affected fields, the only bees that died acutely were the domesticated Italian type used commercially as pollinators on fig, olive and fruit trees adjacent to the lavender. Wild honeybees, smaller bees and the bumblebee types were not affected. The same with the flamingoes..."

Everyone listened intently to the information Jules was providing. Tom scanned the room and noticed that the looks on the faces of each person slowly shifted from interest to concern over the news that only particular subspecies were affected. As though a magnet were drawing his gaze, he stopped on Kate. Her hair was loosely tied back in a low ponytail and she mindlessly played with a pesky loose strand that kept falling from behind her ear. She wore subtle makeup with just a hint of blush to give her a sun-kissed glow. The navy, fitted V-neck she wore would have had any man steal a second glance, but it was her hair that had Tom mesmerized. She had every shade of brown in her locks and it reminded Tom of the colors of the rivers near his home in Wisconsin. There's something beautiful about a flowing river and Kate's hair emulated that perfectly. As his gaze lingered, Kate looked back at him. He gave her a quick, sheepish smile and quickly looked away. *Nice one, you idiot. Now she thinks you're a creep,* he thought. A short moment later he looked back and noticed a deep blush had spread across her cheeks.

Dr. LeClerc was wrapping up his presentation from a seated position now with his legs crossed expertly as he leaned back somewhat casually in the chair, "Our testing of specimens included all the standard pathology tests from gross to submicroscopic, which yielded no information. Bacterial, viral, fungal and testing for prions were also negative. We injected mice, rabbits and two chimps with a composite of the dead animal's tissue. We then aerosolized a dilute suspension of tissues and fed test tissue to these laboratory subjects. With the exception of mild lung inflammation from the suspended proteins in the aerosolized tests, we saw no adverse effects. We are not currently a field-investigating facility. We only examine problems brought to us. For this problem, we have no answer."

He stood as he finished with, "It seems death here, is its own disease," and returned to his seat.

By this point, Kate had regained her composure and stood to introduce the next presenter. "Dr. Boskoff, would you add to our discussion about the experience of your findings at the Institute of Bio Pathology?"

The older, severe-looking Russian took the podium, not looking up from her notes, which appeared to be on simple index cards. Tom decided it was due to her age that she used notecards, though the gray-haired woman was decidedly nervous speaking in front of the large group. Her hands gave a slight tremor as she continually checked the state of the low bun that contributed to her severe look.

"The Russian Federation is actively investigating number of field reports from both inside our country and our neighbor, which had been part of old USSR. Our suspicions are these attacks are... uh... how do you say... target? Exact precise down to DNA of the species attacked."

Her English wasn't as good as Dr. LeClerc's, but she spoke well enough that everyone could understand. Dr. Boskoff hesitated and looked up from her notecards, pushing her readers up her nose, suddenly determined. "No more example. We feel it is an intentional bioweapon capable of exterminating selected species, culling or controlling populations of animals with the final attack being directed at Homo sapiens. It is not nature, but quite possibly from Hell. We must find answer!"

Kate was a little taken back by the warning in Boskoff's summary. To make the claim that humans are the final targets was extremely concerning. She quickly thanked the Russian representative and moved on to Dr. Bruce Bentley.

Bruce Bentley looked more Scottish than English with wild reddish hair and a well-groomed beard. If it weren't for a distinct British accent, Bruce could easily pass as a Scot. He was tall and seemingly well built for a scientist. Tom half expected to see him dressed in a tartan honoring family colors. Contrarily, the only average thing about Bruce Bentley was the business slacks and classic blue button-up shirt he wore.

"So on that happy note," he started sarcastically, "last, but not least, I'll share our experience in the U.K. We are also dumbfounded concerning all the worldwide reports of die-offs and the lack of a reported common etiology." Dr. Bentley began his discussion before he even made it to the front of the room. He was the kind of presenter that never stood in one spot. He roamed the room forcing the audience to crane their necks to get him in their line of sight. As he moved toward Tom's table, all eyes moved with him, including Kate's. Her eyes met Tom's and, again, she took on an uncertain look that had Tom wondering if he had food stuck in his teeth.

Dr. Bentley began making his way further toward the back of the room, and Tom took this as an opportunity to turn away from Kate. "We did, however, find one unique aspect to a kill of pigeons in London. As you might know we have security cameras all over the city and we happened to record on February 13 last, an acute kill of 280 pigeons in an exactly 100 square-meter area. We determined that by using the cameras to measure the kill perimeters. Quite cutting edge stuff and the measurements were precise down to the centimeter. We also feel, as Dr. Boskoff and the Russian Federation does, that this is a bioweapon. A weapon of unknown strength. The ability to focus and destroy individual species based on DNA coding could redefine life on Earth as we know it. Very Hitler-like…"

Many of the members in the room were shocked to hear the correlation to an event like the Holocaust. It was a bold statement that put this situation into a more crucial place.

He sat and Kate was again at the podium as the images of the pigeon kill faded from the screens and the CDC logo reappeared. "So, we have opinions, but very few facts to back them up. Obviously, these are not naturally occurring events. They are targeted and extremely sophisticated. To our knowledge, no government currently has the capacity to develop and deliver such a weapon in such a stealthy fashion. Future attacks could be more widespread and devastating, so you are here to be our eyes in the field to look for the less obvious and recognize the obvious. Look at this as specie assassination. Mankind could be next.

"We will now adjourn for lunch and return here precisely at one thirty. Please take the time to enter your questions now so they can be collated and we will open up with a Q & A session after lunch. I know the computers might be a little intimidating, but I promise, they will amaze you. By the way, you break it, you buy it!" Kate smiled as she left the podium while the rest of the room gathered their belongings to break for lunch.

Chapter 11

Kate met Brad and Tom at the conference center cafeteria after fending off numerous attendees attempting to ask her questions instead of waiting for the scheduled Q & A session after lunch. She was polite, but reminded them to use the format already established.

Brad and Tom were in line as she joined them near the head of the queue. She smiled at the friendly faces of the two men.

"Well, what did you guys think?" she asked.

Brad smirked and teased, "Please submit your questions through your nifty…"

Kate rolled her eyes as she gave a more-than-playful jab to his arm.

"Okay, I get it, Mr. Smarty Pants."

"*Doctor* Smarty Pants to you, missy!"

"*Doctor* Missy to you, buster!"

Tom intervened, "Am I missing something here?"

"Kate and I dated for about six months after we met at my training session. She couldn't resist my charming personality or the fact that I was a hunk back then."

Kate added, "Turned out we really liked each other, but couldn't take it to the next level. Now that my 'hunk' is a 'chunk,' maybe I can get over him and move on." They all laughed.

"How about you, Tom, do you have a significant other?" Kate asked.

"I'm in dairy practice so I have barns full of significant udders. But if you want to know if I am married, no, we divorced three years ago. My ex had a real struggle with the loneliness the profession demands of our spouses. But now I have a partner. His name's Jed."

Kate gave Tom a suspicious glance that, if he didn't know better, almost looked a little disappointed. He quickly added, "By the way, he's a black lab."

"Yeah, keep telling yourself that, buddy," Brad poked.

Tom chuckled as he watched Kate's facial expression turn from what he thought was disappointment to something he couldn't quite make out. Relief? Pity?

The three made their way to the front of the food line, and Brad and Tom picked out typical male carnivore treats while Kate was all about salads and whole grain bread. She was health conscious; they were typical men, enjoying a 'whatever' unconscious lifestyle.

Kate led the way to a table in the far corner of the cafeteria courtyard. It was a somewhat secluded spot out of the hot Georgia sun.

Tom started on his food and glanced over to Kate as she prayed a brief grace over her meal. She finished, looked up, met Tom's eyes and blushed again. Kate was making a habit of blushing, but he didn't mind. Kate, on the other hand, was aware that she was losing control of herself and it began to frighten her.

"It's something I do both out of my religious conviction to give thanks, but also as a prayer for protection against all the possible bad scenarios I have investigated over the years," she explained.

Tom liked that. His ex-wife, Sara, wasn't much into the formal tradition of attending church. As a kid, Tom was heavily involved in youth groups, Sunday school, and Bible summer school. As a young adult he continued to attend Church almost every week. He enjoyed the structure of traditional services, and his wife did, too. But shortly after he married, Sara insisted they needed to spend more fun time together and less time going places even if it was to church. The demands of a veterinarian were 24/7 and that was hard on their marriage.

Brad asked, "Kate, any word on the lizard work we did yesterday?"

"The only thing I heard was that all six were male. We have people now at the kill site to see if they can locate some living females. There are also herpetologists and zoologists getting involved to determine if finding only males in one location is normal. The good news is that all six are in great condition, and they should be able to do complete testing on them," she continued enthusiastically. This was obviously good news to have specimens in a condition that was conducive to testing.

"You guys are going to be so impressed with the program we have put together here. It goes way beyond just the science of fieldwork and tissue collection. You also are to receive firearms training, basic military self-defense, and will eventually be deputized federal agents with a federal conceal carry license. Under most circumstances, you will be able to fly commercially under that permit and carry on your handgun. You are also receiving a salary so you might be asked to travel anywhere in the world using a type of diplomatic passport."

"Cool!" Brad exclaimed. Brad turned from thirty-something to twenty-something in the blink of an eye. He acted like he was just asked to join a secret undercover mission.

"Do you really think we will need all that authority… and weapons?" Tom asked with a sense of concern. "I mean, aren't there more qualified agents out there who are trained to handle this?"

"When this hits the fan, there will be all kinds of bad scenarios we could get involved in. You might be asked to arrest and detain," Kate answered elbowing Brad in the arm with a knowing smile.

"Will I be able to do strip searches?" Brad mused as he took another bite from his burger.

"Only on the jackasses, jackass!"

Chapter 12
Fort Peck Indian Reservation

Northeast Montana

"Grandfather, are you alright? I'm here and will help you. Please wake up!"

Joseph Blackfeather waited to see if his great-grandfather was responsive to his voice. His frequent dreams and night terrors were getting worse and taking a physical toll on the very old man. It was frightening that his only living blood relative, a Sioux Shaman, had to experience these nightmares. They had haunted him for decades, but only now were intensifying to the point Joseph feared for the health of the old man. The term 'fragile' fit the senior Blackfeather, who was nearing one hundred years of age.

The Blackfeather family had once numbered close to forty at the start of the twentieth century, but had dwindled down to just six. Only two, Joseph and his grandfather Nelson, still remained on tribal grounds. The sprawling Fort Peck Indian Reservation, where they lived, covered some 3300 square miles north of the Missouri River in northeast Montana, where about eight thousand Native Americans lived. Almost one million acres were titled to tribal members, who elected to stay on the land, but many young people had left because of the social and economic problems which generations had been consigned to. Of Joseph's family, only two cousins and their parents worked for the Feds in Washington D.C. Content being 'outsiders', they never visited the reservation.

Truth be told, when Joseph's great-grandfather passed, he, too, would escape. At nineteen years of age, he needed to be with new, alive people. He had had enough of seeing depressed people who found their happiness at the bottom of a bottle or at the craps table. Some days, living with his grandfather made him start to feel like the rest of the hopeless souls that wandered around the reservation. Joseph didn't want to fall into that generational desperation which haunted this place.

But Joseph loved the old man he cared for, especially the historical stories that had been passed down to his grandfather about tribal life when they were a free people. About dominant warriors who fought for their way of life and unwittingly traded their freedom on the Black Hills of South Dakota for Montana after the defeat of Custer at the Little Bighorn.

They had won, but victory cost them their homeland and way of life. Grandfather always said that remembering the past was the only real way to connect to their ancestors. Joseph knew those ancestors would have hated this place just as he did.

Grandfather had always been true to the ancestors and the old ways. He could still recall the details of life as it had once been and spoke with pride about the great leaders and families. Tribal prayers and shaman incantations still flowed effortlessly from his lips, indelible memories of what his own grandfather had taught him as a child. True, his own grandson, Joseph's father, pretended to be white and would have nothing to do with the old ways, so his soul then left him because he was nothing, and he had returned to the soil as nothing. His great hope was for Joseph who, since a very young child, he had raised. Nelson knew there needed to be another to remember the past — there always needed to be another, and he made it his sole purpose in his later years to help Joseph learn and understand the old ways and who the Sioux had been. At ninety-nine, Nelson Blackfeather's health was deteriorating and, had he not been the Keeper of Knowledge, he was sure the Creator would have returned him to the earth long ago. Only when his purpose was no more, would he pass.

Nelson began having visions when he was seven after the death of his shaman grandfather. These visions foretold events that affected the Sioux, including visions of his grandfather in full war-dress. Each 'episode' came with a warning. They typically occurred on an irregular basis, but now happened nearly every night with the same message he had first heard as a child: "The Creator and the Destroyer are in battle again. Beware of the Evil One as he will be the destroyer of life. When he returns, the animals will flee and people will cower and bow as life will cease."

He had always thought it referred to the world wars, Hitler, HIV, or any of the major natural disasters the world experienced. The problem was they never ceased to reoccur and 'The Destroyer is coming' message was becoming his personal Hell.

Tonight's message had been different and more ominous as Nelson heard a new warning: "Beware, the Destroyer is here."

Joseph now consoled a frightened old man. A man who had never shown fear before was terrified beyond reason.

Chapter 13
CDC Center for Forensic Investigation

One week into the training, Brad, Tom and Kate had bonded into a tight-knit little group. Kate was masterful at leading the general sessions, answering questions which had now subsided to a trickle since that first day when "we have no answer to that," "we don't think so," "no, we weren't kidding," and "we can't truly rule out aliens," were the typical answers.

The conference attendees had been split into three groups, which rotated sessions through the different training topics. The three musketeers, as they were now called, had just finished 'Principles of Investigative Etiology, Field Necropsy, Gross Clinical Pathology and Toxicology', the most intense of the scheduled weeks, which required passing a proficiency exam with a score of 80% or better to be certified. Tonight, to celebrate being over the hardest academic part of the training, they planned a special dinner at Sosume, a local Japanese restaurant.

"So-sue-me. Sounds like this place was opened by a bunch of New York lawyers," Brad said as the three walked up to restaurant's oversized wooden doors. The exterior was rustic with lots of use of wood and simple hardware, but that contradicted the modern, sleek interior.

"Wow, I wasn't expecting this," Kate mused as Brad headed over to the hostess station.

"Yeah, it's definitely upscale," Tom agreed.

The server in traditional dress motioned for them to follow and she led the group toward the rear of the establishment where the table was a little more secluded. Tom pulled Kate's chair out for her, and she slid in she gave him a shy smile.

As Tom looked over the menu he began talking about the training, "I cannot believe you had to take the test! It seems to me that if the instructors take the test, it would ruin the curve, and Lord knows, Brad and I live and die off the curve. Even a curved 80%!"

"Come on now, you know I really didn't develop these courses, so I learned as much as you guys did and maybe a little bit more because I

41

actually paid attention. You boys shouldn't be so jealous of a female's superior intellect."

"You mean *some* females," Brad added as he flipped open the menu.

"Yes, at least all female veterinarians."

"Let's vote on that. I'm sure you're going to lose in a tight 2-to-1 race. And I suppose you'll want a recount," Brad scoffed.

"No need," Tom declared, "I vote that Kate *is* smarter than you, and better looking too!"

"Okay, I get it. Pick on the old married guy who's no fun."

"Yup," Kate and Tom affirmed in unison. Tom looked to Kate as they teamed up on Brad. He enjoyed having a good time with a woman for a change. And Kate was a beautiful, intelligent woman. Kate seemed to enjoy the company, too. She stole glimpses of Tom when he was single-handedly ribbing Brad.

Now that the initial fun was over, the three got down to the business of planning their meals. Seafood in the form of appetizers, sushi and entrees appealed to all of them, so they started with a good selection of cooked and raw sushi, Kirin beer, and Miso soup. Tom noticed Brad was really into the shrimp dishes.

"Brad, why don't you try something other than the shrimp?"

"Because," he explained, "I learned in high school that the Pilgrims came to this country on the Mayflower, but that the midgets came over here on the shrimp boats and I think those little people deserve all the support I can give them!"

"Lord, help me," Kate groaned laughingly.

When they settled into the meal, Brad's phone interrupted Tom as he asked Kate about the next sessions.

"Sorry, let me take this call real quick. It's someone from the car agency," Brad explained as he stood to leave the table. Tom nodded to Brad as he made his way to a quieter location.

"So, Kate, now we move to the sessions on bioterrorism with instructors from Homeland Security, the FBI and NSA, right?"

"That's right, and it's intense," Kate warned.

"The scuttlebutt I heard from the group that just went through was that it scared the Hell out of them. Most had no idea so much evil lurked out there, or how much technology is needed to thwart those threats. MacHenry told me these mass die-offs are such a big concern to the government because they are so 'occult'. We have no clue as to why, what, who or where a new attack will occur. Or what species could be the next target," Tom said as he expertly picked a roll of sushi from the platter with his chopsticks.

"It is pretty frightening to be in the dark with all of this right now. But with all of the brilliant minds we have together, we'll come up with answers," said Kate confidently.

"Can you imagine a weapon that could be programmed with specific DNA markers to take out only males of a specie?"

"No, it almost has to be a weapon of some kind because this isn't something from the natural world."

"What if it is a weapon and has the ability to identify individuals with specific ethnic DNA? We could potentially be talking about another Holocaust. On the flip side, this type of technology could be focused narrowly to kill cancer cells, bacteria and parasites. In the benevolent hands, a Godsend; in the wrong hands, we could be looking at Armageddon!"

Kate added, "Right, I've been to more meetings in the last two months than I had been in the previous ten years. The USDA is afraid that entire segments of our agricultural economy could disappear overnight, or perhaps even a simple threat could hold the nation hostage for fear the terrorist could starve us into oblivion. Nobody should underestimate the enormity of the potential disaster we face, that's why the 'Threats' section of this training was designed."

"The bottom line is, we should all be scared shitless," Tom suggested.

"Yep," she continued, "and we spend the next week being terrorized about terrorism and then we move on to legal and self-defense. Two more weeks to mature our ideas and thought processes that will hopefully lead us to a resolution or explanation. We need answers and maybe someone in this eclectic group will find one."

"Hopefully lead us to a *who*," Tom interjected as Brad walked up with a look of distress on his face.

"What's wrong, Brad?" Kate asked.

"Some bozo down at the hotel backed into my rental car. I hate to run, but I have to go deal with the rental company and straighten everything out with insurance," Brad expressed. "Don't get frisky, Tom. Kate's not that kinda girl."

Tom noticed Kate blush slightly again when Brad made his remark. He was really starting to love that about her.

Brad left the two of them alone, and the conversation quickly turned from shoptalk to a more personal level. Being around Kate was so natural, it's almost like they've been friends for years let alone a few days. Kate seemed to find the conversation with Tom easy, too.

"So, what made you want to become a veterinarian, Tom?" Kate asked.

"Well, it wasn't my intention, but I just discovered the passion for caring for animals during my undergrad at University of Wisconsin. I originally went to school to be a teacher. That just wasn't in the cards for me and I couldn't be happier with my work. What about you?"

Kate thought for a moment and said, "I don't know, I just always loved science and animals and wanted to help them because they need us. We're the ones destroying their habitats and I wanted to be a part of the world that does something about it."

"That's understandable. What about…" Tom nervously cleared his throat, "What about kids? A boyfriend? Maybe a lab of your own?"

Folding her napkin in her lap and eyes locked on Tom, she boldly stated, "I'm available."

Chapter 14
CDC Center for Forensic Investigation

Final Day of the Conference

The three weeks of training, education and new friendships was coming to a close. Kate stood before the attendees as she had on that first day, and called the group together for the final time. Today Kate donned a soft yellow cardigan over a black and white striped tank dress that fell to the floor as it hugged her hips. Her hair hung loose and she applied just a touch more makeup than usual. It wasn't like her to put this much effort into her hair and makeup, but then today wasn't like any other day. Today she felt possibilities of something open up for her. She glanced toward Tom who returned the look.

The attendees quickly responded to her request, returning to their seats, all of them anxious to return home to their families and normal lives. Though normal was now an understatement as each of them understood exactly what they were recruited for. Now, normal meant they could confidently mount a structured scientific response if called upon. They were a trained 'army' of soldiers equipped to hopefully stop this enemy of life. Any mistakes or missed cues could spell disaster.

Kate addressed the group with a new type of confidence, "First, I would like to sincerely thank you all for your patience, dedication and diligence over the course of this training program. You are now an elite group of professionals who, on very short notice, can be mobilized to help diagnose, cut short, or prevent these attacks. You are, more or less, veterinary minutemen in this new era of biologic threats," she smiled as she looked directly at Tom. He returned the smile. Brad saw the exchange and rolled his eyes.

"On your desks, you will find a sealed folder containing your certification credentials, federal CC permit and firearm registration, federal emergency contact call lists, SAT phone information, easy passes for your vehicle, TSA priority credentials, and a personal PIN number. Memorize that number and destroy the original card. Also you will see a USDA badge.

When on official business, wear it with pride because you are now part of the USDA."

Brad passed a note to Tom that read, "I was a minuteman in the sexual revolution!" Tom crumbled the note and bounced it off the side of Brad's shiny bald head.

"So," Kate continued, "a couple of nice surprises for you. First, each of you will receive, after your return home, a vehicle equipped with all the tools you will need to do your job. You will be totally ready to go after that, and will kinda be like veterinary *Men in Black*. Don't let that go to your heads. These vehicles are tools of the trade, not to be used to take the little ones to McDonald's.

"The last thing in your folder is an envelope that contains a check to help reimburse you for all your time and trouble during the last three weeks. The check is yours to spend, but understand it covers this meeting expense and any time you devote to this project for the next six months. It is non-taxable and is a sort of retainer. It comes with our thanks."

Kate watched as the group tackled the envelopes. There was an audible gasp as they started to reveal the check amounts. Tom was startled to see a check for $100,000 made out to him. He started counting zeros to make sure he was seeing it correctly, and leaning over to Brad said, "You'll only need one hand to count the zeroes, man."

"Good one, Casanova," Brad retorted as the people near the exchange chuckled.

"These are extraordinary times and the funds are to cover the personal expenses and sacrifices you have made and will make again for six months. After that, if we are still an active group, you will receive a monthly stipend. Anyone who feels their economic loss exceeds the check, you can document and submit a claim to the main office here in Atlanta. So, in closing," Kate finished, "please use the skills you have learned, and for God's sake use those resource numbers if you question anything. I wish you all well and am now pleased to send you all home. This conference is closed and go with God's blessing!"

Kate looked out to where Tom and Brad were shaking hands with some of other participants, happily saying their goodbyes. She was focused on Tom because she had found herself attracted to him like no man she had ever know before in her life. He was a good man — kind and honest. Tom was someone she could make room for in her career-driven life, and not feel like she was giving up to get him. She also was totally happy when with him and missed him terribly when they were apart, even for short amounts of time. So here they were, going their separate ways and desperation was nagging her to tell him exactly how she felt. For a person who was never afraid to tackle any topic, this need for intimate conversation was making her feel like a sixth grader going to her first dance. It only took one dinner together and she knew without a doubt that she was in love with him. And, for the first time in her life, was afraid of losing what she wanted.

Chapter 15
Fort Peck Indian Reservation

A mist hung over the low pastures as the sun breached the hills on an unseasonably cold, late spring morning. Joseph loved this time of day when, with the morning, came playful dogs barking, multiple roosters competing to announce the new day, and the fresh smell of wood smoke as families brewed their morning coffee. Despite the beauty of the morning, Joseph knew that today would be a carbon copy of yesterday, and could easily anticipate the questions he would be asked, and the answers to be given, as he moved through his mundane day.

With a tall, slender frame, Joseph was every bit Lakota as his distant ancestors. He wore his black, shoulder-length hair pulled back in a leather band that accentuated his high cheekbones, long nose and wide, brown eyes. His square jaw and long, muscular build belied his youthful years. Joseph's countenance was mirrored in his great-grandfather Nelson. Though Nelson Blackfeather had evidence of much more life lived in the lines of his face.

His great-grandfather had another troubled night, and woke once again in a terrified panic. Joseph had become a light sleeper with his senses focused on the old man, who had become both a burden and a joy to him. He needed his great-grandfather's connection to his blood, but perhaps more than that, he needed the outward strength his great-grandfather showed in his people's proud history. It was, in a sense, something that Joseph couldn't explain or ignore.

Nelson had drifted asleep, once again, in the well-worn recliner across from the rabbit-eared television set. It was a set that looked like it was out of the sixties. Joseph quietly left the trailer to do the morning chores, which included feeding the livestock, and grooming and mucking out the horses. He had forgotten to call the farrier to schedule a change out of his horse's shoes — something he had planned for today — and was now kicking himself. Many of his people did not manage their horse's feet properly, so when they rode, it was often painful for both the horse and rider. Joseph appreciated comfortable shoes and he wanted the same for his paint gelding, Wakinyan, which meant 'Thunderer' in Sioux. His great-grandfather's old horse was, of course, named Lightning, slower than sin, and hadn't been ridden in years due to Nelson's age and physical abilities.

Two hours later, he returned to the ancient trailer to find the old man up and slowly gravitating to the coffee pot. Grandfather liked his coffee hot, black and a little on the thick side. He claimed it was the secret to a long life and keeping a woman happy. Joseph couldn't argue the longevity part, but doubted the virility claim because, since his great grandmother died, no other woman had been able to interest the old Indian.

"You had another bad dream last night, do you remember?" Joseph asked.

"Of course I do! I might be old, but there is not a senile bone in this thick skull of mine," the old man defensively replied, "Last night was absolutely the worst one yet! It felt like I had left my body and was floating with our ancestors, looking down at the world from above. I wanted to puke as I heard the words 'the Destroyer of life is here'. I heard them over and over again, louder and louder each time. The voices were English, Sioux, Blackfoot, Cheyenne, Shoshone, and other tongues — all speaking in unison! I heard the animals plead for their lives and understood them. The message was one of fearful power. I was born to hear it and understand it. No question, it was intended for me," Nelson said with certainty. Though the old man physically quavered and appeared feeble, his voice emanated strength and resolve.

"So it was a clear message that you were meant to hear and act on. But why? And by who? Just the Ancestors, and to what end? We must still be missing some key part of the puzzle. He is 'here', but where?" Joseph questioned.

The old Indian shook his head in a gesture of frustration, desperately searching for an answer that made sense. His body was shaking a little and he seemed slightly more unsteady on his feet than usual.

Nelson shuffled over to the trailer door leading to the deck outside. Joseph walked with him to try to steady him, but the old man shook him off. Outside the sun shone brightly in a cloudless, endless blue sky.

Facing west, Nelson looked skyward, his deep-set eyes squinting into that brightness. He extended his thin, heavily veined arms, raising them toward the heavens. Head tilted back and palms rotated to catch the warmth of the sun, he started praying in ancient, timeless chants. His voice was strong and resolute, like it was coming from somewhere other than that frail, old body. "Eternal ancestors, honor me with your wisdom and guidance. Tell me what to do for I heard your message that the Evil One is now renewed and will destroy all that lives and breathes. Help us… help us for the love of all life. Please help us!"

While Joseph's great-grandfather was chanting, he stood behind him and closed his eyes letting each word reverberate from him toward the heavens. He allowed each meaning, nuance and ancient tradition to flow from Nelson through himself and back out to the eternal. It wasn't just Nelson chanting, but eventually a nation of ancient Lakota speaking through him. It was a connection that would span through time.

Chapter 16
Rural Northwest Wisconsin

Tom would have had no problem sleeping in his own bed except for an overjoyed Jed bouncing off and on in celebration of his homecoming. After settling down, Jed positioned himself on the pillow next to Tom, something that was not usually allowed because it meant several wet licks a night, a liquid reminder that he was sharing his bed with a canine.

When the alarm rang at five a.m., Tom found it a little difficult to roll out of bed after those weeks of late eight o'clock starts, but the need to return to his regular routine was a strong lure.

This morning he was to meet with Dr. Bob Kane, his relief practitioner, for breakfast to go over the field journal and accounts before Bob left in the evening. Even though Tom was happy to be back home, the thought of fixing any problems that could have occurred in his absence and returning to the daily grind left him a little apprehensive. Strangely, he would miss the excitement of new responsibilities and learning, not to mention the friendship shared by the 'Three Musketeers'. Most of all, he would miss Kate with her intelligence, sense of humor and beauty. He was very drawn to her and felt a powerful urge to call and ask her on a date. It was becoming more like an obsession for him and he regretted not asking her out before leaving Atlanta.

They met at Betty's, a local diner and meeting place in the small community. Tom had reviewed Bob's field journal and invoices and, at least on the surface, looked like he had done a productive job. The real test would be on today's calls when Tom could see the farmers' reactions to his return and Dr. Kane's presence. He found Dr. Kane, a sandy blonde, twenty-nine-year-old, sitting in the corner booth hiding his compact stature. He had strong hands, which was necessary in this line of work, but Tom wanted to get to know the real Bob. Was he a solid fill in, or did he cause more harm than good?

Bob Kane was a recent graduate, the son of a small animal veterinarian. He had been active in 4H and, despite his family's roots, decided to become a large animal general practitioner. Horses, dairy, beef cattle, sheep, pigs, llamas and alpacas were all species that interested him. General large animal practice was his goal, so he could have the variety of cases that would challenge him. After two tries to enter The Ohio State College of Veterinary Medicine, he was admitted with the fall class. Shortly into his second year of study, a drunk driver tragically killed his parents. Devastated, he left school and wandered around the Midwest trying to lose the anger that haunted him in an attempt to find new purpose in his life.

On his way through Wisconsin, he passed field after field of Jerseys and Holsteins and smelled the fresh-cut fields and spread manure. A realization came over him that this is what he was born to do and what his parents would want for him — peace in his life in a rural community.

Shortly after this awakening, he decided to stay in Wisconsin and transferred into the veterinary school at UW. He worked hard, but when he graduated the Midwest dairy economy was not good, so he took a job in a large commercial dairy in California. There he was promised a good salary, lots of experience, and fair hours. It turned out to be a way too commercial operation where there was no real love for the cows, just a love of butterfat percentage and milk volume production profits. These cows weren't the happy California cows advertised in television commercials, but bovine slaves tied to rotating milking carousels, which broke his heart. These cows experienced a higher percentage of the common feet and udder problems that plague milk production and since pregnancy was necessary for lactation, he became a whiz at bovine reproduction. It was not, however, the way he wanted to practice so he returned to Wisconsin when his contract was up.

As a relief veterinarian, he filled in when practices were short-handed due to vacations, injury, illness or any other reason that left these twenty-four-hour-a-day businesses wanting. The time he spent working Tom's practice was the first time he had really felt like a veterinarian and not a hired mechanic as he serviced family farms that had strong generational connections to their land. Although they were in business to make their living, they truly understood the value of their lifestyle. These families were producers, and to them, work was a blessing. He would miss this place.

Betty's was a small restaurant with a lunch counter and laminate counter booths that had butt-worn burgundy vinyl seating. The eatery had served as an essential gathering place for as long as anyone could remember, and was as much of a place to get a bite to eat as it was a place you could discuss the market prices, who was ill, or having an affair — a kind of rural hometown goggle spot.

As Tom expected, the place lit up with good-natured ribbing when the two of them walked in.

"Hey, Doc, that Dr. Kane is a keeper. He fixed my scouring calves just fine," said John Baker, a local farmer who Tom checks in on almost weekly.

Even if there isn't a professional need for Tom's visits, he always makes a point to stop over and see John. Bonnie, John's wife, passed away a year ago from ovarian cancer. Tom can see on his face how lonely it gets for John.

"I'm glad to hear it, John," he replied.

John slapped Tom on the back and suggested, "In fact, why don't you give this boy a permanent job? Lord knows we could use a good vet around here!"

"You keep that up and I won't be stopping by to see you anymore, Old Man!" Tom shot back.

Sally Taylor piped in from the booth next to Tom said, "I agree with John. Keep 'im. He don't charge much as you and he's prettier to look at." Sally was always nosing her way into other conversations and had a knack for gossip. That's just what Tom needs is a rumor going around that he's hiring Bob Kane as a full-time employee. Heck, she'd probably tell everyone that Bob was taking over the practice.

That set the stage as everyone, smelling blood in the water, joined in. It became like an old rerun of *Hee Haw* — they all thought themselves a comic.

By the end of breakfast, it was apparent Bob had won the hearts of the community, and he was also starting to grow on Tom.

They started the daily calls and talked a lot as they drove from place to place. Bob seemed to have something on his mind.

"I really appreciate the fine job you did running the practice while I was in Atlanta. It really meant a lot to me not having to worry about the shop while I was on vacation," they both laughed as Tom put air quotes around the word 'vacation'.

"I met a girl when I was at the Purcell place. She was a knockout and we got along great," Bob confessed. "Her family even had me over for Sunday dinner last week. Nice folks!"

"So you met Beth! You know, she has had more suitors than probably any other young lady in the county. She was the Dairy Princess at the fair I'm guessing seven years ago, before she went off to college to study Dairy Science. She probably knows more about genetics and milk production than you and me combined," Tom offered. "She's one hell of a nice girl."

"We plan on seeing each other again so I kinda wondered if you could use some regular help, you know, answering the phone, mopping the floor or shining the truck?" Bob joked. "I think it's about time for me to settle into a practice and I know we could work well together. Grow the business and share the duties. Just think, not having to be on call very night," he said nervously.

Tom smiled. He might have really lucked out finding a solid individual to work in the practice and potentially become a partner. Plus, he might be called out by the USDA at a moment's notice and he hoped to spend time with Kate. This seemed like a perfect opportunity. He couldn't have been happier.

Tom extended his hand to Bob and said, "The truck really could use a good cleaning, I think you have a deal!"

Chapter 17
Chicago

Late August

Nearly four months had passed since the training in Atlanta, and there had not been a single incident around the world that merited investigation. All the trained responders were fully equipped with their new USDA vans with portable laboratories, but no one had had a reason to use it. Brad was still stuck on his alien theory and Tom was beginning to believe that maybe it was just some kind of a weird cosmic event like sunspots.

As Tom was grabbing his truck keys to head out on an emergency call, his cell rang. He saw on the caller ID that it was Kate. He stopped dead in his tracks and checked his reflection in the hall mirror.

"You fool, she can't see you," he teased himself as he readied the phone. On the third ring he picked up, "Hi Kate."

"Hi to you, Tom," said Kate. "What are you up to?"

"I'm just heading out on an emergency call. I have an injured calf that may need some stitches." Tom opened the front door as the sunshine immediately warmed him.

"I have good news. At least I hope it's good news. There's a conference I'm attending in Chicago and I thought it might be a great opportunity to mix a little business with pleasure. What do you think? Can you get Bob to cover your workload for a couple nights?" Kate asked not even attempting to hide the hope in her voice.

"Absolutely! That sounds wonderful. I'll swing by and ask him right after I take a look at this first call. I'll let you know what he said later."

"Great! I can't wait to see you," Kate said coyly.

"I already have ideas for an incredible weekend. Actually, I've been thinking a lot of a weekend with you ever since I left Atlanta," Tom admitted. He felt a little embarrassed that he told her that, but it was too late to take it back.

"I've been thinking of you, too," Kate said.

"That's good to hear. Listen, I gotta run, but I'll call you this evening with more details." Tom revved the engine as he backed out of his gravel drive.

After Bob agreed to cover for Tom and he gave Kate the all clear, he got down to planning some fun starting with dinner and a Broadway show. She would, he was sure, fill him in on any new information on the die-offs, but most of all he hoped the spark between them he had felt in Atlanta was still alive. He had missed her horribly.

Tom arrived at the hotel in Chicago just ahead of rush hour on a Friday afternoon. Despite missing the notorious peak rush hour traffic, he was still frustrated by the city congestion. That impatience was the direct result of rural life where he never had to wait at a stop sign for more than a split second.

He pulled into the hotel and handed the valet the keys to his old Subaru. He was a little embarrassed to be driving the old 'beater' to such a nice hotel, but in reality, he spent 99% of his time in one of the Vet Body trucks they used for farm calls. The old car was reliable and got good gas mileage, but it made him nervous on the Chicago freeways with the space intimidation of the eighteen-wheelers and other manic drivers. He preferred to think of the old SUV as vintage, paid for, and economical. Not sexy, but reliable, like him.

He checked into his room and took a long hot shower to help erase any lingering aromas that he might have carried along on him. Satisfied he looked good, well groomed with a new haircut, and clean-shaven, he texted Kate his room number and confirmed their rendezvous in the hotel lounge at six. He hoped a little relaxation time in the lounge would give them time to talk and he did have a lot to confess to her, if he could find the courage. He had purchased great seats to *Les Misérables* at the Chicago Broadway Playhouse Theater and had reservations for after the show at Katsu, a well-reviewed Japanese restaurant in downtown.

A few moments after his text, Kate called and sounded wonderful as she laughed and told him how much she had missed him since Atlanta. Tom listened, detecting possible nervous anticipation and realized she was as anxious as he was. All he could think was, *Don't blow it, don't blow it!*

The lounge was modern, cozy with seating areas placed strategically to provide maximum privacy for intimate or business conversations. Tom located a corner table near the large marble fireplace with a street view reflecting in the opposite wall's mirrored panels.

Kate entered the lounge shortly after six and she nearly took Tom's breath away when he saw her. She beamed when he stood up, and gave him an extended warm hug, clinging to him, letting him know exactly how much she had missed him.

"My God, you look incredible," Tom stated. "I really missed you and was so glad you had your conference in Chi-Town. It's really just in my back yard."

Kate flushed red and smiled, "I missed you, too, Tom. Seeing you here, looking very handsome is just what I needed," she said, "I can hardly believe it's been almost four months since we were in Atlanta and because there hasn't been any documented die-off events since we adjourned, my life was just starting to get back to normal. I am so glad we could meet here, I think about you often!"

"I would rather you call it a date, it makes me feel younger and actually gives me a little hope," Tom replied.

Kate blushed again, adverting her eyes, "Sorry, I have been looking forward to our date also. No more business tonight, I promise! Let's enjoy our drinks and do some catching up. No more shop talk," she reaffirmed.

"Well your shop talk would be a whole lot more interesting than mine, but I am afraid I will bore you to death on our first date without interjecting a little bit of what's going on down on the farm," Tom said.

"I told you about my good luck in finding a real nice, competent associate because of the conference, so if nothing else, the three weeks in Atlanta has dramatically affected my professional life for the better."

"How about your personal life," Kate teased.

"I do have one prospect who has affected me in ways I haven't felt in years. Someone I would drive hours to see and who never ceases to amaze me with her beauty, intellect and sense of humor. In fact, I plan on meeting up with her this weekend."

"Well, don't let me hold you up!" Kate replied, laughing.

"No, only you and you alone could hold me up, Kate." Tom smiled.

The evening Tom had arranged for them included great seats at the show and an unbelievable dinner of some of the best Japanese food in Chicago. Tom called the meal 'clean food', because it was presented beautifully and left the palate craving more of that unique, fresh flavor.

Kate was thoroughly enjoying herself and could tell Tom was trying very hard to impress her and that was making her even more sure of the feelings she had for him. She loved those schoolgirl feelings.

As promised, they avoided discussing the die-offs, but did find time to plan another weekend together. Tom realized this new freedom he was enjoying was the direct result of Bob Kane joining the practice and would never had happened without that USDA training trip to Atlanta. Tom found himself subconsciously staring at Kate, gazing into her beautiful eyes, which caused Kate to flush and advert her eyes when she realized it. There certainly had to be something special happening.

In the cab on the way back to the hotel, Kate rested her head on Tom's shoulder as he held her hand. She felt better tonight about herself than she had for years. Tom seemed to be the missing piece of her life's puzzle.

At the hotel, the doorman opened the cab door and assisted Kate out as Tom paid the cabbie. Tom followed her through the quiet lobby as they walked to the elevator bank. At the elevator, Kate turned quickly and made a suggestion. "I really can't remember when I've had such a wonderful evening. Plus, we even avoided the dreaded talk of work! That was refreshing! I really don't want to lose this feeling and wondered if you would like some company for the rest of the evening?"

With that, Tom embraced her and they kissed with a depth of passion that pleased and surprised them both. They would not part tonight.

Chapter 18
Fort Peck Indian Reservation

Montana

Joseph had left his great-grandfather in the big easy chair sleeping deeply and breathing slightly irregularly. The old man had really deteriorated in the last few months as he approached his one-hundredth birthday. The dreams continued to haunt him, but he rarely shared their disturbing content with Joseph. He did, however, record these events in his life journals, like he had for the last seventy-five years. He also sketched his visions in penciled detail in the composition notebooks like those used by students. His bedroom contained over twenty-five volumes of these writings, and Joseph had never dared to open even one out of respect of the old man, but also because he was afraid of what he might find written in them.

Joseph exited the old trailer. The near-evening air was dry and crisp, as it often was in this climate where severe heavy thunderstorms in summer would wash across the normally dry landscape. In the winter, blowing blizzards could isolate them for up to a week. It was the land of extremes. They rarely received less than twenty-four inches of precipitation, and snow could be in the forecast eight months out of the year. The landscape of the reservation reflected that semi-arid climate, with plains of wild grasses and clusters of forested areas. Cattle and sheep now grazed on these areas that once were dominated by vast herds of Bison. Pronghorn antelope still ran in long groups along the horizons and often parallel to the lonely roads, while wolves, cougars and bears hunted any life they could find. It was as it had been for thousands of years, but now a dramatic change was upon the land as geological expeditions were discovering and extracting shale oil, promising new wealth and employment for the area. Man was meant to serve the land, not the opposite, and those evolving changes worried Joseph that white men, with no cultural connection to the land, would rob the area of its natural wealth with no regard for his people or the animals.

Joseph walked the cinder-lined path from the trailer to the horse paddock and placed a bridle as the paint Indian pony gently nuzzled him in anticipation of an excursion into the grasses. He was meticulous about caring for the animal and groomed the small horse, looking him over carefully, picking his feet clean as he did every evening. He then saddled him up with his well-worn, but comfortable saddle over an old, thick, multicolored Indian blanket. He double-checked the girth, clinched it up a little bit, and then mounted up.

"Let's go find Custer," he whispered in Wakinyan's left ear, patting the thick neck gently and controlling the reins to signal a westward route toward the setting sun.

Joseph gave Wakinyan his head and the horse followed the route that they had traveled so many times, a loop west then north, then west again before heading south and east. This route followed the course of the Missouri River. It was a route they could navigate in the darkest night or in a blinding blizzard. Tonight, though, he broke off the traditional path and looped more to the north where the great grazing areas of the bison had been and where they had started to repopulate their ancestral home. The bison, unfortunately, carried brucellosis, commonly called 'Spontaneous Abortion', so they were monitored and kept away from the cattle grazing areas where they could transmit the disease to their bovine cousins. Bison, over the generations, had developed immune tolerance to the disease seemingly affecting them less. Unvaccinated cattle, however, if infected, would abort dead calves.

It took Joseph about thirty minutes to arrive to the bluff where the bison grazed peacefully, and the hundred or so in this herd didn't even acknowledge the horse and rider. Joseph sat back in the saddle sipping from a water bottle and watched as a band of pronghorns burst from behind a distant small oasis of trees into the scene, obviously running away from something. Maybe the wolves were working this direction or someone on an ATV was having some fun.

The sun stood lower as he turned Wakinyan to cut to the west and in about thirty minutes at a brisk canter, he saw the outlines of cattle, cows with their spring calves and the obvious bulk of the herd servicing bulls. They also seemed oblivious to his approach as they leisurely grazed in preparation for the evening. Joseph sat and watched the cattle for a few minutes then said to Wakinyan, "Time to go home, my friend."

With the sun now behind them, Joseph restrained Wakinyan's gait. The horse hurried back in anticipation of the good rub down and bucket of grain that always followed their evening ride.

Joseph could see the horse's heavy breath in the frosty air as they arrived home, the promise of a clear crisp night and the big sky above filled with bright stars and planets. In the distance, Joseph heard dogs carrying on like crazy, barking and howling in an unusual frenzy, just like the night when an earthquake shook them all out of bed. Maybe, he thought, they just wanted to get off their chains and run like the wolves that they were.

Chapter 19

Tom returned to Wisconsin happy, excited and determined to keep Kate part of his life. In Chicago, they had nearly expressed their love for one another when they parted on Sunday evening, but neither could find the courage or right words. They did, however, eagerly make future plans for a long weekend on Cape Ann near Boston to enjoy the early fall foliage, whale watching and enjoy great seafood. Tom had already found accommodations at a small B&B near Cranes Beach where they would have access to the villages of Gloucester, Essex and Ipswich, but close to Maine and New Hampshire if they decided to explore up the coast. Because he had hired Bob Kane, Tom now was blessed with time to develop his relationship with Kate and, fortunately, she had lots of accumulated personal time. Things were working out great for them.

Dr. Kane was also happy with his situation in the practice and was doing his best to convince Beth that he was the man of her dreams. She was heavily involved in the family dairy business, so their dates were primarily talking over simple dinners or during long walks. Beth's family liked him a lot, especially her younger brothers who teased her relentlessly when Bob was around. Her family knew about his parents' tragic death and tried real hard to make him feel like part of their family. It was working and he, too, was feeling blessed by this kind family, his new job and, especially, Beth.

The Monday after Chicago, Tom and Bob met at Betty's for their customary breakfast strategy session for the day and plans for the rest of the week. Tom lightly touched on his time with Kate and listened as Bob opened up about Beth.

"I sure wish that girl would get off the pot and get me a recognizable signal about how she feels about me! All this playing hard to get is becoming hard to take!"

"Come on, Bob, you're already way ahead of all her former boyfriends because her brothers haven't tried to beat you up yet. Plus, when I saw her last week in town, she gave me a big smile and a nice hug, so I figured either she was thanking me for hiring you or was dumping you and going after me."

"Well, boss, when you got it, you got it," Bob laughed.

Tom paid the check and as they were leaving to start their rounds, his government satellite phone started its sterile ringtone, which startled Tom since it was the first time since he left Atlanta that it had rang. He answered it warily.

"Watson, are you there?" Brad's voice boomed out.

Tom smiled and replied, "Sorry, mister, you musta got the wrong number," and immediately hung up.

Tom laughed as it quickly rang back and Brad shouted at him, "It's me, you stupid SOB!"

"I know who you are, but who in the hell is this Watson guy?"

"Okay, okay, I get it. Guess what?" Brad said conceding to Tom's tactics.

"I'd guess, but I already know you're just gonna tell me," Tom said offhandedly.

"You're right. I am. Kate just got a call about a cattle kill in remote northeast Montana, and wouldn't you know, one of the few areas we don't have a team in place. So, Kate will be flying into Bismarck, North Dakota tonight and she wants us to motor up there in your CDC mobile, and pick her up at the airport around seven," Brad explained.

"Why didn't she call me?" Tom said a little disappointed. He could hear papers shuffle on the other end of the line so he knew Brad was catching up on paperwork. That's Brad, always putting paperwork off to the last minute. "And when will you learn to do paperwork more often? You let it pile up and pile up, and then you're stuck doing it for hours at a time," Tom teased.

"Yeah, yeah. You know I've never been one to push a pencil. Besides, paperwork isn't what gets the job done. Being in the field gets it done. Anyway, Kate said she tried to get you on your cell, but it goes directly to voicemail. Since when did you become a recluse and turn your phone off?"

"Since I learned that it could be you calling me at any time!"

"Well, since you blessed me with answering your phone, you better go ahead and get the van ready. Kate's foaming at the mouth to investigate this."

"Well, it is the first incident since our training," Tom reminded Brad.

"I know, and she wants to see firsthand if our protocols work well in the field. Bring your service revolver because there are bears up there."

"OK, I'll bring Bob up to speed and get the van ready. Where are you now?"

"I'm at a dairy about an hour south reviewing some tests but I have to go home and see Ellen, pick up some clothes, shaving kit, gun and credentials — just in case. Maybe Ellen can put up some coffee and sandwiches so we won't have to stop for lunch. I'll see you in about two hours."

"Roger that," Tom said in a serious tone.

"Who's Roger?" Brad joked back.

Chapter 20
Fort Peck Indian Reservation

The word spread quickly about the dead cattle, which had been found by an after-dark coyote hunter. Reservation leaders immediately called the authorities and then sent four tribal police deputies on ATVs to secure the site until the USDA could arrive. The investigation wouldn't begin until well after midnight.

The state road department was sending large mobile LED work lights and several generators so the work could start whenever the investigators arrived. There was, however, a real fear on the Reservation that this was a contagious disease event. There was already a push from the people to burn or bury the remains of the dead cattle despite firm orders not to approach within two hundred yards.

Joseph heard the reservation chatter on their old CB radio go back and forth and he wondered if it was the same group of animals he had seen the afternoon before. Curious, Joseph mounted up Wakinyan and rode out to the area he previously visited. This time, he reversed the route. He hoped that by taking that less obvious approach, he could avoid contact with the authorities, get a decent look, and return home without being noticed.

It had been a very restless night for his great-grandfather who was up and about the trailer shortly after two a.m., pacing and chanting softly under his breath, looking out the windows, going through his personal things and checking this and that. He set to writing in his journal with a renewed vigor and, at times, sketched intensely. When the sun came up, the old man made his toxic coffee and seemed more rested and at peace than Joseph had seen him for months. And for the first time in months, he didn't feel guilty leaving him home alone.

The ride up to the grazing area seemed to take forever and was a strangely silent course. The prairie birds who flushed from the grasses when they rode weren't calling or moving at all. The cloudless blue sky was absent of the raptors that drifted overhead calling out to each other. The deer and rabbits that normally were abundant, were nowhere to be found. The predictably alive and vibrant environment seemed dull and placid as if the whole area was drained of life.

Joseph pushed Wakinyan on and gave a silent shiver as the horse startled, nervously darting his eyes and snorting in a form of equine disapproval. Death was in the air and the horse knew it.

As they got closer, Joseph could feel his heart starting to race in anticipation of the two hundred plus dead cattle he had heard were at the site. The rumor he had heard was that only cows and heifer calves were dead. The big bulls and spring steers were reportedly still alive, but grouped away from the dead animals, staring blankly in disbelief at the bovine carnage.

Nearing the site, Joseph could see tribal police ATVs patrolling, and he pulled Wakinyan up short. He reached into his saddlebag and removed a compact spotting scope that he used when hunting. That saddlebag also contained his basic first aid kit, flint and fire starting tinder, a space blanket and beef jerky. He never left home without it, just in case.

He pushed his hat back and pulled the scope up, surveying the scene. The instrument put him at 450 yards out and he could clearly see the carcasses steaming as their body heat mixed into the cool morning air. Some of the cows still had long prairie grass clutched in their mouths, which reminded him of the illustrations he had seen at a museum of the sudden deaths of the dinosaurs, when the toxic cloud from the earth-smashing meteorite engulfed the creatures.

Joseph started feeling a little sick to his stomach viewing the change he saw in less than twelve hours since he had left. He pulled Wakinyan around to return home. He had had enough of this mystery and just wanted to get back and tell his great-grandfather what he had witnessed. He would have some insight or reassuring words. *Yes, Grandfather would know,* he thought to himself.

Chapter 21
Rural Northwest Wisconsin

Brad arrived in two hours, just has he had promised, and they started putting together everything they hoped would be needed for the emergency trip. Brad had brought his camping equipment, including sleeping bags that they used on family vacations. Because he was an off-again-on-again believer in being prepared for a disaster or the end of the world, he also brought two cases of drinking water and some 'gourmet' freeze-dried rations in case they ran into problems. He thought this would be a great time to see how 'delicious' they were.

"I have a real treat for you Tom!" Brad exclaimed. "Meals from my private collection of disaster preparedness dinners so all we have to do is add warm water and eat. I have been looking for a good excuse to break into my supply and try these babies!"

"Gee, thanks, Brad, but I don't think we are going off the map or anything. I think there will be food and water and possibly even bathrooms."

"Damn it, I forgot my composting porta potty," he lamented.

"That's okay, Big Guy, I think we'll survive," Tom laughed.

When they were all loaded up, Tom took the driver's seat and buckled up. Brad warmed the passenger side. The large crew van was a new Mercedes Sprinter 2500 series. It could seat five easily and had been modified to provide ample room for the diagnostic lab equipment, and even had a built-in refrigeration system and diesel-solar generator. If necessary, they had the capacity to operate off the grid for up to seven days.

The van's navigation system started to politely give them directions as they pulled away from the clinic. Next stop: Bismarck. Tom was having a hard time containing his excitement to see Kate again. He nervously tapped a pencil on his knee, and Brad said, "You're pathetic, you know that?"

"Sorry, man, I'll stop. I'm just really looking forward to seeing her."

Shortly after they pulled out of the driveway, Tom's cell rang. It was Kate. He put the phone on speaker.

"Hi, Tom, I just wanted to see how you two were making out and if you think you can make the airport before I land," Kate asked sounding a little flustered.

"You sound a little out of sorts," Tom said. "Are you OK?"

"I guess so, but since I received news of the emergency call from the Montana Public Health Service, I have had to make dozens of calls and talk to all kinds of different bureaucratic services. You know that was the plan. Anyway, some were helpful, but most had no idea what I was talking about. All those connections were supposedly confirmed by the CDC after Atlanta so there would be a seamless flow of information. We needed all the right people to be kept in the loop if an investigation was initiated. Apparently, there is no loop, just loopy people. I'm mad as hell," she explained.

"So, is the USDA still in charge of the investigation?" Brad asked her.

"Hi, Brad. Yes, in fact, we are totally in charge right now. It seems the CDC overspent their budget by zillions and they are tightening their belt. They will provide diagnostic help only and really no help in the field. Evidently, they are involved in something bad going on in Africa that will make this look like small potatoes. It's in our laps now and we have to make a good show of it."

"How come you're flying commercial? I thought they would hustle you up here in a turbojet helicopter, you know, boots on the ground," Tom asked.

"There are two reasons for that. First is the cost. Second is they would have to find someone else because I am terrified of flying, in general, so there is no way I'm flying that far suspended above the ground by vibrating rotors. I would need a medevac helicopter with a rubber room."

"And besides," she added, "your van is a mobile diagnostic lab that needs to be tested. You boys just get your lily white rears up to Bismarck on time. I will probably need a drink by the time I hit the ground."

"I think 'hit' may be a poor choice of words," Brad offered.

"You're right. I'll save 'hit' for when I see your goofy face," she laughed.

"Don't worry, Kate, I'll probably clobber him before we get out of Wisconsin. Besides we don't need a chaperone on this trip!" Tom laughed.

"That's not what I heard! Chicago may still be talking about you two for weeks to come!" Brad chuckled.

"OK, OK, you boys just meet me at seven. We will figure everything out from there while we continue on to Fort Peck. Be safe. I love you guys!"

"Love you, too," they answered in near unison, though the meaning behind each remark was vastly different.

Tom smiled thinking about being able to work with Kate after just seeing her for their romantic weekend. It was like a dream come true.

Brad kept the jokes coming as they passed Eau Claire and moved onto I-94W on their way into Minnesota. They needed to keep moving to reach the airport by seven so Tom pushed a little harder than he liked. He wouldn't keep Kate waiting. After picking her up, it would be an all-nighter of driving, but he figured if the GPS was correct and they didn't make too many pit stops, they should arrive on tribal ground by five a.m. That puts them on the actual site by daybreak.

There were also two USDA technicians coming in from either Wyoming or Colorado, he wasn't sure exactly. When they got closer, Kate would start making calls to the Reservation leaders ensuring all the equipment they needed to move carcasses was in place. With that many posts to complete, he didn't want to struggle physically with each one to get the required 10% necropsy rate completed. He was figuring that with the two additional techs, they could get through the majority of the gross work in one day. Fortunately, the weather had been unseasonably cool, so he hoped the cattle carcasses would still be in good condition and not a putrid mess. The job should be 'cookbook', in that the protocol manuals and guidelines left very little room for thinking outside the box. He remembered from Atlanta, 'Fresh is best, less of a mess'. Exactly how fresh was the question.

Brad and Tom arrived at the Bismarck Airport with about thirty minutes to spare, so they went to the Starbucks and bought enough coffee and sweet rolls for all of them and at least one refill. Because the van had a small microwave, they could reheat if necessary. Tom wondered if that was one of the intended uses for the small appliance.

Kate's plane was twenty minutes late because of strong headwinds and rough turbulence. She looked pale and spent as she moved toward the receiving area. They waved as they saw her, and a relieved look came over her that they actually were already there.

"At the risk of sounding like a complete baby, that was without a doubt the single worse flight that I've ever had to endure. For a while I thought I would need an airsickness bag. I tried to focus on you two traveling in that Mercedes coming to rescue me, but that only made it worse!" she joked.

"We love you, too, Kate," Brad offered, giving her a big hug.

"You know how I feel," Tom whispered as he embraced her, feeling their special connection.

Kate feeling better, got them back on track.

"OK boys, let's get a move on. We have a lot of ground to cover before morning and we better try to each get a couple of hours of sleep before we get there. If it's OK with your male egos, I drive first. I've got so much adrenaline going from that flight, I'll probably set a new overland speed record, especially since, from this point, we will be driving in very rural areas."

Brad volunteered to take the first rest shift and made himself comfortable on the second row bench seat. It only took him a few minutes to settle into a peaceful — for him — snore. Kate looked back at the big man and smiled at his ability to drift off so fast.

"Well," she said in a low voice, "it looks like he will be well-rested when we get there. I'm not so sure I could rest like that with what we are facing in the morning."

"Me neither," Tom replied, "so I'm OK letting sleeping beauty rest till we get close. At least one of us will then be working with a full deck and alert."

"I'm not so sure about the full deck thing, but you're right, one of us should be fully rested because it will be a full day. We are the first guinea pigs of this program so we can't screw up. All we have to do is come away with one solid lead or new piece of information — anything — so the geniuses can solve the mystery of these die-offs. I have a gut feeling it is going to hit the fan soon and I sure as hell don't want us downwind."

Chapter 22
Fort Peck Indian Reservation

Joseph Blackfeather was restless all that night, waking and thinking several times about what he had witnessed on that north prairie. The sheer waste of those animals he had seen laying on the sea of grass shocked him. The sadness he felt had to be similar to what his ancestors had felt when their beloved Tatanka or bison were slaughtered on vast killing fields just for their hides. That was a blood memory that lived in the soul of each Lakota. *Perhaps*, he thought, *what he had just witnessed had something to do with grandfather's persistent night visions.*

The sun hadn't yet risen, but he couldn't lie in bed any longer, so he decided to run down to the small twenty-four-hour market and fill up the pickup from one of the two old gas pumps that warned 'Cash Only!' Thirty bucks topped off the tank and he went into the store for coffee and a donut. Old Pete was at the register as usual and was anxious, as he always was to share gossipy news in his rapid squeaky voice. Old Pete was a squat guy who looked to be in his sixties, though Joseph knew he was actually in his mid-forties. Pete lived a hard life like most people on the Res and it showed on his face. He let his hair grow long despite the early onset of male pattern balding. With a round midsection, Pete didn't appear to be too malnourished and the lack of physical exercise was apparent. He lived with his ailing mother and was her sole caretaker. He did what he needed to do to make sure she received the meds she required for the arthritis that plagued her days. The fact that he was either at home with his mother or working at the store left little social time for Pete. So, he made do and talked up everyone who walked through the glass front doors.

"You going down to the village hall to see all the commotion Joseph? They said there are some Feds down there right now to sort this thing out. I guess they're vets, you know animal physicians, not the army type. The people are asking a lot of questions of them while they are packing up, you know, to see the north plains area. A bunch of people want those cows in the ground or burned. Not going to happen, they said, at least not yet. Pissing a lot of people off!" he gasped, catching his breath.

"Hi, Pete," Joseph started, slowly, calmly, "A little too much caffeine this morning?"

"Well, you know, stuff like this makes people nervous, and what if it is contagious to us or wipes out the Tatanka or hits the horses? And what if they take over this place, you know, the Reservation?"

"Not possible, Pete. This is sovereign ground. They need our permission to even be here, let alone isolate or quarantine any part of the Reservation."

"You really believe that, Joseph? After all they have done to us and all the broken promises, ca- ca- can you truly believe that?" Pete replied, stuttering nervously.

"I'm not sure what to believe except we can't live in the past. I think I'll run down there and see for myself what's going on. Then I'll find out what Grandfather has to say," he grabbed the coffee and donut and headed to the door.

On the way out, he pushed the door open for Betty Eagles and smiled at her as she passed him into the store. Immediately, Pete started with her.

"You going down to see..."

Joseph started the pickup and stared over the steering wheel as the orange and pink sun broke the eastern horizon. He was curious and what was the worst that could happen? They would just send him away, right?

It took less than a minute to get to the village center and Joseph could see a lot of activity going on, but no commotion like Old Pete had described. He saw the vets in their coveralls with 'USDA' emblazoned on the back and what looked like an ID and badge on the left and right side of their chest. They wore a type of deep blue baseball cap and had white, knee-high Wellington style rubber boots on. They appeared to be explaining something to several of the Elders and to the chief of police. Two other men in coveralls were nearby loading up a couple large four-man ATVs with trailers containing plastic encased equipment of some sort. Looking around he noticed several bystanders recording the scene with their cell phone cameras. It seemed everyone was getting along, so he decided to move in closer and see if maybe he could overhear some part of the conservation.

When he was close enough to hear, it was apparent that they were negotiations between the Elders and the one woman in coveralls. He overheard her say several men were needed to work the heavy equipment the state had brought in last evening. His ears perked up when he heard the words 'trustworthy and reliable', and $150 an hour. He had worked construction and was a safe, certified operator. Plus, he was curious as hell about what had happened out there. He worked in a little closer and signaled to Bert Eagles, Betty's husband, that he wanted to talk. Nodding, Bert excused himself from the group and moved over to where Joseph stood.

Bert had the classic features of a Plains Indian — heavily weathered face, deep-set soulful eyes and abundant gray and black hair carried proudly in a braided ponytail. He never said much, but was a great listener and he acknowledged Joseph with only a nod of his head when Joseph asked him to put a good word in for him.

Joseph watched as Bert said something and then pointed over to him as the group turned to look. One of the men broke off from the assembly and started toward Joseph.

"I'm Dr. Tom O'Dell with the USDA. Mr. Eagles said you were a reliable man," Tom said extending his hand. "That's what we want, but how good are you at keeping your mouth shut?"

Joseph grinned slightly, "I'm as good as you will get around here, but you will find that if any one of us promises something, that is how it will be. The only exception is the drunks, and I don't drink."

"OK, I buy that. Here's what we need. We have a major kill of beef north of here and we need to investigate it in a very specific way to see if: one, we can find a cause, and two, relate it to recent major die-offs of different unique species around the world. The Government feels this is an actionable security threat and could result in human as well as other specie's destruction. What we are doing here is very important."

That word 'destruction' hit Joseph hard. A destroyer creates destruction, so his great-grandfather's visions could have a direct connection to this.

"We need you today and maybe several more to deal with the clean up and securing the area. Also, the site will need to be monitored for about a year. How does that work for you?" Tom inquired.

"I'm available for whatever you need. I only have to run home and pick up a few things, feed and turn out the horses, and tell my great-grandfather where I will be. I'll also need to explain to him again how to us his cell. He's almost one hundred and I worry about him, of course."

"Is there anyone else you feel that is reliable and can handle that equipment?" Tom asked pointing to the large CAT dozer.

"I know Billy Eagles is good and he has two cousins that might want work. I'll check in with them. Either way I will have two more here to help within the hour."

"Good," Tom said, "then I will make you in charge of this part of the investigation. That means you're responsible that it is done properly. No screw ups, OK? There is way too much at stake."

"Yes, sir, Dr. O'Dell. I won't let you down."

Chapter 23

Billy and his cousin Rick jumped at the chance to work the heavy equipment and make some 'easy' money. Both were older than Joseph and had families with hungry kids, so for them this was a windfall. Joseph asked them to meet him at the equipment in a half an hour and then hurried to finish his chores so he would have some time to explain to his great-grandfather what was going on. The old man seemed frailer now than he had been in a few weeks and that concerned Joseph, but the he shook off Joseph's worries as he was quizzed about the cell phone over and over again. Joseph asked him a final time and he angrily responded, "If I can't get the damn thing to work, I'll send up a smoke message. I'm OK, have been for nearly a century, now you go and do your job." That ornery reply brought a smile to the younger Blackfeather's face.

They met by the CAT equipment and waited for their instructions. In about five minutes, the good-looking woman who appeared to be in charge, motioned for them all to assemble by the van. There were ten total in the group, including the five Federal agents, two reservation police and the three of them. It didn't seem like enough to Joseph for the job that lay ahead of them.

"OK, everybody, I'm Dr. Kate Vensky, and I am in charge of this rodeo. It is extremely critical that all of you understand that this project is under the authority of the United States Department of Agriculture and we are duly deputized to arrest and detain anyone who challenges our authority or decisions," Kate warned in her most authoritative voice.

The group sensed the severity of the warning and a couple of the guys shifted nervously from side to side.

Kate moved closer to the group, "You should be aware of this up front. We will not tolerate any bullshit. If you don't feel you can keep a confidence or complete the job at hand, you best leave now." She waited for anyone to decide they'd rather head on home. This time no one moved a muscle. They stood like statues, perhaps out of fear, but more likely out of resolve.

"Great. Then if all of you are on board, I will give you an overview of what is up and how we will proceed. First, to my left is Dr. Tom O'Dell and on my right is Dr. Brad Upton, both of whom are veterinarians," Kate said as she motioned toward Tom and Brad. "Behind me are veterinary clinical pathology technicians Sean Thomas and Rob Yeary."

Brad chimed in hoping to break the tension a bit, "They are really good with knives so don't mess with them."

Kate smiled seeing the new members of the group relax slightly, "So here is our agenda for this morning. We are going to caravan up to the site led by the police officers on their ATVs followed by Sean and Rob on their ATVs pulling the trailers. Tom, Brad and I will follow in the van, and you fellows will trail us with the heavy equipment. Once everyone is on site, we will survey the kill zone, document any gross findings and select the animals for necropsy and testing. Be sure to wear your coveralls, boots, gloves and face masks at all times. If you see something you think might be significant, don't touch, just call one of us over." Kate had a confidence that was unmatched when leading a group, even a group of all men. Tom admired that about her. She wasn't afraid to be herself even if it meant having to be a little authoritative.

The group nodded their heads in understanding, and maintained attention on Kate's instructions.

"Basically, we will review the site and then start breaking down the carcasses. While we are doing that, Joseph and your crew will dig and prepare the burial trenches to receive the remains. At the end of the job, the carcasses will be incinerated in what will be the largest BBQ these parts have ever seen. You will then carefully backfill those trenches and restore the landscape. Tom, do you want to describe what we should expect to see in regards to the carcasses?"

Tom nodded in agreement and addressed the group, "Sure. We have been fortunate so far that the weather has been unseasonably cool, so those carcasses should still be in relatively good condition. However, it is going to warm up dramatically later today so it's best if we get going now." Tom was pleased with how smoothly his part went considering he spent most of his time having one-sided conversations with his patients.

"Alright, I just want to thank you ahead of time for participating in this investigation. What we are doing here may have profound consequences for every living thing on the planet," Kate concluded as she shook hands with each of the workers.

They traveled for about thirty minutes and pulled right to the edge of the police perimeter, which was flagged out about one hundred yards from the dead cattle. The bodies were grouped in a football field-sized area and contained Angus, Hereford cows and calves that were either all black or black with white faces. A large group of mid-sized spring steer calves and four Black Angus servicing bulls held in a group that stood silently a fair distance west of the kill site staring dumbfounded at their approach. Kate had the work crew gather for her instructions.

"Well the first thing we have to do is try to isolate the living from the dead so Joseph, will you and your men put up that orange vinyl snow fence on the west, north and south sides of this mess to keep those bulls away from here? While they are doing that, the rest of us will suit up and do a walk through."

After everyone had donned the protective clothing, she led them over to the nearest of the dead cows. She was on her side with her head pulled back, her legs straight and rigid from her sides. Next to her was a spring heifer calve, probably weighing three or four hundred pounds that lay dead in a typical sleeping position with her legs folded under and head curled to the side, nose laying in the hollow of her flank. It seemed the cow had been standing by the calf in a maternal protective position when she died. Both appeared to have died instantly and unaware. Everywhere they looked, that same scene was repeated over and over again.

Kate spoke first, slowly, "Well, now, I guess we better get out there. I would like us to line up about equal distance apart and walk from here to the west. I want to look for any animal that looks different or unusual in relation to the others. Look also for blood, indications of trauma or any other dead species like field mice. Use your spray paint to mark anything weird and photo or video it. I want all of us in there because the more eyes we have, whether they are trained or not, the better our chance for success. Let's go."

They spread out and started to weave their way through the dead animals, all focus on the cattle and the ground around them. Tom could feel the sun to his back as the day was brightening and warming as it rose. Here he was in the middle of a major investigation, working with the woman he loved, hundreds of miles from his home. The sweet smell of the prairie grass was helping disguise the emerging gaseous odor of the dead ruminants, but it was apparent that by later in the day, this was not going to be a pleasant place. He witnessed death in his practice on a regular basis, but never more at one time than a half dozen or so that had been kill by a lightning strike gathered under an old maple tree. Unlike this, easy to explain and understand.

They walked silently and respectfully through the field stopping here and there to document an animal with a photo or write down an ear tag number. When they reached the western edge of the kill, they went north and did the same walk through procedure heading south. After finishing that pass, Kate dismissed the Indian crew for a coffee break and gathered the rest for a strategy session. There was a look of concern on her face.

"Well, that was interesting. I wasn't sure what to expect, but all this death is hard to comprehend. I just received a text about the satellite surveillance of the kill zone that indicated 209 dead here of which 49 were juveniles. From what I saw they all appear to be female. The bulls and steers didn't seem too affected. Bizarre. So using the Atlanta protocols, we need to post 16 cows and 5 calves. We are also to draw blood, fecal and urine on two bulls and two steers. We will do that last as they will need to be darted with chemical restraint. I'm afraid this is going to take a lot longer than we anticipated. Sorry."

Kate's SAT phone started to ring in weird sterile notes. Tom reached for his phone, but saw Kate put hers to her ear pulling her hair back to hear better.

"Kate Vensky," she smiled, "ah, Jules, Bonjour! Comment sa va? Oui, nous sommes ici. Combien? Tout? Bien. Merci. Au revoir!" she folded the large phone over and placed it in her pocket.

"That was Jules LeClerc from the Pasteur Institute in Paris. He was notified about this kill and is following the investigation closely. He just made a small request for some additional sampling. It seems they are working on a thesis that will require us to sample CSF and core cardiac muscle samples for their study. We are to also to draw CSF on the dead animals and sacrifice one steer as the control animal with that being a complete necropsy."

"How many animals does he want those samples on?" Tom asked.

"All of them," Kate responded reluctantly.

"What? Is he friggin' nuts? That will take forever! We don't have the manpower to collect all those samples. Those animals will be degraded and the samples worthless," exclaimed a frustrated Brad.

Kate had a plan. "Here's what I think we should do. We will select the animals for complete necropsy and mark them with green paint. Tom, Brad and I will do gross necropsies and collect the tissue samples and cultures. We will use Joseph, Billy and Rick to assist us. Rob and Sean, I would like you to start the CSF testing on the non-posted animals and, since most of these cows are in full rigor with their heads thrust back, I suggest doing lumbar punctures — it should be easier. Everyone you complete should be marked with a big red X. The police officers could also help us get this done. If anyone balks or gives you a hard time, threaten them. I think that covers it. Now, let's get rolling."

Brad turned to Tom and grumbled, "Who's going to threaten us?"

Chapter 24

The individual teams fanned out so that each was working in a dedicated area. Kate worked with Billy, Tom with Joseph, and Rick was to work with a still-grumbling Brad. Sean and Rob off-loaded the equipment bundles for the gross necropsies and unfolded the compact workstation carts. They left the large water bladders and a gallon of a Class 1 disinfectant on each cart. They also set up a main solar/propane generator to charge the battery packs for the power saws. Tom decided that he and Joseph would start on an easy-to-process calf because it might be less likely to discourage the young man than breaking down a full-size cow. He hoped to essentially ease him into the task.

"I know you all didn't sign up for this, so I'm surprised no one has protested this change of job description," Tom started.

"Doesn't bother me. Work is work, and this promises to be more interesting than sucking in diesel fumes all day long," Joseph replied casually. Joseph wasn't a man of many words, but he had so much to tell behind those eyes.

"Right..." Tom said with unease. He brushed it off. "Everything we do in a necropsy has a logical reason and for this type of mass death scenario, we need to work fast before the samples we collect break down and therefore have no diagnostic value. I will do most of the cutting and collection of the tissue and cultures. You will help me balance and support the carcasses with those large wedges over there. You'll record and document on the Path sheets the samples and place their preprinted accession number labels on every bottle or tube we collect. So, the first thing we will do is photograph the animal with a visible ear tag number and assign the accession number to that individual. After that, the rest is cookbook. I have a protocol to collect samples and that flat Styrofoam container by the saw has the tubes and bottles we are to use. They're pre-labeled 1 through 28 for each tissue sample — like kidney, liver, or heart. So when I start the cutting, you will call out the tissue to be collected. For example, you'll say 'Vial 1: trachea.' I collect, place it in the vial and you then document it on both the computer and the path sheet by placing the label in the correct spot. Then you scan it like you were checking out of a grocery. Where it says BY, place my initials TO. Also, be very careful, as these saws, knives and needles are extremely hazardous. Work smart and don't rush, alright? You don't want to pick up the nickname 'stubby' after working this job. Any questions, Joseph?"

"No, as long as you watch me and talk me through the first couple, I'll be fine."

"OK, let's set everything up on that white plastic folding table and inspect to be sure we have each item on the laminated visual check list. You will need to fill the buckets and put two gel packs and a good splash of disinfectant in each one. The orange bucket is for equipment and the green is for gloves and boots. Avoid getting those chemicals on your skin as they are caustic and might give you a good burn or bleach mark."

They made sure everything was ready and then positioned the calf on her back with the wedges supporting the stiff carcass from rotating or shifting while they worked. Tom took the large necropsy knife and split the animal in half from the chin to the pubic bone of the pelvis, releasing the postmortem gasses from the abdomen with a tympanic *pop* as he entered the abdominal cavity.

Joseph started reading and calling out the tissue names on each vial starting with number one, carefully holding open the vial while Tom placed the sample in it. Though they were onto a good pace and the slots in the foam specimen holder were soon filling up, Tom couldn't help but think there was just something more to Joseph. He felt like Joseph was too perfect for this job, but he just wouldn't admit to it. Tom chuckled as Joseph struggled with pronouncing some of the medical terminology, but he was a fast learner and soon picked up the lingo. The final step in the tissue collection was to split the skull down between the eyes to collect brain tissue and upper respiratory cultures. The new stainless power saw cut the cranium like butter with just a little smoke spiraling off the blade. Tom looked up and the young Indian was looking a little green.

"You OK?" he asked.

"Yeah, I'm fine. I hunt so the rest of this is fine, but that's the first brain I've seen. A little weird, you know?"

"You did great. Most would have passed out or tossed their cookies," Tom replied.

Despite Tom's failed attempts to get to know Joseph, they worked well together. With the first necropsy done and everything checked and rechecked, Tom gave Joseph the honor of spraying the big red X to signify a completed necropsy. One down and six more to go for Team O'Dell. They probably would need those lights tonight because it was promising to be a long day.

Chapter 25

By eleven a.m., Kate, Brad and Tom had processed four heifers and three cows — about two an hour. At that rate, they might be finished by midnight. The CSF samples had been collected so Kate put Sean and Rob on the job of positioning and pre-splitting the next carcasses ahead of each necropsy to cut down time. She then sent one of the tribal police to town to find three men who could work the heavy equipment so they could start the trenching to burn and bury the bodies.

They took half an hour for lunch, which had arrived from the village on schedule. Hot chocolate and coffee with ham and cheese subs were the main course and a large box of peanut butter and chocolate chip cookies would provide dessert and energy into the afternoon.

Kate, Tom and Brad sat off in one group to eat and the vet techs and Indians sat together in a group a short distance from them. They could hear the techs and Indians break into laughter as each shared stories or some line of BS.

"I think they are finally getting my jokes," Brad mused.

"Yeah, they are such great humor, it only takes three hours and a group analysis to get the punch lines," Kate retorted.

"Well, if you ask me, they are a great group of men — solid, hardworking and honest. My only concern is that Joseph is so very quiet; it's almost like working alone. He only talks when addressed, so I'm not sure if that is how he always is or if this whole thing just really bothers him," Tom said.

"You should try to engage him and see what is concerning him, if anything. Try some small talk, maybe he will open up to you," Kate added.

"Well," Tom said, "if something is bothering him, maybe he'll be better after lunch. There must be something going on."

The half-hour lunch went by fast and they had just gotten right back into the rhythm of the processing when the additional heavy equipment operators arrived from the village. Surprisingly, two of the new operators were female. Billy's sister and an aunt and uncle showed up ready to work wearing worn leather gloves and heavy work boots. Billy and Rick verified their ability and Kate directed them over where she had staked out the large trench site. Three hundred feet by one hundred feet and sixteen to twenty feet deep was to be a big hole. She hoped the thick prairie would give up its hold on the soil once they busted the carpet of sod. Her main concern was to get the dead cattle in that hole quickly and incinerated so they could close it up. It might be difficult to keep the other cattle at bay and the last thing she wanted was a pile of dead or broken bison in the trench.

The equipment started to roar, breaking the prolonged silence of the morning, as they positioned themselves to work. The backhoe started by breaking the perimeter surface and large chunks of the ancient perennial grasses gave up their hold on the earth allowing the smell of fresh dug soil to escape. Once that surface was cracked, the two bulldozers started pushing the dirt up one side of the designated area. The trench was on a slight rise that hopefully would be drier, easier to work and backfill. After a few minutes, it was apparent to Kate that the three understood what she wanted to accomplish and seemed to work well together. She hoped the pit would be finished ahead of the last necropsy so that the dead unprocessed cattle could be moved out of the way since the smell of death was increasing as the day warmed and the relentless, annoying blowflies had arrived to do their job.

The pre-splitting of the carcasses was cutting the sampling time in half and the repetitive cookbook nature of the sampling was becoming automatic. The teams were gaining on the job and Kate was becoming hopeful they might finish before nightfall.

Tom and Joseph worked well as a team and were flying through each animal. Tom decided to slow it up a little and try engaging Joseph in conversation.

"I really appreciate your hard work, Joseph. It looks like we will finish ahead of the others," Tom praised as he continued with a specimen sample. "How do you feel about what happened here. Do you have any ideas?"

"I dunno, I guess it's sad to see a normal animal die for no reason, and…" Joseph trailed off.

"And what? Have you ever witnessed anything like this on the Reservation before?"

"No."

"You just seem significantly affected by what happened. Do you want to talk about anything?"

"I guess it's just weird to know this herd was alive and well the evening before they died," Joseph admitted.

"You saw them the night before? Did you notice anything out of the ordinary? Was anyone around?" Tom was trying not to show his excitement.

"See anyone? No. It was just my horse and me. All I saw was a herd of healthy animals one day, and dead the next. But my great-grandfather... well... he is very bothered by the whole situation, too."

"What specifically is bothering you and your great-grandfather? Maybe I can help?" Tom offered. He wanted to try to get more information from Joseph to see if there was anything that could help them determine the cause of this particular die off. Joseph stared at his hands while he picked at the skin around his thumbnail. Tom tried another tactic. "You said you were with your horse when you saw the herd. What's your horse's name?"

"I call him 'Wakinyan'. It means 'Thunderer' in my native language, though I really don't speak much of it. My great-grandfather guided me more toward perfecting my English and studying. He didn't want to see me fall into the cycle of living on the Reservation," Joseph told Tom. He was proud of his education. Just one more reason his great-grandfather was the most important person in his life. He gave him a way out, a way to fight against the injustices that are handed down to children growing up on a Reservation. "I guess giving my horse a native name was my attempt at acknowledging my heritage and honoring my ancestors."

"That's a great name for a horse, Joseph. I'm sure you take great care of him, too." Tom was working to get Joseph's trust. He decided that Joseph wasn't going to spill his guts to someone he didn't feel comfortable with. "You know, I can relate to connecting with an animal. I have a dog back home named Jed. He's my constant companion and a lot of days my confidant," Tom gave a quiet chuckle. "There's just something special about a man and his animal. Nothing quite like it..." he trailed off hoping to give Joseph a chance to talk. Fiddling with a few of the specimen jars just to keep his hands busy, he waited in silence.

"Hmph. Nothing quite like it," Joseph repeated quietly. "You know, Doc, this has bothered me a lot for a couple of reasons. Wakinyan and I ride here often, and I saw these cows alive and well grazing the evening before they died. There was nothing out of the ordinary then and I left that night feeling at peace seeing them out here on the grasses. Now, I'm here at this... this... murder scene." Joseph's anger became physically evident, his voice quavering, but Tom didn't dare stop him. "You and I know both these animals were targeted. I am so angry at the sheer waste of these animals. It doesn't take a rocket scientist to figure out this was not a natural occurrence."

His anger continued to build as he motioned toward the dead animals still on the ground, "Not one animal we opened up looked to me to be anything but normal and healthy. I know you are just doing your job, but you know that this was an execution of these cattle, just like one of the events my great-grandfather has been warned about. He predicted this was coming."

81

"Whoa, whoa, whoa, wait a minute," Tom interrupted, "your great-grandfather predicted this and was warned? By whom?" Tom grabbed Joseph by the forearm out of shock. He had an incredulous look in his eyes, and with his free hand, ran his fingers through his hair.

Joseph wasn't affected by Tom's grasp, but took a deep breath and explained, "My great-grandfather is very old, almost one hundred, and has great spiritual powers which puts him in contact with the ancestors who look over us. Since he was seven years old he has received periodic warnings as disturbing dreams or visions of death and carnage. A 'Destroyer' was coming to wreak havoc on the earth, its animals and people. He has kept detailed journals where he documents these events going back decades. He shares some of it with me, but most he keeps private in his journals. Recently, these visions have become more vivid, detailed and disturbing. He is a man who is frightened of very little, but these recent visions have scared him shitless. What frightens him should petrify us."

"How much detail of these visions has he shared with you? Have you actually read his journals?" Tom asked. He didn't really think this was at all related, but thought the information was interesting to hear.

"He has never offered to share them so I have never dared to look. That is his burden and I would not offend him by looking at something so sacred without his permission or blessing. But when he passes, I will have to continue his legacy and maintain those records, something I'm not sure I'm ready for... or even want," Joseph admitted. He wasn't standing with the confidence he previously held, but rather with a submission to something he had no control over. Tom realized that Joseph truly believed he would begin having visions once his great-grandfather passed on.

This intrigued him and he thought it might be worth looking into. "Do you think your great-grandfather would talk to us? I think it's possible he could shed some insight on this problem of the die-offs. I agree with you that what we are doing here probably will lead to zilch, so we need to think outside the box if we are to get to the bottom of what's going on. If your grandfather is frightened and only knows a fraction of what I know about the magnitude of these die-offs, then I'm worried more than ever."

Joseph replied, "He needs to talk to someone about it other than me. He might feel that, until he passes on what has been revealed to him and unburdens his soul, he will be trapped in that old body forever. I'm just not sure if I'm strong enough to take it on."

Tom could sense Joseph's uneasiness, something he now shared. He offered one last comment, agreeing with the Lakota, "There may not be anyone strong enough. This is evil, pure evil."

Chapter 26

By 8 p.m., they had finished harvesting the samples and finally took a break to eat the left over sandwiches, cookies and some fresh coffee the town had sent out along with a box of fruit and a large pot of venison chili. They fired up the lighting cranes, and the bright LED lights made the field of death and large trench seem unreal, almost artificial. After they ate, Kate gathered the crew together for a review of the final steps they would take to complete the job.

An exhausted Brad still offered humor as they gathered, "Why do I have this overwhelming feeling that I'm in a stadium witnessing the results of the world's largest bull fight? I think it's called Déjà Moo!"

"No, Déjà Moo is that overwhelming feeling I've heard your bullshit before," Tom teased.

Kate laughed and took control.

"Well, I'm glad you boys are still able to joke after the day we just had. This had to be the most effective and efficient day of field pathology in the history of veterinary medicine. We managed to pull it off without any injuries, which in itself is amazing. Now we can close the book on this mess, clean up the site and get the heck out of here. Everybody be aware that I want us to move these remains respectfully into that trench. Also, I just took a call from the EPA and we are NOT to burn the carcasses. Instead, they want us cover them with hydrated lime. They shortly will be delivering one hundred and fifty impact-sensitive bags, about three tons. All we will need to do is push the bags with the dozers or toss them from the perimeters of the trench. They will open on impact and spread the chemical. The stuff is real dusty and caustic so I want everyone in full protective gear, including the respirators. Finally, I want to thank you all for your extreme hard work today, it was amazing to witness such a strong professional effort and I'll see if I can finagle a bonus or something else to reward you for that effort. I couldn't be more pleased."

As she finished, they could hear the distant beating blades of the approaching helicopter. Kate had Billy, Rick and Joseph set three flares on the north, east and south perimeters of the trench for drop locations thinking the west wind would blow any of the dust away from the dozers pushing the carcasses. They watched as the pilot of the big Montana National Guard Chinook Ch-47 F helicopter maneuvered the huge craft over the first flare and dropped the palate of lime right on target with a small puff of lime dust. Within twenty minutes he had off-loaded all the palates and the pilot waved off a goodbye with a thumbs up gesture.

The trench had been dug as a gradual ramp down on the west with a deep center and a sharp cliff-like wall on the east. Most of the spoil had been pushed north and south of the hole providing easy access to backfill the cattle grave. A dry, granular disinfectant would be broadcast over the actual necropsy area after all the animals were interred. That powerful disinfectant would be activated with the next rain, which was predicted within forty-eight hours. Unfortunately, even with reseeding, the prairie would take generations to recover the broken sod.

The bulldozers started the movement of the mangled remains, pushing deliberately to the back wall of the trench and as soon as they had all the remains in, the lime came raining down, bags exploding in white clouds turning the black carcasses a ghostly gray color as the Indians made a game of hitting every area of the trench. Once all the lime had been distributed, the backfilling began. By midnight, all the soil had been replaced and the disinfectant spread. It was pointless to do anything else as the tired crew was starting to move so slowly. Kate was afraid that they were accident victims waiting to be injured.

"We are going to call it a day," she started. "It's amazing, but we pretty much accomplished a couple of days of work in less than one. Tomorrow, we will meet at noon at the Sunrise Café and a few of us will return here for a couple of hours of dressing up the site. Doctors and techs, please see me so we can make sure all the specimen boxes are secure, labeled and ready to be shipped. Twenty-one for the CDC, and that one with the CSF tubes for shipment to Dr. LeClerc at the Pasteur in Paris. Thanks to all of you for your very appreciated efforts."

She started to clap in recognition, which rose to a cheer among them. Maybe what they had done here could make a difference. Joseph, and now Tom, weren't convinced it would.

Chapter 27

They loaded up the van and ATVs and shut down the big mobile lights making the area around them eerily dark, but the expansive sky was lit up with bright twinkling stars animated with brief flashes as many shooting stars appeared and disappeared in an instant. They left the windows of the van open to enjoy the clean crisp smell of air uncontaminated by death or chemicals. The clear skies had brought a frosty crust to the prairie grasses and the exhaust from the caravan of vehicles hung like a mist over the cold ground.

When they reached the village, surprisingly, the mayor and two council members were waiting for them having been alerted by the tribal officers that had participated in the investigation. They asked several questions and exchanged handshakes, happy that the dead cattle were in the ground. While they waited, Kate took contact information from each of the contracted Indians so she could forward their pay and bonus. She thanked each of them and sent them home. Except for Joseph.

"So, Joseph, have them at the Sunrise at noon. We will be at the Fort Peck Hotel if you need to contact us. Call my cell listed on my card or call the desk at the hotel. Thanks, you were a big help," Kate said, giving him a warm smile.

Kate felt a sense of relief to have finally put the day behind them. She had reserved five rooms at the historic hotel before they arrived for three prepaid nights, but now it was likely they wouldn't need them for all three nights. Tom entered the address in the van's navigation system and they started off to find the hotel with Sean and Rob following behind.

"I can hardly wait to get into a hot shower and wash this smell of dead cows off of me!" Brad exclaimed, "All I want is plenty of steaming hot water and a good bed because I am dog tired."

"Well, the hotel has good reviews and was recommended by the locals even though it is an old place, built in the 1930s. But it's in the middle of a park by a lake — quiet and fairly remote. By the way, it's said to be haunted!" Kate laughed.

"As long as they don't mess with my sleep, because if they do, I'll personally exorcize them out the door," Brad promised.

"I second that," Tom grunted wearily. "Spooks don't mess with me tonight."

They arrived to a deserted front desk and had to ring up the night desk clerk, who gave them a dirty look after getting a good whiff. While they waited for the clerk to finish a quick general orientation of the hotel and grounds, Tom softly brushed Kate's hand. She didn't look back, but he could see her smile. The clerk handed Kate the room keys and she passed them out, along with their remaining cache of cookies.

Cunningly, Kate had carefully selected the rooms so that Tom's was across from hers. The rest were down the hall, which suited her just fine. They made their way up to the third floor in the elevator and Kate secretly slipped her hand in Tom's. He traced the length of her forefinger as the elevator came to a sudden stop.

He was anxious to have some personal time with Kate and needed to inform her about what Joseph discussed with him. As the others made their way to their rooms, he signaled Kate to enter his. She stole a glance down the hall to make sure the others were in their rooms and darted in through Tom's door. She tossed her bag and room key to the floor and jumped into Tom's arms. With both hands on the side of her face, he leaned in and passionately kissed her not caring if anyone was watching.

"I've been waiting for that ever since we left Bismarck!" Kate admitted.

"Me too," Tom whispered in her ear, holding her tightly to him.

"I think we should get cleaned up and then get together for some cookies," Kate purred.

"Right, some cookies and then I have something kinda crazy to share with you that Joseph told me today. I hate to mix business with pleasure, but this may be too important to ignore."

"It better be important, buster, because I've had just about all the business I can stand for one day."

Chapter 28

They met in the lobby of the hotel at ten a.m. looking a little hung over from the previous day's hard work. Brad was, as usual, the last to show up as he tried to milk as much sleep out of the morning as he could. The group started to harass him playfully.

"I know, I know. But, you see, I didn't get much sleep till I chased Custer and Sitting Bull out of my room. They just kept shooting and punching each other. I think they need to move on and get over it. For God's sake, it's been over one hundred years, you know, smoke the peace pipe."

They all laughed at Brad's excuse with Tom calling Brad 'Sleeping Bull,' but deep down they appreciated his type of comic relief which helped get through the craziness with their sanity intact.

Kate gave the order to load up the vehicles and they headed back into town. After a brief stop at a McDonald's for breakfast, they entered the village and started their final review of the sample boxes, crosschecking ear tag numbers with the written manifest. There was to be a priority pickup from FedEx at eleven thirty a.m. so the samples could be in Atlanta and Paris by the next morning. The three vets and two techs planned to travel back to the site to create a checklist for Joseph to complete so they could be sure the primary site work was monitored as it recovered. After they finished the onsite inspection, Kate hoped that Joseph would arrange a meeting with his great-grandfather to get his insight on the die-off. She wasn't sure it had much to do with the cattle, but she was very curious what a nearly one-hundred-year-old Lakota holy man could add to their investigation.

When they arrived at the kill site, Kate was surprised how good it looked in the daylight compared to how it looked under the large LEDs. The green chemical granular disinfectant was visible on the ground and looked evenly distributed. Kate was relieved there was no evidence of any animals working the site, and happy her premonition of piles of dead, disinfectant-filled birds wasn't happening. The dirt that had formed the crown of the mass grave may have settled a little overnight, but she was planning on having the soil over the trench compacted today and grading the excess soil up over the necropsy area to cover the disinfectant area with a couple of inches of soil. That would take about an hour or two, and then Kate hoped they could meet with the old Indian before going back to the hotel for their final night before leaving in the morning.

The final dress up of the site went smoothly and Kate felt confident that everything reasonable was done to restore the environment. The USDA was to send a team to create a barrier fence around the site and would seed and mulch the exposed earth with prairie grasses and a wildflower mix. Then it was just a matter of time. The large grave held all the victims of the incident and the one sacrificed control steer. That steer was the one they felt the worst about. All three of them understood the need for a control animal, but it didn't make sacrificing an animal any easier. A life was a life, and in their profession, they saw their fair share of animals in death.

At four p.m., Brad, Tom and Kate left and followed Joseph's directions to his trailer. His great-grandfather had requested they bring along a recording device so that his words would not be misquoted or misinterpreted. He didn't have the time or energy to repeat himself he said.

Joseph greeted them and led them out to a west-facing deck. There was a small fire going in an open metal fire pit with rough handmade wooden benches surrounding it. His grandfather physically looked all his years, but had clear, sharp eyes which reflected all the wisdom of their years.

The old man was staring to the west and slowly looked up as they approached him. He rose, half standing, and shook their hands with the strength of a man who had done hard labor during his life. As they sat down by the fire, they could see the flickering flames reflected in those sharp eyes. He was solemn, but seemed energized by their presence.

They were about to hear a story that would change their lives.

Chapter 29

Nelson Blackfeather sat on a faded camo canvas folding chair that appeared nearly as old and worn as he did. His hair was a pure white that was striking against his leathery bronze skin, which was heavily wrinkled around those deep-set eyes — eyes trapped in his old shrunken body. He sat there projecting the calming feeling of ancient wisdom. Joseph was seated to the old man's right and quietly attended the fire, adding small pieces of wood to make the flames start to dance wildly. Kate, Tom and Brad pulled the wooden benches a little closer to the fire facing Nelson. To their backs, clouds on the western horizon began to block the low-setting sun and the fire cast shadows of flickering light back and forth around the group.

Nelson spoke, his voice low, resolute and clear. "My grandson has told me about cattle which died here and the other creatures which have also been killed. I know that these things have happened many times, in many places and were foretold throughout the generations. Life is always created and then always becomes destroyed. That is the truth of nature, but at times, that balance between these forces shifts as destruction outpaces the creation of Life which then becomes a consuming fire that is uncontrollable. We are now experiencing a cycle where the Destroyer of Life is testing the strength of Life's Creator.

"Every culture has stories of the creation of man and the start of time. Their stories may have different names and titles for the characters, but the common threads are the tales of floods, wraths of their god, and the constant battle of good versus evil. My ancestors have told me the truths of our world in visions and dreams from the time I was very young. I have been warned of these events and watched the faces of evil that causes them. These things I have recorded in the volumes of my journals and they will become Joseph's responsibility to do what he wishes after my death, but my hope is he will use them to solve mysteries like these animals dying. Many things in my journals will be self-explanatory when you place them in a historical perspective, but Joseph will see my knowledge always came before the actual events. The years 1938 to 1945 of my journals are a good example of how evil breeds destruction. There is always evil waiting for an opportunity to rise and destroy again. This I have been told, this I believe to be true.

"I am convinced that, what you call 'God', is the balance between the Creator and the Destroyer. The Lakota are not historically a traditional monotheistic people, but feel the Creator is the summation of all that is good that we believe in as a people. When the good or Creator favors us with peace, love, good weather and abundant supplies of food, Life is good. When we become the target of a rising Destroyer, then we struggle to survive — to exist. There has to be a balanced existence in all things, including living and dying."

The veterinarians sat mesmerized by the words the old man spoke. The truth they were hearing was penetrating into their souls and sent spasms of recognition up and down their spines. Nelson continued to speak.

"My life journals can help you, but they will belong to Joseph only. Seek his help with the problem you face as he will inherit the power that comes from our ancestors. They will bring to him their warnings and insight. There is no one but him to do this, the rest are not worthy. It will be a blessing and a curse for him, so you must help him as he helps you. Why do you think you are here right now? It is because it is a struggle between good and evil, and you four together will restore that important balance between good and evil, which is the only reason you ended up on this Reservation. Understand this: I am not long for this world and when I give up my spirit, this race to restore that balance begins. You must not fail."

The sky in the west started changing from a dark gray to near black, as the wind sent gusts of cold rivers that flooded past them with the ferocious tympani of thunder. Lightning flashed like gigantic sparks that cast brief shadows before them.

Nelson Blackfeather nearly sprung from his chair, surprising them all and stood erect, slowly lifting his arms skyward, casting his head back as pellets of rain started to fall. Holding that position for what seemed to be an eternity, he rotated his face back from the west 180 degrees to the east and then north and south, releasing a great sigh. At that, there was a direct tremendous crash of thunder that nearly put them off their feet.

Nelson turned toward them and said matter-of-factly, "Tomorrow is a new moon." He returned to his trailer without saying anything else.

The lightning and deafening thunder intensified as the day had become the color of night and the rain stung as it was forced down to the ground. Kate led the way as they made a mad dash for the safety of the van, frightened by the storm and intrigued by the old Indian. Something strangely mysterious and powerful had just happened.

Chapter 30

Brad was the first to speak when they got into the safety of the van. "What in the Hell just happened? That was the craziest and scariest ten minutes of my life, excepting my wedding, of course. I thought I might wet my pants when that deck lifted up after that huge crash of thunder. My ears are still ringing!"

Kate answered, "It was incredible! Crazy as it seems, I think we were just handed an unequivocal commission to save the world. That old man has some kind of power, I don't know exactly what, but he meant business. I felt like something entered me when he raised his arms and then it gave me a chill down my spine. I'm afraid our job doesn't end here, not today."

"I felt that same energy whack me, too," Tom said, "but it gave me a feeling of strength and energized me. I almost felt like a know-it-all teenager again, you know? Invincible! That was magical! I feel like a warrior!"

Kate proposed a new plan for the next day, "Originally, I thought we might leave tonight, but I think we should rest up today, put together some questions for Mr. Blackfeather and visit him first thing in the morning. Maybe he can share some specifics, if he has any, about these die-offs. Then, we need to keep Joseph and his great-grandfather as a resource so if more events occur, they can help us or offer their unique perspective. This was a little too weird to just be dropped in our laps like that. There must be a lot more to it that we are meant to understand right now."

They headed back to the historic hotel and by the time they arrived, the storm had driven its way to the east leaving a magnificent rainbow refracting in the face of the western-setting sun. The sky now seemed at peace with itself.

After an enjoyable dinner, they spent time discussing over and over again what they had experienced in the last two days. Everything they tried to reason through scientifically seemed to only be answered by the old Indian's powerful explanation of the Creator and Destroyer. Plans were finalized and questions developed for their visit to the trailer in the morning. Brad suggested they provide the Blackfeathers with a computer and Skype account so they could communicate face to face any time.

They were exhausted after dinner and the brainstorming, most of their adrenaline spent from two exhausting days. The vet techs had left earlier in the day to travel back to Wyoming and all the samples had been shipped. The 'Three Musketeers' would head back home after seeing the Blackfeathers in the morning. Then they would drop Kate off at the Minneapolis airport. They would then wait on all the tissue sample analysis from the CDC and Jules' tests at the Pasteur, but that most likely would take two weeks or so to get.

Kate and Tom spent that last evening together talking about their future as a couple. Even though they loved their professional lives, there was a passion for each other that left their traditional common sense behind. Kate said it and Tom knew it — they were soul mates.

By eight a.m., they had checked out and stopped at McDonald's for coffee and breakfast. Because they had a long trip ahead of them, Kate was anxious to see Joseph and Nelson Blackfeather to find out if what they had experienced the day before was as real as it had seemed, and talk to them about resourcing those journals and Nelson's insight. Then she wanted to get on the long road home.

When they arrived at the trailer, there was a tribal police SUV parked in the driveway so they pulled off to the side of the road and walked through the weedy yard to the front door. Joseph answered the knock at the door, looking upset. He spoke before they could ask.

"My great-grandfather, Nelson Blackfeather, Lakota Shaman and spiritual leader of this community have entered the world of our ancestors."

He motioned for them to enter the trailer. They saw the police officer, hat tucked under his left arm, writing on a clipboard. He looked up, nodded to them and then spoke to Joseph. "I'll call Johnson's and have them pick him up as soon as they can. You said his wish was to be buried today before sunset, so when you know the service time, call me and I'll have the radio station announce it. I will arrange an e-blast announcement with our emergency notification system. You know, that reverse 9-1-1 thing?" The officer started to turn to leave, but turned back and said, "Again, sorry for your loss, Joseph, he was a great and special man. The last of our ancient ones."

He shook Joseph's hand and gave him a pat on the back as he left, replacing the ivory colored hat on his head.

Kate spoke for all three of them expressing their sympathy and asked if they could help in anyway. Joseph politely refused.

"What happened after we left last night, Joseph?" Tom asked, concerned.

Joseph walked to the old discolored bookshelf that held worn books, family photographs, and a few Indian carvings.

"After you left he looked like all the life had been sucked out of him. Pale and kinda gray, but at the same time at extreme peace and very calm. It was very strange. He started showing me all his hiding places for his personal stuff. He was like a squirrel. There were places with cash, places with important papers, including a life insurance policy from a company that probably doesn't even exist anymore. He showed me birth certificates, the deed to this place and one to 160 acres he homesteaded during the Depression. I had no idea about the homestead. He smiled and told me it was probably wooded now and should have good hunting on it. All the deeds and insurances were in an old rusty lockbox with a lot of old gold coins from the 1800s," Joseph rubbed his face with both hands as if he were trying to wipe away his grief.

"He said the coins were taken from dead soldiers at the Little Bighorn. There was a box that held ornate beaded baby moccasins that he said went back to eight generations of firstborn males in the family. They are very small and quite beautiful."

Joseph moved toward the single-paned window and stared, as if searching for something. He stared past his land, past the Reservation, and into his ancestor's souls. "The problem with people is that they often refuse to remember, and then they don't learn from their past. Grandfather said the past is the future and the key to the future is contained in the past... whatever that meant." Joseph turned back toward the three sitting on the old, dusty couch that had faded over time. He walked back to the bookshelf and picked up a tattered notebook.

"He showed me his journals, which he had on shelves and under his bed in neat bundles of dated gallon Ziploc freezer bags. Look at this one," he said as he handed the notebook to Tom.

"Wow, this one dates back to the late twenties," Tom said as he skimmed through the pages of the old man's mind.

Joseph looked over Tom's shoulder as he said, "They contain his personal thoughts on life as a Lakota, as he experienced it, and was told to him by his great-grandfather, grandfather and father."

"That's quite a valuable item, Joseph. Not many people have journals that go back that many decades. What a great family heirloom," Kate offered consolingly.

"It is. But it has value for another reason. They also contain the dreams and visions he experienced," Joseph said. "He illustrated many of his entries and was quite a good artist," he added this as an afterthought, smiling at the still-fresh memory of his great-grandfather.

"He carried a small paper checklist and went through each item on it with me till he reached the end. Then he grabbed me at arm's length and looked me directly in the eyes and said resolutely, 'never forget'. He gave me a shoulder pat and turned toward his room. I knew then it was his last day." Joseph allowed himself to weep in front of the group. Brad reached out and put his hand on Joseph's shoulder comforting the young man.

"He loved you like a son, and he knew you loved him," Brad said showing a side of him not many people have the privilege of seeing.

"Thank you. Well, after that I didn't know what to do so I tried to sleep in the chair I kept outside his room for the days he had a lot of bad visions or dreams. I just sat there and listened to him breathe until I must have fallen asleep, because I was woken up by a voice that called to me, 'Joseph, wake up, you have a job to do. Don't you remember?' Scared the crap out of me. I sat up and listened and couldn't hear him breathing. That was four a.m. and then I knew he was gone. The night before he told me he was born at four a.m. on a new moon."

"A new moon just like this morning," Brad said nearly inaudibly.

Joseph nodded, "I got up and checked on him. He looked at peace. The trailer was so quiet I had to leave, so I went out to the horse stalls to muck them out and groom them, something that relaxes me. Wakinyan was restless when I entered, so I went over to him and talked to him and he settled down. Then I went over to my grandfather's horse Lightning's stall, and there he was on his side, dead. The funny thing was he also seemed at peace. I guess the two of them went off together."

Kate gasped as she heard this last bit of information about Lightning. Tom grabbed her hand in response and she held tight to him.

Kate asked, "What will you do with your grandfather now?"

"My people will return him to the earth today and I will try to bury the horse, if I have time. We will honor him today and then I will start on the things that he asked of me, and try to get you some answers from his journals. We are now linked by his spirit to locate this evil, this Destroyer, and then find a way to restore that balance he called God. Fail at this and we will have allowed the Destroyer to win. I pray that we are as smart, strong, and humble as he was. Otherwise, the world as we know it may be no more."

Chapter 31

They expressed their sympathy and apologies for not staying for the funeral service and having to leave and head back home, but promised to stay in touch.

In the van, Brad was the first to comment on what had happened, "This whole thing is getting creepier and creepier by the minute. Now we are knights on a crusade, commissioned by a now-dead centurion Indian, against this 'evil' one, so we can save humanity and all the creatures on the earth. I just want to go home and get back to reality, see my wife and kids, and then kick back and watch a Walking Dead marathon." Brad clicked his seatbelt and quickly added, "Oh, yeah, I forgot, in my underwear."

"Now that's creepy. Maybe when we corner this evil one, the 'Destroyer', you can challenge him to a best two out of three Sumo matches, winner takes all. Just think, you can wrestle in a diaper," Kate said, trying to sound lighthearted.

"The last thing I think we should to do is trust the fate of the universe to this guy in Pampers. We better come up with a plan B," Tom scoffed.

Their joking was helping relieve the tension over Nelson's death and the unequivocal commission he had laid at their feet. They now had less of an idea on what they were facing after this trip than they had when it started. How do you stop something called the 'Destroyer'?

Tom started the engine and Kate clicked her seatbelt as Brad commented, "This sounds like a job for Superman, not a job for three vets and an Indian."

Around noon, Jules LeClerc called from Paris to inform Kate that the samples had arrived safely and they would start their testing first thing in the morning. Kate explained briefly to Jules what had transpired with Nelson Blackfeather and that she would call him on Monday so she could go into more detail. She spoke in fluent French and their conversation was rapid and seemingly exact, with lots of affirmatives. Kate was smiling, looking beautiful and very smart as she talked. Tom loved to hear her speak in French. It made him think of Gomez Addams' reaction to his wife's French on the old sixties TV comedy. Sexy — that was the word — she was very sexy. Kate then used the one word that Tom recognized in the conversation

— Destroyer. He was now way too familiar with it. Kate repeated it several times because Jules seemed particularly interested in it.

Tom was driving and Brad had stretched out on the bench seat. Kate finished the conversation with a 'goodbye' to Jules in English and closed her phone. She immediately started busily typing some notes on her personal iPad. He smiled, having no idea what she saw in him.

"So I'm writing down everything I need to get done in the next week. Because we are getting together for that trip to Cape Ann in less than two weeks, I want everything well organized and documented this week, well before we leave. I'm not sure if I have a basis to include what Nelson told us in my summary report, because it's not based on fact or science. It was incredible, true, I'm just not sure it's credible. When we understand it better, I might submit it, not before. I don't want to be known as 'that crazy Vensky'."

"So why was Dr. LeClerc so interested in the 'Destroyer'?" Tom asked.

"I'm not sure why, but he asked if I could get copies of those journals written during the Second World War up to 1948 forwarded to him. I'm not sure Joseph will go for that, are you?"

"No, I don't think those journals are going anywhere without Joseph attached to them. They are way too personal and I'll bet until Joseph has a chance to grieve and settle things out, he'll keep them private. Period," Tom offered.

As he spoke, he watched a strand of hair keep falling from behind Kate's ear. She absentmindedly tucked it back as she said, "I'll inform Jules on Monday. Maybe he can figure out a way."

"Right now my focus has to be getting back to work and giving Bob some relief. I feel real guilty shoving the entire practice workload on him. I hope we don't have anything else to investigate for a while because time wise, I need to be with you, and I want to be fair to him. I better start thinking about offering him a piece of the practice, maybe then he will feel more invested in the business, not just like he's being used. He might be my only shot at a 'normal life'," Tom said.

"You best look into it because I have a feeling, call it a woman's intuition, that our meeting up with Joseph and Nelson plus all the other stuff we experienced this week has some significant purpose. What happens from this point forward might be part of something so big and bad we could be consumed by it. I want us to be prepared for any potential outcome," Kate explained.

"Now you're scaring me!" Tom answered only half kidding.

"Me, too. Scared for us and for the rest of the world," Kate said seriously.

Tom continued heading south while Kate typed away on her computer. Despite the mundane tasks they were both doing, the thoughts racing through their minds were anything but.

Chapter 32

Joseph tried to keep himself busy in the days immediately following his grandfather's death. There had been a great celebration of the man's long life with full tribal honors and a traditional burial ceremony. The number of people who showed up to pay their respects, especially considering the short notice given for his burial service, amazed Joseph. Several families had traveled over one hundred miles to honor him immediately after hearing of his passing.

Billy had helped Joseph bury the old horse, which turned out to be a real chore. When Lightning had passed, he was laying on his side fully stretched out to the width of the stall. The horse was stiff and impossible to turn, even hooked to the John Deere tractor. To get him out to the freshly dug grave under the big old apple tree the horse had loved so much, Billy and Joseph cut though and braced the back of the stall so it opened to the pasture. Then, with heavy construction chains, they dragged the horse's remains. Something that should have only taken a couple of hours stretched into a six-hour ordeal, all the while Wakinyan expressing restless grief at the older horse's death. He seemed agitated and swished his tail aggressively while pawing the ground nervously. It was apparent to Joseph that he would need to find a stable mate, either an Indian pony or a goat to settle the horse. Well, maybe not a goat because Joseph disliked the goofy way they acted, but mostly he hated how they smelled.

Now he spent his time going through his great-grandfather's belongings, constantly being amazed at the volume of stuff that the old man had collected. There were old license plates going back forty years, family records, old photos — some black and white and some with faded color. On the back of each photo in scribbled handwriting was the who, what and when. He found prescription vials with pills disintegrating that dated back to the sixties and a pack of condoms that had to be fifty years old and probably needed to be in a health museum. As he uncovered each of these treasures, a new window was opened to the life the man had led.

The first journal entry was dated May 19, 1928 and was written the day that Nelson's own paternal grandfather died at the age of eighty-eight. The story he recorded about being a warrior survivor of the great battle between George Armstrong Custer and Sitting Bull at the Little Big Horn, described how the eighteen-year-old had fought, celebrated victory and then ran for his life with the assembled Lakota from a United States Army seeking revenge. He had witnessed glory become disaster and he made sure his grandson understood how they lived as a people and how they were systematically domesticated on a 'Reservation' by ignorant Federal policies. Nelson had sat as a child by the knee of this man who was a wise shaman, intent on passing on the knowledge of the old ways, and with it the responsibility for tribal integrity. The stories Nelson had heard repeated over and over again became the fiber of his soul and he never forgot what he was told. That first journal contained recorded history, folk stories and remembrances. Page after page revealed the basis for that next tribal shaman to function, including the Creator/Destroyer story, how the Lakota received their souls, and what the afterlife was to be. Great tales were recorded about the bison herds, which covered the plains. It recorded patterns of duck, geese and pigeon flocks, which could darken a sunny day as they passed overhead, and of a people that were content and self-sustaining before the white man forced their will. The story evolved to one of a decline of their people, of battles lost in keeping their lands, of those vast herds of bison sacrificed for only the skin on their backs, and how that great victory over Custer became a curse on their people, of flight, fear, starvation and the humiliation of total defeat. Joseph read the words, which had been written passionately, with sadness and such beauty that they brought tears to his eyes.

The record on how the people lived and died was as exact as the description on how Custer had died. It also provided the family names of the braves who had directly been responsible for the soldier's death, and a detailed record on what they had done to him after the battle. Gruesome, but they had been battling for their very survival as a people, as a culture. Nelson had also recorded lineage of the family Indian ponies that went back to the horse which had carried his grandfather into battle and who had also been called Lightning. That made Joseph smile thinking that the horse he had just buried was also joining his ancestors.

After his recording of family stories subsequent to the death of his grandfather, came the beginning of the dreams and visions that would haunt him for the balance of his life. Initially, Nelson spent his efforts recording the most important ancestral history of his Lakota kin, but as the dreams presented new messages, he took to putting them down in great detail in his journals. He recorded his family triumphs on the farm and the tragic deaths of three of his four children to measles and influenza. Nelson's sole surviving son was Joseph's grandfather who grew up and lived on the homestead during the Great Depression. The family survived on that farm — poor, but happy until Nelson's wife died of pneumonia in 1938. Nelson could not reconcile her loss and moved the family off the homestead to a wheat-producing farm near Bismarck. Here his visions and dreams became much more vivid and disturbing after his son left for the army at the start of World War II as the stories of death and destruction became disturbing daily headlines. Those dreams contained images of unbelievable violence, fires, human bodies piled high, and billowing smoke. He would wake, terrified, with the smell of smoke and death filling his nostrils and the lifeless eyes of the dead haunting his mind. Other times he would see fields of dead bison surrounding destroyed Indian villages with bodies of women and children staining the snow with their blood. At times in the dreams, he ran in the cold, deep snow, his legs leaden from the effort to escape a revenging Army. He rarely had a peaceful night during the conflict years of the Second World War and constantly worried that he had lost his sanity.

When the war ended and the evil of the Nazis was revealed to the world, he started believing that what he was receiving were visions, not nightmares. The immediate years after the end of the war were some of his happiest with the return home of his son, then the marriage of his son and birth of his grandson, Joseph's father. Those happy days changed to another cycle of visions of burning jungles and incinerated bodies that correlated days in advance of news reports from Vietnam. About this time he moved to Fort Peck, bought his trailer, in hopes that tribal life would relax his troubled soul.

Then his life started to change dramatically. He lost his son on an icy road after a night of drinking in 1985, and ten years later, Joseph's father from suicide brought on by the despair of an alcoholic life. Joseph's mother had fled years before from constant drunken abuse, so Nelson adopted young Joseph and swore to never let him fail, as the others had done, and to live a life of truth and self-respect. Joseph became his mission and, although they were separated by decades of age, they became true brothers bound by their blood. Nelson made sure the young boy had the tools he needed to understand who he was and also the history of their people, so that he would never forget. In his heart, Nelson knew that someday this boy could make a real difference in the world.

His most recent entries revolved around the 'Destroyer'. Again, with more recorded scenes of death and destruction, including swastikas on every page and several sketches of a man he had recorded once before in a 1943 entry. The images were similar to that of a police mug shot with front, right and left profiles. The face was of an intelligent looking man in his late twenties or early thirties with close-cropped hair and small wire rim glasses. Surrounding this last image, written in bold red ink — the only entry that he had ever seen not in pencil — was a message all in caps, 'DESTROYER, DESTROYER MUST BE DESTROYED.' They were the last words he wrote.

As Joseph closed that last journal and placed the notebook back in its plastic bag, he stared out of the large picture window, which looked out over the deck, to the west. A large orange sun was rapidly setting and it was then he realized he had spent the entire day absorbed in his grandfather's writing. He felt strangely proud and somewhat saddened, but at the same time energized. He knew the old man's burden was now on him, possibly to help solve this strange die-off mystery. He reached in his back pocket and retrieved his wallet and located Kate's business card. As he dialed, he mumbled to himself, "What in the Hell have we gotten ourselves into?'"

Chapter 33

When Kate received Joseph's phone call, she was leaving the office after a meeting with her superiors on how the new investigatory process had proceeded in Montana. She had everything well documented and was asked to prepare a PowerPoint presentation for the various agencies, including the foreign participants in Atlanta. She also included the processes used and the results of the tissue analysis. While in her meeting, she received authorization to send checks to each of the non-governmental workers who helped on site for $2500 each. When her phone rang, she was a little surprised to be hearing so soon from Joseph.

"Hi, Dr. Vensky," he started.

"Hi, Joseph, it's good to hear from you. What can I do?" Kate happily replied.

"I need to talk to you about Grandfather's journals. There appears to be a ton of information, which in some strange way I feel may be relevant to your investigation. I think we need to focus on what he called the 'Destroyer'. This consumed grandfather in his last months and there must be a reason for that. Also there is a lot of real nasty stuff that revolves around World War II."

"OK, well, first of all, please call me Kate. So, Joseph, I'm really not sure where we go with your information, but I agree your great-grandfather understood he was given something powerful and mystical."

"Yes, he has a wisdom unlike anyone I know. Well, *had* a wisdom unlike anyone," Joseph added regretfully.

"I'm so sorry for your loss, Joseph, but just remember you're not alone in trying to figure this out. Tom, Brad and I are here with you," Kate offered before moving on with the conversation, "Our work on these events has gotten us nowhere so far, and our standard and expanded epidemiology processes have not been helpful at all. To top all that off, we just learned today of a pig farm kill in the Ukraine and a zoo in Brazil where the entire chimpanzee population died under mysterious circumstances. Alive one minute, the keeper turns his back and all 17 are dead as door nails in a split second. The chimp is our closest biologic relative, so those dead chimps are hitting quite close to home. I wondered if you would mind sending me the journals so I can have them analyzed?"

"No, sorry, Kate. They are way too important to me to leave my possession. It's a life's work and I just can't chance something happening to them. If they were lost or destroyed there is no way they could be resurrected. Besides, some of it only I would understand because it comes from a Lakota perspective, his perspective."

"Can you scan the pages and send them to me?"

"Nope, I don't have a scanner." He reluctantly added, "I might be able to photograph some pages with my phone, create a file and email it to you. That way you could see if they have anything relevant to your agency's investigations. Just remember that they belong to me and me alone, not for public review. I don't want people passing judgment on Grandfather, you know, thinking he was nuts or something."

Kate could sense the wariness in Joseph and reassured him that the files were safe with her. "I promise no one other than Tom, Brad or me will see it without your consent. Try to send the email to me before tomorrow and I'll start working on it immediately," Kate responded.

They agreed to conference a call after she, Tom, and Brad had the chance to review what he would send. Having been on the Reservation and meeting Nelson, Kate understood Joseph's concern over the journal's potential exposure to 'outsiders'. They had been private for a lifetime, but now needed outside analysis to see if they really had value, or if they were just the rambling of a crazy old Indian. Would the conclusion be that Nelson was just that, an insane old man, or might he be a modern day messiah, saving the world from biologic Armageddon? Kate feared that he was that prophet, and the evil he spoke of was going to draw them in and try to destroy them in the process. Something powerful and unstoppable? She feared for the love that she and Tom now shared, that it would vanish, being destroyed by their pursuit of something evil. Or worse, maybe they would be killed or severely injured. It was something for them to seriously consider.

All the things that were happening started to remind Kate of old cartoons of the bearded long-haired man in a nightshirt carrying a placard announcing 'Repent! The End Is Near!' She wondered how many of those signs were being shouldered around the world right now, because maybe they were spot on. If any species could be selectively eliminated or gender specific assassinations possible, then 'the end' could be imminent for any living, breathing thing on the earth. An ultimate weapon. The harbinger of death and the end to natural selection. Mold the world you want and pick only the playmates you want on your block. The idea of it sent a rapid shiver down her spine.

The next morning, the email with photo attachment from Joseph was in her phone inbox. Still in her pajamas, Kate grabbed an apple as she waited for the computer to finish printing the pages. Fresh off the press and warm in her hands, she sat down with her coffee and fruit to look them over. The quality of the photos was really pretty good and she was impressed with the detailed writing and artistic interpretation of the visions. Nelson had captured the crematoriums of the Nazi death camps with their tall smoke stacks, even though at the time he drew the images, he had no idea of what he was recording. The faces of the dead with their emaciated bodies had been drawn in horrific detail, as they appeared stacked like winter cordwood. The faces he drew appeared to be vainly pleading for justice. All these images were dated pre-1943, at a time when the horrors of the camps were unknown to the general public. By the time the world gasped at the revealed atrocities in newsreels, Nelson had lived with the images in his mind for three years. Kate empathized with the burden he must have felt. His personal strength had to have been incredible.

With a never-ending list of questions and very few answers, Kate needed to clear her mind. She pulled a green performance tank over her head and pulled on black running capris before lacing up her running shoes. She would head toward the city limits for a long 10-mile run. This was Kate's way of making connections and sifting through the information that gets jumbled in her mind. *This just doesn't make sense*, she thought as she headed down her driveway toward the street. "Maybe it will in about 10 miles," she said out loud hopefully.

Later that day, Jules called to say hello and ask her about the things she had witnessed in Montana. They playfully argued in French and English about which language to speak in, with each professing they needed to practice in the other's native tongue. Jules said her French was better than his English so Kate gave in under the weight of his compliment.

"D'accord, en Anglaise maintenant," Kate said. "OK, in English now."

"Oui, mon chérie, in English," Jules replied. "OK, Kate, tell me what happened during your investigate... uh, investigation. Any significant findings or leads that might send us searching in new, more productive direction?"

"Well, my friend, we processed the standard ten percent of the dead cattle and that one steer that had not been affected. Other than the normal stuff, like several walled off abscesses from metal foraging and one older cow with a liver mass and some intestinal parasites, nothing stood out. Seemed like a sheer waste of time and effort, but I did enjoy being in the field again. We'll have to see what comes from the tissue samples we collected to understand if it was really worth the time and money."

"We, here in Paris, are working on your CSF samples, but so far they show also nothing. The 'brains' at the Pasteur are speculating that we must be dealing with some kind of programmable pulse of energy that causes death by suddenly stopping the heart or scrambling the brain. After some thought, we decided to concentrate on the brain because these animals never move, they drop dead in an instant, whereas a cardiac event causes the animal to run or struggle until the brain is oxygen depleted and the circulation collapses. If it was the heart, they could run, seize, but death is not instantaneous, it can take several minutes. I am calling our theory a Biological- Electromagnetic Pulse Event, almost like a nuclear EMP event where all electrical circuits fail due to a massive disruptive burst of energy. The CSF samples will hopefully give us a lead on that, plus today we received thirty brains from some Ukraine pigs that died acutely. Also our researchers are testing whether we can shut down the brain's electrical circuit board in mice by using various microwaves, sound pulses and electrical pulses. So far, we have nothing but a bunch of unhappy rodents. That is OK because, as you Americans say, Rome wasn't burnt in a day."

"Interesting theory, but the phrase is 'Rome wasn't built in a day'," Kate teased.

"Sorry, you see, my English is not so good."

"Your English is better than most Americans, silly. There is, however, something more on this 'Destroyer' than we spoke about when this all started. The Indian who explained to us about this evil entity, heard about it from his great-grandfather, a Lakota Sioux shaman, who kept meticulous records of disturbing dreams and visions that had haunted him for decades. We met this man the evening before we left and it was a surreal experience to say the least, and very, very scary. That old man died in his sleep that very night after we had listened to him explain what we were facing and why it was so important to eliminate this threat. He also gave us an unequivocal commission to do just that. Early this morning, I received some copies of his journal entries revolving around the Second World War and there has to be some connection to Nazi Germany, just I'm not sure what it might be..."

Jules interrupted her, "Perhaps you can send them to me so I can run them though my government's resources as we have a lot on the Nazis and there are still many in my country who survived those dark days who take a personal interest in what those bastards did."

"It's possible, but I may not be able get him to release them to you. You see, he only trusts Tom, Brad and me to review his grandfather's archives. If he gives the OK when I call him, I'll get them to you ASAP."

"Bon, but what is this word *ay-sap*?"

"It means 'as soon as possible'," she answered.

"You mean très vite!" Jules replied.
"Oui, mon ami, très, vite!"

Chapter 34

When Kate had convinced Joseph that they would have access to a huge resource by sending the selected journal entries to Dr. LeClerc, he agreed, anxious to get some answers himself. Because it was 1 a.m. in Paris on a Saturday morning when she sent the email and attachment, Kate figured that Jules would review them in his office on Monday. However, her phone rang barely five minutes later showing an international phone number.

"Jules, I'm surprised to hear back from you so soon. Was there something wrong in how I sent the information over to you? And isn't it, like, 1 a.m. in Paris right now?"

"Oui, et Bonsoir, Kate. My wife and I just returned from a dinner with friends at a small fabulous restaurant on Ile Saint Louis. I'm fairly strict about reviewing my email a couple times a day, every day, so I was eager to see what you had sent. Ils sont trés intéressant, n'est-ce pas? Very impressive art work and writing by Monsieur Blackfeather and also very disturbing and unsettling. That Nazi imagery seems vaguely familiar so I just sent the sketches to a good friend whose father was a famous Nazi war criminal hunter and is still alive, but very old. Perhaps his father can run the images through his facial recognition program to see if the images are of a person of interest. The old Nazi hunter is in his nineties, physically a little feeble, but his mind is very sharp and his long-term memory is especially good. Maybe if he puts a name to that face it could shed light on the rest of the mystery we are facing. We should know in a couple of days and I am thinking, based on what we learn, you and this young man should come over here so we can see the original work and do a complete analysis. The Pasteur will arrange your transportation, credentials and pay your expenses, if we decide that is necessary. I will handle your superiors so they understand why we must do this and I think you should bring the other two Musketeers with you, also."

"You know about the Musketeer thing?" Kate asked.

"Mon Chérie, I am French and when I hear, I listen. And I hear a lot. You are very good friends, Non? Especially with Dr. Tom!" he chuckled.

Kate felt a rising blush come upon her.

"Yes, especially with Tom. He is the person I've waited for a long time and, without a doubt, the best thing to come out of this investigation process. But now I'm scared that the world is changing in a way that we don't understand or can possibly stop. I don't want that change to prevent us from having a wonderful life together."

"You need not worry, Kate, because we will find the answer and, with God's grace, solve the problem. Man has always faced insurmountable challenges that appeared unsolvable. Look at the Black Death that swept through Europe in the Middle Ages, the major Flu pandemic of the early last century where millions died, the world wars and genocide, and the cyclic starvation in poor countries. Those challenges were defeated by the good gifts given to us by God. Good will always defeat evil for it is in God's plan. The only thing we must do is use those gifts He has endowed us with to find that answer. It could take us multiple baby steps or perhaps it will come in one giant revelation, but we will prevail with His help."

"You sound so confident, Jules. Do you really believe we can do this?" she asked.

"Oui, Mon Chérie, with God's help, who better than us?"

Kate hung up with Jules, but couldn't get Tom off her mind after admitting how she felt to Jules. She dialed Tom's number, praying he would answer.

"Boy am I happy to hear from you," Tom said as he answered the phone.

"Oh, goody, you answered!" Kate exclaimed.

"I was just making dinner thinking to myself how much I would love to make dinner for you sometime."

"I wouldn't mind a handsome guy making me dinner," Kate laughed.

"Just *any* handsome guy? Ugh, straight through my heart..." Tom pretended to sound hurt.

Kate played along, "Of course not, but since Jed can't cook I'll settle for you." Kate twirled a strand of hair around her fingers while she talked. She felt so comfortable talking to Tom, and it was something she never wanted to stop doing. This was much different than any of her past relationships, not that they lasted a long time. Kate had been always so goal-oriented and focused on her work. Nothing else was as important to her. Until now. Tom was now her life, and she wasn't going to let him go.

"Jed just may have better luck with cooking, to be quite honest. I never got around to perfecting the skill since my stomach isn't picky about what it gets," Tom said. "But if I want you to stick around, I'm going to have to take a couple lessons."

"You want me to stick around?" Kate asked, a little uncertain where this conversation was heading.

Tom sensed her uncertainty and was afraid he said too much. "Well, sure, you know, I love..." He cleared his throat. "I mean, I'd love to see more of you."

Kate wasn't sure if he almost told her he loved her or if he just misspoke. She felt mixed about the exchange, but brushed it off. There was no sense rushing things. It was better to take it slow and really get to know each other.

They talked for another forty-five minutes, and when she hung up the phone, she knew one thing for sure. She loved Tom and she needed him to stick around.

Chapter 35
Paris, France

Jean Baptiste DuBois opened the forwarded email from Jules late that Saturday, after returning from an afternoon in the Luxembourg Gardens with his two grandchildren, Louisa and Philipe. They had had a perfect day with clear blue skies and a gentle early fall warmth that made the park a perfect place to run toy boats in the large fountain pond. The laughter of children, as they dodged tottering cane-wielding seniors, always reminded him why this was his favorite public park in Paris. The City of Light had been his family's home over the centuries, and he loved sharing all its special places with his grandchildren.

As Jean read through LeClerc's email, he began to understand why it was sent to him.

Hello, my friend!

I hope this message finds you well. My apologies for disturbing you over the weekend, but this is a matter that just could not wait for Monday.

Attached you will find scanned files of sketches that I have come across. An old American Indian who has visions of major world events — visions that far precede the event itself, drew these sketches. They are drawings of possible Nazi war criminals, which is why I thought to send them to you.

Perhaps you could review them with your father? I would be very interested to hear what you both think.

All the best,

Jules

Jean's family — really his father — was understood to be the preeminent European experts on Nazi war criminals. He clicked on the attachment and was immediately looking at the image of a man who appeared familiar in the way most of these criminals did — with dead, lifeless eyes. As he continued to click through the images, an odd feeling of déjà vu came over him leaving him wondering if he had seen this face before. Was it from his father's work or at his position with the Archives Nationale? Strangely, these images were chronicled years before general knowledge of Nazi atrocities were publicly made available. No one outside a limited circle of intelligence field agents knew of the slaughters, so either they were fake or hugely significant. The possibility of them being real did not seem reasonable. His father would have to review them for authenticity. He forwarded the information to this father's computer and then went out to the garden to find the old man.

As Jean entered the courtyard leading to the stonewalled garden, he saw his father snoozing, seated in his worn wicker rocker and covered in a gray woolen shawl, strategically positioned between the small herb garden and the multiple bird feeders. He gently touched the old man's shoulder to wake him.

"Pardon, Papa. Wake up. I have something important to show you. A mystery that only you can solve."

The old man gasped slightly, being startled from a deep sleep. One good thing about being ancient was that the lack of solid hearing gave him the ability to sleep without being disturbed by ambient sounds. That gave him a quality of sleep that he rarely experienced during his active years.

"Jean! The house better be on fire because I was just putting my signature moves on Bridgette Bardot!" the old man hissed.

"Je suis désolé, Papa," Jean said. *I am sorry, Father.* "There is something you must look at. I'm not sure what to make of it."

The old man struggled to rise from the creaking wicker, balancing himself on his silver-handled hickory cane that was a gift from President Dwight Eisenhower. It had been given in gratitude of his apprehension of a prominent war criminal in 1960, one who had tortured and executed captured American soldiers in lieu of transporting them to POW camps. The cane was a prized possession that, for years, sat only as a trophy in his study, but now was the tool it was intended to be. As he started to move forward, his shuffling feet kept a delicate balance on unsteady legs, and although it would take time to get from one spot to the next, he understood that travel safe from falls was essential for a prolonged vertical existence. His fierce independence and active mind were the tonic that kept him functioning. He had conquered greater enemies in his lifetime than just the ills of chronic age.

Jean followed his father into the study, watching his progress, ready to assist, if needed. The study, with its gray filing cabinets that were once filled with dossiers, intelligence reports, newspaper clipping and correspondences, now only held his unresolved files where the physical evidence of capture or death of the criminal was not reconfirmed by official sources. All the rest of the files, the confirmed captured or executed, had been taken by Jean for permanent storage in the Archives Nationale. The remaining four locked cabinets still held information of some of the worst of the worst that had escaped detection and their final justice. There had been so many with their inflated sense of righteousness that had conspired with the insanity that became the Nazi agenda. During the war there were three kinds of Germanic people. The first was the citizen who had been conscripted into service, but had no love for the Nazis or their dream of world domination. The second were the believers who blindly, mindlessly followed their orders because that dream had corrupted them and destroyed their souls. The third were among the evil elite leadership, which had insane satanic designs on the world without any concern for how that goal was accomplished. They destroyed without conscience, and consumed anything or anyone who stood in their way. All were now probably dead, but not having verification and complete closure haunted the old man. Soon, he, too, would be dead, and all this would be forgotten.

"So, what was so important that you felt compelled to wake me from a beautiful sleep?" Jean's father chided as he eased himself into the chair behind the old curly maple desk.

"Jules LeClerc, you know, my friend who works at the Pasteur, has been involved in a worldwide investigation of mass animal die-offs for which they can find no cause. Some Americans who were also working on that same problem on an American Indian Reservation in Montana were given information through journals written by a nearly 100-year-old Indian. The journal entries that he documented had Nazi references that greatly predated any general knowledge of the events. There is a face that you may be able to put a name to, so Jules wanted you to take a look. He feels there is some connection with what has been happening to the animals."

Robert DuBois pulled the ragged dish towel he used to protect the old television-like screen from dust, and struggled to adjust his reading glasses as he fumbled with his hands to find the on switches. The dated CPU whirled as it started up, as if it, too, was waking from a deep sleep. The screen lit up gradually and then, with a slight pop, was up and running. With the green screen waiting a command, his fingers typed in a series of passwords with speed that denied their age. He went to his email and looked for Jean's forward.

"I don't see yours, Jean, but I do have several love letters from Bridgette. She wants to meet me in Nice for drinks and a little hanky-panky. I'll take the TGV in the morning if she can wait that long. Alors, here is yours, in my spam file."

He clicked on the attachment.

"When was this done?" he asked in a serious tone.

"The journals are continuous from 1928 until the man's death last week at age ninety-nine. According to Jules, he was a shaman, or spiritual leader, who had dreams and visions throughout his life. They were mostly general history, but became more and more adamant about a destruction that was coming. Very vivid and detailed. These pages represent the years 1938 to just after the war. It's very detailed and in exact chronological order, so they don't think it is a fake."

His father read forward to the point where he reached the pages with the facial image. He studied the screen and clicked back and forth as he studied the screen.

"Mon Dieu! I know this face! Jean, go to the second file cabinet from the right, second drawer down and look for Wilheim Berhetzel. It shouldn't be a big file because he was only a secondary assistant to Adolf Eichman and Henryk Goldzmit, and I believe he died in a small plane crash over Switzerland in the days immediately after the fall of the Reich. Because he was a relatively unimportant person, his death was never confirmed by medical records. Just one of the rats escaping the sinking ship."

Jean went to the file cabinet and found the dossier exactly where his father said it would be. He walked over to his father who took the yellowed file and slowly, gently opened it, his hands shaking from anticipation, not age.

Both men focused on the old documents. The official German government photos of Wilheim Berhetzel were an exact match to Nelson Blackfeather's hand-drawn images, accurate down to the small scar on his right forehead and mole over his left cheekbone. They were absolutely the same individual. Robert stared at the underlined title attached to the image, DESTROYER, and shook his head in disbelief.

"God must have given us this information for some very important reason, otherwise none of it would make any sense," Robert mumbled.

"But what connection can Berhetzel and the old Indian have?" asked Jean, perplexed. Jean looked to his aging father and suggested, "I'm sure it's just a coincidence."

Shaking his head slightly and standing with difficulty, Robert looked straight into Jean's eyes with an intensity he hadn't had in years. "I don't know, but my gut is telling me there is far more to this than some coincidence. God has a purpose for everything, Jean. You know as well as I do that this is troublesome. I fear this man is not dead and his evil has been returned upon us again!"

Chapter 36
Amazon River Basin
Northwest Argentina

Same day

The rainforest was always more alive at this time of day as lengthening shadows started a cooling transition under its dense tree canopy, allowing the heat of the day to escape and change into the pleasance of the more temperate evening. The loud and noisy insects, birds and small primates gave way to the more subtle nocturnal sounds of the creatures of the night. Some enjoyed that daytime concert, while others preferred the cooler subtle evening symphonies, but Wilheim Berhetzel disliked the rainforest day or night. He was a Northern European and enjoyed the cool of the day and the cold of the night. This place had been his personal Hell for nearly seventy years, but being in Hell did seem appropriate for him because his soul had, in reality, belonged to the Devil. Ever since he chose to be part of Hitler's Final Solution for the opportunity to freely experiment under the guise of science, Wilheim believed he was doing humanity a favor. The things he had done left no question that he was a war criminal of the worse kind. Good thing the world believed him dead.

Now, when he wasn't working on his experiments and refining his discoveries — those twenty-hour days when he rarely ate but drank gallons of coffee made from the beans grown in his own plantation fields — he sat under the house portico thinking, with the overhead fans humming softly as they pushed the moist air around him and kept the insects disorientated when they tried to land for a hot meal. The large shaded porch was where he drank the wine he produced or the bourbon and cognac he imported along with a good supply of Cuban cigars once a year. It was also the place he would regularly sit and review the events that had brought him to this awful place.

When he joined the Nazi party, Berhetzel was a second-year medial resident at the prestigious Berlin Academy of Medicine and was at the top of his class. He became part of a youthful group of extremely well trained doctors who had been seductively recruited into the Party with promises of wealth, power and cutting edge medical excellence. The medical students and residents were broken into groups of about two-thirds field surgeons and one-third researchers. That initial group of researchers was then divided into two smaller elements, some working on lethal toxins and biologic weapons, and the other group, led by Berhetzel, researched healing medications and longevity drugs. He personally supervised about fifteen medical researchers who each had five assistants. Their efforts were focused on finding an immortality formula — the Fountain of Youth drug — to extend longevity to the leadership of the Reich, primarily Adolph Hitler who was pathologically obsessed with his own immortality. They were sworn to secrecy upon the penalty of death, and even though they initially worked as a group in one location, when the death camps were established and occupied, the best researchers were dispersed to and around those camps to continue their work on the readily available human subjects.

Berhetzel started his own research working on chicken embryos where he would take fertilized chicken eggs, incubate them for ten days and then experiment with hundreds of the embryos at a time by fenestrating the narrow crown of each egg to view the developing embryo with a stereo microscope and then apply his experimental compounds to observe how the developing chicks were affected. He processed thousands of eggs a week, which were never wasted but incorporated into feed for the camp pigs kept for the SS officers' mess. That protein source alone could have sustained hundreds of prisoners in the camps, but it was considered much too valuable to be wasted on the doomed.

Every result was carefully numbered and recorded in the Thomas Edison style. That endlessly repetitive process was rewarded one day when Berhetzel applied a compounded wild mushroom mix of toxic and non-poisonous alpine fungi that did not kill the developing chick, but slowed its rapid growth within the eggshell. Feeling he was on to something crucial, he secreted his results and began experimenting on juvenile rats and rabbits, which showed similar promising results. He then moved on to human subjects and became a war criminal.

Berhetzel was an exacting man and transferred his experiments far away from the main camps for security, but regularly visited the death centers to select a fresh supply of near-term pregnant women coming off the arriving transport trains — women that would have labor induced to harvest his newborn test subjects. The postpartum lactating mothers were fed well and the infants given the optimum nutrition and vitamins to maximize their physical development. However, these children did not grow and develop while receiving Berhetzel's compound of mushroom extracts. They remained newborns until the formulation was removed from them and then they grew and aged at an astounding rate. However, with the Russians winning the war on the eastern front, he realized he would soon need to flee, and arranged to systematically loot the spoils of war in the form of gold and diamonds from the SS stores in the main camps. All he needed to do was to split the cache with the guards providing the valuables and then provide falsified papers that would get those men safely out of a post-war Germany. Berhetzel's extensive contacts gave him the power to threaten, intimidate and, in turn, allowed him to amass a huge store of stolen wealth.

Berhetzel's formula and data had been kept ultra-secret and only he knew exactly how well it worked, but his associates understood the implications of what they saw in the children. The mothers had long before been returned to the camps for extermination and, with the abandonment of the death centers occurring, and the Allies closing the noose on Germany, it was time for him to take his formula and his stolen valuables and disappear into the chaos of the approaching defeat.

He called an emergency meeting of his research associates to allegedly say goodbye and close down his experiment station.

"It is apparent that due to the fortunes of war," he began, "we are about to be overrun by men hostile to our beliefs and values. Our work here is done and there will soon be a Red Cross ambulance arriving to move the children to a refugee orphanage. I was fortunate to be given a couple of bottles of champagne, left by the camp SS Commandant Erich, our liaison officer. He suggested we toast to our work, our past and to our uncertain future. So, let me pour a little into each of your coffee cups so we can make our final friendship toast."

Each cup filled, they raised them to their lips in a solemn toast, drank greedily and fell to the floor in near unison, seizing in terrible, terminal pain. The poison Berhetzel had used was a rapid solution to prevent his identity and his life's work from being uncovered.

He now had one last detail to complete. Each child was given the same toxin extracted from his fungal collection in a bottle of sweet apple juice. Soon the nursery was dead quiet, his task accomplished.

He was considered a secondary figure, which should have made him a footnote in the post-war hunt to find those who tortured and exterminated millions of innocent human souls. It was true, he had started at Treblinka where 850,000 had died in the forests of Poland, and that he had worked under the supervision and with the blessing of Dr. Henryk Goldzmit performing gruesome experiments on the living and dead, but his super-secret laboratory was off from the main camp and because of that, he was somewhat of an anonymous figure. Few knew that much of his initial efforts included work on an offensive weapon death ray that could drop soldiers in their tracks. The term he coined for the device was an HDL weapon — High Degree of Lethality weapon.

When Treblinka closed in October of 1943, he was moved to a similar lab near the Dachau death camp. His 'Thousand Year Reich' project to sustain the Nazi leadership, had transitioned from the embryo testing stage to human testing because, he told his superiors, the chicken embryo results had not been repeatable, which was a lie, and he wanted to research on humans so see if his results might become more predictable. He secretly knew he had discovered a 'body preservative', which seemed to delay aging by 80-90%. He just had no idea how good it really was.

At the same time, while Berhetzel was pushing to refine his discovery's reliability, one of his associates who had worked on the death ray project, stumbled upon the structure of DNA after reviewing the work of Friedrick Meischer that had been done in 1860. Their relatively new electron microscope was cutting-edge technology, the latest model of the 1931 German invention, and this associate was an expert at using it. Berhetzel took his raw data and was able to expand it and describe the DNA double helix structure, calling it the 'Ladder of Life' ten years before Watson and Crick described 'their' double helix discovery. He laughed out loud upon hearing about their announcement in 1953.

It was unfortunate that the war was being lost before he could complete all his work. When he terminated the research group and test subjects, it was with an understanding that he would immediately need to escape Germany to survive. Arrangements had been made to leave by plane with his lover Anna, and then, by using false identities to be purchased in Switzerland, find their way to South America through southern France.

He had that large cache of plundered gold and diamonds, which would fund his new research life that he hoped would last for an eternity. His volumes of data had been condensed and microfilmed, so the primary weight of what he would be transporting was the gold. He and Anna went into hiding, anxiously waiting for the pilot to contact them with a departure date and time.

When the end finally came to the Reich, Germany was not just defeated, she was crushed. Their pilot never contacted Berhetzel and they guessed the flight had been sold to a higher bidder. Extremely eager to leave, and with the Russians closing in, they were barely able to find another pilot — and much smaller plane — to get them out. The problem was that the small-sized plane was to carry four people and there were limits on how much weight they'd be able to carry on with them. No gold was going to leave with them, so Berhetzel located a secluded place to hide the gold bars in a remote farm's stone fencerow. In the dead of night, he secreted the gold and his service

Luger behind the ancient granite rocks and made sure the location landmarks were permanently etched in his brain. He would return in two or three years and retrieve the gold when the world returned to normal.

When the plane was finally set to leave, it was over capacity with three passengers, the pilot, their scant personal belongings and limited petrol. The other passenger, another German, appeared to be hiding his identity with a minimal disguise and was most likely another war criminal, also escaping for a new life. They all were now refugees from their past, anonymous travelers flying into an uncertain future.

Berhetzel remembered well the death rattle of the plane as they took off, sputtering and coughing as its fuel, as most had been towards the end of the war, was likely a very poor quality or contaminated with products intended to stretch its use. The pilot who looked to be in his late forties and smelling of alcohol, assured them he had flown for the Luftwaffe and had mastered flying with worse problems than dirty fuel. Besides, he thought, he would be a very rich man once he landed this flight.

The plane struggled as they made their way south and after a one-hour battle to keep it flying, they could see the Alps rising to their south, and knew that freedom was just over that first range. They would land outside a small remote village and be out of harm's way.

The pilot started to push the engine to gain enough altitude to cross the jagged mountaintop and, as he did, the plane stuttered and stalled, dropping several hundred feet at a time. A terrified Anna started crying and was screaming hysterically with each drop while the other passenger vomited violently into his lap. The pilot commenced breathing rapidly, almost gasping each breath, was pale and held on to the yoke and throttle like they were going to fall from the plane. Directly ahead of them stood the north face of last rise of stone before they could land at the opposite side's plateaued village. They were at a point of no return and the plane, it was apparent, was unable to gain enough altitude to rise above and over the mountain.

"Scheisse! Scheisse!" the pilot cried out. *Shit! Shit!*

"Gott! Mein Gott!" Anna pleaded, shielding her face with her hands. *God! My God!*

On impact, the world went black for Wilheim Berhetzel. The plane cartwheeled and slid down the rocky face of the mountain grinding and screaming sparks as it slid down one-third the distance from the peak to where a very large, deep ridge of glacial snow slowed and then stopped the descent.

When he regained consciousness, Berhetzel could only see from his left eye, as a large scalp wound was covering the right side of his face with a

118

sticky blood clot. The pilot and passenger were obviously dead as their heads hung loosely by skin and sinew, as their skulls had luxated 180 degrees from the vertebrae. When he reached over to check Anna and rolled her face toward him, he was greeted by glassy, lifeless eyes staring blankly back at him. His own neck and head hurt tremendously, but otherwise, it seemed he had survived reasonably OK. He pushed his way out of the wrecked fuselage after carefully exchanging his papers for the pilots and searching both the passenger and pilot for valuables. He found and pulled a small inflatable rubber raft from the baggage compartment and inflated it so he could use it as a sled and makeshift shelter. In the raft, he placed his and Anna's secreted diamonds and the planes emergency canned water and biscuits. The first aid kit allowed him to clean and patch the scalp wound with loose sutures, and he found a rubberized, olive-colored poncho to wear, pulling the hood up to hide the bandaged wound. A chilling rain was starting to fall and made the crusty snow surface slick, so he moved down to the valley below, through the wilderness, deciding to avoid any public place until he could figure out a secondary escape plan. He would build a shelter, rest and heal until he felt safe, and then following the topographic map flip book the pilot had carried, work his way around the mountain by following the river that drained to the south. On that valley floor were tiny villages to rest and provide transport to Bern, where he could establish his new identity papers and then meet a predetermined contact to guide him through the process of getting to the Port of Marseille. After that, he would locate a merchant vessel to take him to Argentina.

Smuggling war 'refugees' of all sorts had become a very lucrative business and fortunes had been made, without prying questions, built on Germany's looted wealth. Berhetzel knew there would be a bidding war for passage to the Caribbean islands, Cuba and other similar 'look the other way' countries. He fortunately had the ability to pay handsomely and could purchase a low-profile passage on a freighter as the sole passenger along with the four or five bodyguards that he planned on hiring to protect himself.

He eventually found passage on a freighter and hired four former German soldiers who also were running away from their past but, unlike Berhetzel, were doing so without financial resources. Being well conditioned, they would be his good soldiers, obey orders and not ask questions or divulge his secrets. The commercial freighter was destined for Porto Alegre in southern Brazil, which would give him easy access to the Amazon River, their highway into Argentina, where he planned to build a secure compound to continue his research. He would start over in the Nazi-friendly country, and some day, rule the world in ways no one could ever have dreamed.

Chapter 37
Atlanta

Early Monday morning, Kate received a call from Jules, and for a man who was generally calm and reflective, he sounded excited with overtones of urgency.

"Bonjour, Mon Chérie," he started. "I hope I did not catch you at a bad time. We have just finished déjeuner and I am on my way back to the Institute."

"Bonjour á tu, Jules. No, it's good timing, I just got to the office. I like an early, quick start to my day. What did you think about the Blackfeather journal pages I sent?

"They are unbelievable! My friend Jean's father, Robert DuBois, a Nazi hunter, feels that there must be a direct connection to the mystery we are working on. He recognized the man in the drawings almost immediately as Dr. Wilheim Berhetzel, who did research for some of the most horrible war criminals like Eichmann and Goldzmit involving bio weapons, genetics and possibly longevity serums. It was felt that all his research was destroyed with the approach of the Allies, and it was also believed that this man died escaping Germany in a small plane crash just after the collapse of the Reich. It seems skeletal remains with authentic IDs were found on a Swiss mountainside in May 1946, something that was fairly common at the time because all of Europe was littered with bodies and remains, which, for the most part, were just buried and forgotten. Anonymous and unremarkable, except in this case, the three complete skeletons in that plane all had papers or passports and were buried by local villagers with gravestones to identify each corpse. Case closed, non? Now, we have a monkey wrench in the soup and we will have to find a way to have this man's grave exhumed to check it against Berhetzel's official medical and dental records. If they do match, then we are only chasing the wild goose. If they do not, then it is very probable there is some connection between this man and the die-offs. Robert DuBois is convinced, instinctively, that the man still lives. Jean says he has not seen him this excited since Bridgette Bardot sent his father an autographed photo wearing a bikini in the late sixties. You understand that Robert DuBois was a very famous and respected Nazi hunter who brought many evil people to justice?"

"Yes, I googled him and was truly impressed. It seems he is still revered in the States for his tireless efforts and has been honored here by several American presidents. It's great he is able to help with this because he understands more about that era than most anyone now alive," Kate replied.

Jules added, "I've known the family for most of my life and he truly is amazing! Remember the word 'Destroyer' that was so prominent and focal in the journals?"

"Yes, what about it?"

"Monsieur DuBois remembered several sources that mentioned a project called 'The Destroyer'. He said that after the war, the military felt it referenced some sort of super ship with rockets that would put their offensive missiles' destructive power within easy range of most cities. Something great like their massive battleship, Bismarck. Now he is not so sure. So. Jean and he are going to do some more research at the Archives Nationale today. Perhaps they can uncover something there to help us."

"So what do you want me to do at our end here?" she asked.

"I would like you to talk young Blackfeather and your friends into coming to Paris next week. If we are able to get the forensic work done to prove the body is not Berhetzel's, and if there is no reference to the 'Destroyer' actually being a project involving a physical ship or the like, then we are going to have a bit of work to track this man down and stop him, if he really is the source of the die-offs. I remembered what Bruce Bentley said in Atlanta about this problem being very Nazi-like and now we have, by the grace of God, identified a Nazi who did genetic research. A person, I might add, if still alive, has had nearly seventy years to perfect his work. Or perhaps he has an heir or protégé. Either way, if we aren't 100% positive he is dead, then we must find out exactly what happened to him and where he is."

He continued.

"Like I told you before, we will pay all your expenses while you are here. I have a very nice apartment for you on Rue Kleber that belonged to my mistress until she said she found a better lover. I ask you, how is that possible?"

"Jules, I am surprised and a little shocked! I always thought of you as a family man!"

"Oui, that is true! I do love my wife and adore my family. But, sadly, I have the weaknesses of a French man. I love the women and they love me. Do you think less of me, Mon Chérie?" he asked.

"Non, Jules. I understand you are a man of many passions. I just hope you can turn all that energy into an answer to help save the world from this crisis."

"Trust me, Mon Chérie, I will."

Chapter 38
Amazon Rainforest

Argentina

Berhetzel had built for himself, over the years, a large self-sustaining compound in the overgrown rainforest of northeast Argentina. The area was as remote as he could stand to be in, but had close access to the Amazon River for easy travel, and he even had a small landing strip and helipad carved out of the jungle. This allowed his needed supplies and equipment to be delivered quickly, as well as provide him with means to escape to cosmopolitan areas to relieve his other needs — personal or professional. He regularly attended scientific conferences in South America and Asia, using his new identity as Dr. Josef Von Braun, research biologist. Those gatherings of the world's best minds kept him current on the latest discoveries in genetics, medicine and pharmacology, filling his world-class library.

Berhetzel, or Von Braun as he had become accustomed to being called, built his compound out of over six-hundred acres of raw jungle rainforest and now it was his personal, secure sanctuary, protected by razor wire topped fencing, electronic surveillance and at one time had Alsatian canines patrolling the perimeters. It was overkill to be sure, but as the man came closer to fulfilling his goals, the more paranoid he became about being discovered.

The compound had a resident population of native Indian workers along with the four men who had escaped with him, three with mixed Aryan-Indian families. He made sure they were self-sustaining in most things with extensive gardens and livestock providing a majority of their food, and a diesel power plant that had recently been converted to mostly solar, saving the expense and trouble of hauling the fuel up the Amazon. A school was once built for the children of the house servants and the laborers, and Berhetzel even had a small chapel constructed outside the compound, so the once monthly circuit priest could hold his services under shelter, out of the persistent rain. That priest, now long dead was the only visitor to ever come and go safely.

Isolation was really his true security asset, and over all the years, only one curious government environmental engineer and a federal drug agent had tried to determine what the hell they were actually doing in the middle of nowhere. Both had 'accidentally' drowned in the all-consuming Amazon and were likely entrees for the multitude of gilled carnivores that patrolled the river's muddy waters. Mostly, the government and locals looked the other way and left him alone, some thinking him eccentric. Others, the Devil incarnate.

The isolation of the place he had called home for nearly seventy years protected him and his extensive research from outside interference. Initially, as he settled into his new laboratory, he found most of the original theory work for a Death Ray Super weapon had been flawed and misdirected, and so he started over from the beginning, using bits and pieces of the original human experimental data to guide his new premises, eventually utilizing the advances found in computer technology. His first attempts yielded a weapon using high-frequency radio waves and then microwaves that had the ability to kill or cook a mouse, but only if held stationary for a minimum of 5.8 seconds. Not satisfied with just inventing a murine torture device, he refocused on a programmable, selective weapon that could be used on whatever, whomever, and as many targets as he chose. It had to cause an instant 'drop in your tracks death' and be portable, but he was in no hurry because his longevity drug was working better than he ever anticipated. He looked and felt like a person in his thirties, even as the decades passed. The mushroom spores he brought from Germany flourished at the compound and he made sure the SS guards who he had found in a Marseille bar, along with their adult families, received his special 'vitamin' pill that he told them would keep everyone young and healthy. No one really questioned him because he had total power over their lives and they, being good Germans, showed absolute loyalty out of respect and fear.

Most of his experimentation was done in solitude, eight to ten hours a day, but on occasion, when he felt he was on the verge of a breakthrough, he would work continuously without stopping for up to two days. He relied on amphetamines to fuel his energy, but then used barbiturates to finally extinguish the effects of the 'speed' and give him the rest his body craved. Through his work in genetics, he created super crops and gigantic strains of livestock to sustain the sixty-five residents living in the compound. There were chickens the size of turkeys, turkeys the size of goats, and goats the size of cows. The corn grew twenty feet high, had the fiber strength of bamboo and produced grape-sized kernels on three-foot ears. Everything they grew or raised was at least double in size and matured in half the normal time. When the residents questioned such a miracle garden, Berhetzel would only point skyward to the sun, then to the earth and finally to the mushroom mulch spray they used on the crops. Since the livestock ate the crops produced onsite, it was obvious that they also were affected in a beneficial way.

He became an expert at creating and modifying life through his science, but initially his work on destroying life by weaponizing energy was not proving to be an easy task. He reasoned obsessively that if you could turn life on, you should be able to just as easily turn it off. The evil that controlled his being seemed to have unlimited patience, so he continued his experiments year after year, all the while using the advancing world research data, and applying each fresh new idea and thesis to advance his own work. His self-taught ability to perform computer modeling of experiments allowed him to investigate and discard many of his theories before he took them into the lab. Never closer to finding how to move his death machinery forward, one day, after watching a goat suffer a seizure, he realized that the abnormal electrical impulses in the brain that caused the seizure, might be redirected and targeted to a specific functional area of the brain, and actually cause it to shut completely down. Every brain, he theorized, had the wiring to respond to that electrical stimulation, and he wondered if it was just as susceptible to a specific energy termination of its function. There were, he remembered, the experiments in the camps where the technicians would administer blows to prisoners' heads to gauge helmet material strength, and to find the design that would best protect their soldiers from injury. There was, he remembered, a very fine line between simply stunning a person and providing a final deathblow. Berhetzel decided he needed to find a way to traumatize the brain's own electrical pathways just enough to cause instant stunning and death. He refocused his research on locating the brain's own 'turn off' switch.

In his fifth year of this new path of investigation, he discovered that each specie had their own unique switch point that was linked to that animal's specific brain DNA, and could be narrowed even more to particular sexes, breeds or subspecies. Rats were different than mice, hooded rats different from Norway rats, and male rats different from females. His breakthrough occurred while he was investigating the use of non-harmonic nano-frequencies directed, and computer guided, to affect specific DNA identified 'GPS' points in the brain. Much like the radiation gamma 'knife' used by modern medicine to kill tumor cells in the brain with exacting precision, this was a self-guided energy burst that attacked a specific source of DNA in exact areas of the brain. The more complex the brain tissue, the more effective was the targeting and killing function. For example, it was more effective on a human than a chimp, a chimp more than a dolphin, a dolphin better than a pig, and a pig better than a dog. By the time you got down to rudimental brains like fish, reptiles and insects, there was still death, but target selectivity became more difficult. He started testing that first device around the world on multiple species, collecting data and refining the experiments to get to his real goal, a weapon to be used against mankind. His tool to rule the world.

He produced solar-powered drones to patrol the world and sent them to remote areas to destroy specific DNA targets, such as Monarch butterflies, fur seals, caribou, and other species that he had been able to obtain requested blood and tissue samples from universities and zoos around the globe to aid in his genetic research. Those worldwide requests for samples provided him with the basic information he needed to hunt for specific target points to gauge the effects of his life's work. His compact hawk-sized drones sent back video surveillance that validated his research with images of dead targets, and would leave the compound and return on a regular schedule, often traveling thousands of miles on their trips. As more DNA samples accumulated in his secret Porto Alegre post office box, his target base continued to increase and aided his manic research.

As Berhetzel became more confident in his data results, he started manipulating the device's energy bursts in length and intensity, and found he could pre-program the devices to be lethal to an individual, or create a maximum unique kill zone of up to one-hundred square meters. The real beauty of his drone prototype weapon was that it was small and fast, fueled by small solar super cells and microprocessors. It could be, as he had demonstrated, flown in a stealth fashion to remote areas to assassinate individual species, attached to rifles for battle much like a bayonet, assembled into grenade-style weapons the size of golf balls or mailed disguised as a radio or cellphone and never leave a trace or raise a thought that it might be a lethal device. The perfect weapon — his weapon.

His first human test was done at a local Indian village, where the lead participant in a frenzied sweaty voodoo ceremony, dropped like a rug had been jerked out from under him. That visual stunned both Berhetzel and the villagers. All he needed to pre-program the man's sudden death was his DNA, which he had obtained the week before at a vaccine clinic Berhetzel had performed to protect the villagers against a 'new' disease. The only catch was that he was the author of this new instant death disease and there was no vaccine to prevent it.

Confident, he decided to test it on the world stage by dramatically assassinating a world leader. Berhetzel chose to kill the President of the Republic of France, an easy decision because he had always hated the French. All he would need was a small sample of the president's DNA to make his plan succeed.

Chapter 39
Paris

Jean, his father and Jules discussed what they needed to accomplish to determine if the man depicted in Nelson's journal matching their file on the war criminal Wilheim Berhetzel, was really dead and in his grave. Robert decided they should travel to that small Swiss village cemetery and use the archived medical and dental records to determine if the man was actually buried in his grave. The exhumation of the remains took the approval of the Swiss government, which came quickly because of Jules' contacts. But it was the local authorities who had the final say in the process, and they insisted that the investigation be graveside only and that the remains must not leave the village where they had rested for nearly seven decades. What this meant was a field forensic team from the National Archives in Paris would have to travel to the gravesite along with Jean and Robert so that the determination could be made under the village's jurisdiction. If the remains had been originally handled properly, the dental records would most likely be all they would really need, but a lot depended on the overall condition of the skeletal remains when they were found in the crashed plane. An Archives forensic dentist and an archeological pathologist would travel with the father and son team and, hopefully, make that determination rapidly because, if the corpse's remains in the grave — that were supposedly the Nazi's — did not match, then the other two graves would have to be opened and tested, and they dreaded that thought. It would mean more time away from home, more legal work, all while stuck in a very remote village in the Alps.

Their drive from Paris in the Archives mobile forensic lab van took the better part of a day, and when they arrived, a thick evening fog was rolling into the plateaued valley and with visibility near zero. They struggled to find the village center and the small B&B where they reserved every bedroom.

That dense fog covered the region until late the next morning, delaying the opening of the grave because the excavator refused to work on the hillside without reasonable visibility. Finally, close to noon, the sun burned through and the excavator began delicately moving the heavy, graveled soil. Village records indicated that the skeletal remains had been interred in a simple hardwood box, and the slightly sunken grave gave evidence that the small wood coffin had most likely decayed. After the backhoe surface work was completed, two village workers jumped into the opened gravesite to carefully hand dig the balance of the earth, hoping to preserve the integrity of the remains. They exposed shards of the rotted wooden lid and then recovered a double sewn, heavy wool blanket that the bones had been sealed in. The thick material was remarkably intact, considering nearly seventy years had passed. The workers respectfully placed the woolen package in a large, white plastic bin, while a village official kept busy photo documenting the process, almost falling backwards into the open hole as the pebbled dirt started to slide away from under him. When the village official was satisfied he had enough photos to justify his job, he signaled to the French team to start their investigation, and Jean and the forensic dentist carried the bin to the van to begin their work. The village police chief stood watch, making sure all the remains would stay with the village because every speck would need to be returned back to the grave.

Jean cut the thick woolen blanket with bandage scissors to expose the bones. They appeared complete and in very good condition. The first to offer an opinion was the forensic pathologist.

"This is NOT the man," he declared looking at the file photos, "his forehead and cheek bones do not even come close to matching the picture profile of Berhetzel." He rotated the shiny amber-colored skull, inadvertently brushing several strands of brittle brown hair and skin off a large compressed defect in the fore-skull as he investigated the probable cause of the man's death.

The dentist then pulled the dental record from the file and picked up the mandible from the pile of bones. He briefly studied the jawbone and then flipped the skull over to look at the inside base of the skull and the maxilla.

"He is correct, look, these teeth are repaired for the man we seek and there is no evidence the person before us had any work done in those areas. This mouth doesn't even come close to that of Wilheim Berhetzel."

"Merde," Jean mumbled under his breath. *Crap.*

His father smiled a little, the plot thickening, and said, "D'accord, let us now get permission for the opening of other two graves."

Twenty-four hours later, that permission was granted. With everyone already in place, they quickly determined that in none of the graves rested the war criminal's remains.

Jean DuBois turned to his father and the two Archive doctors and said, "I think we are going to need a better perspective on this mystery, so I will contact Jules and see if he can get the Americans to give us the old Indian's original documentation to validate it and see if there might be more to it than

128

meets the eye. The Archives will need to develop a deeper profile on Berhetzel, such as relatives, business or professional connections. It is possible he still uses the name Berhetzel. Remember that Josef Mengele reverted back to his real name after decades in hiding. Maybe this man has done the same. Also, we need to really look at the reference to 'Destroyer'. I think possibly even take a trip to Berlin to see what they may have archived in their extensive records. Jules LeClerc is correct, this smells rotten and we better find an explanation fast!"

Robert turned and looked back toward the mountain crest towering behind them. "While we are here, we need to look at the original crash site. Maybe we could find a small piece of information overlooked in 1946 that might indicate their plans or where they were headed. There were four passengers on that plane when it crashed and only one survived — Berhetzel."

"But how did he manage to get away undetected?" questioned Jean brushing his hand through his hair in an act of frustration.

"Let's think this through," suggested Robert. "What do we know for fact?"

"Well, we know there were four passengers on that plane, and only three bodies are buried here. We determined that none of them are, in fact, Berhetzel," Jean said beginning to see the answer clear as day.

"Yes, my boy," Robert smiled proudly.

"Berhetzel must have taken the pilot's papers!"

Robert suddenly became very youthful in appearance as the excitement grew on his lined face, "Perhaps there is a registration number or scrap of paper that has survived identifying the pilot or indicating where they were headed and is still in what is left of the wreckage. Ninety-nine percent of the war criminals left by ship from southern France or Italy. Find a name or a dated document such as a newspaper on that plane, and it may be possible to locate records or a manifest to tell us how he left and to what country or port. Like everyone who was scrambling to escape justice, Berhetzel would have needed to get out in a hurry, secretly, as I'm sure he carried many valuables that he wanted to protect. No one left empty-handed."

The chief of police was the only person in the small village still alive who had personal knowledge of the crash site. His father had also been chief in the spring of 1946 when the wreckage was discovered, after the melt off of the deep alpine snow cover. He had been only six years old at the time, but the skulls he witnessed with pieces of clinging hair and flesh, haunted him for years. He thought he knew exactly where the plane rested, but had doubts much would have survived the decades of heavy snow and countless avalanches on that side of the mountain. In the right location, it might be possible some of it could have survived. As they talked, he suggested using a helicopter to survey the area, and if the plane's fuselage was still there, try to find a landing area or return on a couple of ski rescue all-season snow cats to check it out.

It was mid-afternoon before the white, red and black helicopter arrived, landing on the village soccer field. They quickly loaded themselves on board and held their breath as the sleek Medical EVAC H17 rapidly ascended and shot forward toward the mountain face. It was extremely powerful and fast, built to evacuate medical patients from the small villages, and pick up countless injured skiers. It could land on a dime. The Swiss mountain pilots were the best in the business.

Once they crested the mountain, the chief directed the pilot to come down lower and start a zigzag pattern to survey the area. He had only seen the spot once and then from the ground only, so as they made pass after pass, he was becoming less and less sure of his memory. Then about a third of the way down, they caught the slight reflection of the aluminum body remnants of the plane, its canvas and paint eroded away decades before from the extreme elements. The chief signaled to the pilot to put the chopper down. The pilot made only one pass and then lowered the helicopter down on a large gravel and snow outcropping, testing its support several times for stability before letting his passengers out. They exited with small utility shovels and flashlights in hand.

Despite his age, Robert led the way, supported by Jean and the police chief, and started probing around with a walking stick to the upside down cabin hull, or at least what was left of it. The wings, propeller and tail were missing, but the cabin doors were closed. They popped off their old hinges and fell away when the chief pulled to open them. They attempted to look around inside, but the old roof of the plane was buried deep in gravelly rock and stones. The pilot quickly returned to the copter, sliding down on the unstable gravel, and retrieved a gas-powered Sawsall that was kept on board to cut up crashed autos to free accident victims. With a loud puff of blue smoke, he started to open the fuselage like a can of sardines. Soon he had it in two pieces, a top half still buried in the mountainside, and the bottom half with the remnants of the passenger seats and pilots area peeled off and laying upright for the first time since the crash. They starting checking every nook and cranny, and eventually found two scraps of paper with faded writing in the pilot's glove box. One appeared to be a pilot's license with the name Ivan Mueller barely readable, and a second was a note with "Marseille, 14.00hr, 2/8/45" written on it. Robert was overjoyed, they finally had their lead and he was back in the game. The hunt was on.

Chapter 40
The Port of Marseille, France

Two days later

Jean called Jules LeClerc that same evening with a report on their investigation, telling him they were sending the two forensic doctors back to Paris to oversee a more in-depth archive search. He also informed him that he and his father were on their way to Marseille.

"You must get all those original journals in our hands so we can do a proper analysis of them by looking for hidden codes, messages or directions," he told Jules. "Papa and I are going to visit the Merchant Marine and Port Authority in Marseille and go through their stacks of documentation to see if this Ivan Mueller impersonator purchased any passage on either a freighter or passenger line around that time. It may be a long shot, but Marseille seems to be his logical exit port and father is absolutely convinced that we are being directed to locate this evil by a higher power."

"Be careful Jean," Jules replied. "He may have paid for protection by his contacts and, if so, they could inform him or possibly harm you. I would not mention any name, perhaps offer to them that you are doing an historic review of something post-war. You know those Nazi sympathizers are still everywhere, including in every level of our government. Silent, but always listening and protective of their pack, and still dangerous if threatened."

"The most difficult thing for me may be controlling Papa. He is really charged up and said when we finish here, he wants to swing by Cannes for a drink with Mademoiselle Bardot. He says she is calling to him!"

Jules laughed at the joke.

"Non, Jules, he is serious. Wants to stop at a pharmacy on the way over, just in case. I pray we find something in Marseille that will take his mind off of her."

The Port Authority Archives was housed in a large windowed, centuries-old brick building with six floors that contained the port history going back to just after an 1879 fire. Each level of the building contained a chronological arrangement of records, starting with the oldest on the top two floors, 1879-1914. The third down housed records from 1915-1939, and the fourth and fifth floors contained records from 1940 through 1969. The ground floor was home to the digitalized, modern microfilm and computer records from 1970 to present day. They easily received passes to the fourth and fifth levels, and were given a passcode for the computer's general records because Robert's reputation gave him Carte Blanche at the facility, with offers of assistance from nearly everyone they met.

Each floor had five hundred square meters of shelved cardboard filing boxes. The individual waxed cardboard containers displayed the file start and end date of its contents, and a modern bar code label that helped verify the box's ID because much of the original writing had faded in the sunlit room. They had been given a bar code scanner to use just in case there was a question on a particular container's ID. The records organization was a testament to French bureaucracy, so it was easy to locate three boxes dated 01/06/45–01/06/47. Jean carried each container over to a large, oak library style table by the massive lead-paned windows overlooking the docks.

"What we must do now, my son, is to each take a box, pull a handful of files and scan them for the name 'Mueller', or 'Berhetzel'. Take your time and use that magnifying scanner, if need be. Just keep them in order so they can go back in as they came out, we don't need to upset anyone." Robert set his cane aside as he pulled a file from the front of the cardboard box. He settled in for a long day of search. "Take a file and let's get started. Tell me what your first file sleeve looks like."

Like his father, Jean sat in a comfortable position ready to dive in to the several files that sit before him. "D'accord, Papa. This file is a log showing each ship that entered or left the port on the first of June 1945 — its name, country of registration, vessel type, and primary purpose or cargo. There is an attached personnel sheet listing officers, crew and non-crew passengers, along with their passport registration. There is also a series of license numbers and certificates of use. It all looks very official and in order."

"Yes, it would on the surface, but these ports were a sewer with much of the world's human excrement finding their way here to escape the manure pile where they belonged. We only need to find one name on the crew or passenger manifests. Just one of the millions of human turds, like the socialists in Paris. You know what I always say, Jean?"

"Yes, Papa, the socialist turds are nothing more than communists in thousand Euro suits. And you can put lipstick on a pig, but it is still a pig. Put lipstick on a politician and you still have a pig!" Jean said as he noticed his father's shoulders set firmly in place. "You smell blood in the water, don't you?"

Robert looked up at his son and pulled off his half-size reading glasses. He gave a deliberate response. "These men we have searched for since the war were the worst evil that modern history had thrust upon it to that point. Since then, Stalin, Pol Pot and the Khmer Rouge, the Chinese Cultural Revolution, the African genocides, and God knows how many others have imitated their brand of evil on human society. The price to stop these fanatics is the soul of mankind. They need to finally be eliminated from the earth with a cry of, 'Jamais plus! Never again!' Berhetzel is a murderer and will mass murder in the future unless we find him. I am as confident of this as I am of Bridgette's love for me!"

Jean smiled at the old man's conclusion. Humor probably helped keep his sanity knowing his intimate understanding of what these evil men had done.

They continued their searching, struggling with the volumes of faded documents and the handwritten 'adjustments' that were made to the original documentation, with name strikeouts and corrections that probably occurred after a new false identity was established or a bribe paid. The human disruption caused by the destruction of genocidal war had made refugees of all sorts of people from peasants to politicians to war criminals. They all needed to escape their past and would do or give anything to accomplish that end. Old fortunes were sacrificed and new ones made in pursuit of the common goal to survive.

Robert found the file after several hours of searching.

"Jean, here it is. Ivan Mueller was registered on a ship called La Loba — The She Wolf — a Brazilian freighter carrying olive oil, wine, Egyptian cotton, wool and other commodities. It returned with similar unfinished products, tobacco, leather, coffee and dried beef. The vessel traveled probably six times a year to Porto Alegre, Brazil, as this was the fourth crossing in 1945. He was listed as crew so he would have needed to go through immigration services to stay and it's probable they would have a handwriting sample. That needs to be checked out!"

"There is no possible way for you to travel to Brazil to dig through records which I think wouldn't even exist now. It could kill you," Jean complained.

Robert stared out the window for a moment and then turned, facing his son.

"I have contacts in South America that I'll call. They are second generation, but still hate the Nazis as much as their parents did. If they can confirm Berhetzel immigrated as Mueller in '45 or '46, then I don't care if it does kill me because I will pack my sunscreen and bags, and go down there with or without you. You can come along if you think you can keep up with my ancient body."

Determined as he spoke, Robert no longer looked very old to his son.

Chapter 41
Atlanta

Sitting in the shadow of a giant, live oak, taking a break from her daily early morning run, Kate was slightly out of breath, but excited as she punched up Tom's phone. She had just finished a call from Jules who had asked, very politely in French, that 'Le Musketeers' come to Paris with Joseph and the journals. He had also given her a quick overview of what had happened with Jean and Robert's Switzerland investigation of Berhetzel's supposed grave. There seemed to be a lot more questions that needed answers.

"Hi, Kate," Tom answered. "You caught me just leaving the house to start my rounds. I'm heading out to look at a possible LDA, which, if my phone diagnosis is correct, I'll operate on after lunch. I love fixing cows with displaced stomachs because most seem to recover immediately. Plus, it pays good Moo-la."

"Is that panting sound Jed or are you that excited to hear my voice," Kate joked in her best Mae West impression.

"Hmmm, a trick question! BOTH of us are panting from the sound of your voice — I have you on speaker."

"Well, I don't want to upset that goofy dog, but we were just asked by Jules to come to Paris ASAP. He also wants us to bring Brad and Joseph with all of Nelson's original journals. Jules wants us to provide an American perspective and, hopefully, bring useful additional brain and manpower to help in any direction their investigation leads. It seems the man in question is not dead in a Swiss grave and the French investigators think that since his original work during the war was on a super-secret death ray weapon — not to mention he was a genius in genetics — that he is the probable architect of these die-offs. The real questions are, is he still alive and working because he would have to be in his late nineties, or is he dead and has an heir or associate carrying on his work? We also need to know if he's working as an individual or with the backing of a government or political group, like the New Nazi Party. The French are afraid that he still works as a Nazi sympathizer, which limits who they can trust because Nazis are still found everywhere in Europe. Being Americans, we are seen as free of those political connections, although Jules said our Space Administration was at one time full of Nazis, and may still be."

"So I guess this means no long weekend in Old Montreal, with those incredibly difficult-to-get hotel reservations, Bistro dinners, show tickets and NON-refundable airfare. At least I'll still get to listen to my sexy girlfriend converse in French. You know, your French makes me a little crazy, like Gomez from the Addams Family."

That made Kate laugh. "Now I'm blushing, stop it. Flattery will get you nowhere except to the City of Light — Paris."

"I don't think Brad is going to be too happy about leaving his family to travel to Europe, and I'm not so sure about Joseph either. He might want to keep those journals private," Tom said as he gave Jed a pat. Jed returned the affection by nuzzling Tom's leg, which left a nice smear of drool and black dog hair.

"Brad will be easy. French wine and food, and the ability to watch *The Walking Dead* in French is a no-brainer. Maybe throw in a nice beret. Joseph is the one I'm concerned about."

"So all this depends on Joseph agreeing to pack up on short notice, fly to a foreign country just so his grandfather's journals can undergo a rectal exam. I best not cancel our plans yet!" Tom lamented.

"I'll handle Brad and Joseph, you work out your business schedule with Bob. Jules said he will arrange all our travel needs. I'll call you tonight when I have the details. I have to get going and head back to the office. Love you!"

"Love you back. Bye," Tom exclaimed happily.

That evening Kate called Tom back with the itinerary Jules had given her.

"So it looks like we need to be at D.C. Reagan International in two days to catch our ride on the Pasteur Institute's private jet. Jules is arranging French diplomat status for us, and he said it would supersede our passport requirements for entry into most countries," Kate informed him.

"A private jet? Sounds fancy."

"Jules knows how to take care of us. Anyway, the plan, for now, when we get to Paris is to help analyze Nelson's journals, and try to match the journal images to other people or places in Europe," she said as she stretched out her hamstrings to keep them from a post-exercise cramp.

"What will I be doing while we're there? Besides kiss you all night," he said, insinuatingly.

"You and Brad are not coming for your good looks — or brains, for that matter," Kate admitted.

"Ouch," Tom faked a hard blow to his intelligence.

"You have to come because Joseph only trusts you. And, of course, I can't live without you. So it will be up to you to convince Joseph; I haven't called him yet. I thought it might be better coming from you."

"I'll give Joseph a call as soon as we hang up. Give me the information I'll need to persuade him. Because he's not easily persuaded, you know." Tom remembered how difficult it was to get Joseph to trust him when they first met. Now, Tom was the only person Joseph truly trusted. It made Tom happy that Joseph felt that way.

"Well," she continued, "that face in the journal belongs to a man named Wilheim Berhetzel. He was a Nazi medical doctor and researcher who worked under or for the infamous war criminal doctors Goldzmit and Eichman. He was thought to have died in a small plane crash while escaping Germany in 1945. The remains in the plane were found the following year and the bodies identified from the official papers found on their bodies. Locals buried them at a small nearby Swiss village close to where they crashed. Jules' Nazi hunting friend and his father went there with a couple of forensic specialists to match physical records to the skeletal remains but, turns out, there was no match to any of the three crash victims. They think he must have survived and traded ID papers to make it look like he died in the crash."

"That's not surprising to hear of a suspected Nazi war criminal," Tom interjected.

"No, it's not. Jules says he most likely escaped Europe and found a way to get to South America, probably Brazil or Argentina. His friend is contacting some affiliated colleagues in South America and sending several computer-aged photos along with Berhetzel's fingerprints for them to use."

"If my math is right, that would mean the man is in his late nineties. Aren't the odds good that he is dead or drooling in some rest home?" Tom asked, seriously.

"Yes, but Jules says the Nazi hunter father is convinced Berhetzel is alive and behind all this. Very convinced. Jules himself is more concerned he has collaborators or another government is involved. That is another reason he wants to keep this a closed investigation. Outside of us, only a few in our government or in Europe will have any idea what we will be doing. Everyone in the investigation has to have impeccable security clearances. To a large degree, we are on our own."

"So," Tom added, "in the event any of our team is caught or captured, the secretary will disavow any knowledge of our actions."

"It may be an impossible mission, but if this man has developed a weapon that can take down groups of select animals or humans, then the description 'evil genius' is going to be spot on. This must start as a narrow investigation and then expand with government resources if we are out of our league. The NSA and CIA have their hands and ears everywhere so it is possible they already know what we are up to. That's almost as scary as our small group scratching the surface trying to get to the real dirt. The only way to stop him might be surprising him because if he has escaped detection for over six decades, then either he has been incredibly lucky or has unbelievable security," Kate answered.

"Or both," Tom added.

They said their goodbyes and Tom called Joseph's cell. He picked up after the fourth ring and Tom started by asking how he was doing.

"I've been fine. I didn't think I would miss that old man so much, but I have his journals to read and that has given me insight into the world he lived in. And it's given me a real feel for the true soul of my people that goes back before Custer, which I would call the start of our 'modern history'. In our post-Custer world, we have been made to pay a price with the arrows of humiliation heaped upon us by the White world and by our self-inflicted wounds occurring day after day, year after year, decade after decade. We paid a terrible price for defeating a terrorist government in a single battle, a government that had lied, stole and cheated us. By defending ourselves we were very nearly exterminated by the flames of hatred, fueled by sensationalism in the press. These journals of grandfather's are a priceless record of the rise and decline of my people..."

"Well," Tom interrupted, "the journals might be more valuable than he suspected. The folks in France think they matched the face from his journal to a Nazi war criminal named Wilheim Berhetzel. He supposedly died in a plane crash escaping justice at the end of the war and was buried in a Swiss grave. An exhumation of his supposed buried remains to verify his death resulted in a 'no match' on physical or dental forensics. The French feel he survived that crash and switched IDs with the pilot, then escaped to Brazil or Argentina. We need your help to find that man by using Nelson's journals," Tom said.

"I don't know, Tom. I really need to be here to tie up loose ends with my great-grandfather's financials. He didn't have much, but the banks and insurance companies still ask for the same amount of paperwork," Joseph was clearly not going to agree to this easily.

"I know this is asking a lot, but they would like all of us, plus the original journals, in Paris for an indefinite period of time. We could be there days or for weeks, we just have no good idea," Tom mentioned hoping Joseph didn't hear the "for weeks" part.

"For weeks?"

He heard it.

"It could be a real adventure and I think you will like France, good food and cute girls!" Tom finished his sales pitch.

Joseph went silent for a moment and then replied, "Alright, but only because I truly think our solving the 'Destroyer' mystery is why grandfather was driven and haunted by all those visions. This must have been his purpose and therefore now my purpose. Fill me in on the details and I will be ready whenever you need me."

Chapter 42

Berhetzel became fixated on a second human test of his death machine in France. Well, he thought, maybe not a human test as he held the French just below the level of dogs. He felt that from an Aryan perspective, he would execute a subhuman, and he saw no moral dilemma in completing that task. Only those of pure blood, his blood, could cull the specie without guilt, as they had done for the Third Reich. In fact, any death of a non-Aryan to him was a neutral emotional exercise — he couldn't care less whether it be man, woman or child. Eliminate the weak or inferior, and breed to preserve the superior. He truly felt they had had the right ideas during the war, but had left too many important decisions to the emotionally weak, often drug addicted or insane men. Berhetzel believed if the Nazi leadership had been patient and waited just one year to start the war, they would have had the time needed to produce their super weapons and rockets. They could have had the bomb long before the Americans finished theirs, and then destroyed Britain in short order controlling the majority of Europe, Asia, and Africa. They could then monopolize a majority of the world's natural resources and wealth. They also could have crippled the United States to the point where she would have had no choice but to become a colony of Germany. But the crazy ones in Berlin didn't have patience, believing in their own rhetoric. That cost them the war, but now he would be the heir to a world power they could have only dreamed of. The enemy would have to figure it out before they could look for him, and he knew that wasn't going to happen. He was dead in a Swiss grave and nothing he had done in the last decades could point to anything other than an anonymous man minding his own business in the jungle, feeding and treating the very poor. He had been declared a saint by the local priests who relied on his generosity but, in reality, he was the angel of death stalking the rainforest, undisturbed and undetected for all the decades he had lived in hiding, out in the open.

Now, the fruit of all his years of research was a sophisticated, highly functional weapon, which modern technology had made possible. He was able to refine his original designs down to a compact, powerful piece of equipment that had taken all of his extended life to develop into the several different forms he perfected. He had two versions he liked the most: the handheld cell phone lookalike, and the remote-controlled drone that was designed to appear and move like a raven. All of this was made possible by nano processors, high capacity solar sensitive battery power and advancements in robotics. He also had purchased, through Argentina's endlessly drug-fueled black market, a 3D printer giving him the capability to incorporate his technology into any design he chose to produce. The key element was his portable DNA analyzer that incorporated small test strips, much like the ones used for home pregnancy tests. This allowed the small test samples to be placed in a 2.5 ml reagent solution vial, easily incubated at body temperature for ninety seconds by placing it in an armpit or aside the tongue, followed by a quick dip of the test strip in that solution. Then the last step was inserting the strip in an electric toothbrush shaped analyzer, which would complete the data collection and then wirelessly transmit the target ID information to the actual delivery device. The total targeting time was fewer than five minutes once the DNA sample was acquired. The coded energy pulse produced by the weapon would effectively be like a laser beam directing that lethal energy burst to the coded DNA tissue only, which would scramble that brain's DNA, shutting off its electrical activity, stunning it permanently. At best, if the victim was placed immediately on life support, the body could be artificially maintained, but the person would become a permanent resident of Mr. McGregor's vegetable patch. The insulted brain was fried and would never recover. Its ability to think and control life's functions was over.

Berhetzel had developed the device to either kill individuals or, more broadly, kill specie-specific zones of up to 100 square meters with the pre-programmed DNA coordinates of humans, dogs, horses and birds. The weapon was good for only two narrow, or individual kills, and one broad shot, which he intended to be used to create a diversion or clear an escape route. The device had nearly unlimited storage capacity, so it was possible to preload it many times with a specific target's DNA data for future reference. The only thing that limited its functionality was the power sourcing — the size of the super batteries limited the number of 'shots' he could take without a full recharge. Solar recharging took six hours of bright sunshine and a standard plug-in charge was at least a 45-minute wait.

Berhetzel was anxious to test his weapon on the world stage and had set upon a plan to collect some DNA related to the French President. He had searched Parisian social media for young, beautiful escorts to recruit for the job of collecting the sample from the President's only son, a known womanizer and party-goer, who had been involved in several scandals involving cocaine and impaired driving. He seemed to be an easy target with either drugs or women — an easy lure to capture the needed sample. The male DNA that he would identify and extract would match the French President, and that would be all Berhetzel would need to target and kill the leader of the country he hated the most. Finding the right woman to collect the sample might be a task, but he was confident that, in a country of 'whores', purchasing a suitable agent for this task would be easy, especially if she had no political or moral limitations. Not knowing who he could trust to contact the young man after hours searching on social media, Berhetzel took a chance and called a professor of genetics at the Sorbonne who he had met at a Vienna conference. The professor had told him, in bragging confidence, of the many female students who would seek him out for 'extra credit', and if he was ever in Paris and needed a student for companionship, call and he could give him a dozen names. That contact paid off and through Facebook, he located one of the recommended girls who looked perfectly capable, beautiful and, most importantly, desperate for money since her Papa had cut her off for drug use and poor grades.

The woman, it turned out, was willing to find a way to collect a DNA sample and hold it until he needed it. He wired her 1,000 Euros with the promise of 4,000 more when he had the sample in hand, and after he reviewed the recordings of their liaisons to verify the identity of the donor. He also implied to her that he was part of the Russian mafia, which should have scared the crap out of her. At least enough to assure she kept her end of the bargain.

When she finally confirmed she had the sample and sent a reasonable amount of documentation, he made his plans for travel to Paris. The upcoming G8 Conference would be a great platform for the tragic, sudden, unexplained death of a major world leader, and an appropriate event for initiating his personal reign of terror. A bloodless coup. No heads rolling, but nonetheless, a political decapitation.

Berhetzel would now fly to Germany for the first time since he fled her in that small, doomed plane, and travel to the Bavarian farm village where he hoped his cache of gold was still safely hidden. That stonewall was surely several centuries old and fortunately the area had not been developed since the war. He checked the field fence almost weekly on Google Earth and it always looked the same from space. He hoped it looked as good in person because he had stashed fifty kilos of gold bars worth over two million Euros that he planned on selling on the black market. This would convert the gold to Euros and he would deposit the cash in a Swiss bank account. After he had secured the funds, he would travel the two hours to his gravesite to pay his respects to his three 'relatives' who had died so tragically in that plane crash.

He would thoroughly enjoy standing by that grave and laying flowers, as a tribute to his superior nature.

Then he would catch a train for Paris, where the real fun would begin. *A dead Frenchie on a world stage*, he laughed to himself, *he would be croaking a frog.*

Chapter 43
Wisconsin

Tom received his marching orders with a tight schedule from Kate, and he quickly arranged a partnership agreement with his overjoyed young associate who was eager to propose to his dairy princess, Beth. At least now if something happened to Tom, Bob's future would not be in question.

Brad traveled to pick Tom up the next morning for the drive to the Minneapolis Airport to catch their direct flight to Washington, D.C.

"You know," Brad complained, "if I didn't need a job, didn't like my job, or didn't have an interest in finding an answer to this 'Destroyer' business, I would tell the USDA what they could do with my job. And there is no way I'm going to eat snails or horse meat or wear one of those funny hats. I'm definitely a naysayer to the nag slayers."

"Come on now, don't be an old fart," Tom said, "the food and wine is the best in the world and there is no way a beret will stay on your shiny dome anyway unless you Velcro it down. Besides, you're always saying 'Oui, Oui'!"

"Only when I've been drinking beer then, I go wee-wee all the way home!" Brad offered as he pulled onto the expressway.

Joseph had left to meet them at the airport several hours before they had and was pushing his old pickup to its physical limit as he had a lot of road to cover to be there on time. This trip was a huge adventure for someone who had never been more than one state away from his home and with the importance of grandfather's journals, suddenly he was thrust into an unfamiliar spotlight. He brought pretty much all of his clothes, which wasn't anything other than lots of denim, western boots and his best ivory ranch hat. He had run down to the mercantile and purchased new underwear and socks, two new string ties, a good leather coat that could double as a sports jacket and all the travel size toiletries he thought he could carry. Everything fit nicely into his old camo duffle bag except for Grandfather's original journals, which he carried in the old man's leather Samsonite suitcase that was probably from the fifties. He had thought about photocopying the text, but that would have taken way too much time, so he swore to never let that old suit case out of his sight. He had wondered for years why grandfather had suffered so from the visions, but now it was reassuring that maybe he wasn't just a crazy old Indian. He truly received a gift from his ancestors. This convinced Joseph that that spirit would travel with them, protect and guide them to an answer.

Kate had several conversations with Jules to make sure all the arranged travel was in order. She asked her best friend Julie to watch her apartment and take care of the cats and plants, and then went out on a shopping spree purchasing new clothes and shoes, and buying the latest perfume from Paris that promised 'passion as a pastime'. Tom wouldn't stand a chance in the City of Light — maybe, she hoped, the romance of Paris would spur a proposal from him. She wasn't going to drop a hint or suggestion, but if he asked, she was ready to say yes. Definitely yes!

Jules called early in the morning and told Kate that the Pasteur Institute 737 had arrived at Reagan International and would be ready to board immediately after they arrived. There was a crew of six, plus two diplomatic assistants assigned to the jet on a permanent basis to service the passengers' needs and clear any governmental issues that might arise. Jules would be providing French diplomatic credentials to the four of them so they could clear all screening processes with minimal delay. One crew member was a Michelin-qualified chef and was cooking a gourmet meal on the eight-hour flight. The French liked to impress, and Jules would make sure that on their Atlantic crossing, they would experience the best he could offer.

Tom, Brad and Joseph arrived on schedule at the Minneapolis-St. Paul International Airport and were at the Frontier Airline kiosk at almost the exact same time. They greeted each other heartily and then checked in for the two-and-a-half-hour nonstop flight, so Tom figured that if all went well, they would arrive in Paris Orly Airport by eight thirty or nine in the morning, just in time for breakfast. They proceeded to the TSA screening area.

"Well, Joseph, are you excited about heading over to Paris?" Tom asked, "It promises to be an exciting adventure — your grandfather would be real proud of you, taking on this responsibility."

"It's a little scary, but I think all of this is being overseen by the Ancestors. I'm just their mechanic. I hope all this analysis uncovers some significant answers or directions that you can use. Funny thing is, I've not felt this much like a Sioux in my life, so these journals have opened a whole new world to me," Joseph answered, dodging a golf cart carrying several gray-haired passengers.

Brad had to add a comment.

"Well, I haven't been this excited to be a veterinarian since my first job offer out of school. Tom, you know, the one at the Milwaukee Zoo."

"That's the one where you were going to specialize in circumcising elephants?" Tom asked.

"Yeah, I unfortunately had to turn them down because it didn't pay too well, but there were *big tips*," Brad laughed, finding himself exceedingly funny.

"I think Brad deserves an honorary Indian name. How about Running Bull, Bald Bull, or Buffalo Bull?" Joseph offered.

"I think that last one fits the best, but any name with 'Bull' in it describes him to a 'T'," Tom said.

"OK, OK, I'm fine with Buffalo Bull, but my wife would prefer Raging Bull. You know, 'I'm da boss, I'm da boss, I'm da boss!'" Brad answered.

"This is going to be a loooong flight," Tom lamented.

Chapter 44
Reagan International Airport

Washington, D.C

"I am Louis LaFleur and I represent the government of the Republic of France. I am assigned to the Pasteur Institute as a diplomatic liaison. My job today is to get you out of the United States with as little problem as possible, and then when we land in Paris, be sure that your entry goes smoothly. That is, think of me as your personal problem solver and concierge. If there are no questions, we will now be escorted by Monsieur Andy Franklin from the TSA who is going to take us to a special screening area where we can move the process quickly to get you boarded. There will be one more passenger on this flight, a geneticist and biochemist from The Ohio State University who also will be working with Doctor LeClerc. OK, Monsieur Andy, s'il vous plait."

The procedure was just a formality where their baggage was x-rayed, and a special government tag and barcode applied to each bag. By placing their coded USDA personal identifier in a tag generator, a two-sided, laminated luggage tag was produced with all their personal diplomatic clearances and luggage data covering either side. Included was the bag's weight, description, measurements and photo, so that any significant variation could be flagged and investigated. It was a fast process that took less than twenty minutes for all four of them, and would provide their expedited passage into France or any other EU country. Louis directed them past the security room and with Andy's assistance, walked them to the massive jet that sat by itself on a far corner of the tarmac.

"As you will see," LaFleur described as he pointed around the jet's interior, "this beautiful vessel has been modified to carry up to forty passengers with sleeping berths, two executive suites, full bathroom facilities with showers, a small isolation suite, and two hospital suites with life support capabilities. Our cargo bay also contains a morgue and lab where necropsies, autopsies or other biochemical tests can be performed. These beautiful cabin seats are arranged so they can be rotated 90 degrees so that the cabin can become a class or conference room with lectern and large video computer screens that fold up into the ceiling. Our galley is a full-service kitchen where we will produce gourmet food for you and we have a full service bar. You will be traveling state of the art, and dare I say in luxury?"

Kate had a beautiful, almost blissful smile, expressing her obvious excitement about the trip, and being with Tom. All her favorite things in one package: romance, travel, Paris and her passion for science. Tom sat next to her on the starboard aisle while Joseph and Brad sat on the opposite side, each taking a window seat. Louis introduced them to the gracious staff and, immediately, Kate was off having a fun conversation in French with the crew. She looked radiant with a new stylish haircut and travel outfit she had purchased for the trip, but it was obvious it was her stunning, vibrant personality that captivated the crew. Tom was suddenly jealous of the crew who was obviously enthralled with Kate. He decided he was a fool for not having spoken of marriage with her.

In the rear of the plane alone was the professor from Ohio State, who had his head buried in a laptop, oblivious to their boarding and the conversations around him. Tom kept looking back toward him with a ready smile, but he was bent over the computer so that the light from the screen reflected off his glasses. Tom excused himself and walked to the rear area to greet the fellow 'Big 10-er'.

"Excuse me, I wanted to introduce myself. I'm Dr. Tom O'Dell from the USDA. I guess we are headed to the same place," he said extending his hand.

The man was about fifty, medium build with salt and pepper crew cut hair and wore khaki slacks, white shirt and a scarlet and gray checker bow tie. He looked up from his laptop, pushed his tortoise shell glasses up his nose to get a clearer look at Tom and smiled, "I'm Fred Garrett. Sorry I didn't get up to greet you, but I'm right in the middle of a data stream review and wax list for my work. I think it's called tunnel vision — a byproduct of continual concentration and tuning out the rest of the world. My wife yells at me all the time about it, but I rarely hear her," he laughed.

"Don't apologize," Tom replied, "we all have workaholic tendencies here. I guess that's why Jules has called upon us. Two of us are USDA veterinarians, that's Dr. Kate Vensky over there speaking French and loving it, the big guy is Dr. Brad Upton, and in front of him is Joseph Blackfeather, a Lakota Sioux from Montana whose grandfather produced the journals which may be the key to solving the mystery that we are on this picnic for. This promises to be real interesting involving a Nazi bad boy. I'm a large animal veterinarian from Wisconsin and currently assigned to work with the USDA on the die-off mystery. So far, it's been a very unusual investigation."

Fred leaned back in his seat and ran his hands over his face in an attempt to revive himself. His height was masked by the fact that he was seated, but

Tom could sense Fred Garrett was an athlete in his not-so-distant youth. "That's why I'm traveling with you," he replied. "Jules sent me some porcine brain tissue to analyze and I think there are some subtle changes in the nano particulate DNA. It almost looks like it is melted down or fried. It was probably an accident we noticed it, but when we went back to check the previously processed samples, we found the same minute changes in all of them. To give you a general idea, the amount of relevant tissue involved would be like filling a major college football stadium with, I guess, beer since its college, dropping a ping pong ball in, and then trying to find it in the dark. All while staying sober!"

"Now would that be Buckeye or Badger stadium?" Tom joked.

"You can take your pick. However you cut it, much more difficult than a needle in a haystack!"

Tom took Fred forward to meet Brad and Joseph, and was dismayed when he started a conversation with Kate in fluent French while the crew started to pass out champagne to toast the flight, apparently a French preflight tradition. They all raised their fluted glasses to 'Salut'. Tom noticed they all drank, but Joseph who handed his glass to Brad since he had gulped his glass down quickly.

They settled in their large seats as the crew prepared for takeoff. Tom could sense Kate's normal confident persona morphing into a child-like fear. She hated air travel, but since he had never flown with her, he had no idea how bad her anxiety was. The jet rumbled down the runway as the engines whined and strained. Kate took Tom's hand and squeezed tightly. He turned to her and as their eyes held contact, their souls became one in the same. He was determined to find a ring in Paris and a romantic way to propose. There would be no way he would let her slip through his fingers by procrastinating. Kate smiled and relaxed as she laid her head onto his shoulder as if she suddenly realized they would be together forever.

Chapter 45
Porto Alegre, Brazil

Berhetzel stood in the security line at the Salgado Filho International Airport, nervously watching the screening process, always aware that someone from his past might recognize him because he looked essentially the same as he had decades before. Each contact with authority, every person present in a congested area was a risk, although minimal, and presented that chance of discovery.

The queue for the five a.m. flight to Miami was long and moving slowly due to security removing food, liqueur and oversized bottles of liquids from carry-ons. Passengers argued their cases in a stressed, rapid Latin cadence. This screening in Brazil would be minimal compared to that in the U.S., so any problem he experienced here, might be magnified many times in Miami.

The Nazi was traveling relatively lightly, carrying his disguised equipment on board and keeping a small quantity of reagents in his carry-on bags, and in his checked bag, he portaged a larger quantity of raw reagents in shampoo and toiletry bottles. If need be, he could fabricate enough finished reagent to last several months. He also packed his extra high-capacity batteries in various electronic decoys, from electric shavers to cameras and carried a couple of solar and plug-in battery chargers. Even if he was off the grid, he could produce enough power to use his weapon multiple times. Both his carry-on and checked luggage also contained his longevity formula capsules disguised as simple brewer's yeast in large amber plastic bottles.

The first security screener didn't even look up as he checked his passport against the boarding pass, making small red check marks as he verified information. He then looked up, glancing back and forth from the passport photo to Berhetzel's face verifying identity and comparing the date of birth with the man's face. There was something in those eyes that bothered the screener. They seemed too old. Berhetzel's eyes looked as an old man's eyes should though everything else seemed in order and correct. The officer did several double takes, then subconsciously shrugged his shoulders and passed Berhetzel through.

Berhetzel had been able to continuously produce and backdate his counterfeit passport that he had purchased for his first major trip out of the continent in 1992. His identity as Dr. Josef Von Braun was a safe ruse that gave him just enough of an air of authority to intimidate most people who crossed his path. It was apparent that this distain for the common man, which he could turn on and off as necessary, would subjugate most, especially in South America where many had inferiority complexes. But then, when necessary, he could charm anyone that he read as strong, confident or difficult. In the U.S. and Europe, charm would serve him best. That evil Nazi nature made him a resourceful actor.

He had left his compound fully prepared to destroy it if he was unable to return, and had set up two drones which he could activate remotely from anywhere in the world capable of destroying all life in his Argentina compound, La Lupa. There were also remote devices that could be used to burn and destroy all evidence in the laboratory. If he had to go into hiding, nothing would be left to identify who he was or what he had accomplished. He was a self-described 'genius' and this residual paranoia would assure that his life's work would remain secret until *he* was ready to reveal it to the world.

Now, all he had to do was enjoy his seven hour layover in Miami, and then get past the TSA screeners for his secondary flight to Stuttgart, Germany. He was going to South Beach to do some plasticized people watching, and test his device one more time. He pushed his way past the confused sheep in the coach line to the first class queue, and rapidly boarded the plane for the trip north, a sinister smile trying to escape from his stern Germanic face. He felt a mixture of determination and disgust at the undisciplined weaklings that seemed to be everywhere — zoned out, sporting earplugs and headphones while talking to unknown entities. It was obvious the species had deteriorated during his lifetime by the number of these inferior beings that seemed to be wandering haplessly. There was no survival of the fittest in this modern world and these people seemed to reproduce like rats. At least rats knew when to eat their young.

His first class ticket put him in the nearly deserted premium section of the plane with only three other seats occupied. He had reserved the first row port side aisle seat, which kept him away from the three men in the rear of the section who appeared to be traveling together. After he had settled in and asked the steward not to be disturbed unless he asked for assistance, he pulled out his laptop and sent a simple message to his Parisian contact about the DNA sample. He wrote:

Dear trusted friend,

I am on my way to visit and hope you and your boyfriend have been happy and well. Are you still planning a child?

W.VB.

It was Noon in Paris, and since these young people seemed to check their email every thirty seconds, he expected a quick reply. It came within two minutes.

Dear W.,

We are certainly trying to produce a child and you will see evidence of that from the present I have for you when we meet to exchange our simple gifts.

V.

Good, he thought. The message meant she had seminal DNA, which would allow him the next best specimen for rapid data extraction other than blood. He summoned the steward over to order beer, cheese and bread, and ate the light snack before he drifted off into a restless sleep. *Perhaps*, he thought, *if I am lucky, I will dream of a State funeral procession down the Champs-Élysées.*

When the jet landed at Miami International on schedule, he was rested and ready to head to South Beach. After an easy trip through passport control with his bags, he made his way to the ground transportation area where a man dressed in a white shirt, black tie and black trousers waited for him holding a white piece of cardboard with 'Dr. Von Braun' printed on it in bold lettering. He gave over the larger bag to his dark-skinned driver, but controlled the critical smaller carry-on. He asked to be driven to the main beach area where the driver was to drop him off and then go park off Collins Avenue to wait for his pickup call. The driver knew his way well and negotiated the hectic Miami traffic in silence.

Berhetzel strolled up the overheated street and passed dozens of nearly naked sun worshippers of different nationalities. He heard French, Spanish, Portuguese, German, Australian and America English spoken at nearly every spot he stopped, and he hadn't even gone a kilometer! He felt slightly obvious and out of place in his white tropics suit and Panama hat, so he looked for and found a shaded table near a busy beach volleyball court, where muscular young men and women played intense thirty-minute matches. They then retired to nearby shaded tables under bright orange and royal blue canopies, where the drinks where as cool as the women were hot. After watching several matches, he picked his target — a muscular, bronzed, Hispanic looking man who appeared to be extremely fit. The young man had

151

a routine of returning to his table after a match and wiping his mouth and body perspiration off with the table's paper napkins and then relaxing with a juice cocktail of some kind before he happily sprinted out for a new game. When he and his friends headed back on the beach, Berhetzel causally went to their table and retrieved the sweat-soaked napkin. Careful not to contaminant the tissue with his damp hands, he carried it to his table and carefully pulled a one-centimeter piece off, then balled up the rest on the napkin and laid it aside.

He looked around at the other tables and saw that everyone was on the beach, and the bartender was busy trying to score with a girl whose alcohol-enhanced laughter sounded like a goat being goosed. He turned his chair slightly away from the bar and pulled a pair of rat tooth forceps, a reagent vial and the small microprocessor — that looked like a mini electric toothbrush — from an old, worn, leather eyeglass case. Berhetzel took the piece of napkin and placed it into the 2 ml liquid reagent vial, inverting it several times. He then placed the vial in his mouth, aside his tongue to incubate it for two minutes. He carefully wiped the vial dry and noted that the reagent fluid had turned a very pale blue indicating a successful incubation. The next step was to take a diabetic-like test strip from a small opaque tube and dip it into the blue fluid. After that, he inserted the strip into the analyzer and pushed the start button. There was a soft humming noise as the data was collected and, after a very short time, the apparatus' LED indicator flashed green, signaling completion. Berhetzel then took a short black cable and interfaced the analyzer with the actual delivery device, which mimicked a cell phone or small camera. He was a great believer in camouflage, and these everyday objects would not raise anyone's concern.

With the device loaded, all he had to do was wait for the man to return to his seat and activate the device. He might have taken him out at up to one-hundred meters, but he wanted a ringside seat for the chaos that he was sure to unleash.

The man and his three friends return laughing and flirting with each other, obviously happy with the last match and each other. Berhetzel waited until they ordered their refreshments and then pulled the device up like he was snapping a photo and pushed the start button. The imaging screen lit up with a three-dimensional image of the man's skull that rotated in a clockwise circle. Suddenly, the screen flashed 'Completed and Acquired'. Berhetzel slipped off the device's safety feature, and completely depressed the 'on' button. There was a barely audible high-pitched whine, and a quick flash of lethal energy projected forward at the man's skull. The man jerked, quivered and fell forward, his head crashing loudly onto the metal table. Then all Hell broke loose.

"Alain, my God, Alain, are you OK?" the blonde girlfriend screamed, and then broke into hysterical rants as she rolled his head over and recognized lifeless eyes.

"Call 9-1-1! Get the lifeguards!" the other male friend shouted, "he's had a stroke!"

The screams went out for help and the lifeguards quickly ran over to start CPR. Only forty five seconds went by before they began the life-saving method. People were in hysterics, but the lifeguards were trained to remain calm.

In a matter of minutes the paramedics arrived, sirens blaring, and worked to shock the corpse back to life. Shouts of 'clear' were followed by sobs and crying as it became obvious he could not be helped. The EMTs shook their heads, indicating the hopeless situation.

Berhetzel slipped away from the chaos and pulled out his real cell phone to call his driver.

"Thomas, I am ready to be picked up now, I will be approximately four intersections north of where you left me. I want to go now to Coco Beach for dinner. Get me a recommendation for an excellent restaurant, please. Thank you."

He walked north through the curious migrating crowd who pushed to see what all the excitement was about. *If I could create this much chaos eliminating a pretty boy beach bum*, he thought, *just think what would result from the televised, unexplained death of Le President.*

He had processed and executed his target in less than twenty minutes. It would be explained as natural causes unless they found drugs in his system. *Ironic*, he thought, *an unnatural death to bring natural order back to the world.*

Chapter 46
In Flight

Pasteur Institute Jet

The flight to Paris was to be just over eight and a half hours long. The Michelin qualified Chef prepared a great meal of Coq au Vin, delicate asparagus with white truffles, arugula salad with candied walnuts, and a fabulous cheese and potato dish. The dessert was a white chocolate mousse with a touch of orange liquor. There were several courses of outstanding regional French wine served before, during and after the meal and a final glass of relaxing cognac, which afterward, had Tom, Kate and Brad feeling no pain. Aviophobic Kate couldn't have cared less if she had been asked to do a wing walk, and probably would have slept through the rest of the flight if she wasn't having such an enjoyable time, unwilling to miss what was coming next. Joseph was the only non-drinker, but definitely enjoyed the fine food. He and asked for additional servings, after commenting that 'this was the best chow he had ever eaten!' The chef, understanding that he was serving a relative food virgin, accepted the compliment, smiling proudly, and replied, "This is just a small sample of food delights that await you in France. The best is yet to come, Monsieur!"

"Then I likely will gain twenty pounds," Joseph replied.

"I already gained that, but who cares," Brad slightly slurred.

After the meal, attendants dimmed the cabin lighting and passed out soft cashmere blankets and down pillows. They quickly slipped into an alcohol-and-food-induced coma, with even the excited Kate drifting off into a relaxed state.

About one hour from Orly Airport, they were politely and gently awakened with a refreshing 'Bonjour', and the smell of freshly brewed coffee and warm croissants. They took turns cleaning up in the in the large en suite bathrooms and returned to find a continental style buffet laid out with all the fresh fruit, baked goods, cheeses and juices that you could want. Next to an arrangement of cream and pink orchids was an open bottle of champagne in a sterling silver ice bucket waiting to be served.

"Oh, look, ginger ale," Brad joked as he poured and gulped a glass of the bubbly liquid before the distressed steward could do his job, "and look, here is an outstanding 'fromage' from a small Israeli cheese factory that I am familiar with."

"Non, Monsieur, respectfully, all these cheeses are from my country," the steward said, correcting Brad.

"Darn, I would have sworn this stinky one was from a company called 'Cheeses of Nazareth'," he said waiting for riotous laughter to erupt. It didn't and Joseph nudged Brad in the back.

"White man speak with foot in mouth!" he said.

"Some people just don't have a sense of what funny is. Like when I saw your sorry face this morning, I grabbed at my scalp and, sure enough, it was gone!"

"That is only because the fertilizer is in your skull, not on it, so it couldn't do any good."

"I'm doomed," Brad lamented, smiling, "not only am I saddled with a smart ass Indian, but also one with a sense of humor."

Brad had his glass refilled and gathered a plateful of pastries and several tiny jars of fruit preserves. He moved over to the opposite side of the cabin with Joseph and sat with Kate and Tom.

"You know, Brad, maybe it was lost in translation, but the French are supposed to have a great love of comedy," Tom commented.

"Maybe if I had hair, messed it up, crossed my eyes while wearing thick black glasses and had buck teeth like the nutty professor, they would laugh."

Kate shook her head.

"Yeah, as they pushed you out of the plane over England. I don't think a Jerry Lewis impersonation would improve the punch lines, except the line waiting to punch you out."

That created a good laugh. It was obvious that there was something about Kate this morning that had all the men on the plane envying Tom. When she had returned from the en suite bathroom, she looked unbelievable and all the men's heads were turning in admiration. Tom shot a couple of them 'eat your heart out looks' as he handed her a champagne glass. She was a very special lady and everyone on the plane knew it.

After the 'petite déjeuner', it was time for Kate to address the group.

"Bonjour, Mes Amies! It appears that we are very close to landing at Orly and I wanted to give our itinerary for the day. When we land, after customs — which Monsieur LaFleur has told me will be very easy—we are to meet Jules with an Institute van at the Orly ground transportation area. He will get us to our housing to settle in. At one p.m., we will be transported to the Pasteur Institute for lunch in the cafeteria. Then we are scheduled to conference with the Institute and Archives Nationale investigators to discuss what their understanding of the situation is and afterward, we may have time to get into some of Nelson's journals. Joseph, you are critical to this investigation so you will have Carte Blanche for anything you need. I suspect you will be working very closely with the Archives staff, possibly without all of us present, so if any of that makes you uncomfortable, one of us can stay with you," Kate informed him.

"I think I can manage on my own," Joseph said confidently. "As long as someone there speaks English!"

The group chuckled and Kate said in a business-like tone, "I know you understand the seriousness of what we are facing and I believe the information your grandfather left in those journals will be key to us resolving this mystery. The trained investigators that will be working directly on your journals are the best in the business, and will be treating them carefully as historical documents. Every sentence on every page will be scrutinized so we can find the man depicted in his illustration."

"If you trust them with Grandfather's journals, I trust them too," Joseph nodded his head in agreement with Kate.

LaFleur spoke up sensing the opportunity to get his voice in, "I hope you all have enjoyed the flight as much as it has been our pleasure to have you with us. And on behalf of the Captain and rest of our crew, we thank you for flying with us. As a reminder, those luggage tags need to stay on your bags at all times so please don't discard them. If you need to fly somewhere else, they will make your life a lot easier, especially reentering the U.S. Now, please return to your seats and buckle up, we will be on the ground in about fifteen minutes. Merci beaucoup."

Brad turned to Tom and said, "Well, if this is any indication of what we're going to experience on this little excursion, I'm going to be one happy camper. I even think Joseph is enjoying the royal treatment. I just have to figure what to tell my wife to make it sound like I'm about to suffer a horrible death by guillotine. I really like this being 'Pasteurized'."

Tom patted the big man on his back and said, "If you don't tell her the truth, I will have to find a way to make it sound even better, although that might be difficult to do."

The plane landed at Orly, France's second largest airport that saw 28 million passengers jetting in and out annually. The Pasteur jet-taxied over to a designated area for corporate jets, well beyond the nearest terminal. It was an uncommonly bright, sunny day, not the characteristic gray misty day that Kate was often used to seeing. She smiled as she looked out her window at the beautiful weather and watched a white passenger van with flashing yellow-orange lights rapidly approach the jet.

Louis and another crew member cracked open the hatch and the warm, early morning sun lit the front of the plane brightly as they waited for a ground crew to position a portable set of stairs up to the exit door.

"OK, we can leave now. I see Doctor LeClerc is here now," he said.

Jules stood at the bottom of the stairs with a wide smile and gave Kate a customary kiss on each cheek, pulling her close to whisper something into her ear. Tom could see a blush rise on her face as Jules smiled softly. Suddenly he was jealous of Jules even though he knew that he had no rational reason to be in envy. He decided right then that waiting to put a ring on her finger wouldn't be a real bright idea while in a country of slick, romancing Frenchmen looking for conquests. Paranoia? Maybe.

After Jules greeted each of them and had a short conversation with the university professor, they loaded the Mercedes van and sped off to a terminal exit where Jules flashed an ID. They passed without any scrutiny. No customs today, they were diplomats.

Brad, Joseph and the professor were driven to the new five-star Peninsula Hotel on Rue Kleber, where each were given a glamorous junior suite in the Parisian version of the internationally famous hotel chain. The location put them a short walk to the Arc de Triompe and the Champs-Élysées, and reasonably close to the Eiffel Tower. Every part of Paris was available to them with a nearby metro entrance.

Jules then took Tom and Kate to his Rue Copernic apartment, a beautiful fourth-floor penthouse with a rooftop terrace complete with a potted garden and dining area. It was stunning, but the most breathtaking feature of his apartment was that it overlooked a prominently visible Eiffel Tower. The sun warmed the breezy outdoor space as sparrows chirped in their universal voices from hidden roosts.

"As you can see, this apartment should give you two your privacy and provide a comfortable stay." Jules knowingly winked at Tom. "My last mistress lived here for three years and left about a month ago, so disregard any personal things you might find. Her name is Lynnette and is the jealous and crazy type, but it was she who left our friendship. Call me if she shows up. The locks are changed so she cannot get in. You have a maid, Maria, who will be here from Noon to two, except Sundays, and anything you need, just leave her a note and she will get it for you," Jules said as he moved from window to window drawing the floor-length drapes.

"Any good bakeries?" Tom asked. He was anxious to get his hands on more croissants.

"Oui. Just around the corner. You'll also find a small market where you can pick up anything you want. Just charge it to my account. Anything else

— meals, wine and the lot — save your receipts and I will make sure you are refunded."

"Thank you so much, Jules. That's very generous," Kate said appreciatively.

"It's the least I can do. I really appreciate all of the sacrifice you made helping with our investigation and hope all of us can figure it out. I will let you settle in and pick you up at Midi. Au revoir."

He gave Kate a pair of parting cheek kisses and waved goodbye to Tom.

When the door closed, Kate turned to Tom and nearly jumped into his arms. They kissed a lover's kiss, as both could feel the heat in their bodies rising from their passion. Kate had always dreamed of being in Paris with a true love, but never envisioned that it would be under these circumstances — work-related and investigating such a critical mystery. This was probably a once-in-a-lifetime opportunity and she planned on making the most of it, both professionally and personally.

Tom held her tightly as he whispered a couple suggestions in her ear.

"Since we have several hours before they pick us up for lunch, I think we have a couple of choices. Plan A would be to go take cold showers and nap for a couple of hours, or Plan B, we could forego the rest and check out those thousand-count sheets in the master. I really don't think they were made for sleeping on anyway."

With that, Kate took his hand, smiled coyly and said, "Any plan but A."

Chapter 47
Miami International Airport

A smug and confident Berhetzel politely pushed through the TSA security line that was moving at a snail's pace. He didn't receive even a second glance as his carry-on bags were being screened, his devices safely disguised as common items people carried with them on a plane. He boarded the Lufthansa 777 and was escorted to his first-class seat that was as far forward as possible. Unlike the flight from Porto Alegre, this jet was filled with Germans returning home from their South Florida vacations, second homes or businesses. Their wealth was worn like a proud uniform. Expensive suits, jewelry and watches shouted to the world 'We are the economic power of Europe!' He felt that old familiar nationalistic pride rise in him as he listened to the numerous conversations in his native tongue. To him, it was like listening to a Wagner symphony, each word a pure and true musical note, not the irritating Spanish and Portuguese garble that reminded him of a persistent yapping dog. That's probably why there was a waiting period to buy a gun.

His return to the Motherland to reclaim the looted gold would close that chapter of his life and fund his new army of assassins, assuring a rise to world power and confirm that a superior people, the Aryans, would finally dominate the lesser races. Each step had been carefully choreographed and he was ready to do the dance.

By the time they landed at Stuttgart, he had replayed the plan over and over again in his head to the point where each step had been dissected and analyzed for any flaws, hopefully preventing stupid errors.

He planned to rent a van at the airport and then travel to the stonewall hiding place. He would carefully observe the area to determine the safety and timing needed to remove the looted wealth. When he felt he could start securely pulling the gold bars from behind the granite stones, he would remove a third of them at a time, and go to a pre-determined meeting place mutually arranged with a Russian black market agent. The conversion of the gold to Euros would allow him then to easily transport the cash to his private Swiss bank and deposit it. From there, he would wire transfer funds when needed to anywhere in the world without fear of governments tracking the transactions. Since gold was at an all-time high, and even with the hefty 25% lesser market price he would suffer, there would be millions secured to fund his plans. And when his power grew, he would sell his services to the highest bidder and buy the bank.

After his arrival, he set his plan in motion.

For a man with few emotional moments, his nationalistic pride rose higher as he traveled further into the rural German countryside. The neat, clean villages, well-paved and maintained roads were a far cry from the wholesale destruction he remembered at the war's end. The German people had lost the war and nearly a complete generation of their youth, but had survived to yet again take their rightful place as a world economic power — although stripped by the Allies of any future military might. Berhetzel now planned a future reining over the world from his beloved homeland, not dictating from some third-world outhouse of a country.

Upon arriving at the small farm village where the stonewall hiding place was, he was very surprised to see how little it had changed since 1945. It was as if his gold had frozen the place in time, the village refusing to grow or die. Not a tourist village, it remained a small farming community, relatively isolated in the hills, and there appeared to be no modern development other than some newer tractors in the fields harvesting the barley and baling its straw.

The Nazi located his way back to the old tree lined, narrow farm lane, which led to his hiding place, the van rocking and rolling to the pitch of the rutted old graveled surface. He passed the stone farmhouse that the fence connected to and, when he saw that it appeared abandoned — probably for quite a while — a momentary panic came over him. Maybe they had found the gold and left? The adjacent fields were overgrown from lack of attention, but the more distant fields appeared to be cultivating maize. He pushed down the dirt lane, which ran parallel to the old rock wall, and saw that the rutted surface didn't appear as if it had been used for quite some time. Weeds and grasses were growing upright in the lane's compacted uneven surface. He recognized his marker rocks and slowly traveled past his hiding place where the gold was cached. Stopping a couple of hundred meters away, Berhetzel did some reconnaissance, with the van's motor running. The ground on either side of the lane was soft so if he stopped close to or adjacent to the spot and pulled off the lane, he would leave plenty of evidence he had been there. He decided to park about a half-kilometer away from the treasure and use a hiker's backpack and Ziegenhainer walking pole to appear to be a nature-loving tree hugger out for a stroll. He carried with him a bottle of Riesling, a loaf of dense, crusty brown bread and a wedge of buttery Weisslacker cheese.

A pretend picnic would provide him a good cover. Besides, he wanted it to be a memorable day. He would settle in close to his cache and be sure when he left to litter a little bread crust and paper so anyone happening by would assume the ground disturbance was the result of a benign picnicker.

There was silence except for ravens cawing and the sparrows chirping. He sat on the wall to eat and looked over the countryside checking for any human activity. All he saw was a hound running lazily, nose to the ground, away from him far up the lane. A bull bellowed in the distance, but he heard no noise that he could identify as human. Satisfied he wouldn't be discovered, he carefully started to remove the stones as not to disturb the lichen coating so, when he was done, he could reassemble the stone puzzle exactly. Finally, he exposed the tight hollowed cave that hid the gold and his old army issued 9mm Lugar. He had wrapped the army issued gun in two layers of oilcloth, placed it in a medium-sized crock and sealed the whole thing with paraffin wax. The exterior of the wax seal had flaked away, but the lid seal was still intact, though brittle. He popped the lid, recognized the familiar odor of old engine oil and found the weapon in amazing condition. He checked and found a shiny cartridge chambered, ready to fire, just as it had been in 1945. Berhetzel wiped the gun down with the oily cloth, and then rewrapped it and returned it to the clay sarcophagus. It would provide a nice backup weapon when messy didn't matter.

The gold bars were still shiny and bright, stamped with a Nazi Swastika, production date, serial number, and camp where produced. They would be damning evidence in the wrong hands, but his Russian buyer would ask no questions. Each bar sold at 75% to market. Face value would yield $40,000 Euros per bar or about 1 million Euros for each third sold. The entire inventory would be sold and converted to cash over a six-day period. Berhetzel would make sure to protect his interests by taking various complicated routes to retrieve, sell and then deposit the cash for each transaction. He was relying on honor among thieves, and had greedily considered taking out his contact after the last transaction, but since this was the dangerous, far-reaching Russian mafia, he thought better of it. He was sure they were thinking the same thing, as they hated the Germans as much as he hated the French. To protect himself, he explained to his contact that there was more gold cached than he had remembered, and they would need four transactions to safely move the full quantity of the precious metal. Unknown to the Russian, they would only see him three times, each time disguised as a very old man.

After he sold that last third, Berhetzel traveled two hours on narrow, winding roads from Bern after his last deposit, to the tiny remote village where he was supposed to be buried. As he approached the town center, an early morning fog shrouded the village like a heavy curtain, so he had no idea where to begin to find the grave. He did, however, locate the village police office near a small B&B, parked his van and entered the station.

The modest office was dark with stained wood timbers, two ancient heavy oak desks with computers that looked several generations old, and a freestanding copy/fax machine. It smelled faintly of age, coffee and pipe tobacco.

An older officer, the chief of police, looked up as the bell on the door tingled cheerfully, and seemed to have a brief instant of recognition when he saw Berhetzel. He stared at the Nazi in a way that left Berhetzel feeling exposed and naked.

"Güten morgen!" said Berhetzel cheerfully. He planned a ruse to steer any suspicious people off track. "My name is Von Braun. I'm here to pay respects to a family member who died in a plane crash shortly after the war."

"Ah, yes, you are referring to the small aircraft that crashed on the mountainside, correct?" questioned the chief. "What was the name of your relative?"

"Berhetzel. Wilheim Berhetzel."

"What relation is Herr Berhetzel to you, sir?"

"He was my mother's uncle. She was told by her father that his brother is here, buried in a pauper's grave. For some reason, she is now obsessed with finding him and moving his remains back to Germany to be interred into the family graveyard before she passes." Berhetzel wasn't keen on the amount of questions coming from the police chief. He would need to be on guard and gain the chief's trust quickly. "Would you be so kind to please direct me to the cemetery? I would really like to photograph the site. If nothing else, I would hope a photograph would put her at ease."

The elder police chief studied the visitor carefully. Berhetzel could see the quizzical look begin to fade on the chief's brow. "Sure, I'll be happy to walk you over, but you won't find your uncle buried there. Seems to be a lot of interest in that grave."

"Interest? What do you mean?" asked Berhetzel, careful not to sound too worried.

"Well, there was a French government team here just last week and they exhumed that grave along with two others," offered the chief. "They were specifically looking for a man with your great-uncle's name — Berhetzel. Had his medical and dental records, but he is not buried in this village."

Berhetzel began to understand that the chief was too trusting. Getting information out of him would be too easy. He prompted the chief, "Why were they here?"

"Well, like I said, they were looking for this Berhetzel fellow. Even went to the crash site on the other side of the mountain. Opened up the plane's fuselage like a sardine can. Found something, but I'm not exactly sure if it's of any real value." The chief swiveled in his chair and looked out the window toward the mountainside where the graves were located.

The normally controlled and calculating Nazi doctor suddenly felt the wind was knocked out of him. For nearly seven decades he had been dead and buried, secreted in these isolated mountains. Suddenly, just when he was about to unleash his life's work and assume world power, he was no longer dead or anonymous. How was that possible? He rocked back on his heels slightly and looked at the chief with a surprised look and said, "It seems rather unbelievable that if he is not in that grave, that he hasn't contacted the family after all these years. He must have died by now, as I believe he would be in his nineties. Mother mustn't know of this, it would unsettle her tremendously. If you don't mind, I would like to see the original site and photograph the marker, maybe that will put her at peace and she would be satisfied."

"Ya, I can do that, but the stone is down and broken so we will have to assemble it for your photograph, and it must be a close up because the maintenance crew has not cleaned up the exhumation mess yet," the chief explained.

They walked through the cool, heavy mist up to the hillside graveyard. The Nazi took his photos and turned to walk back to the van, thanking the village officer. The old cop turned to return to his office with that familiar unsettling instinct that something was wrong, nagging at him. Back at his desk, he located the business card for Jean DuBois. As he started to dial, the welcoming doorbell jingled, and at the door stood Von Braun.

"May I get a photo of you next to the village sign so mother may have one more thing to perhaps placate her," he asked. "By the way, is there enough crime way up here to keep you busy?"

"We mostly help people out of ditches in icy weather, help move injured skiers out. There has never been a murder in the village," the Chief said as he hung up the phone and moved to the wall next to the hand-carved sign. He removed his readers, brushed back his white hair and stared back at Berhetzel with the sober Swiss look. The Nazi lined up the man like a firing squad against the wall, and triggered a non-specific human burst from his camera appearing device. The old man instantly crumbled to the floor, hitting his head on the worn bricks with a loud crack. Berhetzel smiled at this effect, that instant lightning-fast death, the village's first murder, and then went over to investigate the chief's desk. He easily found the business card of Jean

DuBois, scrutinized it for a second and put it in his wallet. Now, he would find out exactly who these bastards were.

Chapter 48
Paris

The Pasteur Institute

The lunch in the cafeteria was probably as good as many of the fine restaurants that populated Paris' neighborhoods. Served on fine bone china with sterling silverware, the artistic food defied the definition of cafeteria food. The wine was extraordinary and the dessert of creme caramel was a delicious finish. Brad and Joseph laughed and joked as the meal progressed, obviously pleased with the gourmet treats. After the almost two-hour lunch, they moved to a small conference room where Jules introduced Jean and Robert DuBois, the Archives forensic team and the Institute support staff that would work with the Americans. Jules then took a position by the small lectern, fiddled with the mini remote, and started his presentation.

"I think by now we all know the story behind why we are here today."

Photos of the mass carnage of varied animal species flashed across the screen with PowerPoint speed.

"These incidents started over two years ago and have been investigated by the United States' CDC and USDA, and British, French and Russian public health agencies. No credible answer for the original die-offs has been offered by any of these elite scientific agencies. We did, however, receive one non-scientific possibility when Drs. Vensky, O'Dell and Upton were assigned by the USDA to investigate this domestic cattle die-off in Montana. There they became acquainted with Joseph Blackfeather, seated here, and his grandfather, Nelson — there's his photo — a man who, over the decades, had recorded visions and dreams that may now provide needed answers as to who could be behind this mystery. Unfortunately, Nelson Blackfeather was of advanced age and died shortly after commissioning the veterinarians and Joseph to find this 'Destroyer'. And as you can see from his hand-drawn depiction, it is a man named Wilheim Berhetzel, a Nazi medical doctor and researcher who worked in at least two death camps. When I became aware of his journals and their significance, I asked Joseph for a copy of this drawing of a then unknown man, which I forwarded to Jean and Robert DuBois. Luckily, Robert found the man's identity in his old war files. He had his service photos, medical and dental records, along with an educational resume. You can see these file photos are identical down to the small scar on the man's right forehead with the depictions drawn by Nelson thousands of miles away, a man who had no idea of why he was recording the face in his journal. Here you can see an Archive's computer-aged rendering of how the man would look today if still alive, at age ninety-five. The wrinkle here, if you pardon my pun, is that the man is supposed to be dead and buried in a Swiss graveyard after the plane he was escaping Germany in, along with three others, crashed into a mountainside in 1945. Jean and Robert have just returned from that Swiss village in an attempt to verify his death by exhuming his remains, but it turned out, our archived records did not match any of the three buried after that crash. We feel he survived and switched his identity, most likely with the pilot. Now Jean and Robert are investigating where the man may have settled after the war and what he has been up to. It seems to be mostly likely Brazil or Argentina, where the majority of these criminals fled. We are focused there currently."

"Personally, I'm convinced that Berhetzel is the 'Destroyer' who haunted Nelson Blackfeather for all those decades, and that our connecting with the Blackfeathers was a gift from God, our Creator. When we find this Nazi, his heir, or protégé, we will put a stop to what we think now is a weapon of mass extermination, designed to target humans, not animals and therefore might be the so called 'ultimate weapon' that Hitler sought. So, now you can see why we asked you to participate in this critical search." Jules moved from the podium as he clicked to the next slide, "Jean, you can take it from here."

Jean DuBois stood and took the podium. He was of medium stature, trim with thick salt-and-pepper hair styled neatly. He had a bit more of a French accent than Jules, but he was grammar deliberate when conversing 'en Anglais'. He cleared his throat and started.

"Merci, Jules. Bonjour and welcome to this prestigious Institute where I hope we can collaborate successfully to solve what appears to be not only a crucial problem, but also an interesting enigma. The best of both worlds!

"Over the millennia, mankind has faced many challenges. War, tyranny, and pestilence have, at times, caused whole civilizations to disappear."

He turned toward the screen and started his PowerPoint display.

"Witness Easter Island, the Inca Civilization, mythical Atlantis, Pompeii, and the South Pacific Islanders who were destroyed by exposure to European diseases. Large populations wiped from the face of the planet from natural and possibly supernatural causes. As plant and animal species go extinct on a regular cycle, others fill their void. Dinosaurs vanished according to popular theory from a cataclysmic collision of a large meteorite with the planet. The point being, life is destroyed and replenished both naturally and by the hand of a 'Creator', which can be, on occasion, human intervention. The discovery of DNA has led to defining individual unique life, the capturing of criminals, freeing the innocent, and genetically modifying plants and animals to resist disease. The question is, can DNA be weaponized? Can it be utilized as a tool to destroy life? The answer to that is a simple yes because cancer starts as nothing more than an abnormality in the DNA of a single normal cell. It initiates destruction of life around it and, in the end, destroys itself by overwhelming the unaffected cells causing the death of the host. Science leads us to believe that all forms of life evolve through DNA by its ability to adapt to its environment, so according to them, there is no Creator or author of 'intelligent' design. What happens is solely the result of chance encounters or outside influences. If that were the only way life progressed to change, there could be only primary or dominant species and eventually life forms would devolve to a more singular version. Therefore, instead of having thousands of species of birds living in the jungles, there would be only a handful of variations. For example, you would see a rainforest of all large singular color, say green birds, medium brown birds and perhaps black small birds. Variations within groups would no longer exist. Species would become as homogenized as processed cow's milk! Dominant phenotypes could result in a few highly effective predator species, one of which would be man. Void of variation, these dominant species would eventually fail because of lack of difference, lack of adaptation and failure of being the fittest to survive.

"My father and I are Jews, our good friend Jules is a devout Catholic, and despite our faith's differences, we believe we are in this life to serve God, our Creator. Monsieur Blackfeather also believed in a Creator, but was haunted by his visions of this great 'Destroyer' of life. My father and I believe that we are searching for a man, or his student — a trained Nazi doctor — who possibly discovered how to use DNA markers as a weapon to terminate life. We know without doubt that he was a death camp war criminal who performed cruel experiments in at least two camps. Perhaps at the time he was a secondary figure, but somehow, we think, he stumbled onto that piece of critical information that has brought us here today.

"My father has pursued Nazi war criminals all his adult life and he believes that this type of evil doesn't die on its own, it must be rooted out by any means necessary and completely eradicated.

"So, tomorrow we will dissect Nelson's journals for other valuable cues and try to learn more about our target by traveling into Germany to interview any relatives we can find. We think there is at least one cousin who would have been old enough in 1945 to have some knowledge of the man. Pray we succeed. Merci pour votre attention."

Jean handed the laser pointer back to Jules and returned to his seat.

"So," Jules announced, "tomorrow we will meet here at nine a.m. and the Archives staff and Joseph will start on the journals and travel over to the Archives as needed. Fred, you will use our support staff here and tackle those porcine brains, which I understand will be very time and labor intensive. Brad and Jean will travel to Dachau to see what they can uncover about Berhetzel's life and work there. Kate, Tom and I will take a similar journey to Germany to interview that cousin. We'll also get into the War archives in Berlin to see if they may have anything else that could aid in our investigation. We cannot afford to overlook or dismiss any potential lead so be critical of everything.

"I know you all must be tired from your travel and the time change, but we must find this monster. We will get as much done as we can today, and then tomorrow we can dive in deeper. We must not fail because just as Nelson Blackfeather was warned, 'the Destroyer is here' and I, too, fear a catastrophic end. Pray to God our Creator to give us strength, intelligence, and the tools we need to solve this mystery. Without His guidance, I fear we will fail!"

Chapter 49
Swiss Alps

Berhetzel left the tiny village, descending slowly down the narrow winding road that led to the valley floor and the main roads to Bern. His mind and his heart raced as he tried to sort out this sudden loss of anonymity with his identity's reappearance into the twenty-first century. This was the very first time since the plane crashed that he had felt not in control, his immortality threatened.

The French hounds were on his scent and although it seemed reasonable they think him dead of old age, there had to be a serious reason to suddenly confirm his demise. Perhaps there was a bounty on him, otherwise there was no possible way anyone would know of or even understand his work, especially those in Argentina. He had always made sure that absolutely no communication with the outside world ever occurred, even with his ex-Nazi staff. The penalty for going against any of his policies at La Lupa was merciless death. Every person there understood that. When he returned to Bern, he would call Hermann Schmitt, his second-in-command, and find out if anything unusual had occurred in his absence.

At the Grand Hotel Bern, he entered the lobby extremely self-conscious, nervously aware of everything occurring around him. Gone was the quiet confidence of Dr. Josef Von Braun and on alert was the Nazi survivalist Wilheim Berhetzel.

He went up to his room, carefully checked to see if anything had been disturbed and then poured himself a large glass of brandy. He sat down in the plush brown leather chair next to the fireplace and pulled out his encrypted satellite phone. He rolled the phone between his hands for several seconds thinking, and then called the only phone in his Argentina compound. On the second ring, Schmitt picked up and answered.

"Hallo, Herr Doktor."

"Hallo, Hermann," he said cordially and calmly.

"How have things been since I have been away? Anything occur out of the ordinary? Is everyone healthy and accounted for?" Not that he actually cared.

"Ya, everyone is fine and in line with your orders, no one has left or entered the compound except Willie." Before Berhetzel could reply, Hermann said, "We did have two visitors at the gate yesterday, an old man who claimed he was a Catholic missionary and his Indian guide. That 'priest' was a lying Jew, I was certain of it. Wasn't even wearing a Crucifix. I attempted to contact you for orders, but could not connect because we were having severe thunder and lightning storms at the time."

"What did you tell the visitors?" asked Berhetzel with an air of concern.

"I told the imposter you were upriver collecting medicinal plant samples and vaccinating the locals, and that Willie would take the two of them upriver to meet you. Willy ran them up a small remote tributary and introduced them to the Lord. By the time the piranhas and other carnivores are finished with them, not even their bones will exist."

"Ah, good. Quick thinking."

"We then used his phone to text a message to his primary recent contact, a Frenchman named DuBois with a Paris area phone number. We sent a simple 'still searching' message and then intentionally garbled the remainder, but indicated they were heading deeper into Brazil in search. Willie took their phone fifty kilometers in that direction and then sank it in the river. If it was being tracked, that is where they will start their search. A Jew and a Frenchman spells trouble, does it not?"

"You're right, but any uninvited guest could be problematic. What you did was, without question, correct. Thank Willie for me and give him some of my good Cuban smokes. You take some, too," Berhetzel replied. "We can't be too careful. They hate all Germans and, if they could, they would stop our work out of spite to prevent us from continuing our research on our life-sustaining compounds and food animal improvements. I hope my work can be a gift to the world to make up for a fraction of the suffering our Germany caused in the war. I'm not ready to release our findings yet. Our work must be absolute, undeniable and stunning to humanity when we reveal it. And if we make billions for our efforts, so be it. We surely have earned it!"

"I understand, Herr Doctor. I will protect our interests here."

"But be very careful and keep me informed if anything else happens. We still have many enemies and they must not win. Danke, my friend."

A stunned Berhetzel was now convinced he really was being targeted, but he had no idea how anyone could have had any clue to where to look for him. It was possible that it was just a weird coincidence and possibly Hermann was wrong, but he just couldn't take chances. The business card he had taken from the Swiss police chief's desk belonged to Jean DuBois of the Archives Nationale in Paris. He opened his laptop and Googled the name.

There didn't appear to be any significance to the historian except a small footnote that he was the son of famed post-war Nazi hunter Robert DuBois. He then searched the father and was overwhelmed at the man's accomplishments. All the 'criminals' he had captured or aided in the capture read like a Who's Who of the Third Reich. Most had died in prison or were executed. *Why now would he have interest in me? I should be dead or a very old, helpless man.* Berhetzel felt exposed and very vulnerable. He needed to travel to Paris to find out about these men and eliminate their threat. It was the fox and the hounds, after all, but now he had a fox's advantage. Suddenly he looked forward to killing a couple more pompous Frenchman. What's one or two more?

Chapter 50
Paris

The large white Mercedes van offered a panoramic view of the city as the Americans traveled back to the hotel and Jules' apartment. They sat in silence staring out at the busy streets with their plethora of small neighborhood shops and cafes, locals mixing with tourists at tiny tables, people watching and enjoying the warm sunshine. As usual, it was Brad who broke their trance.

"I don't know about the rest of you, I love both the food and the city, mostly the food, but I'm not getting good vibes on doing a 'Where's Waldo' search across Europe for a mad Nazi scientist. I don't think it's anywhere in my job description. And there is a phrase popular with the twenty-something's that keeps popping into my mind: 'cluster' attached to the F-bomb. This could be a good example of what that word intends to express."

"Every June 25th, we celebrate something called 'Custer' attached to the F-bomb," Joseph joked, referencing the famous Battle of the Little Bighorn.

"OK, boys, settle down," Kate admonished. "I think our goal here is to do our tasks in a calculated, professional manner and see what happens. Nobody will get screwed."

All eyes were quickly now on Tom, and Brad reached over laughing, and slapped Tom on the back with a hearty "Sorry, Buddy!"

That had Kate blushing, embarrassed at her little miscue as the men roared with laughter.

Tom quickly changed the topic to protect Kate from more of their good-natured ribbing.

"You guys better be kind to the lady. Remember, she *is* your boss and can make sure your searching for Berhetzel is in a place you'd rather not be, like those famous sewers you've heard about."

Brad, Joseph and Fred were dropped at their hotel, and the driver returned Kate and Tom to Jules' apartment though they didn't go in. Kate's excitement was palpable and she said to Tom, "Now I am going to show you some of *my* Paris." Grabbing his hand, she led him down to Rue Kleber where they took a left turn and walked up to the Champs-Élysées. The Arc de Triômphe stood proudly as cars spun wildly around the surrounding traffic roundabout like wooden horses on an out-of-control carousel. Kate led Tom to a wide crosswalk where they pushed with the crowd to the other side descending down stairs to an access tunnel designed to safely protect touristy pedestrians from the traffic chaos going on above them. At street level of the monument, Kate purchased tickets for the short elevator ride to the top.

"Close your eyes before the doors open and keep them shut until I tell you to open them," she told Tom.

She led him like a blind man dodging excited children and couples walking arm in arm, taking him to the walled edge.

"OK, you can open your eyes. Voilà, Paris, my love — my Paris!"

Tom opened his eyes to a panoramic view of beautiful tree-lined boulevards fanning out diagonally in all directions with the Eiffel Tower standing guard resolutely to the south. The wind blew steadily with air that was fresh, not the street-level mixture of food smells and exhaust. The sun shone down brightly and appeared to magnify the city's beauty. Suddenly he realized why Paris was Kate's favorite place on earth; it was like nothing he had ever seen before.

Kate took his hand as they descended back to the street, squeezed it gently and mouthed the words "I love you!"

These were the very words he had laid awake at night trying to find the right moment to speak. He embraced her and, with a kiss declared, "I love you, too! Marry me?"

Their eyes locked on each other and the rest of the world faded out as they melted into one soul. She didn't have to respond since the answer was written all over her face — yes, yes, my love!

She did whisper another answer in his ear in French, "Bien sûr, mon coeur!" She now clung to him, savoring the moment as they walked up the stairs from the access tunnel onto the Champs-Élysées.

"Let's go find a ring. Tell me a good place," Tom suggested.

As they walked to a nearby taxi stand, Tom's phone signaled the receipt of a text. He opened it and laughed.

"It's from Bob. He took Beth to dinner just now and proposed. She said yes. Says he is on cloud nine!"

Kate laughed, "Good for them. Looks like you cowboys have finally got your acts together."

Chapter 51

They ended up on Boulevard Haussmann with the grand department stores where you could literally buy anything from a baguette to a Bentley, and Tom found a 'reasonable' engagement and wedding ring set for a mere $27,000 dollars, but a large portion of that price would be reduced when he was refunded the heavy VAT tax that France levied on purchases. The ring sparkled in the sun rivaling Kate's radiance as they exited the store.

They strolled down the wide, busy street, arm in arm, literally window shopping as they passed the elaborate displays of seasonal merchandise that filled row after row of dressed store windows. Kate's cell phone rang with Jules' personalized ringtone, '*La Marseillaise*', which had several shoppers glancing over at her. Kate answered, listened for a moment and started to speak in rapid French. She was smiling, almost beaming and seemed to be agreeing. Tom felt again like a fifth wheel, odd man out, but loved to hear Kate's mastery of the language. She ended the call with flowery "Merci, Jules."

"Let me guess," Tom offered, "that was your favorite man this side of the Atlantic."

"No, that was Jules, you're my favorite man on either side of any body of water. That man is a very dear friend who called with our plans for tomorrow. It seems we are flying the Institutes' Learjet early tomorrow to Berlin so we can try to locate Berhetzel's two nieces and an uncle who would actually be younger than him because of a post-war remarriage. If the supportive data is there, we will try to meet with them. Jules said the Germans are sticklers on record keeping, even when it is incriminating. He feels someone has to know something and, by the way, he says you are the luckiest man in Paris. I tend to agree with him."

"Today, I am the luckiest man on Earth," making his voice reverberate like an old stadium PA system, quoting Lou Gehrig.

"He is also buying us dinner this evening at the Jules Verne Restaurant, in the Eiffel Tower — the most difficult reservation to get in Paris. He has a good friend who manages the restaurant and he assured me that it is a wonderfully romantic experience. It will be made even more unbelievable because of his friendly connection. We should head back to Printemps to get you appropriate clothes for fine dining."

"A monkey suit?"

"Yep, and new shoes, a tie and cologne that is definitely not Old Spice!"

Jules had his driver pick them up at nine, with champagne on ice and a single red rose in a thin crystal vase greeting them on the passenger bar. The chauffeur took the small limo off the main boulevards through very upscale residential neighborhoods, and somehow managed to get to the iconic monument without the normal noise and congestion found on the more direct route. He held open the door of the limo for them and walked them to the restaurant entrance at the base of the tower, and led them inside to the elevator. The manned elevator rapidly took them to the second level, where the restaurant overlooked the Seine with the whole of Paris spread around it. Jules' friend, Maurice, was at the door as the elevator opened to the restaurant.

"Bonsoir, docteurs! Welcome to Le Jules Verne. We have a very special table for you!"

The restaurant appeared to be very full, but had a reserved, dignified ambiance except for several tables of loud Americans which was an irritation for Kate. It was obvious from Maurice's actions they were going to get the star treatment this evening, and he led them to a quiet corner table with a panoramic view of the river and its illuminated bridges, Bateaux Mouches cruising up and down the waterway, and the ant-sized pedestrians staring up at the tower.

"This table has a long history of famous entertainers, politicians, wealthy citizens and some dubious characters enjoying its privacy," Maurice said as he seated Kate, "We reserve it for the very special and Jules tells me that describes you both. My congratulations."

"Merci, monsieur!" Tom offered, surprising Kate with his foray into French.

"Je vous en prie," Maurice responded. *You're welcome.*

"Wow! I'm impressed! I'm actually engaged to a bilingual man."

"Wait a minute now, I've never even looked at a man in that way," Tom joked.

"And besides, I think we will most likely visit here on our honeymoon and probably often after that, so I best get with the program. Plus, it sure would be nice to understand what you and Jules whisper about."

After champagne, the meal was presented without a menu, Jules having put his trust in his friend to offer the best cuisine available. Course after course was presented, paired with wine, and each a special treat made just for their table.

By the third course, Tom, a beer drinker, was feeling no pain and was tired, basically having run out of gas. Kate caught him staring out the large panoramic glass window at the people below.

"A centime for your thoughts, my love," she asked, grasping his hand and pulling it toward her.

Tom realizing his inattentive pause, smiled and said, "I was just thinking about what Brad said today. What in the world are we doing here chasing a Nazi ghost that could destroy millions of people and change the world forever? I mean, I prefer my arm up a cow's rear, but now we might be on the receiving end. Not a pretty thought."

"Let's put that behind us, so to speak, because once we figure out this mystery, I'm sure Jules will hand it over to a higher power. Right now, his concern is with all the Nazi sympathizers that populate Western Europe, and how dangerous they might become if we do something too obvious or stupid. I thought the war ended all that stuff, but it's still a dangerous movement that has people occultly in place to move on a government if the opportunity arises. Berhetzel may be their Messiah, God help us."

As they left the restaurant, they were glowing from their love and the French wine. Their limo driver was at the elevator as they exited and walked them over to the car, and waited with the opened door till they were seated. The driver started back to the apartment just as Kate's phone started playing *La Marseillaise* and she answered, greeting Jules with their thanks for the wonderful evening. She listened to Jules explain something and wished him 'Bonsoir'.

"There has been a change of plans. We are now going to Switzerland instead of Germany, and our train isn't leaving until 1 p.m. so we can sleep in tomorrow. He sounded very concerned, but glad we had a great evening."

The apartment was lit up with candles, champagne was on ice, and the bed turned down. Kate put the wine in the refrigerator, gently blew out the candles and led her future husband to the only room that was still illuminated with a single flickering candle, to express her love for him.

Chapter 52
Paris

Next Morning

Joseph was up and out of his hotel before dawn, needing to move after a night with a disturbing nightmare. He walked the near-deserted streets observing the on goings of a waking major metropolis. No roosters crowing, horses calling or dogs barking, just the diesel smell and gear shifting sounds of delivery trucks making their rounds, trying to beat the morning migration of the citizens of Paris. In Montana, silence was interrupted by sound; here, silence was in the background only to occasionally be heard. He watched the curious movements of motorized street cleaners moving back and forth, zigzagging to remove yesterday's street trash, and listened to the banging as dumpsters were engaged, lifted, emptied and dropped without ceremony.

He carried no map as his sense of direction and orientating skills were extraordinarily honed though generations of survival and self-reliance. He had never been lost once in his life. Perhaps a little confused here or there, but never lost. The idea of a GPS satellite system telling him where to go with a blind faith, disheartened him. He could navigate a blinding snowstorm, live off the land while getting back home with a fresh deer or antelope on his back. His ability to survive and function was innate to his DNA, a treasure from his ancestors, a gift from the Creator. He cherished those abilities and walked the Parisian streets with a quiet assurance in his denim shirt, jeans and ranch boots. He looked like a classic Native American, with jet-black hair, dark brown eyes, straight nose, high cheek bones, and a long-torsoed, lean muscular body. The only thing lacking this morning was he hadn't worn his yellowed western ranch hat with its single turkey feather.

As he walked, he passed several bakeries that already had customers lining up for the first 'pain' — bread — of the day. The delicious aromas of the busy boulangeries had his stomach complaining. He entered a fairly busy shop and muddled his way through purchasing a short demi baguette and large, dark hot chocolate. He reversed course and headed to a small public park with a quiet trickling fountain and several wrought iron benches. There, he broke the loaf of bread in large pieces and dipped it into the hot rich liquid.

The small city birds began dropping from their roosts to pick at the breadcrumbs and hopped from morsel to morsel enjoying the leftovers.

He finished his early snack and started to head back to the Peninsula Hotel just as the sun cut in and around the trees and buildings drying the damp, cleaned streets. It warmed the morning air, bringing people out of their apartments and hotels. He felt alive now, tuned into the city, feeling better after a restless night where he had experienced a nightmarish dream.

He had been exhausted last evening after the travel and long day, so he had fallen into a deep trance-like sleep quickly, cooled between the sheets of 1200-count bed linens on a premium mattress. He enjoyed mindless sleep until a vision stirred his subconscious awareness. It was that rerun dream he had had off and on for years, where he was hunting on the prairie with his great-grandfather. In the dream they were always stalking a large fat pronghorn antelope buck, a long, painstaking process where they relied on crawling flattened in the tall grasses. They were dressed in camo and stayed well downwind from the easily spooked animals. As always in this particular dream, he carried his old Savage 270 and grandfather used another old ranch gun, a Mossberg 30-30 lever action. Both guns were very accurate and had fed the family for decades. In the dream, he could feel the reassurance of the worn stock and weight of the weapon.

But this time the dream didn't end with the usual outcome — a shot fired, the solid whack of the clean lethal impact, blue gun smoke and an animal down, harvested. But then, always, strangely, when they walked up to the kill, the antelope disappeared in vapors, totally from sight, no evidence of it ever having been there. A ghost. Last night in that dream, however, the buck was still lying there, head folded around and under the chest, and when Joseph grabbed the horns to straighten the neck preparing to cut the jugulars to exsanguinate the carcass, the antelope's head morphed suddenly to the visage of a devil-horned Berhetzel, who blinked glowing green eyes, growled and bit down on Joseph's wrist ripping away flesh. Searing pain raced up into his torso and jolted him fully awake, heart racing, covered with a cold sweat. After that, he was awake the rest of night, afraid of closing his eyes. The Nazi now haunted his dreams much like he had his grandfather's.

Upon his return to the hotel, he showered and put on clean clothes. He opened the old medium-sized suitcase that held the thirty-five pounds of his grandfather's journals to verify that the demon last night hadn't stolen the valuable evidence of his existence. Joseph peered in verifying the contents were still secure, and pulled out the yellow legal pad that he had used to record his interpretation of his great-grandfather's writings, sort of a Cliff Notes version of the complicated work. Only Joseph, of everyone here, could understand all of the subtle references to the things a blood relative, a Lakota, would have written. His analysis, he hoped, would make his grandfather proud and open doors in the investigation.

At eight thirty a.m., he was picked up by an Institute driver and sped off to the Archives Nationale in the Marais district of Paris. The gigantic storehouse of national treasures and documents contained historical items going back hundreds of years. Primarily a document warehouse, it also served as a facility to analyze, restore, preserve and collate generations of history and knowledge into an understandable and secure format. Administrators from the Ministry of Defense had sent a dossier on Berhetzel and the camps he worked in over to the Archives. It looked like it might be a long, tedious day.

Robert met Joseph at the main entrance and welcomed him to the historical preserve.

"Bonjour, mon ami, welcome to this great mausoleum of French history. I hope you had a pleasant evening and a good rest as we need to get a lot accomplished today," Robert said.

"Bon-jure, Mon-sewer Do-Bwah," Joseph replied slowly, his first try at speaking polite French. "Thank you for inviting me here. I am excited to offer my grandfather's help. He will also be here with us in spirit."

"Très bien! We are going to need all the assistance we can muster, whether it be worldly or not. Now, let's go to our conference room where I'll introduce our team and you can get some coffee, if you like."

The conference room was modern with large video computer screens, projectors, and scanning microscopes among the equipment. Joseph could sense the slight musty smell of old documents stored in cardboard containers. As he walked in, five old men respectfully stood to acknowledge him. He definitely was going to be the youngest in the group.

The five elite researchers were in their mid-eighties, Robert in his mid-nineties. These men should have been retired, living in a socialist country where most quit their work in their mid-fifties. The difference here was that, for these men, justice meant no rest until every Nazi war criminal was captured, killed or accounted for. These men lived because of that passion, employment was just a means to that end. Fear that the horror that was the Third Reich would be forgotten, kept the old men alive.

Robert did the introductions and then gave Joseph the floor, asking him to explain his great-grandfather's journals. Joseph, a little nervous, cleared his throat and began.

"Thank you for inviting me here. My great-grandfather would be very proud that I would be in Paris sharing with this group something that haunted him for decades."

"He took me in when his grandson, my father, died. As tribal shaman, he raised me, counseled me in the culture and ways of our people, and gave me a spiritual grounding. The American Indian, in general, has lost cultural identity becoming more of the world than part of their natural world. This, unfortunately, separates them from long traditions which reflect their heritage and connects them with their ancestors, where we receive our real strength. Underemployment, poverty, under education, poor health care and alcoholism often destroys their ambition and breaks up families. Some of our Indian nations have turned to gambling casino enterprises and now prosper, but these are the exception and only provide financial reward. This does little for their spirit. My grandfather was a pure spiritual soul, connected to powers that would scare most of us to death. What he recorded is the truth.

"I am a direct descendant of the Lakota Sioux that defeated George Armstrong Custer and the Seventh Army at the Battle of the Little Bighorn. It was a complete annihilation of the troops under his command, with no survivors. After that victory, the United States Army pursued us to Canada, defeating us physically and spiritually. Eventually, we were relocated to a large Reservation in eastern Montana. There, life has been difficult, living years under virtual house arrest, so we have paid a heavy price for defeating Custer and his army."

"Being a holy man, my grandfather was taught all the stories of the great years of our people — those being the years before the White man. As a young man, he was mentored by the elders and became familiar with the cycle of life, the Creator and the Destroyer. He became convinced that the balance between these forces is what we call God. The Creator is always establishing new life and protecting the life He creates. On the other side, the Destroyer ends life cycles and keeps balance in populations. Man can co-op the process, sometimes destroying that delicate balance by war, disease or toxic environmental change. At one time, man was controlled by his environment, which killed off the weak or unfit making the survivors stronger. Now, man survives these challenges so the Destroyer establishes new ways of population control with plagues, cancers and famines. Evil people want to become junior Destroyers to control others and, with the spoils that come with that power, become invincible. In the end, however, the Creator must prevail because man was made in His image. The war between these forces is an endless battle. My grandfather feared this 'Destroyer' had developed a new means to destroy and became afraid of his power, all the while our ancestors repeated their messages to him—find and stop him. My ancestors have warned us, and my grandfather received that message and passed it on. We must now stop this man before he multiplies the power of the Destroyer. Failure could result in species genocide on a magnitude that might dwarf previous mad men's efforts."

Joseph was now speaking in a manner that he knew was being directed by his ancestors. Tears formed in his eyes, his voice trembled as the passionate plea overwhelmed him.

"I hope with these journals you can discover new answers to stop this insanity." Joseph exhaled the last of his plea and returned to his seat.

Joseph had just addressed a group of very educated, war-hardened, dedicated professional investigators in a country where he couldn't even speak their language. As he walked away from the lectern, they rose to their feet offering unified, unqualified applause. He had spoken the ancestor's truth and now had become a true Lakota warrior against evil's disciple.

Chapter 53
Eastern France

Secondary Route to Paris

The pounding rain was making navigating the back roads out of Switzerland into France a slow and nerve-wracking journey. Berhetzel had decided to avoid the security camera scrutiny that came with the easy travel on France's AutoRoute, and stick to the slower secondary roads where he could travel anonymously from village to village, department to department. Slow, but safe. His first planned overnight stop was to the walled city of Avignon in the Rhone Valley, where he could clear his thought processes about what had just happened with his sudden resurrection from the grave, then rest for a day or two. With a change of plans, he would ditch the van and take the TGV into Paris. That would put him in Paris at least five days prior to the end of the G8 meeting, where the world's economic powers were meeting, and would display their unity in a summit ending photo op. His best opportunity to hit his target. But he needed some time to develop a basic disguise to thwart the security cameras that were sure to be everywhere. If someone was interested in him, the last thing he needed was to be picked out of a crowd by cameras with advanced Facial Recognition Software. Because he looked a great deal like he did in 1946, he felt it was likely they would be looking for a very old man, but this certainly was a good time for a little extra paranoia. Plus, there were a lot of questions he needed to answer before he left for Paris about the French investigators who were in the Swiss village trying to confirm his death.

Avignon was the old walled city of the non-Vatican popes — when the Catholics had two ruling leaders — and was a good place for him to rest and hide out. It put him near a reasonably good airport, on the main TGV train line to Paris, and close to many small villages and mountain hideaways that, if necessary, he could escape to relatively unnoticed. He also was close to Italy, Spain and the Mediterranean, if he needed to move by sea.

After he rested, Berhetzel planned on scrutinizing the next week's plan and then make contact with his Paris connection to finalize her delivery and payment for the DNA-rich material of Le President's only son. He also needed to produce a fake American ID or passport to use just in case the security was more stringent than usual for the meeting. He knew the bulletproof blast barriers that would surround the G8 leaders could not stop his weapon, because he only needed to get within 100 meters of the stage. The only possibility he could fail is if he couldn't get to that perimeter to acquire a firm target confirmation on the victim. Otherwise, he would surely deliver the death blow.

The southern part of France was busy this time of year, but he had been fortunate to reserve a room in the five-star Hotel European and received a suite-sized room overlooking the garden courtyard. Berhetzel showered and shaved for the first time in thirty-six hours, and had the hotel valet pick up his dirty clothes to be laundered. He then hung the 'Do Not Disturb' sign and walked down to the hotel restaurant, and ordered a beer and the Plât du Jour—steak et frites. He observed, as he ate, a predominance of Americans and Italians staying at the hotel, with several sitting in tables adjacent to him. All seemed nicely involved in their own affairs, so he eavesdropped on the Americans, trying to pick up on their accents, just in case. Americans, he felt, still received more respect than they deserved and often got a pass when undergoing official scrutiny in passport or other foreign government security checkpoints. Since he didn't hear anything unusual, he lost interest in the party of Americans.

Berhetzel finished his meal as the day was cooling to early evening. He decided to walk the town to get some much-needed physical activity and studied the paper map the concierge had provided him. He saw he could take a long loop around the city center and be able to get about an hour's walk in. He started at a brisk pace and kept moving through the tourist and locals as they shopped and found places to dine. He could feel some of the stress from the last several days leave and he warmed with the fast pace he had set.

Eventually he found himself at the long end of the loop in a neighborhood that was looking a little rundown with young men, tattooed, olive-skinned, dark eyes and hair, like gypsies, huddled in small groups looking like they were up to no good. They immediately focused on him, daring him to come deeper onto their turf, shifty eyes darting back and forth as they scanned the area for the authorities. Berhetzel felt their hate and casually turned to reverse his loop back to the hotel. Three young men, wearing white sleeveless t-shirts and dark baggie pants fell in behind him and immediately started throwing insults at him, taunting him.

"Hey, you! Faggot! Monsieur Shithead, we need to talk to you!"

"Douche bag! You need to stop, NOW!"

Berhetzel slowed slightly allowing the men to close the gap, sensing an opportunity. He hated gypsies even more than the French so disposing of

French gypsies was going to be a real treat for him. He made a sharp right turn into a small hidden alleyway to see if they would take the bait and follow him. He reached into his jacket pocket and powered on his death weapon as they aggressively followed him into the dark dead-end alley, screeching to a halt as he brought the camera-like device up to eye level.

"Look, the faggot wants a photo of us for his bedroom dresser to remember us by. Here's a newsflash for you, maggot faggot, by the time we finish with you, you will have no memory," the tallest curly haired punk announced boldly, grinning with tobacco stained teeth.

Berhetzel just smiled back as he heard the device click over to the ready mode. The men darted toward him just as he depressed the trigger, firing the weapon.

"Fromage," he mumbled as the three crumbled, collapsing into a heap of juvenile trash, dead in an instant.

He stepped over them and collected some sheets of cardboard from the dumpster they were near, and covered their corpses. Their mysterious demise would keep the local authorities guessing, waiting for autopsy and toxicology reports and, by that time, he would be back in Argentina. They would soon be forgotten, but he would be an accomplished assassin.

He left the alley and headed back to the hotel. Killing always gave him an energy rush that seemed to strengthen him, empower and validate his work. One thing for sure, this bio weapon was going to make his 'old age' more and more fun every day.

Chapter 54
Paris

Next Day

Jules arrived at the apartment to pick Kate and Tom up at noon, as promised. He hugged and kissed Kate lightly and extended his congratulations to them both on their engagement. Tom had been wary of the Frenchman's feelings toward Kate, but was growing to enjoy the man's openness and generous spirit. He also was starting to like Paris way more than a country boy should have.

Jules' driver sped off to the Gare de Lyon to pick up the TGV train that would take them into Switzerland with only one transfer. The old station was another huge multilevel mausoleum that was packed with travelers coming and going to the south of France, Italy, and Switzerland. The 'bullet' style train would reach speeds of 329 km/hr and could transport them safer and almost as fast as a multi-stop, small plane ride. Jules had reserved an SUV for the final leg of the journey, driving to the small alpine village.

They boarded the first class section and Tom took his window seat. He looked out through the Plexiglas as an oncoming train slowed, screeching metal wheels and locking brake shoes brought the shiny silver projectile to a smooth stop. Tom watched as the passengers rose up, retrieving their personal items to exit the train. For a brief instant, Tom saw the face of a man he thought looked familiar, but then the man was gone from sight—almost like an apparition. He half stood and leaned forward to try to see out of a more distant window, but there was too much interference from people moving into their assigned seats. The man was no longer visible and Tom wasn't quite sure of whom he had seen, or even if it was important. He rolled the brief image over in his head, but came up with nothing. "I must be imagining things," he reasoned as their train started to move deliberately in its escape from the city.

Kate and Jules were engaged in a rapid French conversation about something or other, and Tom was feeling tired, the last two days catching up with him.

"Excuse me," he said, "I am a little tired and hate to be rude, but would it be alright if I catch a quick nap?"

He received a smile with permission from both of his travel partners.

Soon, he had drifted into a deep sleep, and although he was aware of the movement and rhythmic vibration of the train and the muffled background sounds of passengers, he felt paralyzed to his seat.

Short bursts of dreams about Jed, his family, and the cows he worked on daily, flashed through his exhausted brain, but they started to get weirder and weirder. One brief episode had him late for a farm call with a Berhetzel lookalike farmer threatening to sue him while wearing a Nazi army uniform. A large Holstein cow had a prominent black swastika over her white skin on her left shoulder with a Mickey Mouse head and ears on the right chest that started to make silly faces at him. He tried to get away from the cow, but his legs and arms were leaden, like heavy weights. The cow then moved after him goose-stepping like a Nazi soldier. The cow's lips moved and she talked, "Tom, my love, wake up. Wake up... we are here."

"Get away from me, you damn old cow!" he mumbled.

Suddenly he realized it was Kate's voice talking to him, and slowly opened his eyes. He was sheepishly looking into Kate's beautiful face.

"Old cow, eh?" she laughed as Jules smiled with pity for Tom.

"Sorry, Kate. I just had the weirdest dream with a Nazi Mickey Mouse cow in it. Damn thing went after me!"

"Well, Sleeping Beauty, it's time to wake up because we are about to change trains," Kate replied.

Tom had slept for over ninety minutes, but awoke still tired, feeling like he had been drugged. Their train was slowing gradually and the announcements in multiple languages began giving the stop as Dijon, where they would transfer to a slower SNF Berne-bound train. Tom vowed to himself that he would not fall asleep again on the trip, and purchased a double espresso at a vendor's station as they walked to their transfer waiting area. Too much talk of Nazis and not enough sleep, he reasoned, but that face he saw was still on his mind.

The second train was a slower SNF that would move relatively lazily to Berne with several stops in the process. Once in Berne, they would stay overnight and then head by rental car to that small village where everyone had thought Berhetzel was buried. Jules explained to them about the recent unexplained sudden death of the village's chief of police, which had come at the approximate time as a missed call from his office to Jean's cell phone. That had been way too coincidental for Jules' liking. He needed to see the chief's body and talk with the local coroner who happened to be the only doctor in town. He wanted to get specific tissue samples, review the autopsy, which apparently had been only a gross examination. No organs examined, no toxicology done, no tissues presented for histopathology. The examiner was unwavering, the chief, his friend, had died of a massive stroke or had passed out, hit his head and suffered a cerebral hemorrhage. Jules felt a personal approach, rather than a state-ordered complete autopsy, could sway the coroner, especially if he was given the full story of Berhetzel and why this new testing was so critical. Jules was on this trip instead of Jean because of his affiliation with the prestigious Pasteur Institute, and Tom and Kate because they represented the USDA and CDC as credentialed investigators.

They left the hotel in Berne early in the morning under a misting rain. Jules had rented a Mercedes GL 350 and evidently that auto made him feel like a Le Mans driver because he had Tom finger nailing the rich, leather upholstery, speeding up and down the rain-slicked mountain roads. Kate, the fearful flyer, seemed to be relaxed with the frantic driving along sharp cliff drop-offs. Tom enjoyed flying, but not this close to the ground. He stared out of the window as the valleys, with burning off mist, whizzed by. Tom suddenly realized who that Paris face belonged to. Not the computer-aged Berhetzel, but rather a face that matched the younger man in his service photo.

"You remember in Paris at the train station I mentioned a man I thought I recognized? Well, I just placed the face. It's him!"

"Him who?" Kate asked.

"The guy we're after — Berhetzel!"

Jules looked startled as he asked, "You saw the old man at the station?"

"No, what I saw was the same face as it appeared in Nelson's journal. I just didn't make the association until now, maybe because I was so tired. But now, in hindsight, I'm sure of who I saw, I just don't understand it," Tom explained.

"There are two likely possibilities. One, that it was just a person who, in a glance, only highly resembled him. And supposedly there are a half dozen people in the world that could be mistaken for your twin. The second possibility is that it was a close relative, son or grandson of the old man. Jules, aren't there security cameras that could be reviewed?" Kate suggested.

Jules affirmed, "In Paris there are dozens of high-definition cameras in every train station, airport, metro stop, and now at high-crime areas. There will be a record and with facial recognition software that we have installed, we should find the man pretty quickly. I'll call Jean and have him contact the station security so they can forward the digital record over to the archives. You know, there is one other possibility."

"What would that be?" Kate asked.

"That it was him, made up to look younger, thinking no one would expect a thirty-something man. These Nazis were devious, the worse of the worst. We should anticipate anything and everything!" Jules explained.

"Well, I know what I saw. There has to be some kind of connection," Tom declared.

"As strange as all this seems, I want you two to be ready for more confusing things as we close in on the answer to this mystery. Robert has experienced these evil people face-to-face, and you would, on face value, think them average, humble people. The problem is they are just buying time until they can find an opportunity to eliminate you as a threat to their existence. Remember whose side they are on and it's not God's," Jules said.

Tom continued to be unsettled over the brief image he had caught through the train's window. The more he thought about it, the more convinced that it was significant. It was possible it was a ringer he saw, but there was something about that face that screamed 'I'm evil'. He was starting to feel like wheelchair bound Jimmy Stewart in the movie 'Rear Window'. He saw something, but now what could he do about it?

They arrived late morning as the alpine morning mist was replaced by a picture perfect blue sky and pure, white groups of fluffy clouds framing the mountain peaks. The village center surrounded a small, fountained reflecting pool, which offset the flagpole flying the Swiss flag at half-staff. At about two o'clock relative to the flag was the well-marked Polizei station, a small stone building with a solid natural wood door. As they entered, a tiny bell attached to the door signaled their arrival.

The town had had only two officers, the chief and a young assistant who now sat in the chief's desk. He rose to greet them, hand extended.

"Good morning, I'm Frederic Acherin, acting chief. And you are the French and American investigators from Paris, yes?"

"Yes, that's correct. I am Dr. Jules LeClerc from the Pasteur Institute in Paris, and these are my colleagues, Drs. Kate Vensky and Tom O'Dell of the United States Department of Agriculture and the Centers for Disease Control. We are here to meet with Dr. Loomis, your coroner, about the chief's death."

"Henry was already here this morning and told me to direct you to the village clinic. So I'll walk you over now unless you would care for some coffee or water?"

Jules and Kate accepted the coffee and Tom took a bottle of Evian. They then walked across the cobbled square to a small, rustic, wooden A-frame building with a wheelchair ramp leading up to an entirely glassed front entrance that reflected the morning sun like a gigantic mirror. There were three flower planters overflowing with late-season red geraniums. The acting chief rang the doorbell and entered the small reception area with its four simple, straight-back chairs and a coffee table with several well-worn magazines. There was no one at the desk, but Dr. Loomis entered from a side door wearing ciel blue surgery scrubs. Half-frame reading glasses were perched on the end of his large nose, and his neatly trimmed gray mustache was peppered with black. He had a clear rosy complexion, husky physique and appeared to be in his late sixties. He came over to greet the four and Acherin started with the introductions. He then left the four doctors to return to his office.

Loomis started, "For a village that gets very few visitors this time of year, we have had a busy couple of weeks."

"Have there been more visitors since we were here?" asked Jules.

"In fact, there have. First we had all the excitement with opening the graves of the plane crash victims, and the identity conundrum of that one grave. Then we get the mystery visitor to the same gravesite the day Bruce, our chief of police, died. Now you are here, I assume to ask permission to exhume his corpse and examine it, all because of these unusual happenings," Loomis was visibly weary with the recent death of his friend.

"So visitors are unusual around here?" affirmed Kate. Her concern for the unknown visitor was growing and it was rubbing off on Tom.

"Yes, it is all very strange."

"Do you think it could just be a visitor to see Bruce? Something that he was involved in that went south?" Tom asked. It was a long shot, but worth asking.

"No. I was Bruce's physician and close friend for the last forty-five years. I knew everything about him and he wouldn't get involved in something illegal or secretive." Loomis walked to his desk and sat down, staring blankly at paperwork.

"Did you personally inspect the body... er... Bruce?" Tom asked. How anyone could perform an autopsy on their best friend was a major feat in discipline. He tried to be sensitive that it wasn't just a body, but Loomis' friend.

Loomis didn't answer immediately, but shuffled the papers together and set them aside. "I grossly examined his remains within minutes of his death and saw no reason for any comprehensive testing. He appeared to have died of a massive stroke."

"Was it likely that he could have a heart attack? As his doctor you would be the best informed in his health," Kate wasn't buying the fact that he died of a stroke. There was something else going on here.

"He had always been a fit man who skied and hiked these mountains regularly. I know how healthy he was because we did most of these things

189

together, and I would have a hard time keeping up with him. Plus, he had a normal physical three months ago with a perfect ECG, only a moderate increase in his blood pressure at 175 over 100, and a mild cholesterol problem. I recommended medications to lower those numbers, but he was a proud stubborn man who procrastinated on the medications. I felt that a stroke was the most likely scenario so I signed off on the cause of death as a CVA. Personally, I don't want to see him cut up, he was my best friend."

"We are very saddened by the death of your good friend, but we only need to take small tissue samples from three different areas of his brain. We will be fast and very respectful. I can't give you any specifics, but if we find what we are looking for, it will have worldwide implications, and will confirm the chief was actually murdered," Jules said.

"Chief always said there never was a murder in the village, and within the village limits that's correct, but just 250 meters outside the boundary is a different matter. In 1803, the mayor caught his wife in bed with his best friend, the town priest. We still talk about that to this day."

Kate offered, "All we need is to have the exhumation completed, then the sampling will only take a couple of hours. I'm assuming the chief was embalmed?"

"No, his wishes were to be buried within a day, so we held a service the next morning at sunrise and he was interred. I would guess that since his grave is on family land in the high forest about two kilometers from the village, and because it is located on the north side of the valley, he should still be in relatively good condition because it is much cooler there," Loomis replied.

"We would appreciate your answer this morning if you will sign the order to exhume," Jules prompted.

"I don't believe you need to exhume his body. I examined it and made my determination as to the cause of death." Loomis began to get upset. Tom understood completely. He was grieving the loss of his friend, and at the same time, had to stand firm as the examining physician.

"I am not pretending to understand how you feel. It has to be difficult to be in your position as both friend and physician. We believe that someone murdered Bruce. We know there have been murders tied to this same man, and we are trying to do everything we can to stop him before more people, more families, more friends are hurt. If you allow us to examine Bruce, you will be giving us the opportunity to find this man faster." Tom practically pleaded with the man.

Loomis sat back in his chair contemplating. He stood up, reached a hand out for the document and agreed. "I will do it now. I think that is what Bruce would want, especially if there was foul play. We can have him here in the treatment room by noon tomorrow unless the family or a local objects. Are you staying at Hilda's B&B?" the coroner inquired.

Tom answered, "We haven't checked in yet, but yes, that's where we are staying."

"Good, she's a great cook. Be sure to have her Zurcher Gerschnetzelt and Rosti, which is meat and hash browns like you never had before. And don't forget her Carac with chocolate for dessert," Loomis suggested. He was putting on a mask of contentment that Tom could see right through. Tom felt terribly for the man. "Tomorrow for breakfast, skip the coffee and have her double chocolate hot chocolate and homemade hard biscotti for dipping. I guarantee that will get you warmed up and moving. That stuff should come with a warning label," Loomis laughed, forcibly.

After leaving the clinic, they walked around the small village square and made their way up to the hillside cemetery where they found the disturbed earth from the recent exhumations. The headstone with Wilheim Berhetzel's name inscribed on it was off to the side, broken into three pieces and a small wooden cross lay on the stone rubble over the grave, temporarily marking the site. The other two graves were in better shape with the stones upright. A wilted bouquet of wild flowers lay on Anna Steger's grave. Tom found it strange that those flowers were the only ones on any grave in the old cemetery. Kate grabbed Tom's arm and they headed down the hill into the village.

"Now that was a little creepy," she said. "When I see the dates on those stones and then think about the type of evil we are pursuing, I have a hard time reconciling it. I can't begin to imagine what the war did to humanity and how that evil has resurfaced to threaten us again." She shook her head solemnly.

Tom reached for her hand and squeezed gently, "Evil has always been with us in different forms. Nelson Blackfeather and his ancestors understood that and knew it was the responsibility of those on the side of the Creator to resist that power. They called him the Destroyer, but I like to call a spade a spade—Satan, the Devil, or Lucifer. In the end, he will lose because St. John says it will be so in the Book of Revelation. We may lose battles, but in the end we will prevail!"

"What do you think, Jules?" Kate asked as she walked hand in hand with Tom.

"My dear, it is darkest just before the dawn. We are approaching dark times, but in the end, the light will win. And I think I'm getting quite hungry and have the urge for a big piece of Devil's food cake.

They all broke into laughter just as they found Hilda's place.

191

Chapter 55

Paris

Archives Nationale

The Next morning

Robert DuBois, the respected Nazi hunter, met Joseph at the entrance of the Archives after Jules' personal driver dropped him off. The old man who appeared to be energized, walked briskly through the marbled corridors to a slightly musty conference room where five other older men greeted Joseph with a mixture of 'bonjours', 'good days' and warm handshakes.

They immediately went through the obvious journal section concerning Berhetzel, the war years, and then broadened the search laterally with half of them moving back from that era while the rest of them analyzed the more recent entries.

The experience and expertise of these men quickly became apparent as they dissected sentences and paragraphs. Their methodology led to discovery of hidden clues like "mapped DNA" and "instant death" in a 1947 written piece. "Death Ray" was in the same sentence as "Destroyer" in a 1936 pre-war paragraph. Discovery of these disguised clues was because Nelson Blackfeather was a master at cryptic writing. He wrote certain sentences in variations of darker and lighter pencil, which were easily missed because of the nature of recording with a lead pencil. He also noted parts of the script with tiny, almost undiscoverable dots that indicated an important letter or word. These became the key words and Joseph was amazed to watch patterns appear that his grandfather had used to hide critical parts of his journal.

Suddenly, the journal was alive with new information. In areas where he had written about more mundane daily Reservation life, were very little cryptic pieces of information, his style slow and deliberate. In the sections where his focus was on their Lakota tribal history, unusual occurrences or records of dreams or visions, there was a hidden story waiting to be assembled. The French team entered the raw data into three different laptop computers that each ran a different style analysis program. Each unit was interfaced with the others and communicated to a larger central 'brain'. The end result was what Robert called a 'consensus' or agreed analysis. By six p.m., they had scanned and picked apart the most critical years, and critically scanned 90% of the rest.

They retired for dinner after giving the main computer the command to 'execute collation of data', which was to give them that understandable analysis. When they returned at eight, there were a dozen printed reports bound and waiting at the printer station — six in French, six in English. They removed the copies and returned to the oval conference table, the French with red wine in hand, to read the report.

ARCHIVES NATIONALE de FRANCE
Report Number:100793.5
Date: 20/9/16
Project leader: Robert DuBois
Team members: Joseph Blackfeather, Maurice DeNapoli, Thomas Willet, Paul Benoir, George Listere, Peter Monet
This report represents the assembled extracted data from the personal journals of Nelson Blackfeather, American Lakota Sioux Shaman, for the years 1934 to the present. Encrypted data was assembled using ASGP 1.0, ASGP 1.2, and ASGP 1.7 analytical programs. Common data points are collated into this report, and individual program points are submitted in the attached Appendix.

DATA SUMMARY—BLACKFEATHER'S WORDS:
The evil we face (1934) has controlled mankind since our creation. It has provided the reasons for war and the destruction of civilizations. The 'Destroyer' comes with his evil intent and is now rising again in Europe (1935), and will be responsible for millions of deaths. The soldiers of this evil are in Germany, Italy and Japan (1936) and they will spill buckets of pain, suffering and death upon the unknowing. They create new powerful weapons to this end (1936), bombs, chemical poisons, rockets and death rays. Their scientists will make great discoveries, but use them in horrible ways (1936). Their leader will attack to her east and break alliances with nations (1936). Death will occur in great battles and in camps where men, women and children will suffer extermination and the nations of the world will try to avoid their doom. But the plague of the 'Destroyer', his soldiers and plans, are in place (1937). The Secret of Youth has been discovered in a spore by one man. Only he knows of this discovery (1939). He will become all powerful, taking the lives of many from the earth to control it. France will fall, but Britain will not (1940). The U.S. will win this great conflict after much sacrifice and use new weapons against her enemies (1940). The man

who understands the Helix will kill with it (1940), but death will fall from the sky on Britain and many will die at a place called Pearl (1940)."

The report went on and on to chronicle the future war and its major players. He wrote in a Nostradamus-like manner — short, concise phrasing and prophetic verses, which spelled out the future clearly. His most startling statement to be uncovered was from 1944.

"The Destroyer King of the world will be gestated in this conflict. He will survive as a young man, and kill silently and without evidence. The world will be controlled without bullets or bombs. His name is Berhetzel and he is to be feared."

Then, recorded in 1947, these words:

"He will mature in the Amazon and start his reign of terror in Europe, this destroyer of life. He will kill man and beast using the ladder (DNA?), and death will come in an instant. Many will seek him, but he will hide in plain sight, under their noses. He lays not in a grave, is strong and young for one so old."

Then the last and most recent entry:

"You must ask me for the help of our ancestors in your quest!"

Joseph finished reading the summation and shock was on his face. "I'm absolutely stunned. Grandfather said, 'Ask me for help.' He had no prior knowledge of our search. He just confirmed the identity of the man that he drew years before. We need to find Berhetzel fast because it's evident he has already found the way to destroy life. Are you looking in Brazil yet, Robert?"

"Oui," Robert accidentally said slipping into French, "I have a very old friend who is tracking down several possibilities in Brazil and Argentina along the Amazon where local rumors persist of things out of the ordinary. The nature of the area, with superstitions and suppressed people lead to many dead ends, but he has hunted Nazis for decades and understands how to play the game. I should have heard from him late yesterday, but he told me he may not get back to me until he returns to a civilized area. Because even the best satellite phones can fail in that remote region. He called communication 'hit or miss,' especially this time of the year with all the thunderstorms they experience. If Berhetzel is there, he will find him, and most likely try to kill him. The man hates Nazis!

"Today, we were given a gift to be able to work on this historic document. Confirmation of our suspicions about Berhetzel is invaluable and will allow us to concentrate our efforts. So we will meet here tomorrow at ten, and we will pour over these records one more time to be sure we didn't miss any minute clue. All the files on Berhetzel and his known project associates who worked in the same facility will arrive from Berlin when Jean and Brad return. Currently, we have generalities about the man, but need more specifics on the research that went on in those camps. The more we understand him, the better we can fight him. It is a big puzzle. Our job is to assemble these clues, then find and eliminate this monster before he destroys mankind!"

Chapter 56

Tom and Kate met Jules for breakfast in the tiny dining room of Hilda Stromberg's B&B. The aroma of fresh brewed coffee, chocolate and yeasty breads, blended with the unmistakable lure of pork sausage and bacon.

Hilda was a stereotypical villager with her round cherub face, stout frame and braided hair circling above each ear. Expressing her hospitable nature, she proudly treated them to a generous assortment of those baked goods, sausages, eggs and potatoes, followed by large plates of cheeses and fresh fruit. They were the only guests at the small B&B, but were presented with enough food for several times their number. Jules, who wasn't a breakfast eater, managed only a couple of sausages, cheese and some fruit. Kate prayed as usual, which caused Jules to comment, 'Bon' as she finished. She simply looked over to Tom and said, "I have a lot to be thankful for!"

They finished breakfast and each took a large coffee to go before heading out to the medical clinic. The sun was burning off the morning mist and a light breeze was starting to move the warmer air up the hillsides. When they got to the office, Dr. Loomis was waiting for them on the porch, fiddling with a meerschaum pipe, nervously cleaning its ornately carved bowl. He took them into the treatment room where his friend laid covered with a large jade-colored surgery drape.

"This is the best person that I ever knew. Let's get this over with," said Loomis with a sheen of sweat just over his brow. The worry hung heavy upon his shoulders as he stood back.

Jules walked to the table and lifted the shroud, doing a quick gross examination of the body. It appeared in very good condition despite not having been embalmed.

Loomis, who seemed obviously distressed, asked him, "Do you want to tackle this or should I?"

"I would prefer since you are the official coroner that you do the gross autopsy and I will then select the tissue samples we need. I am only interested in the brain, so unless you want to do a complete post, that will be all we need to look at," Jules replied.

Loomis took four pathogen barrier gowns from the wall closet and gave one to each of them. They then put on plastic face shields and heavy autopsy gloves. Loomis removed an instrument pack from an old enameled glass front cabinet, and retrieved a Stryker saw from the bottom shelf. Next, he draped off the Chief's skull and made a careful incision from behind his right ear over the crest of his skull and behind the left ear. He then dissected the skin and scalp from the face to the back of the skull, exposing the boney top of the dome. Wiping the tissue fluid from the bone, he started up the Stryker and cleanly cut the top of the cranium off with light smoke drifting airborne as the saw ground its way around the circumference. Next, Loomis cut away the connective tissue, nerves and dura mater, and cleanly lifted the brain from its protective bowl, placing it in a stainless tray. Visibly upset, he turned to Jules and said, "There you are. I'm going outside for a smoke," and he quickly exited the room after discarding his exam gloves.

Jules carefully examined the brain looking for any evidence of a major bleed from a stroke. Other than a small surface hemorrhage, most likely from hitting his head when he fell to the floor, the brain looked pristine.

"I don't see anything grossly," he said, "I'll get our tissue samples and cultures now. Kate, will you take notes and label everything for me please?"

Jules quickly harvested small tissue samples from each major functional area of the brain, half of each he preserved in formalin, and then froze the others on dry ice. He then removed fifteen millimeters of CSF fluid and cultured all the sampling areas. He would have preferred to have the entire brain, but made sure that he took the medulla oblongata and pons in a singular piece as this was the important involuntary control center of the brain. When Jules finished his work, he carefully placed the brain back in its cranial cradle, replaced the skullcap and neatly closed the skin with cosmetic subcutaneous stitches. He removed his protective gear and went to find Loomis. Loomis was on the porch, pipe in hand, staring at the green hillside. He acknowledged Jules with a nod.

"I can't begin to tell you how many times Bruce and I sat in these old chairs, smoking and drinking, looking at that view, laughing at stupid jokes. He was a good man — the best — and my great friend. If he was murdered, you need to find the S-O-B who did it."

Jules empathized with him, "You should know this, Dr. Loomis, if he was murdered, we will find out who did it and how. Our suspicion is that this goes far beyond what happened here, and potentially could have devastating impact on every living specie. If this hunch is confirmed, your friend may have just helped us solve one of the greatest mysteries of our time!"

Chapter 57
Paris, the same day

Berhetzel was in the City of Light refining his plans for a dramatic assassination of the President of France. He was proud of his decades of endless research to finish developing something his nation had worked so hard to accomplish, but failed in defeat. His so-called death ray, the ultimate weapon, was now in danger of discovery. All his careful plans had so far worked without a hitch until the last two weeks, and now rather than being an anonymous entity, he had been resurrected from the grave. The ruse that had protected him from discovery was now exposed, but why would some Frenchie look for him after being 'dead' and buried for seventy years? He had led a spotless, quiet life in the remotest of areas. It would have taken a world-class psychic to connect all the dots and figure out what he had been up to all these years, let alone tie his name to anything. Now he had to find this Jean DuBois and his Nazi hunter father, Robert, interrogate them and eliminate them from threatening his life's work. He only had a few days in Paris to accomplish that before the G8 leaders would convene their economic meeting at La Défense, the Grand Arch.

So far, he had been able to review the area around the modern structure by using Google Earth and other available public records. He knew the iconic building, whose marble and glass facade glistened and shined day and night, would provide a dramatic backdrop for the assassination. There had previously been a meeting of G8 leaders twenty years earlier, and he had studied the news reports of that meeting carefully and it appeared to him that the very public display of unity that signaled the end of business occurred with a defined security zone of only 50 meters. Beyond that distance, the public was behind barricades standing shoulder-to-shoulder cheering in chaotic nationalistic fervor, the multinational flags waving wildly above their heads. Berhetzel was confident that the same security zone would be utilized since the orientation of the building required the politicians to declare their 'unity' under the Grand Arch to get the maximum effect they desired. All he really needed to do was be among the first waiting at the forward edge of the public area and pretend to be recording the event with his 'camera'. He would snap his 'photo' and quietly vanish into the subsequent chaos. There would be thousands of phones and cameras documenting the unexplained death of 'Le President' and he was anxious to see the evidence of his genius displayed in stories that would be carried around the world. Perhaps after this tragic death, he would travel across the channel and eliminate the British Royal Family. For now, his effort had to be centered on finding his pursuers so he could arrange their own untimely death. The DuBois family was famous in France so hopefully locating where each lived would not be difficult. Finding where they worked, however, would probably be easier.

Berhetzel had been renting a small apartment in Montmartre for nearly a year in preparation for this trip, having it cleaned biweekly and the flower window boxes tended to. He chose this area of Paris because it was the one area where the majority of people minded their own business and looked away when something didn't directly affect them. It also was adjacent to the seedy red light activity that took place in the Pignelle, and known for the abundance of hungry artists and the eternal hilltop beauty of the Cathedral Sacred Coeur. The apartment now gave him an anonymous base to work from in an area of Paris where privacy was expected and respected.

Berhetzel sat at the small, red-painted table of his apartment searching on his laptop computer for Parisian addresses for Robert and Jean DuBois. It soon was apparent that this would not be an easy task as there were nearly 300 'J.' or 'Jean DuBois' addresses and phone numbers, and nearly 500 'R.' or 'Robert DuBois' addresses and phone numbers listed. Frustrated, he decided his best approach would be to stakeout the Archives Nationale and follow Jean DuBois to his home when he left work. After that he could figure a way to get Robert's address. He wasn't even sure if the man drove to work, used the Metro, or walked. He had already decided not to use his weapon to eliminate the father and son. Instead, he could fake a robbery that turned to murder, or perhaps arrange a fake accident. Berhetzel knew he had to stay under the radar and as much as he would love to test his weapon on a human again, it was too risky. He decided a robbery gone wrong was the best option.

Berhetzel pulled up Jean's public information from the Archives website and printed his photograph. He would use that photo to screen people entering and exiting the front of the building when he surveyed the coming and going of personnel. He would try this approach for one day and see if he got lucky. However, the more he thought about his chances of seeing him enter or exit the massive building and then following him though congested traffic, he realized it wasn't an efficient idea. He decided the best way to obtain the information was to call and make an appointment.

199

The Archives phone operator pleasantly answered the phone and transferred his call to DuBois' personal secretary, Babette. Berhetzel, a master of deception, using his best academic voice, spoke.

"Good morning, Mademoiselle. My name is Dr. Fritz Hammerschmitt, and I work at the German Federal Archives. I am in town for a lecture at the Sorbonne and if I am correct, your office has been making inquiries to our office on a particular individual and general war-related issues. I was asked while I was in Paris to drop by a CD with a resource guide for our services and information accessing the secure files once your credentials are approved. I was asked to personally deliver this disk directly to Dr. DuBois, but I am on a very tight schedule. Do you know if I could meet with him very late this afternoon as I must be available for these lectures until after 1600 hours?"

"I am so sorry Dr. Hammerschmitt, but Dr. DuBois must leave a little early today for a dinner engagement. Tonight is his monthly evening at the opera with his father. They never miss these evenings together," his secretary explained.

"Too bad, I would like to meet him, but I'll never make it in time. Perhaps I could drop it at his residence after my meeting? I could call him tomorrow to go over it by phone on my way back to Berlin."

"I'm sure that would be fine. His home address is 2413 Avenue Montaigne in the 8th. It runs just north of the Champs-Élysées. You will find a brass mail slot just to the right of the entry doors and if you drop the CD in, it will be safely delivered. The door latches are antique brass lion heads and his home is on the south side of the street."

Berhetzel smiled to himself as he listened to her directions. This was too easy! He thanked her for the help.

"Merci Beaucoup, mademoiselle, that will allow me to accomplish my task and still make the early evening train home. One less thing to worry about! Auf wiedersehen!"

He put down his encrypted cell phone thinking, *Too bad. She will need to find a new job.*

This satisfied him that this loose end could be tied up quickly. He located his tourist street map, found the street orientation and memorized the Metro stops so he could travel easily to and from the residence. Then he put the address into Google Earth and viewed the property with a street view and the satellite bird's eye view. Fortunately, the house had a large courtyard and a garage with an alley entrance that would provide easy access. From there he would easily find a way into the main house to set up his trap. He then thought of something that might present a problem and called DuBois' secretary back.

"I'm sorry for disturbing you again, but I thought perhaps I would purchase some flowers for the family and give them to Madame DuBois when I drop off the disk. Do you think that appropriate?"

"That would be a very nice thing to do Dr. Hammerschmitt, but he only lives with his father. No staff, wife or children. Don't worry about the flowers, they are men and what would they care?"

Berhetzel put down the phone and broke into a smug feline smile. Now he had all the information he needed.

Chapter 58
Archives Nationale

Paris

Joseph and Robert finished their work with the archivists in the early afternoon and had not discovered anything else of value that would assist them in finding the 'Destroyer'. The young Indian, however, felt stripped naked emotionally while they picked apart his grandfather's journals, trying to discover the elusive clues that he had secreted behind cryptic symbols and Native American syntax. Much of what he had written was uniquely American Indian, such as his emotional commentary on the Wounded Knee Massacre. Names of tribal leaders and his editorial commentary on the true history of the 'White' media-distorted events confused the French, so Joseph spent much of his time explaining references that would only make sense to a Sioux and really meant nothing to the Europeans. His grandfather's feelings for the earth, animals and Creation just didn't connect to them, but were really the beating heart of the history he related. In the end, Grandfather had fingered the present day 'Destroyer' with an eagle's eye, and the wisdom of a wolf in predicting his rise to power and his tools for destroying. All that was left to do now was to focus their search to uncover this evil one — Wilheim Berhetzel.

Jules had returned with Kate and Tom from Switzerland shortly before noon and they sat in on the conclusion of Robert's Archives sessions. Joseph gave them a warm 'get me out of here' smile, distress visible on his face. The young man, who had spent all of his adult life on the Reservation, had never been involved in something so intense or, for that matter, so very critically important. Robert dismissed the participants with considerable thanks and finally sat down with Kate, Tom, Joseph and Jules, feeling all the age he had kept at bay for the last two days' meetings. Jules had just started to share their trip to the small Swiss village when Robert's phone rang. Jean and Brad were back from Germany and Dachau and were now on their way up to the conference room.

When they arrived, the team was intact for the first time in three days and each group had generated some valuable information that could put them closer to Berhetzel. Brad, however, seemed agitated in a way Tom had never seen before. Perhaps it was the result of their visit to the death camps. Brad was the first to report to the group.

"Hitler was a nut about the Fountain of Youth and had a lot of experimentation on its possibilities going on at the camps," Brad started. "Supposedly, he had teams in the Americas and in the Himalayas looking for an actual physical spring, as well as additional teams collecting all sorts of botanical samples, fungal samples and native medicines. His hopes were that his ruthless medical researchers could delay, arrest or reverse his physical degeneration, which was accelerating rapidly during the last years of the war and especially after the failed attempt on his life. We were able to find three documented camp survivors who had given sworn testimony that in the last camp Berhetzel had been connected to, Dachau, they had seen infants who did not appear to age or grow despite receiving the absolute best nutrition available in the camp. We located two of them still alive near Dachau, and they easily picked Berhetzel's service photo out of five other similar official service ID photos. Said he had been the head honcho at the child's medical nursery for a short time. You could feel their hatred for the man, they left not one iota of doubt about how evil he was. I just can't believe he was off the radar for seventy plus years."

This was a side of Brad that Tom had never seen before. The visit to Dachau had sobered the normally jovial big man.

Jean asked his father, "Have you heard from your South America connection? I suspect that is where we are going to find him because that is where the main sewer from Nazi Germany spit out most of these vermin. I'm convinced he has developed some kind of youth potion and may not have physically changed significantly in the last seventy years. And if he is smart enough to accomplish that, then anything else is possible. After all, he had all this uninterrupted time to perfect his evil intent."

Robert answered, "Yesterday I put a call into my friend who is doing this great favor of looking in the Amazon basin for Berhetzel, but I couldn't get through. I then tried his home and office, but they hadn't heard either. Their rule is he must check in twice a day, but some areas are so remote, they may not hear for several days, especially in the rainy season. One text was received saying he was going downriver from Argentina toward Brazil, probably because he could leave that text in cyberspace, but no voice communications. I have a general idea where he started so, if necessary, some of you may have to go and carefully retrace his general route. I obviously can't do it, but most of you could and I would stay armed and equipped to do battle. The local authorities and the majority of the federal forces will look the other way because they are used to being paid off by drug and human traffickers, so we would need a good amount of American dollars to buy information, obtain transport and secure protection. The dollar still opens doors wide in those areas. Whatever that animal has built down there will surely be well defended. He's no dummy so we will need to proceed with extreme diligence. If he is in Europe, then this trip, if necessary, will perhaps serve as a way to keep him cut off from his support and resources. Isolate him either down there, or here if we can, and then track him down like a dirty dog! Once we have an idea of which area he is in, we can bring in some governmental help. Until that time, we best not create too much dust or he will slip into hiding, and Nazis are real good at vaporizing into thin air!"

Jean looked at his watch, "For now we are adjourned for the day. I will be in touch with you in the morning. Please think about your options on a possible trip to Argentina; I will only take volunteers. Merci beaucoup!"

As everyone gathered their things to leave, Jean turned to his father, "Are you ready to leave, Papa? There is nothing further we can do this evening, and I still have tickets to the opera," Jean realized the opera wasn't something that was on their list of important things to do, but there really wasn't anything to accomplish until the morning. A night out would take their minds off the topic for just a few hours.

"Oui. That would do me a bit of good," said Robert as he pulled on his overcoat. "Shall we dine at Chez Paul beforehand?"

"Sounds wonderful," said Jean flicking off the lights as they left.

Chapter 59
Paris

Berhetzel was now glad he had kept his service 9mm Luger taken from the old granite rock wall because with the weapon's untraceable age, he would be an anonymous assassin. In Europe's current gun-phobic environment, there would have been no possible way to purchase a weapon without giving up his fingerprints and DNA. Fortunately, this old, unregistered, untraceable handgun would allow him to eliminate the father and son DuBois without risking leaving his unique calling card of two apparent sudden unexplainable deaths that might result in a serious medical examination, since the old man was a national hero of France. He couldn't chance some pathologist getting lucky and therefore ruining his future plans. Fortunately, he had been able to have the old gun's ammo reloaded with fresh powder and hot primers by a rural gun dealer on a day trip to Normandy. For fifty Euros, he basically had twenty-five rounds of unregistered bullets purchased from a man who ignored the 'do-gooders' from Paris' rules and regulations. Too bad he was going to have to dump the gun after he finished tonight's party.

The opera was scheduled to finish just before 2300 hours and since it was located fairly close to the DuBois residence, Berhetzel felt they would return home before midnight. He planned on arriving after the scheduled start time of the program to ransack the home, providing the appearance of a robbery and to set up his surprise attack on the two men. A master of details, a taxi would transport him to a point where he could walk unnoticed to the home, wearing nondescript clothing like his heavy fisherman's knit sweater, a navy blue Basque beret, pulled down to just above the eyes, and carrying a canvas shopping bag with a baguette and vegetables on top of burglary tools, vinyl gloves, duct tape and the loaded weapon. All of it destined for the famous Parisian sewer system once he completed his evening's work. Excited, he smiled in anticipation of that moment when they realized who he was. *Surprise! And goodbye.*

The alley behind the DuBois house was dark, barely lit except for small gifts of light from the old homes lining it. Entering through a rear entrance leading into the walled courtyard garden, a motion-activated light snapped on above the back door and lit his way in. He checked for any evidence of a security system, but found no signs of contacts, tape or motion detectors guarding the wood-paneled room off the garden, which appeared to be the study or office. Using a painter's tool, he jimmied the door open, amazed at how easily it popped open. A light switch was next to the door and soon, the room was lit by several small overhead lights.

The wood-paneled room was without question the space where the old man worked. Framed, faded black and white photos and yellowed news clippings of captured Nazi war criminals hung from above the two worn, steel gray file cabinets on the only wall that wasn't mostly floor to ceiling book shelves. He decided to pull books from the shelves and scattered the desktop items leaving the old computer alone. Then, he went room to room through the house, grabbing silver, watches, cash and anything else of value to give the appearance of a home invasion. Most likely, since a silver Mercedes was in the small single-car garage, the men had probably used a taxi for transport to the Opera, and he decided they would also return by taxi and use the front street entrance. He pulled a dining table chair and positioned himself behind where the door would swing open, wearing his vinyl gloves and holding the Luger on his lap. Soon, he would spring the trap.

Berhetzel heard a vehicle pull up to the front of the house at 23.10, pretty much when he had expected the men to return. There was a muffled conversation going on as he heard the key enter the door lock and the latch turn over.

"You are always so very critical of the tenors, Jean. I think this evening's lead was exceptionally clean and passionate! Not everyone can be a Placido Domingo. You need to focus more on the story and not concentrate so critically on the singers' mechanics, that way you will be incorporated, not absorbed, into the music!"

"I know, I know, but I get that from Mama. She had an exceptional ear for music and I guess that is why I fuss over it so much."

Jean pushed the heavy oak door open into the foyer hallway, switched the overhead light on and closed the old creaking door behind him, throwing the lock as it latched.

Hidden behind them in the shadows, Berhetzel quickly stood, pointed the Luger at the men and announced with an exaggerated German accent, "Güten abend, meine Freunde! Or should I say, Bonsoir, mes amies! I think we need to have a small conversation."

Surprised and startled, they paled when they turned to see the face of their enemy. Present was the identifying facial scar with the mole on the opposite cheek and other than a tanner complexion, he was an exact match to his service photo and to Nelson Blackfeather's sketch. Berhetzel had not changed in appearance in over seventy years and the proof of it stunned them.

"You see, my friends, I am the man you inquire about exactly as I was when I supposedly died on that mountainside in 1945. I think the proper French word is 'incroyable'. *Incredible.* You see, I am a genius and you were sadly mistaken to look for me after all these years!"

A sinister smile formed as he signaled with the gun for them to move down the hallway to the study. Robert slowly moved down the hall exaggerating aged disability while mentally searching for ways to escape Berhetzel's trap. Jean followed with the gun pushed firmly into his back.

As they walked Berhetzel said, "I have questions for you and perhaps if you cooperate I will spare you, but deny me the truth and I will happily kill you. You see, death is the price one pays for living and it waits for an opportunity to strike. I will happily be that agent of death if you wish it!"

Robert looked to Jean as they entered the study and signaled a negative response with his facial expression. Jean understood. No cooperation could save them or extend their lives. This was the end for both of them and they knew it.

"Now if you will, old man, sit at the desk where you can use that computer, and Monsieur Jean, I put that chair next to the desk especially for you. Sit in it, please."

Berhetzel pulled the duct tape from a book shelf where he had placed his bag of bread and tools and set it on the desk. Then he took three glasses and poured a generous amount of the Martell cognac he had discovered in each one. He handed a glass to the father and then to the son.

"Let's see, what should we drink to? Immortality? Yes, immortality seems particularly appropriate under the circumstances. You will now drink to my toast! To immortality. Salut!"

Jean and Robert drank the liquid feeling the alcohol's warmth offer a strange, hopeful encouragement. The Nazi pushed his drink back with one swallow, wiping his mouth on a forearm sleeve.

"Now we will get down to business," he said. "Jean, take the tape and go around your father's chest and the chair until I tell you to stop." Jean did as instructed and wrapped tape around his father's chest. With each pass, he looked into the old man's eyes, fear quickly growing.

"That's good. Now, old man, lean over and TIGHTLY secure your boy's wrists to the chair arms." Robert took his turn securing Jean's wrists to the chair. He vowed to himself to do anything he could to protect his son.

Satisfied, Berhetzel sat directly across from the men in a worn, high-backed, black leather chair, taunting them with more sadistic smiles.

"Let me fill you in on what I've been up to since my death in that horrible plane crash in 1945. No, I've not been sequestered in a monastery in Nepal contemplating the meaning of life, but I have been actively involved in endless research into the mechanics of life. I'm sure you find my youthful appearance startling considering, I'm sure, you know I am almost one hundred chronological years of age. I am in the same mental and physical condition as I was in 1945 when I escaped your invasion of Germany. Actually, I am in a superior mental state than then. You see, it is not that I inherited superior genes from my Aryan parents, although they were the right gene donors, but rather I am the proof of concept of thousands of hours of research into discovering a longevity serum. What you see sitting before you is the result of my discovery that the simplest of organisms, mold and mushroom spores, in the right combination of toxic and benign types and in specific ratios ingested orally can prevent cellular attrition by over one hundred times, possibly eternally. With my discovery, the immune system is stronger and even cancer cells can't overwhelm so-called normal cells or body systems."

"So, you may be thinking, 'why didn't this genius before you give this product to humanity to save or extend lives?' It is because I have a specific plan to use it to establish a Fourth Reich and correct the degeneration and chaos of the last seven decades. This is not something that should be consigned to the masses anyway. Why preserve inferior peoples and societies? This discovery will allow the new 'Elite', the true heirs to mankind's legacy, to establish that elusive New World Order and rule Earth!

"To help this occur, I have a second part to my plan that will accelerate this pro-evolution. That plan is to exterminate the world's political and military leadership. How, you ask, can that happen? Well, thanks to my brilliance, I have created a DNA-programmable death ray. I, and I alone, will decide who lives and who I destroy. Then Berhetzel will be the creator and preserver of proper life and the judge, jury and executioner of the inferior. My new society will be pure and strong and make up for the evolutionary mistakes of the last five thousand years.

"What I want from you is simple: I want all of your files pertaining to me and my work destroyed, as well as a complete list of all your associates and collaborators who have any knowledge of me. I know both of your wives are deceased — you have my sincere sympathy — but there is a daughter and two grandchildren that I would deeply regret having to kill in a most painful and disgusting way. My time is valuable and at this point of my life, I would have no problem exterminating the entire DuBois family. I must complete my tasks here in Paris and then return to my research and weapon production facility."

Robert and Jean stared defiantly back at the Nazi with pure hatred. Robert broke their silence.

"Doctor Berhetzel, there is no question that you are a genius, just look at my frail old body and compare it to yourself. However, just like the rest of you Nazi swine that polluted Europe in the last century, you are equally insane! What I don't understand is why you are not asking for an explanation on why we suddenly decided to investigate a dead and buried war criminal seventy years after he died in a plane crash?"

Berhetzel took the bait and asked, "All right, I was going to ask after I looked through your files, but I guess we could have that conversation now."

Robert now glared back at Berhetzel, his old eyes locked on his enemy and with a confident and knowing smile said, "Our Lord and Creator God has blessed us with the information and insight to help stop you from coming to power. The entity that controls your so-called 'genius' is the evil one, the prince of darkness or Satan — whatever you wish to call him. Your immortal soul has already paid the ultimate price, our job is to shortcut your descent down to Hell!"

With that, Robert pulled the trigger of an old sawed off 12-gauge shotgun that he had strapped to a hidden cutout he had made in the underside of his old desk. Something he had prepared decades ago when Jean was young and the Nazis were still abundant and dangerous. The deafening blast splintered the old chestnut desk front and blew Berhetzel backward off his chair. As the blue smoke swirled, the Nazi rose like a demon, his eyes alive with rage, staggering up to his feet holding his bleeding left side.

"You bastards!" he shouted angrily swinging the Luger first to Jean firing two rounds into his upper torso, and then quickly dispatched a struggling-to-stand Robert with a clean shot to his forehead. He looked to the files, but knew he had to leave immediately so he threw several decanters of liquor against the library shelves where he had scattered the books and lit a match he found on the desk next to a carved clay pipe. The alcohol ignited with a whoosh and illuminated the walls with dancing flames. The wail of distant police vehicles was faintly, but increasingly audible. He had to escape. Grabbing the old man's shawl, he pressed it firmly against his painful side to slow the bleeding. The fire was taking hold, producing a lot of smoke. It was time to leave.

Carefully he slipped out the back through the garden gate. Now he would have to find a way back to his apartment without anyone noticing his wounds. He would find a way, he always did.

Chapter 60
The Escape

Berhetzel was short of breath and light headed as he rapidly pushed on his escape route. House lights were popping on one by one as the sirens engulfed the quiet neighborhood calling its citizens to arms. Resisting the urge to run with panic, he maintained a steady, metered pace that he hoped would first not draw attention to himself, and second, prevent excess blood being pushed out his wounds. He examined the shawl several times to gauge blood loss, but each check indicated that the bleeding was not increasing, although his sweater was thick and heavy with the sticky liquid. Five blocks away from the DuBois home, he came upon on a small side street cul de sac with a stone bench and water fountain. Berhetzel drank the sulfur tasting liquid from the slow fountain and wet his handkerchief to wipe blood splatter from his face.

Resting was the right choice and he listened, reveling at the sound of panicked sirens as they wailed their way to and from the DuBois neighborhood. A quick look under the sweater showed at least nine bruised BB sized holes peppering the left side of his torso from his waist to shoulder. All the wounds appeared lateral to anything vital and he assumed the heavy sweater had provided some degree of protection from deeper penetration of the lead. Getting safely back to his apartment was now his goal. He needed to get the wounds clean and dressed, and rest up enough to continue with his assassination plans.

As he sat resting in the shadows of an old gas lamp that illuminated just the edge of the tiny refuge, he mulled over the near disaster at the DuBois home. True, he had eliminated the immediate threat to his work, but he had failed to get the names of all his pursuers. There had to be more, but hopefully he had managed to cut the head off the serpent and the rest would flounder without the DuBois leadership. That was something he had witnessed over and over again during the war — sheep must follow a leader, even if it is a Judas goat. Remove the leader and the rest scatter or wander aimlessly, they called it human nature. For him, there was nothing natural about weakness. The weak always got eaten.

After about ten minutes of rest and reflection, Berhetzel painfully twisted to retrieve his smart phone from his pants left rear pocket. The GPS locator APP put him forty-five minutes from his apartment by foot on a direct route, or over an hour if he took a more clandestine approach. He was tired, his adrenaline practically spent and a steady cool rain was starting to get heavier, soaking his sweater, leaving a trail of diluted blood runoff at his feet, and now the chilling of the night rain precipitated an involuntary deep shivering reflex from him. To survive, he needed the refuge of his warm apartment and some first aid. Painfully he stood, walked over to a street sewer port that was receiving a good flow of runoff and dumped the grocery bag containing the Luger and the valuables he had pilfered from the ransacked home.

Berhetzel now was starting to shake violently and his hands were ice cold with blue-tinged nail beds. Shock was starting to overtake him. His phone provided the location of a taxi stand that was only two streets over to a main boulevard. The Nazi slowly walked, pushing himself, concentrating on his dilemma and his options. As he got close, he drove his index finger into his left nostril until he had a good flow of blood started. He approached the first waiting taxicab, holding the bloody shawl to his nostril. The tough-looking cab driver rolled down his window to get a better look at the curious situation.

"Pardon, je suis désolé, anticoagulants," Berhetzel apologized pointing to his nose. *Excuse me, I'm sorry, blood thinners.* "Je suis mal." *I am sick.*

"You are not French," the cab driver said. "Speak English! You have not been recently to West Africa, have you?"

"No, no! I have heart valve disease!"

"Where are you going?" the cabbie asked handing Berhetzel a large wad of paper towels.

"Thank you! But I'm a mess. Can you just drop me at La Sacre Coeur?"

The Nazi slid into the cab, gingerly, trying not to show obvious pain. His nostril had ceased to bleed, but kept the paper towels pressed to his face to help disguise his appearance.

The driver was a typical Parisian cabbie who floored the gas pedal between the street intersections, almost like he was the one being pursued or had a long line of customers waiting to experience his driving skills. Each sudden stop and start were painful jolts that sent hot searing pain burning up Berhetzel's side.

The Eastern European driver negotiated the route on nearly deserted streets in a record eight minutes, and Berhetzel handed over a 20 Euro note for the 11 Euro fare, happy to be out of the danger zone and close to his apartment. The unexpected large tip had the driver happily out of the taxi, quickly opening the auto's side door to help his passenger get out. Under the driver's arm were the paper towels and a foam disinfectant and as soon as his ride stepped aside, he was in, furiously wiping down the interior, like he was expecting a health department inspection.

Berhetzel turned and walked directly away from the location of his apartment until the cabbie sped off out of sight. He then reversed course and walked downhill to the unit, which was only two blocks away. In a couple of minutes, he pushed his way through the heavily painted old oak door and into the safety of the tiny two-room rental.

The apartment was cold, or perhaps he was getting worse? He found the space heater and pushed the control to maximum and then took two Nurophen tablets for the pain and guzzled down two bottles of Evian with a teaspoon of salt in each one to start his rehydration. There was no way he could lift the sweater off by pulling it over his head so a kitchen butchers knife was used to slice up the side to the neck so it would just fall away. He took a wet, warm paper towel and gently sponged the nearly dried blood and clots from his side revealing a dozen holes that peppered the area from his scapula to just above the naval. He also had streaking, claw-like abrasions where the majority of the blast had blown past him. The holes had clotted and several were plugged with wool from the sweater, which may have minimized some of the bleeding. Black and blue hues were forming where the smaller capillaries had burst under the skin from the impact of the blast. This was the first time since the plane crash he had been significantly injured and the stupidity of it angered him. The DuBois men should have been shot as they entered the home. He had let his ego and curiosity about how he was discovered cloud his common sense. He learned nothing and now had to deal with an injury. Stupidity and overconfidence had given Robert DuBois that split-second opportunity to end his life. Just like Hitler and his cronies, arrogance had cost them the war. His arrogance had almost ended his years of scientific breakthroughs. He vowed it would never happen again.

He diligently cleaned the wounds and then prepared a poultice of sugar and water and smeared a thick layer over each small hole. The sugar would pull fluid from each wound almost like a drain and decrease the chance of infection. A bandage wrap made from a pillowcase was placed over several layers of paper towels and tied with strips of cloth from the bed sheets. The support of the wrap was uncomfortable, but it acted as a constant reminder to him to be smarter. Exhaustion then forced him to bed where he gingerly laid on the creaky mattress and fell into a deep, but troubled sleep.

Tomorrow he was to pick up the important Presidential DNA sample. There was no room now for any errors. He could never repeat the mistakes of this day.

Chapter 61
Paris

The next day

Just after eight in the morning, Jules received the shocking news from Le Directeur of the Archives Nationale that Jean and Robert had been victims of a rare home invasion robbery that left Robert dead and Jean clinging to life in the Médical Centre Saint-Lazare with two gunshot wounds to his upper torso and suffering from significant smoke inhalation. He was on complete life support in a drug-induced coma. The Centre's trauma surgeons had removed the two slugs and stabilized him as best they could with fluids and blood, but he was listed as very critical, and given the smoke damage to his lungs, he had less than a thirty percent chance of survival, let alone recovery.

The whole thing didn't add up for Jules. Jean lived in one of the safest neighborhoods in Paris where crime was nearly non-existent, but for the occasional theft of art work or jewelry and that was always a 'cat' type event, never a violent robbery and murder. There had to be more here than met the eye. He called the office of Le Maire in their Arrondissement in hopes of being connected to the police detectives investigating the crime scene. Maybe there was something they overlooked, after all, his whole life had been spent looking for the less-than-obvious clues to a mystery. Besides, he needed to look at Robert's files on Berhetzel if any had survived the fire. The Maire was extremely upset with the whole situation and he asked Jules to meet a Detective Montel at the house at 1100 hours. That gave just enough time for a visit to the Trauma Centre.

Jules called Kate and broke the tragic news to her. Stunned, she handed the phone over to Tom who listened in disbelief as Jules related what he knew and suggested an emergency meeting at the Pasteur after he had the opportunity to visit Jean and then meet with the detective at the DuBois residence. Tom said he would handle the details and set up a 1400-hour meeting unless Jules called with information that would change that plan.

Jules took a cab to the hospital and was met by security at the door, which escorted him to the modern Critical Care Unit, a central nurse and monitoring station surrounded by glass paneled units full of electronic monitoring and advanced life support equipment. He recognized Jean's daughter hovering next to his bed where two IV pumps were connected to each of his forearms, both with a piggyback bag attached to the main fluid bag. He quietly walked in and saw that one bag was antibiotics and the other a cocktail of medication to keep Jean in the drug-induced coma. Only human sound was his daughter's soft sobbing, with the rhythmic beep of the heart monitor, the mechanical click of the respirator and pumping sound of the blood pressure cuff inflating and exhausting its air, creating a discorded symphony through the room.

Jean's daughter, Susan, looked up. Her normally perfect makeup was smeared from wiping her tears, and upon seeing her Godfather, immediately rushed to hug the man she called 'Oncle Jules'. Up to that point, he had been resolute and focused on finding answers, but seeing his friend's terrible condition and holding Susan, feeling her terror, broke that emotional barrier.

"I am so sorry Susan, I don't know what to say. I have never heard of such a thing as this ever in Paris, especially in your family's neighborhood. Your grandfather was a brilliant man and a true patriot who made sure that there was justice served for so many millions of victims of the Holocaust. The Republic has lost a true hero and your father, God bless him, has been my best friend since we played together on the streets by his home when we were mere boys. In my heart I truly feel God will spare him and I vow to you we will find out who did this with the tenacity that is the DuBois legacy."

He did find the words.

Susan held closely to him, crying onto his shoulder, feeling his pain and love.

"Oh, Oncle Jules, look what they did to him. Pourquoi? Why? Just for money and things? Je ne comprend pas!" *I don't understand!*

Jules didn't understand either, but he suspected this was a disguised hit, possibly from a long ago Nazi-related case or more likely what they were working on now. He needed to keep his suspicions to himself. It was better to keep Susan in the dark for now until he had all the facts.

Jules stood by the bedside of his friend, and took his pale cool hand and gently squeezed looking for that phantom response which said 'I'm alive'. Nothing. He bent down and whispered a prayer for recovery and a personal vow for vengeance to find Robert's murderer and his attacker. He stood and wiped his eyes, hugged Susan goodbye and left to meet the detective. Anger boiled in his blood and the pain of seeing his best friend near death was almost more than he could bear. Hopefully a visit to the house would help him channel that anger constructively.

Detective Phillipe Montel was a short, balding man in his forties that was dressed in an ill-fitting navy sports jacket with his official laminated ID badge clipped to the vest pocket. He had the distinct smell of Gauloise cigarettes and eucalyptus cough drops, and held a clipboard under one arm. He appeared irritated to be there.

"Doctor LeClerc, I am Chief of Detectives for the Ninth, Phillipe Montel, and I was told to assist you in no uncertain terms by some very important people," Montel said, juggling the clipboard to extend his hand.

"Pleasure to meet you, Monsieur, despite these difficult circumstances," Jules replied politely, "Have you ever run into a case like this in your career?"

Montel unlocked the front door while responding, "I have not. I mean we always have property theft, but never this degree of violence. It scares me to think this man is still out there and even though he has been wounded, we have no indication he sought any medical attention. The entire city's law enforcement community is on edge."

"How do you know it was a man?" Jules asked.

"We have his blood from the floor and wall splatter where the senior Monsieur DuBois shot the man with an antique sawed-off shotgun that was secured under a desk drawer. Six inches more to the left and had there been fresh shells in the weapon, the perpetrator would now be dead in place of Monsieur DuBois. That is a shame!"

"If you agree," Jean asked, "I would like a sample of that blood sent to my office in the Pasteur so we can test for DNA markers, drugs or other identifying items. Maybe we can use that information and enter it in Interpol's database and possibly submit it to the American FBI."

"Consider it done," Montel said.

Inside, the house smelled heavily of smoke and felt damp from the water used to put out the fire. The once beautiful, hand-painted Trompe L'Oeil walls were obscured by a heavy layer of black soot. Montel led the way to the study, a familiar place for Jules, where he had spent many hours with Jean, sitting in the deep leather chairs, feet up on the desk, drinking liquor while discussing all sorts of important and trivial things, and laughing at each other's bad jokes. The room was in shambles with a melon-sized, splintered hole in the front of the old chestnut desk, the heavy drapes charred and torn from their iron rods, and the beautiful library of rare and old books, many first editions, trashed on the soggy carpeted floor. There was an odd mix of smells and, along with the strong odor of incineration, Jules thought he could smell mildew mixed with the iron taint of fresh blood.

Montel described the scene when his men arrived the night before.

"Monsieur Jean DuBois was over here strapped to this heavy leather dining chair, which I feel somewhat protected him from the flames because somehow he pushed the chair over or it fell toward that patio door with his head nearly touching the glass. See that small hole near the base of the door in the glass? We think that small hole kept him alive by sucking in fresh outside air as the fire consumed the room's oxygen. There is also one other very interesting fact on the wounds he received. The projectiles, 9 mm, were unusually soft lead and we suspect were old, reloaded brass based on the casings we found here by the desk. Very old, heavy brass with modern flash primers. Also, my ballistics expert said the powder used was a very hot modern mixture. He also said the slug lead was so soft that the extreme velocity out of the gun's muzzle caused a reverse mushroom effect on the bullet. In other words, nearly instantly the rear of the slug flattened almost like champagne cork so when it hit your friend, the rear was already flattened and produced a tremendous impact punch, but did not penetrate deeply like modern jacketed ammo."

"Why did you say modern?" Jules asked.

"Because these slugs were produced during the Second World War, probably near the end when resources were depleted and the 9 mm handgun bullets were no longer an alloy, but composed of pure soft lead. The alloys were reserved for rifles, artillery and aerial bombs. Handguns were low on the list of preferred lethal weapons. They could still kill up close, say in a head shots, but their range was severely restricted."

"Is there any way to find out who produced the ammo?" asked Jules.

"That's easy," Montel said, "Nazi Germany. Only those bastards had to produce these inferior slugs near the desperate end of their Reich!"

216

Chapter 62
Montmartre

That same morning

Berhetzel had slept on his right side all night to keep painful pressure off his injured rib cage, and now that sharp discomfort had him questioning if a rib was possibly cracked. Although, as a doctor, he knew the intercostal muscles laying between the bones were more likely the source of his pain. He was stiff and sore, but so far had showed no signs of fever or infection. Slowly easing himself off the mattress and pulling himself upright with a table chair he had wisely positioned next to the bed, he stood and tried to complete a stretch, but was couldn't reach up above mid chest . His walk to the bathroom was more of a slow shuffle and the face in the mirror was a shocking reminder of the events of the last evening. The visage was pale with blue-gray swollen bags under the eyes that had aged his appearance twenty years in less than twelve hours. Cold water to that face revived his senses and he gingerly untied the makeshift body bandage and removed the paper towel dressing with its serum-soaked stains. He lifted his arm painfully halfway to look at his side and there was thin bloody fluid drainage and bruising, but no real evidence of infection or inflammation. He turned the water on to the impossibly small shower until it reached a very warm level and eased in, allowing the comforting stream to rinse and massage his injured side. The water refreshed him, waking a reminder that he had business to do today, retrieving that DNA sample, and there was no way he would let this injury interfere with those plans.

Fortunately, the arrangements for transfer of the DNA had been set up for over a week. Berhetzel had prepaid a bicycle courier service to deliver an envelope to a prearranged meeting place, Le Cafe du Louvre Nouveau, and pick up a small padded manila envelope, exchanging the delivered envelope for the one carried by the young blonde in a red turtleneck sweater. Berhetzel needed only to travel to Le Jardin de Tuileries and position himself prominently, disguised as an old feeble man, hunched with a silver cane, feeding pigeons on a bench by the fountained pond, a role that he suddenly now could play without much acting ability. There he would then receive the

217

exchanged courier-carried envelope. Even though only six blocks would separate Berhetzel from the young woman, he didn't need any further contact exposure in Paris. Anonymity was especially critical now as yesterday's events might trigger a specific search for him, depending on who else was linked to the DuBois men's team. He already had left a potentially large footprint of his own blood and DNA, and there had to be a well-choreographed, aseptic, infallible method to achieve his final goal. Any other stupid mistake might set the hounds directly upon him.

The disguise was perfect and he slipped unnoticed onto the street walking down to the Metro station, one block away. The newsstand by the station stop had headlines that announced his previous night's endeavor. 'Héros Nationale est Morte!!' screamed the red headline in the daily journal Le Figaro. He paid for a copy and rolled it up under his good arm, and continued down the subway stairs to the turnstile entrance. Fortunately it would be an easy ride to the Tuileries station and a short walk to the rendezvous point.

The massive tree-lined park was busy in the late morning and Berhetzel assumed his role as a fragile old Parisian toddling along as runners, cyclists and children moved around him. The park was surrounded by a city alive with the sounds of a vibrant metropolis, but had an innate peace that millions over the years had come to rely on. The park's large shimmering pond with the pulsing fountain was surrounded by lovers kissing and others snacking on food while they reflected on their electronic media. He found a smaller bench facing the direction he felt the courier would come and crumbled a petite baguette he had bought from the boulangerie near his apartment the day before. He tossed a few crumbs toward a silver gray pigeon that bobbed his way over to eat, causing a chain reaction of dozens of hungry avians looking for an easy meal. Relaxing as the sun warmed him, he unrolled the paper and read the story describing the horrific murder of Robert DuBois and the attempted murder of Jean DuBois. Attempted murder? The story went on describing Jean's incredible survival and his tenuous cling to life at the Saint-Lazere medical facility. Suddenly, his footprint had enlarged once again. If DuBois lived to tell of his attacker, the world would find a way to destroy him and end the dream of a Fourth Reich. He swore out loudly, his German pronouncement startling those within earshot. The anonymity of the rainforest suddenly appeared to be his safest, best refuge. He needed to immediately find and finish this DuBois, murder Le Président, and get the Hell out of Europe.

The courier located Berhetzel resting in his strategic location surrounded by the hungry pigeons and sparrows and exchanged the envelope quickly while greedily accepting the large tip with a flurry of 'Merci, Monsieur! Merci beaucoup!'

With the DNA secured, Berhetzel crossed the street at La Place de Concorde and walked up the Champs-Élysées to a public restroom where he ditched the disguise, pushing its components deep into separate trash bins. He exited looking as he naturally appeared with his New York Yankees embroidered ball cap pulled down snugly to cover his forehead and hairline. He dodged and slid past many of the international mix of tourists who walked the city's largest and most famous boulevard in a semi-oblivious state. A far cry from June 23, 1940 when Adolph Hitler led a victory parade on this very street of the conquered city, a street then lined with German troops and subjugated Frenchmen. He had, at the time, been working in the death camps, but saw, as every German had, the newsreel reports of the German revenge for the 1917 humiliation in the Treaty of Versailles, and enjoyed watching Hitler rub their Gallic noses into their conquering. A proud moment for all Germans. He had always felt that one of the biggest errors of the War was not burning the damned city to the ground when they were forced to abandon Paris in August of 1944, something which would have demoralized the French. Perhaps he would lead his followers down this historic boulevard when his power was secured. About halfway to L'Arc de Triomphe, he descended down the stairs to the Metro and headed back to Montmartre where he planned on visiting a local Pharmacie to buy some proper wound dressings, antibacterial ointment and elastic body bandaging. Then he would rest, process the DNA and load the data into the weapon.

The weather was forecast to be sunny, cloudless skies for tomorrow's G8 unity celebratory photo op at La Défense. A perfect backdrop for a bloodless coup d'état that no one would comprehend. A tragedy for some, a celebration for others, including Berhetzel.

He checked online to reconfirm the timeline for the public display and decided that to get to the necessary fifty meter limit to the stage, he would need to line up three hours before the scheduled event. He had purchased two small flags on the Champs-Élysées to wave just like the other nationalistic groupies who would crowd the spectator area just so he would fit in better. He would wave the French flag prior to the assassination and the German after the delivery of the death blow.

He only wished they sold Nazi flags.

Chapter 63

Jules sat in the speeding cab mulling the events of the last week over and over in his mind. If Berhetzel was the one responsible for all this death and chaos, then they all had to be extremely careful because he was connecting the dots much faster than they had been able to do. If he had been able to figure out that Jean and Robert were on to him, then could he have knowledge about the rest of the group? The thought was frightening. How much had Jean and Robert confessed to him? Was there a target on all their backs right now?

By the time the taxi pulled up to the entrance to the Institute, he knew what their course of action must be. Go on the offensive, but split into small groups and coordinate their work electronically. No one should become an easy target, but everyone would still actively seek answers to find this 'Destroyer'. This battle had now become personal and they would need to focus more on finding and destroying the brains behind the killings and less on how it was accomplished.

The reception foyer was alive with security — two guards armed with automatic weapons standing either side of the main reception desk, the two pretty young customer service representatives, obliviously distressed, waved tentatively, but managed a cheerful 'Bonjour, Docteur LeClerc'. Two more uniformed men secured the elevator bank and the primary hallway. Happy to see the increased security, he wondered if it was directly related to the DuBois attack, or if something else had happened that he was unaware of. Security armed with automatic weapons was always unsettling and this level of protection signaled the threat was perceived a real and present danger.

He made his way to their conference room and found a solemn group huddled around the large oval table. The Americans and all the French investigators from the Institute and the Archives were there along with the head of security for the Institute, Thomas Butéré.

"I was just at the medical center where Jean is receiving intensive care in a drug-induced coma. He is on life support and looks like crap. His lungs are severely damaged from the smoke inhalation and the two slugs he took to his chest did a lot of tissue damage," Jules explained, "but did not penetrate deep enough to destroy his cardiovascular structures. If he survives the acute injuries, which the surgeons are estimating at a one in three chance, he will be in rehabilitation for a long time. I just came from their home where I met with the detective in charge, a Monsieur Montel. He seems to be on top of the investigation and has offered complete cooperation with our research and is sending blood and small tissue splatter from the attacker because Robert had mounted an old sawed off shotgun under his office desk, probably decades ago. Robert blew a huge hole in the desk, but probably only slightly wounded the man as it seems the majority of the blast blew past the perp and hit the side of the chair he was sitting in, peppering the wall behind him. The gun used to kill Robert and wounded Jean physically was a vintage 9mm Luger with reloaded cartridges. Because we restrict ammunition sales in France, many will reload their spent casings and apparently these were very old heavy, brass reloaded with modern hot powder and an equally hot primer. The saving grace was the slugs were original to the bullet and made of very soft, nearly pure lead, unlike our modern alloy or jacketed bullets that penetrate with explosive killing power. That high velocity powder overpowered the old, soft lead almost instantly distorting it to a flatter, less lethal form. Montel felt those slugs came from Nazi Germany toward the end of the war when resources were scarce."

Kate interrupted, "So do you think this was the work of Berhetzel?"

"Bien sûr, that is the likely answer because Robert had not been involved in any significant investigations since the late nineties and now, with the Swiss police chief's sudden death, I think our man may have figured out that he was being pursued. Exactly how I don't know. It seems reasonable that Jean would have left his business card with the Chief, and possibly the Chief decided to do some poking around himself. Probably had a fair amount of free time. He may have inadvertently triggered a red flag and Berhetzel could have paid a visit. If the Chief's brain tissue we brought back has pathology consistent with the porcine samples that Fred's technicians are verifying now, then we will have established the first link to a lethal bio weapon, one that fries the brain's electrical system in an instant, shutting it down, like pulling a plug."

"We can't meet here again because it could make us easier targets. I can't be sure if Robert or Jean gave us up, but I seriously doubt it. However, if he has been observing their comings and goings for a while, then he might be able to determine who we are. So, for now, until we eliminate his threat, we will only meet electronically unless absolutely necessary. Montel has the service and aged photo of Berhetzel and the police are going to cover public transportation venues like the Metro, train stations and airports to try to spot him. He was a little confused at having two photos, but I told him that

Berhetzel is a true master of disguise and a very slippery character. The authorities were already on guard at the hospitals and emergency clinics looking for a man with a left side shotgun blast injury and Jean's hospital room has twenty-four-hour security. For that I was very happy. Is there anything else that you feel should be covered?" Jules asked as he finished.

Joseph sat with eyes downcast, very solemn. He spoke.

"I am so sorry for bringing this evil to your doorstep. Robert was very kind to me and reminded me of my grandfather — very old, but very intelligent and driven to find answers. Maybe it was a generational thing because of what they had lived through, but I think they were on similar life paths that intersected and their spirits were joined through their visions and life experiences to bring us to this mission. I had a dream last night that was a warning similar to those my grandfather experienced. A voice that sounded like him, warned that the 'Destroyer' was again active and with the caveat that 'He fears the truth of man and now runs from the pursuit of the Creator and his Angels'. I then saw people running, screaming with flashes of intense bright white light. I saw flames and sensed the acrid smell of smoke. I am fearful of the path we are about to follow, but I know in my heart that grandfather, my ancestors, and now Robert, will guide us through this one way or the other. These 'Destroyers' come and they go, but there is only one Creator who is omnipotent and will lead us, through them, to victory over this evil man. I guess the real question is, how many will die, how many of us may die before that happens?"

Kate jumped in, "So Jules, what is the next step to find this bastard? Do we stay in Europe or should we look to South America for his probable base to possibly isolate him to one continent or the other?"

Jules had already thought this out.

"Here is what I think we should do. I want Kate, Tom and Joseph to travel to South America, and Kate, since you are fluent in French, Portuguese, Spanish and German, you will lead that investigative team. If everyone agrees, I will keep Brad and Fred here in Paris to filter through the leads and help with our communications and to monitor any developments in Europe. I would say you three should try to leave within several days after you get the necessary immunizations, equipment, and clothes, and we put a solid plan in place. Thanks to Jean and Robert's work in Marseille, we have a pretty good idea where Berhetzel disembarked in 1945 — Southern Brazil — so I think that will be your starting point. You will have to be very discrete as that area is full of ex-Nazis and other nefarious types dealing in drugs, human trafficking and kidnappings for ransom. Robert had professional contacts and friends down there he trusted so I will look at his recent phone records and files, if they even exist now, and see if there is someone still active down there that we can co-op with. I am also going to arrange a discreet armed security escort to accompany your team, and we will have very strict protocols for checking in with those of us who remain here in Europe. I think every six hours would be appropriate. We also must develop a good cover story for your trip and you will have to make it real and make it stick if you are questioned, or God forbid taken hostage."

Tom glanced over to Kate and could see the concern on her face. This was becoming a 'beyond the call of duty' situation, but it appeared that now they were in too deep to back away. Besides, they owed it to Jean, Robert and Nelson. He was sure they all felt obliged to finish this job and even Brad, who really missed his family, understood the gravity of the situation and the end result of failure. Failure meant the 'The New World Order' would arrive with a Swastika, not with nations holding hands while singing Kumbaya. Finish the job and then go home.

"So let's adjourn now," Jules finished, "and think about our friends and family and carefully consider how we need to get this accomplished. I will arrange a conference call at nine tomorrow and email you the number and passcode. Be alert of your surroundings, and be aware that Berhetzel is most likely in the streets looking for Jean and Robert's associates. We just don't know if he can identify who we are for sure. If you have any concerns of questions call me directly on my cell. Pray for Jean. OK, that's all, Merci et Bonne Journée."

Tom quickly stood and helped Kate out of her chair.

"So, French, German, Spanish and Portuguese? Are you kidding me?" he teased.

"He forgot Italian," Kate said smiling as she took Tom's arm in hers.

"Just more ways I can say I love you!"

Chapter 64

Kate and Tom returned to Jules' apartment, but immediately left for the streets of Paris to enjoy the beautiful sun-filled day. They started walking toward the main Boulevard Kleber and took the street walking south toward the iconic Eiffel Tower and the river Seine. The air was filled with delicious aromas of the many brassieres, boulangeries, and the small market shops displaying produce boxes filled with colorful oranges, apples, lemons, pineapples and iced trays of oysters, whole crabs with claws banded, and gray black sole with fresh glistening eyes that blended the smell of the sea with the spice of the citrus and fresh green herbs. They were lured in and purchased two fresh ham and cheese baguettes layered with creamy Normandy butter, a half kilo of red grapes, Evian and a nice chilled Sancerre with simple, clear plastic cups for an impromptu picnic lunch adjacent the Eiffel Tower. This could be their last special personal time to share before they left for South America and an uncertain future.

They found a perfect spot to eat under the sycamore-like Plane trees, on a wooden bench in the shadow of the massive tower. They relaxed, settling into a silent, people-watching meal. Individual tourists and those in large groups with tour leaders herding their charges around following waving flags on a large sticks or handheld paddles, mulled around staring up at the girdled steel frame expressing their universal 'oohs' and 'ahs' of wonder. Children frolicked, chasing handmade bubbles while their parents proudly called out their names — Philipe, Marie, Louisa, admonishing them to stay close. Old couples in berets dodged the children adjusting their canes as they moved slowly, walking hand-in-hand as they had in their youth, absorbing the warmth of the sun. It was a perfect Parisian scene and Tom and Kate relaxed, losing themselves in the moment. This world was oblivious of Berhetzel and his imminent danger to every living organism, but for now, that naivety seemed to be a good thing.

Tom had sent Bob a quick email in the car as they were driven back that morning from the Pasteur, explaining that he was being asked to extend his time away from home for an indefinite period of time. He ended the apology with the "I'll make it up to you" statement that he had already used once before. It seemed rather unfair to ask the young vet to manage the practice alone and even though he was with Kate and on a strangely exciting mission, Tom missed his home, his real work, and his dog.

Kate was studying him as they sat and asked, "A penny for your thoughts?"

Tom looked over at her and smiled.

"I'm just worried that I've been away from the practice too long and how it's affecting Bob. I want to be fair and I don't want him burning out like I almost did. And I miss that quiet of the countryside and, believe it or not, that unique smell of manure spread onto the open fields. Also, I really miss Jed. Plus, why the hell are WE going to South America and not the FBI, CIA or some other three-letter government agency that understands better what they're doing?"

Kate picked up his hand and gave it a loving squeeze, smiling as she felt the tension leave him.

"I have the same fears, my love. For me, it's not so much that we heading into an unknown situation, blindly searching for a dangerous man, but more that we aren't even sure where to search. South America has both natural and human dangers, and we will be at risk for both. Finding him would be a piece of luck, but after that, who do we call for help in the middle of Timbuktu? We are not taking an army with us and outside communication probably will be iffy at best. What if we call for help and no one answers?"

"Then," Tom expressed, "we are screwed in a major way!"

Tom's phone signaled an arriving email with a long 'moo'. It was from the young veterinarian in Wisconsin.

"Bob just sent a message. He says quit worrying about him and the practice. He's OK and not crazy busy, mostly feet and teats. Says they set their wedding date for next June 21, and they chose the longest day of the year to celebrate the longest day of their lives together. He ended with a 'Ha ha.' If we need anything just let him know."

"See, you were worried about nothing. What a guy!"

"That does make me feel a little better, but doesn't change the fact that none of this is what we signed up for. We were just supposed to be data collectors to aid researchers in the original die-off phenomena. So far, we have worked on a herd of dead cows in Montana, which morphed into a mysterious set of events that led to pursuing a supposedly dead Nazi in Europe who probably murdered one team member and tried to kill another. Now we leave for southern Brazil in hopes of locating this madman's hide-a-way. I think this is what is called a vortex, you know, sucking us deeper and deeper into God knows what. And truly, why *are* we still involved? Now we are looking for a 'dead' man and not investigating dead animals? We are veterinarians, for Christ's sake."

Tom's venting had hit a cord with Kate.

"I have the same concerns, but remember, it was Nelson who gave us this task to stop the 'Destroyer', not any governmental agency. We are now here to participate in an international coalition to solve a crisis that began as a biological mystery. This could be called now a potential global crisis. Look at the last eighteen months. It was almost cosmic that we started in Atlanta, which led us to Montana where we met a teenage Indian and his Sioux great-grandfather who just happened to be a psychic shaman and had visions for decades containing clues to specifically help solve these die-offs. We find the person behind the events, Berhetzel, we fall in love, end up in my favorite city in the world... Then we turn to with picking apart seventy-year-old graves, failing to find its rightful occupant, and then help remove a dead man's brain to solve the original reason we were assigned this task in the first place. Crazy! I really think we need now to focus only on the 'who' and the 'how', and not worry why we are part of it. It's way beyond our control. I think we need to do what Jules thinks best, but to be sure, I will call Atlanta to confirm we have permission to continue. I seriously doubt they will recall us as Jules has a lot of clout in the global scientific community. I don't think we are heading home."

"I'm sure you're right, but if this madman Berhetzel did find out he was being investigated and murdered Robert and tried to kill Jean to cover his tracks, then he's going to be on full alert and we lose the element of surprise. We end up at his address unannounced with a less-than-credible cover, we are going to be dead meat! The man must be a frigging genius, and whether he is sane or not may be the difference between life and death for us. Jules needs to use all his resources to disseminate our cover story before we set a toenail in South America. I mean major international press like CNN reporting something like 'Three American scientists on an international quest to find Bigfoot, check on sightings along the Amazon basin' and accompany it with an out-of-focus video of Brad in a monkey suit! That would likely put a bunch of nut cases in the field and give us safety in numbers."

"Wow, that's a great idea! Let's open us up to humiliation and ridicule as well as potential death!" Kate gagged as she gave Tom a playful punch in the arm. "You know, maybe if we locate a Bigfoot, he could help us find Berhetzel and recruit an army of Bigfoots to take him down. I think I'm going to cut you off from the wine now!"

Tom laughed and said, "We may all need strong drinks if my instincts are correct. You see, we are going to knock on the Gates of Hell to see if the Devil is home. I don't think he is going to invite us in for cookies and milk."

Chapter 65
Berhetzel Montmartre's Apartment

Earlier that day

Berhetzel woke as the sun's rays poked holes in the darkness through the small apartment's bedroom window and he felt refreshed for the first time since he had been blasted by Robert DuBois. He stretched tentatively at first searching for indication of the burning pain, but was able to move easily with minimal soreness. He smiled at the return of an energy that was being fueled by anticipation of the drama he was about to set in motion on that podium under the Grand Arch. He visualized the rush of security and medical personnel as Le President fell to the ground, panic spreading from the stage to the audience, foreign leaders being hustled away with helicopters flying frantic paths as military teams secured the area while dodging the inquisitive news reporters daring to get the story. They would eventually report witnessed accounts of the sudden tragic death of their beloved President of unknown causes with gossipy speculation on poisons and other secretive murder weaponry. He could almost taste the excitement of that moment — his greatest triumph, salivating at the thought of a personal sweet revenge for the Treaty of Versailles! This would only be a tiny down payment with much more reparation to come at his avenging hands.

He showered in the small stall and milked the last drop of warmth from the weak stream of water that trickled from the tiny shower head. He toweled off gently examining the wounds that covered his left side. The bruising was clearing and he was barely tender when he pushed the holes looking for drainage. The scabs were tight with no discharge and he marveled at the rapid healing, which he guessed was the result of his daily regimen of the secret mold spore longevity capsules that he had tripled in dosage since the injury. The issue now was that he was down to only a week's supply if used at a normal dosage. He needed to return to La Lupa and the source of his immortality, this youth preservative, because he feared the consequence of withdrawal. Would he just pick up the aging process at a normal progression, or would there be a rapid change or death from accelerated attrition of tissues into a frail, shrunken, senile perishing corpse? Prison if he was captured would mean no formula and certain death, something that he vowed would never ever happen.

The celebration was scheduled at 1300 hours and Berhetzel planned on being in position at least three hours prior to that choreographed raised arms of triumph, which signaled the world leaders' public unity. He needed to beat the anticipated crowd's arrival to position himself anterior to the rest of the hoard so as to have a clear line of sight for his 'photo' coup d'état. To minimize scrutiny he cleared his wallet of everything but his new photo Passport ID card as Dr. Von Braun and about one hundred Euros of various denominations. A small plastic bag would carry the two small flags, some water and fruit, but the star of the show, his lethal device, would be hung just like a camera on a lanyard from his neck. His Yankee's emblem ball cap would cover his recently close-cropped hair and aviator sunglasses would obscure his eyes. He would appear as a tourist, possibly a fervent nationalist, which, in reality, he was, but unless someone targeted him specifically, he would blend nicely into the expected international crowd.

The DNA data had been loaded into the device and the powerful battery carried a full charge. There would be one 'shot' at the French leader and then one reserved broad shot if he needed to clear an emergency escape route for himself, which would be an act of desperation that undoubtedly would then trigger a manhunt to bring him down. Because he needed to return to Argentina, the plans he had made to take down the British Royal family were scrapped in favor of restocking the longevity formula and testing system improvements and enhancements to make the device more lethal. More ways to surprise the world.

The early morning sun was almost blinding as Berhetzel left the apartment and hired a taxi to take him over to the La Défense area. The site was cordoned off in a three-block perimeter, and the area secured by Military guards in Kevlar vests and helmets, carrying small automatic weapons and wearing video and communication equipment. Bomb sniffing dogs, primarily Belgium Malinois were zigzagging, patrolling under the watchful eyes of their handlers as drones buzzed through the air doing aerial surveillance. The area was as secure as possible against conventional attack with a near zero possibility that any conventional weapon would go undetected, but Berhetzel was the harbinger of a new death with his stealth-like device from which there was no escape. Murder without a lethal signature.

The admitting point to the viewing area was only slightly busy when he arrived with most of the early birds who flocked to the security station ready to be screened and admitted. Berhetzel sent all his personal belongings in a gray plastic bin through the radiologic viewer and then he passed through the

228

state-of-the-art body scanner. He set off a low buzzing alarm and was stopped and asked to go through the device again, the technician staring intently at the viewing screen. He was pulled off to the side and a handheld scanning wand waved over and around him.

"Sir," the security officer asked, "you were shot?"

"Yes," he replied cordially, chuckling, "a stupid hunting accident where my best friend mistook me for an overgrown partridge."

The guard laughed and replied, "Ruffled your feathers, eh? Tell him that next time he shoots you to use birdshot, not that oversized buckshot unless he intends to kill you and run off with your lover! Go ahead and enjoy yourself, Monsieur."

Berhetzel, relieved, collected his belongings and scanned the scene in front of him. There was a thick line of people crowded to the center of the control barrier separating the anticipated nationalists from their heroic politicians, but the far sides were barely occupied. He decided to test his view from the right corner to see if imaging his target from there was possible. There was security stationed at equal distance laterally across the stage and he took a brief scan from his position of several of the faces, and on each, the device affirmed the acquisition of the target and locked it into the firing system. He immediately aborted each acquired target, secure that his less central position was safer, but would still allow him to complete his assassination.

Soon, the public area filled with people pushing and crowding to get their best view. Eventually they expanded to the sides encroaching on the Nazi's territorial claim. When they pushed, he pushed back harder keeping the immediate area to his left and right visually available, defining his protected zone. Invaders received a curse and look he had used before in the camps that had resulted in submission of even the strongest testing him.

Ten minutes before the scheduled commencement of the 'Unity' display, the crowd had divided into country groups and restlessness in anticipation of seeing their beloved leaders resulted in spontaneously sung national anthems in good-natured competition with each other. The French, who outnumbered the rest of the crowd three to one, waved their flags of blue, white and red while crowing proudly *La Marseillaise*. Each participant was obliviously enjoying the beautiful day and the flags of the world's eight major economic powers waved in a sea of color above the 'chanteurs'. The crowd started to push forward again, straining for a better view, but allowing Berhetzel his corner without testing him.

At last, the world's leaders, wearing their expensive suits and crisp French-cuffed white shirts, sporting the traditional politician's red or blue ties, walked on stage, beaming as the crowd's cheer rose to a roar. The

American and French presidents stood almost shoulder to shoulder as the group moved to center stage. A secondary row of finance ministers and sub-secretaries stood stiffly in the background directly behind their country's Chief Executive. Berhetzel luckily was in a superb position. He quickly raised the camera-like device and acquired and locked his target into the system. He waited, finger nervously poised on the trigger for the exact moment when arms would be raised in a linked chain of economic strength. The device was making a soft whirling, almost moaning sound, flashing 'Acquired and Locked' and was hot to the touch as the energy beam awaited its orgasmic escape. The politician's arms finally went up to the roar of the crowd and the trigger instantly went down producing a nanosecond burst of nearly invisible, lightning-strength energy that was released toward its DNA-matched target. For a moment the French President did not move, but then whirled to the left and stood looking down and behind him. Security rushed the stage with weapons drawn and forced the eight countries leaders off as emergency medical personnel rushed in pushing a gurney while others appeared to be giving CPR to someone who had stood just behind the French President. The circle closed around the downed person with paramilitary police lining the front edge of the stage. Berhetzel couldn't see, and slowly put down the device as the crowd started yelling and screaming in a disorientated panic and stampeded in near unison to the exits.

Angry at his device's targeting failure, Berhetzel joined the herd of bodies pushing their way through and out the disabled security exits as the agents in charge watched helplessly. He knew security camera recordings would, at some point, be scrutinized so he avoided looking up and around and kept the ball cap down over his forehead. He didn't want some computer technician finding that slight burst of energy light and then extrapolate its path back to his profile. With enough of an image to use, the modern computer programs could make short work of finding out who he was. He would need to leave Europe immediately.

He escaped the viewing area spurting out on to the street with news crews pulling aside those who had witnessed the sad event. For now, he would rest, pack up and take the train tomorrow from Paris to Germany and then reverse his last trip back to Miami and then on to Brazil. He would call Hermann Schmitt to inform him of his imminent return and to be ready with the boat barge at Porto Alegre in forty-eight hours. Troubled at his device's failure to complete the assassination, he knew he would have to refine it in the private security of his compound. The only thing that could bother him there would be the heat and the bugs. Anyone who dared disturb his much-needed solitude in Argentina would now be considered an automatic enemy and swim with the hungry fishes in the Amazon.

Chapter 66
Paris streets

The same afternoon

The rest of their afternoon was spent traveling the streets and boulevards of the vibrant city. The couple strolled hand-in-hand absorbing the city's ambience, enjoying their time together before the coming uncertainty of the Amazon. Kate took them up the Seine toward Notre Dame, drawn as she always was to the beautiful cathedral, and to the peace she felt when there. Their walk would be a long one, but worth every step as they passed beautiful monuments, museums, and crossed ornate bridges. Kate always went to Notre Dame when visiting Paris and she wanted Tom to feel, as she did, God's presence and power. She would light a candle and pray for their future together and ask for His guidance and protection as the investigation of Berhetzel continued on to South America. They needed God's help and the great cathedral was the perfect vessel from which to ask for their deliverance from evil.

When they arrived, Kate gave Tom a brief history lesson as they stood outside, including a standard warning for him to watch for pickpockets. She took the cream-colored scarf from around her neck and respectfully covered her head and led Tom through the meticulously carved doors into the sanctuary where a mass was about to start. They sat on two well positioned, wooden folding chairs just as the service commenced.

Kate noted there was an unusual high level of congregant conversations occurring in the typically reverent sanctuary, and then the Archbishop suddenly appeared, walking up to the pulpit along with the Priest who was regularly scheduled to conduct the late afternoon mass. She listened to the Archbishop's announcement, to gasps of surprise, as he announced the sudden tragic death of the Republic's Minister of Finance during the well-publicized G8 Summit. This was the first time Kate had heard the news, but she immediately thought of Berhetzel, an intuitive reaction now to reports of any unexplained death because she smelled a rat. She would need to call Jules about it when they returned to the apartment. The Mass continued with the scheduled priest and the assembled congregation came alive in emotional fervor, strong in their responsive prayers and hymns.

Tom had no idea what was going on in the French service until Kate leaned over and whispered in his ear. When the service ended, Kate led him to her favorite prayer station, located in a dimly lit corner of the sanctuary with rows of flickering candles providing teases of illumination. She had Tom pick a candle and left a Euro in the worn wooden offering box. Lighting the candle from another while she prayed a silent prayer for protection and wisdom, she placed it in its holder with a reverent 'Amen'. Tom suddenly felt an infusion of peace from the power in this Holy place and it humbled him.

Leaving with new questions to be answered but confident that her prayers were heard, Kate gave Tom the option to go back to the apartment by taxi, Metro or to continue walking by following along the Seine. She didn't want the day to end on public transportation and was happy when Tom pulled her hand to his and said, "Let's walk." They put the crowds and congestion of the Notre Dame area behind them, taking the tree-lined walkways that followed the river's path. A cool breeze freshened the air while gently blowing in their faces just as the sun started its slow descent behind the Eiffel Tower. Rush hour traffic sped by on the adjacent boulevards with fast-moving cars and taxis honking and maneuvering around those drivers who valued their lives. Tom watched, amused by the frantic automotive stampede.

"Have you noticed that all these cars are spotlessly clean and newer models? And I have yet to see a junker or a car wash in Paris."

"I guess French cars don't get dirty like plain old American cars!" Kate mused.

"Then I guess I need a French truck to do my farm calls because I'm always washing off mud, road salt or bugs," Tom complained, chuckling.

By the time they returned to the apartment, their feet were sore and swollen and they were tired, but in a good way. The maid had left two fresh baguettes, fruit, cheese and two bottles of wine, so they prepared a snack and went onto the terrace to eat. Kate took her phone and called Jules.

"Bonsoir, Jules," she started, "How is Jean?"

"Bonsoir, Mon Chérie," he said, sounding exhausted, "Jean is still very critical, but fortunately his doctors now believe he will live. However, they want to keep him sedated and on ventilation, possibly for several more days and then recover him."

"Great, then perhaps he can shed some light on what happened and if Berhetzel had anything to do with it."

"Don't bet on that," Jules replied. "The medical staff told me that the sedation drugs combined with the trauma he sustained will most likely result in a complete loss of memory of the events surrounding what happened. We did make sure that particular piece of information was made public just in case the shooter feels the need to finish the job. Unfortunately, our police now seem more focused on the strange circumstances of the Finance Minister's death. I am trying to get a specific sample of his brain tissue sent over here when they complete his post so we can see if they match the pathology signature our Nazi 'friend' might have left. It's a loose end we need to tidy up."

"I heard the announcement in Mass at Notre Dame this afternoon — about his death — and my first instinct was Berhetzel. That was odd and I was going to ask you about it," Kate said.

"I know both the Finance Minister and the President, personally. I see them all the time at state functions and they are never far apart, my understanding is they have been best friends since childhood. They both fell in love with the same woman in college, and it is rumored that they had a ménage à trois that persisted for years, perhaps to this day. There were even rumors that one of the President's sons is not his. Probably a lot of nonsense, but the French have always had an affinity for scandal when it comes to affairs of the heart!"

"So," Kate asked, "you think that if Berhetzel was involved in this, the President was the real target not the finance minister?"

"Oui, or even the American President. They were standing very close, but I think since they were on French soil in front of a largely partisan audience that it was supposed to be a blow to France. The Germans have always hated us, even more since the Treaty of Versailles. It is their passion. I just think he missed his target!"

"When will you know about the brain tissue samples?"

"Fred Garrett said within forty-eight hours of receiving the specimens. But that's assuming nothing else is found on the gross autopsy that would discount our theory on cause of death. By the way, Fred just finished the Swiss police chief's analysis and he had the same pathology as the pigs. It was Berhetzel's work all right. That's why he attacked Jean and Robert. They were getting too close."

"So what do we do?"

"Our plan has not changed. You, Tom and Joseph will be flying to Porto Alegre, Brazil the day after tomorrow. That is a slight delay, but I hope Jean will have recovered by then and perhaps Fred will have an answer on today's death for us. I also need the time to run the G8 surveillance footage through a facial recognition program to see if our friend was actually there. If so, perhaps we can trap him here on the continent. That would be easier, safer and less of a goose chase. And maybe a better look at him will give us an idea what that gander looks like now."

Kate replied, "OK, then I will fill everyone in and call you in the morning. Maybe Brad and Joseph can join Tom and I for a late dinner tonight and we can start making travel plans and developing a credible cover for us to use."

"I wouldn't plan on those two this evening. Brad said he was taking that poor boy over to the Crazy Horse tonight. I suspect Joseph thinks he is going to see a Wild West show, maybe sign some autographs as an authentic Sioux warrior. What Brad failed to mention to him is that it is a gentlemen's club, and that he would be the only Indian there unless they run into some businessmen from Mumbai. I would give anything to see the look on that boy's face when he sees those women only wearing a few feathers!"

"I'm going to kill that Brad! Don't you remember that old World War I song, *How Ya Gonna Keep 'em Down on the Farm (After They've Seen Paree)*? That will probably be Joseph! That Brad is sooo dead!"

Chapter 67

The walk back to his apartment was neither painful nor exhausting for the first time in several days. He had planned a quiet celebratory dinner at a neighborhood restaurant called La Mer. He still planned to go, but the evening would be subdued because of some technical failure of his invention. He had hoped to enjoy delicious French cuisine, something he would readily admit was better than the typical German heavy, fill-you-up fare, drink good wine, all the while listening to the other diners bemoan the tragic loss of their great leader, Monsieur Le Prèsident.

Now he would eat his meal, temporarily defeated and eavesdrop on some curious concern about the Finance Minister's strange death.

At the apartment, he immediately turned on the television and watched the coverage of the assassination. Each channel he flipped carried the story, but stopped at Le Monde, arguably France's premiere news channel. He caught a biographical story on the dead finance minister. The story led by describing the minister as a lifelong friend of the President and his beautiful wife Diana. The story reported both men had courted her in University and the three were very close, traveling and spending vacations together, even providing a guest apartment on their estate for the minister because he spent 90% of his free time with them. Unusual, even for France. Le Monde then showed a recent photo of the first family, with the minister on holiday in Nice. Three children stood between the parents and the minister — three boys. Berhetzel recognized the eldest son, standing next to the finance minister, as the young man his connection had gotten the semen sample from. The two sons who stood on the left of the President and his wife looked like their father. The son who stood next to the finance minister looked like him. It was an ah-ha moment for the Nazi.

So that was the answer to why the President survived the assassination! The male DNA matched the Finance Minister, not him! The son was not a biological match to the desired target, but the device still managed to find, and execute the source of the programmed DNA. There was no need to 'fix' his invention. It had worked perfectly!

He watched for another half an hour to see if any of the cameras showing the crowd reaction had picked him up in an identifiable way. He did not appear on the video and hopefully would remain anonymous.

Berhetzel felt validated for the first time since he had pressed the trigger releasing that flash of energy toward the stage. All his hard work with his discovery that the brain was a delicate harmonic electrical field that could be short circuited with a sudden, intense burst of energy, and once disabled in such a way, the brain could not reconnect the circuit pathways in that millisecond that was necessary to maintain its function. The 'fried' synapse circuitry no longer fired signals resulting in instant, non-recoverable death. It only was HIS genius that produced Germany's long desired 'Death Ray' and only HIS genius that used specific DNA to become its targeting system. He could eliminate an individual, a group or an entire species if he wished. His invention made him a god of evil.

Now, he felt the urgent need to escape possible detection before the French had the opportunity to review the video and possibly put two plus two together, or just get lucky. He needed the security of La Lupa to further refine the killing instrument to increase the lethal zone so he could take down stadiums of people, full shopping malls, buildings full of military leaders, Congress, Senate, Supreme Court and decapitate the leadership of a major government like the United States in one afternoon. All he would need would be a small army of mercenaries carrying his next version of the lethal invention to collapse the nation. All he needed was time, and with longevity capsules, he would have all the time in the world.

His confidence restored, he ordered his train tickets to travel back to Germany and then on to Porto Alegre. He would leave his apartment with a slow gas leak and a tiny broken exposed lamp cord wire with a timer set to turn it on several hours after he left. The explosion would obliterate any evidence he was ever there. In thirty-six hours, he would be back in the jungle, soullessly at work again.

Chapter 68
Paris

Dawn next day

The critical care physician called Jules at six a.m. to inform him that based on Jean's improvement, they were going to start titrating down the sedation drug dosages to prepare Jean for his assent out of the drug coma. There would still be security twenty-four hours a day. Plus, once he was responsive, he would be moved to a step down unit in an exclusive isolated area where celebrities, politicians and foreign dignitaries often were sequestered for privacy. No word on his condition could leak from this highly private area. Encouraged, Jules called Kate.

"Bonjour, Mon Chérie," Jules announced, upbeat for the first time in two days, "my apologies for calling so early, but it appears Jean will start to be recovered from his coma this morning. I will visit and try to see if he could answer any questions with perhaps a blink or finger tap as soon as he is able. Hopefully before you leave. Also if Fred confirms a connection between the pigs and the politician, excuse me for that, I will then sign off on your departure even if Jean is unable to help. Just so you know, you will fly commercial first class because the Institute jet would probably draw excess attention in Brazil. One more piece of information on the perpetrator's blood left in Robert's office — it matched Berhetzel's AB positive blood type, a relatively rare type, and they also isolated a compound called PSP, or Polysaccharopeptide, a compound extracted from the Coriolus Vesicolor mushroom. Why it was there, no one is sure."

Kate jumped in, "Wait a minute, I just heard about that compound. I think it is being used to extend mean survival times in canines with certain malignancies like Hemangiosarcoma. I read it could improve survival times by nearly double. But why would it be in his blood?"

"Fortunately, they are able to run complete blood panels on those nano samples and this was a compound originally unknown to our lab, but they broke it down and eventually put a name to it. Their research indicated it is in human trials for everything from cancer to Alzheimer's disease. Our lab speculated that the shooter may work in research or is currently in some kind of experimental drug trial. Evidently, the mushroom species from which the compound is extracted is very common and found around the world. In the Americas it is known commonly as the Turkey Tail mushroom because its coloration resembles the fantail of a wild turkey."

"If it is Berhetzel, do you think perhaps he is ill?" Kate asked almost hopefully.

"My dear girl, that would be a fairly safe bet. He is, after all, in his late nineties. Probably uses Viagra, too!"

"Jules you shock me. Leave it to a Frenchman to relate something to sex!"

"No, you are wrong, Mon Chérie, Frenchmen don't need such things! We only need the love of a passionate woman, n'est-ce pas?"

"Like I said, leave it to a Frenchman," Kate said, unwilling to let Jules off the hook. "I am going for my morning run so I can stay faster than your countrymen! I'll let Tom and the two 'Clubbers' know what is happening, assuming Brad and Joseph aren't unconscious in some alley in the Pignalle!"

"Bon, so I'll keep checking with the hospital, and call you as soon as I know something. I think perhaps I will use the mushroom as your excuse to visit South America. We might make you and Tom experts on mushroom types, culture and medical usage so if Berhetzel is into fungal research, perhaps we can trigger his curiosity and give you a tactical advantage. Also, so we don't lose track of you, we are going to give you a temporary GPS micro tracker by subcutaneous injection. Ouch! That will provide a level of security and safety in an area that is unsafe and never secure. They are no bigger than a grain of rice and will be removed when you return. We think also that Berhetzel likely had the man Robert sent to investigate in the area killed because he has not been heard from now in ten days. I won't chance losing you or the others. So now your job and Tom's is to become expert mycobiologists, good enough to convince a very nasty man that you are worth inviting into his lair."

Kate sighed heavily, "That sounds easier said than done, Jules. How are we going to become experts in such a short time?"

"You are going to start a crash course this afternoon, remotely, from your laptops where our people will familiarize you with scientific terminology, and common names. Once you are on your own, you have to be experts because, if you can't convince him, you will be dead, plain and simple."

"Plain and simple? You make it sound so cut and dry," Kate groaned. She was very uneasy about this plan but did her best to put on a brave face.

Chapter 69
Lufthansa Flight

Over the Atlantic coast of Florida

"The prisoner will stand for the verdict of the New Nuremberg Tribunal. Wilheim Berhetzel, a.k.a., Joseph Von Braun, you have been found guilty of crimes against humanity and nature, including capital murder, and other heinous war-related criminal activity. It is the judgment of this court that you will be extradited to the nation of Israel for an execution date to be determined after you are put on public display for the period of ninety days so the world can see what evil looks like face to face. The method of your death will be determined by a popular vote of the Israeli people and we are sure that… Dr. Von Braun… Dr. Von Braun, please wake up."

Berhetzel, startled by the Lufthansa flight attendant's gentle touch on his shoulder, gasped and flung her arm off his body with a violent push. Moments later he realized he had been only sequestered in a nightmare.

"Entschuldigung, Fräulein, I was in a very deep sleep. I have been really exhausted from my business trip."

"No problem, sir. Would you please return your seat to an upright position, we are on our landing approach now to Miami. We should be at the gate in forty minutes."

He smiled cordially at the attendant and pushed the positioning button causing the heavy first-class recliner bed to morph back into an upright captain's chair. He shook off the lingering effects of the black dream and accepted his preselected breakfast tray of juice, coffee, sausages, cheese and apple strudel. This probably would be his last real taste of Germany until he returned to her as ruler of the modern world.

There would be a short layover, going through customs, security, and then waiting in the Lufthansa First Class Lounge to board the next jet to Porto Alegre. Arrangements were in place for his men, armed as usual, to pilot him back to La Lupa on his luxury boat-barge which he kept ready at The Premiere, a discreet, high security private boat 'club'. Even though his vessel had sophisticated electronics, radar and an auto navigation and piloting system, he could not risk traveling through the dangerous Amazon River basin alone without a small army. His men would make sure everything he commanded was completed without question because they were former Nazis who understood the German system of command loyalty. They would make sure every order was accomplished whether they agreed with it or not, even if it put them at great personal risk. This Germanic trait was both an asset and a flaw because it could cause good men to unquestionably follow insane leadership, even into hell itself.

Berhetzel had kept tabs on Jean DuBois' condition using the hospital's social media information page, where family and friends could leave encouraging messages, get updates on a patient's condition and receive visiting hours and room locations. Sadly he noted the Frenchman's page indicated he was no longer under their care, no surprise to the Nazi; DuBois had been too ill to move and typically the French police would withhold reports of a death in cases like this from the media hoping to flush out perpetrators. The announcement of his death would only occur when they felt they had exhausted all their leads, all the while hoping the killer would make a mistake or fall into one of their silly traps. He was not stupid enough to be caught, but could not risk the possibility that even a blind squirrel will occasionally find an acorn. It really did not matter now anyway as he was heading home, home to the anonymous safety of the jungle where he had been mostly unmolested by outsiders for nearly seven decades.

Schmitt had a sleek black limo waiting for him in the ground transportation area of the Porto Alegre Airport. The uniformed chauffeur drove silently to the marina, parking close to Berhetzel's dock and his state-of-the-art vessel. He unloaded the bags and several boxes of carefully chosen foods, bottled water and assorted alcoholic beverages, including several good German beers. Schmitt had also cached several 9mm Sig Sauer handguns, automatic shotguns, one stun grenade, three smoke grenades, several machetes and a large amount of American dollars in a heavy locked duffle bag. The items were to purchase influence, or create it depending on the circumstances.

Berhetzel dismissed the driver and unlocked the cabin door's security system by punching in Hitler's date of birth as his passcode: 20-04-1889. The vessel's interior was a testament to his wealth, adorned with beautiful lacquered teakwood and highly polished solid brass. There was no smell of mildew, which accompanied so much of the jungle, but instead, the clean scent of citrus filled the spotlessly clean cabin. A generous, heavily tinted bulletproof glass surrounded the cabin and acted like mirrors, reflecting light away when the sun was its most intense, funneling in exterior ambient light on the darkest night to provide illumination as needed without using the vessel's generator or solar batteries. Collecting panels that lined the flat roof over the cabin provided ample energy for lights, fans, computing, and the air, water purification and conditioning systems. The hybrid engines could switch from diesel to electric automatically — or on demand — and could motor at full power in electric mode, in the tropical sun, silently, for extended periods of time. The boats jet thrusters gave it extreme mobility and its shallow draft gave it unmatched navigability on the Amazon's variable water levels. It could motor almost as fast as a decent powerboat or run in a stealth-like manner against the jungled shore, maneuvering in and out silently. With a camo net deployed, the vessel would disappear from sight, blending into its background.

Berhetzel went to the operations panel and fired up the diesel generator and it started with a soft hum. They would be very comfortable on the return trip in the Kevlar-armored vessel.

Hermann Schmitt, Berhetzel's top man at La Lupa, arrived by helicopter air taxi just as the orange-red sun appeared over the jungle canopy, stirring its noisy inhabitants. He had brought with him one of the original ex-pats and four of their native security soldiers from the plantation. They all were happy to see their benefactor again.

"Good to see you again, sir," Schmitt affirmed, giving Berhetzel a modified body salute — a nod of his bowed head with a rigid body, hands at his side and heals snapping together. The command respect was apparent.

"Danke, Hermann. I trust everything is good at home and your trip here comfortable?" inquired Berhetzel.

"Ya, the trip was fine, however we need to talk privately about a problem we had on the plantation. Can we walk?"

Hermann lit a cigarette, Berhetzel a Cuban Cohiba cigar and they started down the marina's long concrete dock pushing the screaming gulls to the air as they walked toward the clubhouse. There they sat in solitude on the deserted patio after ordering coffee from the only other person in the entire marina, a white-jacketed server.

"Well, Hermann, what is so important that we need a private conversation?" Berhetzel asked.

"We had a problem with the pigs and the crops while you were away. A gate was left unlocked and the pigs got into something or were perhaps infected with a disease, but that evening they went crazy and tore up the gardens destroying nearly all that we had planted. They were salivating wildly, running blindly and seizing. I was concerned about rabies or some other contagious disease so we shot all the field pigs, only preserving the sows and piglets in the farrowing house because they seemed unaffected. We burned the carcasses. They did do a lot of damage, but all the crops have been replanted. However, they also got into the fungus propagation garden.

It was severely impacted as the pigs trampled the patch down after rooting out all the mature plants. Apparently that's about the time they went wild and destroyed the main garden. I have tried to restore the patch by watering and heavy mulching, but so far only a few of the common species are popping up. The rarer ones, those with all the coloration, are missing even after ten days of cultivation. I'm not sure if we salvaged them or perhaps they will need more time to reestablish."

Berhetzel felt like he had just taken a blow to his gut. Those simple plants were proprietary to the manufacture of his life-sustaining discovery. All six fungal species were original, collected from the Alpine hills of Germany in 1943, each crucial to his formula, but since he had never bothered to analyze the role each played, he had accepted the empirical results of his fortieth death camp trial and never looked back. He now might have lost several critical species to the longevity formula and that made him furious.

"Tell me who was in charge of the pigs that day."

Schmitt replied quickly.

"That was Thomas. But I have already taken care of that problem, he joined the pigs in Hell. This wasn't something I could let go, I needed to make an example of him."

"Good, that was the correct response. I hope the bastard goes and burns in Hell, pigs or no pigs. Tell me, Hermann, how much of the processed extract do we have on hand?"

"We have 500ml of the thick concentrate waiting to be dehydrated and placed in dosing capsules. That is approximately enough for the entire compound to last sixty days or, if we limit it to management, then we are OK for about one year. I have already prepared two thousand placebo capsules of tea-stained corn and Brewer's yeast. You really can't tell the difference."

"Gut!" Berhetzel pronounced, pushing a cloud of blue-gray cigar smoke upward. "We must find some way to salvage that planting bed. I think we shall look for rotted tree trunk debris from many different hardwoods along the river as we travel back. Perhaps we will find some specific rotted media that will promote regeneration. If not, I will have to go back to Germany once more to recollect spore stock. I just hope they still grow where I found them!"

Hermann offered some encouragement.

"Those plants were established here for over sixty years, so I think that soil should be loaded with spores. They are our best bet as they have acclimated to our climate. New plants may not establish, especially if they are planted during the wrong season. I say let's concentrate on the existing plot for 60-90 days and, if we are unsuccessful, then go to plan B."

Berhetzel threw down the remainder of the expensive cigar and crush it out with the heel of his shoe.

"I want to get going now! There is so very much more to be done in the lab than I suspected. We'll pick up those rotted logs and when we get back, I want you to work on that bed, extend it and try the new media. Thoroughly vacuum the drying and processing lab with a clean filter bag so perhaps we might find old spores in the floorboard cracks or some other hidden area. We can then incubate the swabs of the bag on agar in the incubators. We must exhaust all our options here first."

Berhetzel then added, "You are a good man, Hermann, I am glad it was you in charge of La Lupa."

"Danke, Herr Doctor, coming from a great man like you, that really means a lot."

Chapter 70
Paris

Jules had been kept busy traveling back and forth between the hospital and the Pasteur. Jean was in a slow ascent from his coma and, although there was the distinct possibility that he would completely recover physically according to the physicians, they were giving a more cautious prognosis for brain function. This hospital was the best at treating the multitude of suicide attempts Paris experienced from failed young artists or desperate rejected lovers, and saved a record percentage of the damaged brains and bodies each year. The heroin epidemic also sent overdosed addicts to their care on a near daily basis so their advanced life support and detox equipment paid huge dividends to France's Life Insurance industry, which had underwritten much of Saint-Lazare's equipment-filled critical care suites. That investment had saved the insurance corporations untold numbers of Euros from being paid to the families of these desperate individuals. Thousands of lives and millions of Euros saved, resulted in the expertise and staff required to resurrect Jean or at least the physical part of him.

The Pasteur had also been using state-of-the-art equipment to analyze the blood left at the DuBois home. The technician's evaluation of the blood from the two victims and the perpetrator generated a lot of excitement when the shooter's blood showed the red cells alive with the reddish pigment hemoglobin so bright it appeared electrified. Those cell's hemoglobin levels were evaluated and then repeated to verify levels at nearly double the normal human sample, coming in at 28.6g/dl, the highest level they had ever seen for blood with a normal red cell count and hematocrit. Blood iron levels were correspondingly high. Jules felt it must be related to the PSP they had found in the original toxicology screen.

Fred Garret pulled Jules aside and walked him over to the electron microscope viewing panel where the screen was split into quadrants, each with a different numbered tissue sample.

"These samples reflect from left to right and clockwise, a normal control brain section, the original porcine sample, the Swiss police chief, and your Minister of Finance. What do you see?"

Jules had spent his post-graduate years studying clinical pathology at the Sorbonne and could recognize the pathology immediately.

"On all the screens, but your control, the tissue appears like scrambled egg whites. There is no cellular integrity or organization!"

Fred smiled, "I didn't think I would have conclusive proof this fast, but there is your evidence that the Minister was also a victim of Berhetzel. He was murdered as surely as the sun will rise in the east tomorrow. I guess now the question is, what do we do with this information?"

"We do absolutely nothing because first, no one will believe us, and second, the more bureaucrats and government types we have mucking about, the less likely we will get close to him and find out how he does this," Jules made his point by gently tapping on the expensive screen.

"And we don't know if he is a solitary madman or if he has an army of followers waiting to unleash this Hell on all of us. Find that out and only then do we cut off the head of this snake. Locate him and then eliminate him. If he has sleeper cells out there waiting for his orders, then we are screwed. We need to be very stealthy in our approach and, if possible, collect up all involved in one push because if they scatter like cockroaches, we could potentially have chaos anywhere."

Fred turned from the screen to face Jules, "Then I guess we had better get cracking!"

Chapter 71
Amazon River

Same day

Berhetzel's men piloted the vessel up the great river, dodging the heavy traffic near the busy port city's freshwater side. Once they had cleared the patrolled sovereign waters of Brazil and entered Argentina, the crew relaxed and pushed forward slowly into the jungled wilderness. They began scrutinizing the near shoreline with binoculars searching for decaying logs and tree trunks, picking up dozens, many sporting their own fungal saprophytes. Soon, the vessel's open stern was filled with the insect- and termite-infested lifesaving spore media, and Berhetzel gave the order to accelerate for the return home. The twelve-hour trip brought them at dawn to the crystal clear waters of the small tributary that led up from the opaque Amazon to the isolated La Lupa compound. As they approached, the compound's gigantic roosters seemed to announce their return as they crowed a loud symphony of welcomes to the awakening day as the new day's sun broke through the river's mist rising up from the cool waters. The jungle birds became alive with screams and nonsensical chatter, and the arboreal primates acknowledged also that it was indeed the start to a new day. These familiar surroundings, the very ones Berhetzel had often felt desperately trapped in during the last seventy years, now provided him a sense of peace and purpose. He was home to his work, his passion.

The first thing he wanted to see was the damage that was done by the pigs to the gardens. The corn, melons and sweet yams had all been trampled and shredded by the twelve-hundred-pound super pigs. Although he had engineered the pigs to grow to a massive size, he had also made sure they were programmed to be docile, easy-to-handle creatures. The toxic effects of the poisonous mushrooms had seemed, according to Hermann, to at first put them into a feeding frenzy as likely their hypothalamus was over stimulated, but after that initial effect, they fell into a blind rage as the brain's neurons started to fire rapidly and irregularly. Unfortunately, the attention of this toxic end stage had been directed back at the source of their illness, the fungal propagation plot. Berhetzel looked down on the once productive bed, and took a bamboo rake and gently pulled back the protective mulch Hermann had laid down to help incubate any remaining spores. What he saw was an area that had been totally uprooted and trampled, compacted down to a brick-like consistency. An anger and fear started to well up and he dropped down on his hands and knees searching for any minute sign of regrowth of the essential plants. There were several of the common varieties popping up through the destruction, a good sign, but none of the rare Alpine toxic plants were growing. He gently replaced the warm, sweet smelling, fermenting mulch with trembling hands and turned to Hermann who had stood back, nervously watching the man he knew only as Doctor Von Braun, fearing his response.

"We may be in trouble, Hermann. Only you and I know the magical properties of these simple plants that have sustained all of us over so many decades. Now most of our family here on La Lupa will have to receive the placebos as you suggested. If nothing else, it will be an interesting experiment to watch, the total withdrawal from such a powerful medication. After you distribute the fake capsules, I want you to search the Internet for potential sources of similar varieties of toxic fungi, although I seriously doubt that they would be available as many people might try to buy them to solve their marital problems, 'Here, my love, a nice mushroom omelet for your breakfast!'"

He laughed at his joke.

Hermann chuckled softly then offered an apology.

"I wish I had cut those animals open and pulled the plants from their guts, but at the time it never occurred to me. I was too focused on punishing Thomas, to make a real example of him! And I did. He squealed just like the pigs before I finished him, so weak and stupid. Tending livestock was all he was suited for and, in the end, he even failed at that simple task. I'm sorry, Herr Doctor!"

"Never mind that, now we must concentrate on getting this bed going again. The rest is history, and if we are lucky, maybe one of those logs we collected will help us get these plants reestablished. Get them up here, grind them up and expand the bed to the northeast. After they acclimate for several weeks we can try to inoculate them with the processing room cleanings and some of the soil from the original bed. We'll make all of that into a slurry and then spray it on the media. If in three months we don't have a positive outcome, then I will have to go back to those Alpine hills again. I want your daily reports on every detail, good or bad. Do I make myself clear, Hermann?"

"I will not fail you, Herr Doctor!" Hermann said, nearly automatically snapping to rigid attention.

Berhetzel turned away from his second in command and walked on the narrow path toward his beloved laboratory. Digging deep into his khaki linen pants' pocket, he located an old key ring that sported only five keys — one each for the lab, the provision storehouse, the weapon arsenal, his common bedroom-library key, and the override key to the alarm and communication systems. He located the one for the lab's rusted old heavy padlock and, after a brief struggle as the lock resisted his effort, it gave way with a solid click. He pushed the heavy, double-thick door open, letting the screened door slam shut behind him. The lab smelled of dead musty air with overtones of solvents and aromatic organic compounds. The old fluorescent lights sputtered, popping on with a groaning buzz and the overhead fans squeaked as they slowly revolved to a workable speed. Berhetzel pulled the bug cover off the window air conditioning, turning the unit on. Soon, cool, fresh air was filling the room.

On his flight home, Berhetzel had made a problem list of things he wanted to improve or change on his lethal weapon to make it more versatile and effective. He went to the blackboard that had been his historic papyrus for over six decades, and with an easy stroke, wrote out a list of problems in order of importance that he needed to solve. He stood back and looked at the tasks, thinking that he really did not care if the answers came in two months or two years as long as he had an unlimited supply of his magic mushrooms.

There on the board were listed tasks like simplify, user friendly, compact, total solar, disposable, mass produce, repeating action, facial recognition or DNA mode and, lastly, an automatic self-destruct feature. Mass producing this upgraded device would allow him to weaponize an army of mercenaries with a failsafe destruct feature that would prevent the invention from being separated more than ten meters from the soldier without Berhetzel's deactivation, preventing a sale of the weapon to be reverse engineered. Separate the man from the machine and both would be destroyed. The army he planned needed to be big enough to decapitate every major world government and military at one time so that in the immediate post-apocalyptic confusion, he could control arsenals, and media and communications, securing his Fourth Reich. Tomorrow's history would be his creation. God help anyone or anything that stood in his way.

Chapter 72
Paris, France

One day later

Jules' cell phone rang at four a.m., the Saint-Lazares Critical Care unit's nursing staff on the line. Per his request to be notified, they were calling as promised to report that Jean was rapidly returning from his medically induced coma. This might be his chance to affirm his love for the man who had been his best friend for so many years by finding out if Jean knew who did this to him and his father. Would his friend's brilliance be erased or would that incredible brain contain a recoverable memory that might confirm Berhetzel as their target? It was critical information that Jules needed prior to sending his American colleagues into the dangerous Amazon.

Susan was standing next to her father's bed leaning down closely, softly talking into his ear. She looked considerably better from the last time he saw her. Glancing up, she noticed him and lit up with a wide smile and ran over to him.

"Oncle Jules! They say he will recover fully and after a couple of months be as good as new!"

Jules gave Susan a fatherly embrace and declared softly, "I knew the good Lord would save such a faithful man! Now, I hope that he might be able to help me find who did this, who murdered your grand-père. Justice needs to be served just as Robert served his. I want the man who did this dead."

The unit nurse waved them over to the bed where Jean's eyes were moving rapidly and fluttering up and down, his jaw rotating, and lips motioning. The airway connector had been pulled from the tracheotomy site, and the small silicon and plastic port was open to room air and made a distinct click as the air mechanically moved in and out through the port's opening. Jean's respirations were becoming more automatic and involuntary as his brain finished freeing itself of the pharmacological cocktail that had protected it. His eyelids finally slowed their fasciculation and separated just enough to see his dilated pupils. Susan leaned over and gently kissed him on the forehead.

"Welcome back, Papa!" she declared softly.

Jules stayed back for several moments until Susan motioned him over to her father. Jean, unable to speak from the tracheotomy, signaled recognition of his old friend with a long blink of his eyes. He looked exhausted, but in those tired eyes, Jules saw a familiar fire that seemed to say, 'Ask me, ask me.'

Susan was crying tears of joy and the ICU nurse choked back her tearful relief. The attending physician entered the room and started flashing a penlight into Jean's eyes, auscultating his chest and checked various brain reflexes with verbal commands to lift or squeeze. The normally somber man broke into a wide smile joyfully exclaiming, "Bon! Bon!"

Jules returned to the bedside and knelt, leaning to whisper a prayer in Jean's ear. He cupped his friend's hand in his and said, "God's love has graciously spared you, my friend. Praise Jehovah and our savior Jesus Christ. Amen. Now, forgive me, but I must ask a single question. Do you recall? Was your assailant Wilheim Berhetzel? If it was him, please squeeze my hand."

There was a pause for several moments before Jean started to press his acknowledgment onto Jules' hand. The pressure was so firm and continuous that it sent a shiver of electricity through him. There was no doubt what his answer was.

Jules decided to try one more question. Again, leaning to his ear he asked, "One more thing Jean. Was it the older man or the younger man from the service records that did this? If it was the elder, please squeeze my hand now."

There was no response.

"If the younger, please squeeze my hand now."

Jean applied all the pressure he could muster in positive affirmation.

"Thank you, my friend, now you rest and tell no one of this. Please, for your safety, don't let on to anyone that you remember anything of that night. We will get him. Believe me, my friend, we will get this bastard!"

Jules only stayed another quarter hour and then excused himself when Jean fell back to sleep. He would contact his American team immediately to plan their trip to South America, because they now would know exactly who to look for and how he would appear — Berhetzel, a Nazi that time had forgotten. He was evil incarnate, evil of the absolute worst kind, and they needed to locate him fast and neutralize this threat to every living thing on the planet. The problem was, where exactly was he and how much did he already know about them?

Chapter 73
Pasteur Institute

Later that day

Jules called and arranged the working dinner for 1900 hours at the Plant Physiology and Pathology Department of the Pasteur now that he had Jean's confirmation of how Berhetzel would appear. After Fred Garrett's verdict about the cause of death of the Finance Minister, he had called Bernard Redare, a good friend that he could absolutely trust. Redare worked in the DGSI agency of France, equivalent to the United States Homeland Security Department, and he agreed to do a private review of the video surveillance that had been shot from every angle and of every square inch of the G8 ceremony. The surveillance had recorded, to a varying degree, every person's face that had passed into the secured viewing area. Jules scanned the service photo of Berhetzel and e-faxed it to Redare's cell phone. Twenty minutes later, his friend asked to meet Jules at his office in the Pasteur ASAP.

"You know, my friend, I could lose my job, my pension and maybe even end up in the Bastille for breaching Level 4 protocols without supervisory permission. I hope this is worth it!" Redare warned.

"I promise you, Bernard, if this wasn't critical to our national security or for that matter the survival of most species on the planet including humanity, I wouldn't ask such an important favor. There are way too many Nazis infiltrated into the fabric of every branch of our government waiting for a messiah to deliver them back into power. This might be their man. He is responsible for killing Robert DuBois and nearly killing Jean. There is a lot more to this, but suffice to say, we are on solid ground breaking the rules."

"D'accord bien," the analyst said placing a small thumb drive into Jules' desktop server, "here is the surveillance footage that the computer thinks shows your man. The software we use combines facial recognition along with behavioral tracing, which will focus, enlarge, isolate and enhance an individual while still reviewing the area for other possible perps. So, here you see a man who arrives before the majority, baseball cap pulled down to eliminate some features, sporting what appears to be a mustache, but when we enlarged that area, you see the adhesive strip just barely showing upper right? No human eye would detect that. Now, he makes a beeline for a spot that isolates him from the majority, while giving him a premium unobstructed view of the stage." He fast-forwarded the images.

"Just before the Minister's death, he pulls up and down a camera anticipating something, which I think was the unity arm link. OK, look at this. There is a nanosecond flash of some sort of brilliant energy from his camera, which was unlike the other cameras that were flashing off automatically, this as you can see, was projected toward the stage. Very fast, very intense. Watch, it looks to hit the Minister in the forehead when I enhance that image. Your man murdered him and only you and I know that. Look at this last image as the audience is pushing out through security. A woman bumps into your man and up goes that cap. He motions up to pull it back and there is the money shot. The computers give a 99.197% probability match."

The incredibly clear image showed a mustached Berhetzel, scar on right forehead, mole on left cheek, blue-gray eyes and sandy brown hair. The computer had estimated 1.93 meters tall and approximately 80 kg. The match to the original photos stunned Jules, the man had essentially not changed in nearly seventy years. He must have found the secret of eternal youth, perhaps it was the PSP. The man could be a genius mushroom head.

"Merci, Bernard. This is much more than expected. I am stunned by your technology. I trust you will keep this meeting our secret?"

"What meeting, mon ami? But if you ever want to know who is sleeping with whom, just give me a call. It's what we do best!" Bernard laughed, retrieving the thumb drive.

Kate, Tom, Brad and Joseph arrived just before the dinner meeting that Jules arranged to be catered in his office. He spoke while they ate.

"First, thank you for your patience over these last days while I sorted out Jean's situation, as well as the death of Albert Valedic, the deceased, or should I say murdered Minister of Finance. I'm going to give you a summary of what I now know and then open up the floor for discussion."

"You will be pleased to know that Jean has recovered enough to confirm with me that it was indeed Berhetzel who attacked them, and that he would appear as he did in the 1940s."

There was an audible reaction from the quartet sitting with Jules.

"He hasn't aged?" Brad asked, incredulous, as he choked on his sandwich.

"Correct. He has unbelievably unchanged after all these decades. I have a friend who works in high-level government security who has identified Berhetzel by using advanced technology, including facial recognition, and confirmed our man was at the G8 unity display. My contact also confirmed that Berhetzel used some device to murder Minister Valedic. He matched, totally unchanged, all the physical data we have from the Nazi service records. There must be a connection of his appearance to the PSP found in his blood from Jean's home. Quite possibly he is using some mushroom derivative to preserve his youth — that would cause a medical revolution, and it also gave me an idea for your cover to go into the Amazon."

"Kate, Tom and Joseph, you are now, by the power vested in me, a field research team from an American university, and will retrace Robert's Argentine colleague's suspected route before he disappeared. We are fairly sure that he located Berhetzel's location in Argentina along the Amazon or one of its tributaries. Satellite imaging suggests six potential sites where he may be located."

"So I think instead of knocking on doors and having possible drug warlords shooting your heads off, we will plant a series of stories in the international and local media about a team of young American scientists investigating the native healing of indigenous Amazon Indians using mushrooms and fungal plants and their potential anti- aging properties. You will be there trying to link North and South American medicinal mushrooms with European or Old World species, searching for a common denominator. Your young Sioux Shaman, Joseph, will be said to have generational knowledge of North American practices, and will help you find these unique species. This all must be done very carefully with attention to even the smallest detail because this is a region of the world infested with people who are hiding for one reason or another, including narcotic traffickers, political terrorists, human sex slavers and satanic cultists."

"So you will need to eat, drink and sleep fungi for the next week as we prepare you through this department to be world-class experts on these simple plants. Your lives will depend on your pulling off this elaborate charade."

"Also, just so you know, this mission is the sole responsibility of the Pasteur. Our goal is at a minimum to capture one of these devices to reverse engineer it. That way, we might be able to neutralize the weapon or build a better stronger one."

"My God, it sounds just like the nuclear arms race of the last century!" Kate exclaimed.

"Oui, that's exactly the scenario we wish to avoid. A new class of weapons, a portable 'death ray'. Mon Dieu!" Jules responded. "But," he continued, "if he has a programmable portable weapon like the one he used at the G8 ceremony, not a single specie on earth is safe from individual or mass extinction.

"There is a flip side, however, to that vision of its use, which is to preserve and develop that technology for good. My colleagues here in the Pasteur, my think tank, suggested that there is the potential to save lives by selectively eliminating diseases such as viral, bacterial or cancer by using the weapon to target and destroy them. The benefit to mankind might be enormous and the benefits to every species on the planet could be incalculable. We only need to figure out how it works."

Brad interrupted, "And whomever controls the technology will make a boatload of money!"

"Yes, my friend. The economic upside is tremendous, but then it would be used for good. Make it a blessing rather than a curse. We, at this Institute, are uniquely positioned to control it to become that blessing. We have the private resources to transform it from a murder weapon to a gift for humanity. However, if any government gets their hands on it, the resulting bioweapon arms race will make no one safe. I would rather see it destroyed than in the hands of the military. It absolutely must be repurposed as a weapon for good, not the instrument of evil."

"Assuming we can survive long enough to capture it," Kate interjected.

"I have arranged for two former French Foreign Legion operatives that will act as your guides, boat crew and protectors. These men are extremely intelligent, intuitive and resourceful. Plus, they are specialists in all types of weapons and explosives and are very, very tough! Like your Rambo."

Joseph was excited for the first time since the meeting had started.

"Back home we call that 'bad ass'. I really like having these warriors cover our backs, but I am concerned that I am the only one here without formal military firearms training. I mean, I can handle a hunting rifle and never miss, but I need to be up to speed on what weapons we will have available. Plus, I need some martial arts training just in case. I should be the one saving Kate, not the opposite. And after last night with Brad at the Crazy Horse, the training would have been helpful fighting off the young ladies. I'm sure things will be worse in the jungle!"

"Yeah, you might have to fight off a monkey or two or some hungry anaconda. Maybe the only squeeze you'll ever get," Brad laughed.

"OK, I'll admit I'm a little shy when it comes to women, but once those men train me, you better hide because I'm going to find you and whoop your ass just like we did Custer!" Joseph said grinning.

"Good luck getting my scalp, Tonto!" Brad said stroking his nearly bald head.

The good-natured ribbing seemed to break the tension of the meeting. Jules looked at the smiles from his group of 'volunteers' and was happy that this collection of intelligent and sincere Americans was going on the hunt for

Berhetzel. He was keeping Brad in Paris with him to monitor communications, GPS tracking, a duty they would share. Brad was the only one with small children so keeping him safe was a priority for Jules.

"There are several tasks to accomplish tonight. First, we are going to place your GPS transmitters just under your hairline on the back of your necks. I am told it is painless, but I would have an extra glass of wine just in case. Just don't quote me on the painless part. After that, we will familiarize you with your itinerary and the main geography, culture, politics, terrorist or crime families, as well as the toxic plants, animals and insects that could harm or kill you. So, if someone offers you a mushroom omelet, you better know whether it was made with a safe specie or not. It would certainly reinforce your so-called 'credentials' to know the difference. All in all, pretty routine stuff for you Americans, non?"

Kate rolled her eyes and gave Jules an 'are you kidding me' look, which caused Jules to burst out laughing.

"One more thing I want Kate and Brad to know is that the USDA has put you on paid administrative leave so you are assigned now to the Pasteur until further notice. Tom and Joseph, you are now considered independent contractors working for the Institute, and technically you could withdraw from the project if you want. I need everyone to know that you will be well paid for your efforts and will receive a very generous finder's fee if we stop this mad genius and recover the device and longevity formula. Everyone could exit this mission heroes and very, very wealthy. Is there any discussion on these points?"

"Jules, since I am technically in charge of our group, I will need to see some paperwork on that please." Kate explained.

"D'accord, Mon Chérie, but I am disappointed that you doubt me. You should trust me. Remember, I am French!"

"I love you and do trust you, but I need to make sure that things are on the level. I just can't risk that, in the end, we find out that we have done something illegal and are out of our jobs or worse," she said.

"I assure you, my friend, there will be nothing we will do that can cause you difficulty. We are in the end doing the work of the Lord. He is really your boss and all He is only asking you to do is a little overtime!"

Chapter 74
Berhetzel's Compound

The jungle felt more welcoming now than it had before his trip to Europe. The events on the continent had been exciting with all the strange twists including the confrontation with the DuBois men, the murder of the Avignon street punks, the elimination of the Swiss police chief, and that poor unsuspecting man in Miami who was the first human test in real time outside the Amazon. The Indian at the voodoo ceremony was calculated and programmed for days prior to that man's sudden demise, but the Miami test was spur of the moment and a bona fide field test using a paper napkin for the DNA source. Much more exciting than the planned execution of that drugged-out peasant.

Now he was going to refine and improve the original device, and began recalling the dozen or so drone versions from around the world that had carried out the original animal testing. He needed parts, and the drones had the basic version onboard that could easily be upgraded to a more effective model.

The small birdlike drones that were the greatest distance away, Berhetzel had self-destructed, only because he feared they could not be depended on to return safely. The others responded to his recall signal and, with the solar batteries charging more than twelve hours a day, they flew twenty-four hours a day at 20-30 miles per hour. All would return to La Lupa within three weeks. Their parts would then be scavenged to begin his mercenary's armory. The overwhelming greed for power fueled his passion to develop this army so when he finally ascended to his rightful throne, the world would worship him and pay untold sums of tribute to stay in his good graces.

One by one the machines returned as programmed to the compound, and Berhetzel marveled at how well they had functioned. Most came in on a full charge looking like the day he had sent the flock off to their GPS coordinates. He was so impressed he decided to scavenge only half of them and began to disassemble them to inspect their components for hidden wear and tear. Most of the parts were either Japanese or German made and he was amused at the irony of two post-war, destroyed nations providing him with the technology of his destructive power.

Berhetzel also made many trips to the mushroom garden where the plants were obviously struggling to reestablish themselves. He checked their progress every day or two by gently lifting and pulling back the old bed mulch and the fresh nutrient-rich plot that Hermann had built. He knew the plots would take time, and several species were reappearing, except the ones that had always struggled in the extreme Amazon climate — the colorful toxic Alpine varieties that would not regrow in either the old or new bed. He needed every one of the types in the correct ratio to produce the life-extending compound. To reformulate the compound could take years or possibly never occur, and without ample stores of the original mix, they would probably not live long enough to benefit from it anyway. It had only been three days off the original product and already the workers were showing symptoms of withdraw including severe vomiting and debilitating muscle cramping. If they declined too rapidly then he would be forced to travel back to Germany to hunt the hills for the elusive Alpine toxic varieties. He would have to have established beds long before he ran out. Otherwise, he could suffer the same fate as the rest of La Lupa.

One week after his return, Hermann came to the lab and knocked with excitement on the old wooden screen door.

"Herr Doctor, I was in the communications room doing my daily maintenance and I was monitoring the world news stations. I saw a story that I felt you would have great interest in! It was on CNN International and may repeat in the next hour. It seems there is a scientific research team heading to the Amazon very soon to try to find similarities between old and new world medicinal fungi."

"Is that so?" he said nonchalantly peering at his specimens.

"They claimed in the interview that the potential benefits from these plants is vastly underestimated and they may hold potential cures for cancer, Alzheimer's and aging, and will be the focus of billions in research in the coming decades." I found on the computer that the story is two days old so they must be recycling it now."

Berhetzel looked up and over his magnifying eyeglasses and turned to face Schmitt.

"So," he postulated, "if the story is two days in the can then it must, at a minimum, be at least three days after the interview. I need to review this story and see if we can use it to our advantage. Perhaps there are fungi right here under our noses that could substitute for or improve my formula. Review the recorded archive. As soon as that story is located, come get me — no matter what time it is!"

For being in the middle of the Amazon jungle, Berhetzel had created a state-of-the-art communication center with all the latest technologies. He understood the need to know everything about the state of the world's politics and especially the goings on in Germany. He studied new scientific postulates, reviewed medical journals and kept up to date on all the general cultural information that he could. He received no mail directly, but kept a post office box in Porto Alegre, where once a month he sent Hermann to retrieve a large collection of scientific papers and journals. He was probably the most remotely located up-to-date scientist in the world. The communication center he built was equipped with the latest satellite, computer and weather technology with upgrades to the system occurring on a regular basis. La Lupa had the ability to stay in contact with the world, but at the same time produce encrypted data and false location coordinates to hide her actual location. Their common GPS address put them 283 km north and 189 km west of their real address, and with their ability to disrupt communications within 50 kilometers at the push of a button, any invasion of La Lupa's security zone by intent or accident could be handled without a traceable electronic footprint. Entry into that secure zone would render any form of communication or navigation equipment useless. A true dead zone.

After a ten-minute search, Hermann found the story in the computer archive which recorded all viewed data for ninety-six hours, and then dumped it to accept new information. Berhetzel immediately came over to see the CNN report. The report was dated four days prior.

The reporter stood next to a sign that read 'La Forêt de Fontainebleau' with two men and a woman. One of the men and the woman appeared to be in their late thirties, while the other man, who looked American Indian, probably was in his early twenties.

The interview started with the reporter, "I am standing just outside one of the public entrances to the forest preserve surrounding the Palace of Fontainebleau just outside of Paris, France. It was the former residence and hunting lodge of French monarchs, but now is a historical reminder of the immense wealth and power that once was held by the aristocracy of France. Started by Louis VII and continued by his generations of heirs, the entire estate and surrounding royal hunting grounds cover nearly sixty-six square miles, and is one of the most revered forests in this part of France. It is home to royal stag, boar and partridge, which are now protected from harm in this recreational park. It is open season, however, for three researchers from the United States who hunt the lowly mushroom in its fields and woods, their last stop on their quest on this continent for potential life-saving fungi. Please tell the viewers why you are on this trip."

The camera panned slightly to the right and had Kate, Tom and Joseph filling the screen. Each had their names posted at the bottom of the screen and the cameraman focused on Kate as she spoke.

"Thanks, Mary. We are here on the second leg of what I would call a quest to investigate both the historical use of simple fungal plants in folk medicine and collection of specimens for propagation with potential medical properties that could lead to treatments or cure for some of the most dreaded destructors of human life. Many of the varieties that were recorded in medieval texts by physicians, scientists and sorcerers — some with detailed descriptions of properties and uses — have been ignored for centuries. New awareness of these ancient healing methods has brought renewed attention to these simplest of plants. Unfortunately, many of these varieties have disappeared from the developed world, possibly victims of acid rain, industrialization and the ravages of world war. We have identified at least ten varieties from this continent that we fear are now extinct. Please put up the graphic. Anyone who believes they recognize these mushrooms or mucors, please contact our project office at www.medicalmushroomssavelives.gov/cdc.us. We are now heading to the Amazon River basin, one of the most complex environs in the world. There, we will search into the interior for new species or others similar to the possibly extinct European types. We need your viewer's help — any regional knowledge could be helpful. To my right is Mr. Joseph Blackfeather, a Sioux shaman with generational knowledge of the vast healing powers of these plants and can detect the medicinal properties by taste, smell and texture. He is our ace in the hole."

The camera went to Joseph as the reporter asked, "How did you acquire these skills, Mr. Blackfeather?"

Joseph looked directly into the camera.

"It is a gift from my ancestors who look over my people. I can sense the presence of the important mushrooms much as the hog finds the truffle. I can't explain it, but am compelled to do it."

Tom jumped in.

"We feel there will be billions spent on these new discoveries developing life-saving compounds, creating thousands of jobs and improving human and animal life by curing cancers, stopping Alzheimer's disease and extending human longevity. Ironically, we may be looking for the fountain of youth Ponce de Leon searched for. So much potential for good from such simple plants."

"Well, good luck to you all in your search for these potentially life-saving plants. This is Mary Imke reporting for CNN International."

The screen went back to the start box and Berhetzel looked to Schmitt and said, "Three of our trampled plants were shown on their extinct specie graphic. That is very bad. We need to find a way to meet with these Americans while they are in the Amazon. Perhaps they can provide for us alternative sources of fungi that we could substitute or potentially improve on the compound. Gather all the information you can on these three, and if they check out, they perhaps will be our first welcomed guests in over sixty years. Yes, maybe the first and probably the last."

Chapter 75
Plant Path/Physiology

The Pasteur

Paris

"Congratulations to you all for completing your crash course in field research protocols, fungal plant identification and propagation, emergency communications and self-defense, and most importantly, how to identify and avoid plants, animals and people that will kill you. Now you can vacation safely in South America," Jules laughed.

"Kate, you are my star student with a near perfect score in all areas of training. You should do most of the talking in any serious discussion about Mycology and keep an eye on these other two.

"Tom, you did well also, and will be more involved in the search and propagation aspect of this operation. Joseph, your research on folk and Native American medicinal uses and compounding will give you credibility if challenged. All in all, you are one hell of a team."

"Damn right we are!" Joseph called out. The trio was very proud of their work, but still a bit unnerved about what they were about to embark on.

"I know you all are apprehensive about the trip, but Brad and I will have your backs. Plus, we are sending the FFL operatives ahead of you, so with your preparation skills and God's protection, you should be fine. I have also arranged a second interview once you land in Porto Alegre. That was Berhetzel's most likely point of immigration in 1945, and hopefully he set up shop relatively close to there. We have set a maximum of twenty-one field days, starting with the initial cover work and then a more aggressive search for Berhetzel. If you fail in your quest for Berhetzel, we may have to turn over everything we have to French and American authorities, and I am sure they will locate him in an unrefined way. Most likely resulting in the loss of important data, but worst of all, sending the discoveries back to within reach of those imbedded Nazis in Paris and Washington."

"I think I am ready," Joseph said proudly, "I am in the best physical condition of my life, I am trained in martial arts and all sorts of weaponry including explosives and garrote wire. I may not be a bad ass yet, but I am at least half assed bad. One other thing I bring with us is my ancestor's protection. We will probably need their help!"

"I wish I was going because I am truly a 'fun guy', but I will be ready for whatever you need, stuck here, lonely, in beautiful, delicious Paris. I'll do my best to put on a brave face. Get it, Hawkeye? A Brave face!" Brad joked.

"Yes, Kemosabe!" Joseph laughed.

"D'accord. I'm glad everyone one is in such fine spirits. I have a special guest now to give you some insight on the type of evil we are facing. She was one of Robert's closest friends, a Dachau camp survivor, who has dedicated her adult life as a psychiatrist dealing with PTSD of those who survived the camps and other atrocities of the war. She had heard the name Berhetzel spoken by survivors over the years, and has firsthand knowledge of the horror factories and the people behind them. Dr. Maria Schencke is now retired, but agreed to speak to you about who and what you face."

The shrunken old woman who had sat away from the group, pushed on her cane, teetering for a moment before she stood, her back hunched, both hands locked tightly on her cane, almost Yoda like. Her eyes were clear and voice steady, resolute.

"You all are so young. This I feel may be both an advantage and a liability for you. On the plus side, he may not see you as a seeker because you are not of my generation. But I also think you may have a Steven Spielberg or Hollywood image of the people who perpetrated this horror on millions during the war. I would toss those cliché stereotypical images from your minds and listen to my advice. You will find Berhetzel to be charming, polite and gracious, but understand that is only the mantel of his evil. To anyone, these perpetrators will not look like an evil entity, but more likely kind, caring and benevolent. Believe me, they will stop at nothing to protect their interests. Your existence means nothing to him — make one simple mistake and I guarantee you will be eliminated. They don't kill, you see, they eliminate. He will have no conscious so don't try to bargain with him. I would say if you have the opportunity to kill him, do it. Do it before he kills you because, in reality, you would not be killing a human, but a disciple of Satan himself."

Kate looked to Tom as the doctor spoke, subconsciously playing with the small crucifix she always wore. She whispered a prayer for protection against Satan and his disciples and for Divine guidance in finding this potential destroyer of all life on the earth. "Your will be done," she finished.

"Remember," Dr. Schencke continued, "these men were trained by the worst of the worst demonic evil doers in the history of the modern world.

They are the destroyers of life and feed their soulless existence by eliminating godly people from their world. God Almighty's prophets have warned us of their existence since the beginning of time. We may never fully stop them all, but each victory we accomplish is a win for the creator God. Assume nothing; take nothing for granted. Your mission is to stop this 'Destroyer'. God bless you in your quest. Listen for His voice, He will guide you!"

Chapter 76
Porto Alegre, Brazil

Two days later

When the trio arrived at the Southern Brazil port city, the weather was changing from warm, late spring to the start of a hot summer. The air was thick with humidity and the temperature stayed above eighty, day and night. People dressed for the near tropical weather by wearing loose, light cotton or linen clothing, and a high percentage sported woven straw or Panama style hats to keep the intense sun directly off their faces.

A major portion of Porto Alegre's population appeared of mixed European descent, as the area had an historic connection to Portuguese settlers and German immigrants that had settled in the area around the mid- to late 1800s, and grew the city to 1.5 million inhabitants. That European heritage was also apparent in the city's architecture and the food people ate — heavy sausages, beef and pork, potatoes, and lots of bread, beer and seafood. The clothing the trio had brought from France was way too heavy, so Tom suggested they find apparel more suited to the humid heat, and something that didn't scream 'foreigners'. A side trip to a small market provided what they needed at very minimal cost.

The two French Foreign Legion men had already been on site for two days, working the docks and marina bars searching for and interviewing local river guides who rented their boats out. They were going to meet with Kate in the evening to discuss their suggested hire and go over their risk assessments. The Amazon was a wide and murky river and once they were on it, there would be little distinguishing one jungled area from another without experience. The region was also notorious for its poor hit or miss communication with even a high fail rate for the new sophisticated SAT phones and SAT-NAV systems. Without a good guide, there was a real possibility you could end up in someone's backyard who may take offense at your intrusion. Deadly offense.

They did their media interview mid-afternoon and it went well with a South American spin, lighter and less dramatic, with the reporter giving a 'don't get lost or eaten' warning. Then they checked into the Hotel Alegre that Jules had reserved for the two FFL men and the Americans, who changed into some of their new clothes for an evening of tapas restaurant and bar hopping. The trio toured the city eating and drinking across the vibrant college district until late into the evening, when Kate insisted that they go into to a rocking dance club. Tom was not a dancer so he sat on the sideline while Kate and Joseph moved to the hot Latin music, blending into the young crowd. After Kate sat, several young ladies kidnapped Joseph onto the dance floor, putting their best seductive moves on the young Sioux.

"I don't think he is getting out of here soon, so I'm going to snap a photo of him and those girls so he can tease Brad later. And just in case they disappeared with him, you know, a photo to show the cops."

Kate giggled, just a little tipsy. She walked onto the dance floor dodging the energetic Latinos and cupped her hand over his ear informing Joseph they were heading back to the hotel, be safe, and slipped him a hotel card.

Tom and Kate left and strolled hand in hand, people watching, back to their hotel. It was apparent from the growing street vibe that the sultry night was just getting revved up.

Back at the hotel, the couple passed through the bar lounge and saw the FFL men they were to meet, sitting with a tanned middle-aged man with a weathered complexion, off to a corner of the bar. The French men stood immediately, almost to attention, as Kate approached their table and the other man stood, removed his Panama hat and bowed his head slightly in a subservient manner.

"Bonsoir, Jacque et Dennis, how is your evening going?" Kate asked.

Jacque, who was the senior operative, responded enthusiastically, "Bonsoir, Doctor Kate, very well, thank you. We are enjoying ourselves, eating fine cheese and sausages, and drinking this very good local beer."

"I'm glad you are having a good experience so far, but that won't last much longer. We need to find that guide and head inland," Kate reminded the team.

"Ah, well I have good news for you! I believe we have found our guide and, with your permission, I would like to introduce the man I think is best suited to pilot us. He has travelled these waters for many years for his business and participated in scientific excursions multiple times. He has a fine vessel that can easily accommodate all of us and our equipment. Plus, he could have us in the field after securing and loading provisions by noon tomorrow. I would like to present to you the man we feel is best suited to provide us safe transport because of his vast experience in the Amazon basin — Monsieur Hermann Schmitt."

Chapter 77

Hermann Schmitt had always been a good listener and was proud of his resourceful nature and intuition when a useful opportunity presented itself. Berhetzel, who he only knew as Dr. Josef Von Braun, had seen those leadership qualities and had put Schmitt second in command, in charge of the day-to-day management of La Lupa. Everything that was asked of him, Schmitt completed ahead of any proposed goal and was always done perfectly. He was a man who could be trusted with responsibility.

As one of the original four men Berhetzel had hired to accompany and protect him on that freighter trip to South America, he had, like all the others assumed a new identity, leaving his past crimes to be forgotten in Germany, a shadowy escape from Justice. Not one of those men ever discussed the war, their families, past lives or, for that matter, the future. They lived in a perpetual limbo, lives extended unnaturally by Berhetzel, trapped by their past in a place with unlimited future.

Schmitt had left Marie, his beautiful wife and three blonde, blue-eyed girls under the age of ten, to fend for themselves in Berlin as the war was colliding to its finish. Each day, he restrained himself from logging on to the compound's computers to find out if any of them had survived the revengeful Russian capture of the Nazi capital. For years trying to remember their faces was a major focus of his down time and each passing year faded that memory. His wife Anna, if she had survived the Russian soldiers, would be in her late nineties, and his daughters would be in their seventies. So thanks to those mushroom capsules, he would now appear like one of their sons.

During the war, Schmitt had been an SS officer whose job was to root out Jews from their hiding places and warrens, and get them transported to the death camps. Initially, he had convinced himself that relocating them was for their own safety, an aide for their survival. In that role he was very convincing, assuring the unsuspecting that he was providing refuge for their survival and that he was not an agent of their deaths. Tens of thousands believed him and were relocated to the camps without much resistance. But as the war progressed, the Jewish population realized they were being systematically exterminated, and his lies were not believed by many. Panic and hysteria erupted, and he became angry, physically abusive, and verbally insulting, never giving his victims a break. He went from a solider just following his orders to an angry man who justified his job by loathing and despising his victims.

It had been his idea to hang around Porto Alegre and wait for the possible arrival of the American scientists. If that happened, he would find a way to gain their confidence and either steer them to Von Braun, if they appeared credible with useful knowledge, or keep them away from La Lupa if they were not going to bring anything of value. There would be some risk putting himself in a situation where, if something went wrong, he would be outnumbered, but he couldn't think of a reason why they would turn on him as long as he kept a humble profile. Only if he determined that their knowledge would contribute to the restoration of the mushroom plot, would he risk exposure and direct them toward the compound.

So far, he had taken them on a route away from the compound and they had found a number of interesting fungal plants that, surprisingly, he had never seen in all the years he had lived in the Amazon. The Americans had a small notebook computer, which they used to photograph the collected specimens and utilizing something similar to a facial recon software, identify the plant and its qualities. The computer gave each a scientific name, class, and properties, and labeled it safe or toxic. Several were listed as unknown and a warning flashed 'ASSUME TOXIC'. They took extraordinary care to package and seal the specimens in what looked to be specialized transport media, and joked often about how many potentially life-saving plants they were discovering. The Indian, Joseph, was quiet and spent time meditating. He was always the first off the boat to start the field work as if he couldn't stand being trapped on the water. One of the Frenchmen that he assumed was a bodyguard against kidnappers or drug warlords, had been bitten by a spider on the first day, and had been feverish and nauseated for twenty-four hours. But he took a pocketknife, cut out the infection and then cauterized the wound using silver nitrate powder without so much as a flinch. Schmitt knew he was the man who would have to be eliminated first if they ended up at the compound.

So far, the easy pace of the trip was starting to bore him. He stayed on the boat waiting while they went out and searched, and that's when he would contact Von Braun and report in. The Doctor was getting very anxious to see the collected specimens and really wanted a look at that valuable identifier computer, which assigned names and properties to the plants. Finally, after Hermann convinced him these scientists were legitimate and had found rare or unknown specimens, he gave him permission to move closer to La Lupa with their exploring..

While Schmitt moved upriver, Berhetzel had rooms prepared for his future guests, and had the main house prepared for entertaining. There they would talk and discuss their finding and drink his imported wine, drink homemade beer and sip smooth maize whiskey. In the communications and computer room, he retested the self-defense radio and satellite signal-jamming program that would cause a dead zone perimeter to extend for a 50-kilometer zone around the compound. In the dense jungle surrounding the hidden compound, they would appear invisible to both the eye and to the ear.

After that first week and with Von Braun's blessing, Schmitt suggested to Kate that they reverse direction and head upriver, bringing them closer to the compound. They continued to make stops on the small tributaries where access to land was easy and more specimens were added to their collection. Kate, who certainly was the boss, called a meeting of the crew to discuss returning back to Porto Alegre to offload the specimens and perhaps return to the States. At that moment, Schmitt knew he had to get them to La Lupa and decided to find a pretense to get them there. He sent a message to Von Braun that he was going to fake engine difficulty and tell them he needed to stop at a client's dock to arrange repairs and to initiate the radio security system. As he approached, he would signal his arrival with three long blasts on the vessel's air horn.

Schmitt was bringing his benefactor treasure in the form of the simplest plants, and five unsuspecting guests who certainly would make the coming days very exciting for him, especially with his plans for the woman.

Chapter 78

Kate could feel the crew's excitement grow with each new specimen of jungle fungi they collected. What had started as a con to validate them as research scientists and smoke out Berhetzel had actually developed into a true voyage of discovery. They literally had a boatload of specimens, many of which the computer had identified as 'unique or unknown'. The pharmacological significance of these new varieties was indeterminable in the field, but each held the potential to treat or cure a child's terminal disease, and that made all the time and trouble they had put into this elaborate ruse worth it. Onshore, away from Schmitt, Kate called the group together for a private discussion.

"Well, everybody, we have been collecting a lot of new fungal specimens that I'm sure the Pasteur will enjoy playing with, but I'm beginning to think either Berhetzel is too smart to try to contact us or we are entirely looking in the wrong direction. Jules' theory was that he would have stayed fairly close to his supply lines in Porto Alegre for the obvious reasons and, if he extended himself farther up the Amazon, he would need a larger staff to run errands and provide security. With a large staff comes the risk that one of the employees could expose them either intentionally or by accident. One man, especially an old man, would have difficulty preserving his anonymity. I don't know about you all, but I'm ready to head home and get a soak in the tub while munching on a McDonald's hamburger and fries. God help me!"

Joseph spoke up. "I know exactly how you feel about home, I'm missing prime hunting right now, but the reality is, if Berhetzel truly is a man of surprises, maybe we just haven't looked in the right direction. No one questions he is a mad genius so maybe he hides away from civilization alone or rules his world with an iron fist. He is a Nazi, for God's sake. Currently, we are only poking here and there while waiting for him to contact us. Well, maybe he's too smart for that. I haven't sensed any evil so far and I've been calling on my ancestors to guide me every day in my meditations. I say turn around, head upriver and check out the larger tributaries that could support boat travel for delivery of supplies. Put a limit on it if you want, but let's stop wasting time pussyfooting around!"

"I agree," Tom added. "This river goes on for 4,000 miles and we have been concentrating on less than five percent of that. I think Berhetzel would have gone well beyond the civilized zone in 1945 because he had a lot to hide and an agenda to accomplish. I say we head the opposite direction, up this damn muddy highway, to a point three times the distance we have already probed. Then work our way back down checking the tributaries for evidence of human activity or settlement. Keep up the ruse of field sampling, but only in what we will call unique environs to the ones we just explored. Kate, I would contact Brad and ask him to have Jules find a way to rerun both interviews and perhaps produce an audio version for radio broadcasts. Maybe put a spin on it that they have lost contact with us and are concerned. You know, let's stir the pot a little!"

"No one should be discouraged," Kate said, "look at what we have accomplished. Thirty-one new or unique fungi, the variations among them are astounding! Some really beautiful, and others pretty grotesque in appearance. I particularly like the petite toxic, red-orange inverted umbrella mushroom, and those strange exposed brain tissue forms that look gross but smell seductive. The mucors that seem to slide along from spot to spot are intriguing. We have done a good job propagating them on that specialized media we brought and all our observations on soil pH and canopy cover will help in their propagation, so we have not wasted our time here. Someone will benefit from our efforts!"

Back at the boat Kate called Schmitt over and gave the order to head upstream until she told him to stop. He immediately obeyed putting the vessel on a rapid push upstream.

He did so smiling to himself. His cherries were now ripe for picking and on their way for delivery to Von Braun!

Tom watched the jungle become more of a wilderness as they moved away from the coast into the interior of Argentina. They were now in a literal windless steam bath with hoards of biting insects obscuring their vision, discouraged but not repelled from feeding on their blood by the military grade DEET they applied several times a day. Ticks would still find a way to attach, dropping on them from the tree canopy like a drizzling rain so they all took oral Doxycycline and sprayed permethrin on top of the DEET as a precaution. The FFL guard who had taken the spider bite also had several leeches attach near his groin after spear fishing for dinner, earning him the nickname 'Unlucky Pierre'.

The torrents of rain became refreshing breaks as the clean water cooled them and obliterated the clouds of insects. After three days motoring into the interior, they had made 500 kilometers of upstream movement and Kate gave the stop order. Joseph who had experienced two restless nights with visions plaguing his sleep, believed they must be getting close. He didn't trust Schmitt because he wouldn't look the young Indian directly in the eyes. The dreams seemed to be warning him of multiple dangers and his gut told him Schmitt was involved in some way. His grandfather seemed to be near, his presence shadowing the trio.

They started short excursions into the abundant tributaries that drained into the main artery stopping to search for fungal plants, but eyeing the areas for evidence of recent human activity.

On the fifth day they returned to boat in a heavy drenching downpour. Schmitt tried to start the engine and pull away from the tie-up when the engine started to cough and miss, chugging irregularly, pushing thick, black smoke out of the tall exhaust pipe. He stopped, tried again with the same result. Feinting concern, he let the vessel drift into the main river and dropped anchor. He then disappeared into the sub deck engine area with an old beat up tool chest.

After two hours of tinkering with the engine and failing to get any kind of normal power, covered in grease, he called the group together. "I apologize for the trouble, but it appears we have a defective valve at minimum and some water in the engine block. I can tinker with it, but we really need a good diesel mechanic and there are only two choices for that. One, is to return to Porto Alegre using my two electric trolling motors I keep for backup power to assist the diesels, not a bad choice since at least the current would be in our favor. My guess is about five long days, no stopping. There is an alternative place we might try, about 60 kilometers upstream from here. It would take about twenty hours or so of travel. It belongs to an old client who keeps a diesel mechanic on staff to be sure his many boats and generators are always up and running."

"Can we make it against the current?" Tom asked.

"I think if we hug the shoreline, out of the main force of the river, we can progress nicely. That also would put us close to shore if the engine problem gets worse," Schmitt replied.

"Well, I would rather try to fix it locally than risk the five day trip all the way back to Porto Alegre, which would essentially end this project, so let's go," Kate ordered.

Schmitt fired up the diesel amid a cloud of smoke and exaggerated engine chatter. He set the two trolling motors close to each other and plugged them into the boat's electrical system and set one of the FFL men to guide their push upriver.

Tom, who had been in the main cabin, came out and moved the on-deck cots and seating around to reduce the clutter. He turned to Kate who was talking to Joseph and smiled at the cloud of black exhaust barely clearing their heads.

"Why do I feel I'm in the movie 'Jaws' with the great white chasing the Orka dragging those yellow barrels behind him? You hear it? That's John Williams' score playing," as he mimicked the famous theme. The analogy was more real than they knew.

Mid-morning the next day, Schmitt informed Kate that the next tributary would lead them to their repair dock. She hurried to get cleaned up a little and asked the men to do the same.

They noticed water at the mouth of the feeder river entering the Amazon was clear, clean and churned in clouds as it married with the great river. Moving slowly with the diesel engine off, the Americans marveled at the crystalline water with all the visible fish, crabs, crayfish and bivalves living in the water. Turtles and frogs littered the downed trees and multicolored lily pads. A cooler wind pushed down the waterway and it seemed fresh and pure. This Eden-like feel gave Joseph the surreal sense that the spirits of this place were welcoming them, the question was whether they were friendly or evil?

Schmitt let loose with three long blasts on the boat's horn, and the jungle became alive with the protests of the Psittacformes, fluttering about in a verbal chaos. Monkeys howled while positioning themselves to get a better look at this invader. Two European looking men carrying shotguns appeared running toward the large dock and, recognizing Schmitt, shouted greeting in a German dialect Kate was unfamiliar with.

They sprinted to the dock, tying the boat securely and leaned down, shaking hands with Schmitt while eyeing Kate and the others. Schmitt turned to his passengers and smiled widely announcing proudly, "Welcome, my friends, to La Lupa, the home of Dr. Josef Von Braun."

Chapter 79

Schmitt was the first off the boat, grabbing one of the men's hands to steady him up the dock's metal ladder. After greeting each other with funny lighthearted insults, he called to Kate and assisted her and the others up and off the boat. The birds and monkeys had settled down by then and the area assumed a peaceful, refreshing ambiance. The ground around the dock was covered in a course dark green St. Augustine type of grass, and had been cut and maintained like a fine golf course. A long lane of this grass led away from the dock providing them, for the first time in nearly two weeks, a place to stretch their legs without vegetation obstructing their movement, crawly things trying to bite or vines tripping them up. Both sides of the lane were protected from the sun by huge moss-laden live oaks, which cast inviting cool shadows.

"Come on," Schmitt said, "I'll take you up to the compound. Everything on the boat will be safe."

After walking up the cool lane about 300 meters, they could see an old high perimeter fence of heavy gauge metal pickets, covered in flowering vines, topped with two strands of rusted razor wire that spiraled down its length. Two thick solid wood doors of what looked like mahogany, sported huge hand-forged hinges and locks, and was colored with tangled flowering vines. The hinges were badly rusted and it was apparent the doors hadn't been secured for years. Two guard towers above either side of the old doors were deteriorating from age. It looked like, at one time, this had been a heavily defended facility.

Schmitt walked them through the main gate and into the beautifully landscaped courtyard with its marble water fountain, statuary and majestic royal palms. Giant peacocks strolled leisurely across the lawn exposing their mammoth fanned tails while parrots sat on perches preening nervously while keeping one darting eye on the visitors. The red clay-tiled, stuccoed house was surprisingly large, but modest in design and sat just behind the courtyard. The door and windows were protected by decorative, blacksmith-forged iron bars. They could see behind the house a smaller building with solar panels on the roof and multiple antennas sprouting up like weeds from around the panels. Wires ran up to a 30- to 40-meter high red and silver antenna tower that sported several small satellite dishes pointed toward the heavens. Directly behind that building, was a second more modern electrified fence with sliding operating gates that was separated into two areas. One side looked to be a cultivated garden with rows of very tall corn and trellises of cucumber-sized pole beans, and on the opposite side was sub-fencing with paddocks and pens for livestock. There appeared to be cow-sized goats foraging between the pens, and turkey-sized chickens that pecked alongside the goats, greedily eating the insects the hungry goats flushed out. Tom and Kate stood drop jawed staring at the overgrown animals while straining to get a better look. Schmitt laughed at their amazement, but directed them to the house entrance. He reached through the Iron Gate, and hammered a greeting on the portico door with its heavy brass gargoyle knocker. A slender, older native Indian man dressed in a clean, white linen shirt and pants pulled open the wood door and unlatched the protective Iron Gate.

"Herr Schmitt, it is so nice to see you! The Doctor is so very pleased you are here. The dock has already sent word up to him of your arrival and he is finishing his day's work in the laboratory, so he can greet you and your friends properly." He was playing his part perfectly.

"Gracias, Ramon, we are going to need some help from Carlos on my engine, but I think he is already down there tinkering. May I present Dr. Kate Vensky, Dr. Tom O'Dell and Joseph Blackfeather, who are on an American expedition collecting potential medicinal plants. I'm sure Dr. Von Braun and they will have a lot in common! Now, I must go to my vessel to see what Carlos' diagnosis is."

"I am pleased to meet you and if you would be so kind to relax in our courtyard, I will bring refreshments. Then if you would like to clean up, the house will be at your disposal."

The trio walked over to some wooden lounge chairs with rush seating and backs, and relaxed under the cool shade of the tall palms. Kate looked to her watch to check the time in Paris and decided to call Brad to let him know they were OK and would appear stationary on the GPS for a while. The call failed.

"I guess we are still in a dead zone," she complained. "Brad will just have to figure it out for himself."

"The sooner we are out of here the better, this place gives me the creeps. You know the 'Island of Dr. Moreau', Man and Beasts? Just what the heck are those animals? Joseph said.

"Good question, we really might not want to know. Hopefully we will only be here a couple of hours, then I say let's go home. I'm tired, dirty and since we have had no luck contacting Berhetzel, I think it's time Jules turned this over to the professionals who I suspect will get the job done with drones or guns blazing," Tom added.

"Well at least the specimens we collected might do some good. I'm fine with that. How about you Joseph?" Kate added.

"I say let's get the hell out of here. Nothing good is going to come from persisting. Besides, I need to ride my horse."

Ramon exited the house balancing an enormous sterling silver tray full of plates of sausages, cheeses, fruit, fresh warm bread, butter and jam. He then returned with ice cold sodas, tea, lemonade and beer. He smiled as he watched the first guests he had ever served at La Lupa dive into the delicious treats.

After they ate, Joseph and Kate pulled their hats down and drifted to a light nap. Tom got up and decided to go to the dock and see what the diagnosis was from the mechanic. As he approached the boat, a plantation guard sat in the wheel house and he could hear some universal curse words coming from the bowels of the boat, and Jacque, who was at the stern of the vessel dragging on a cigarette, shook his head in obvious frustration when he saw Tom approaching. He motioned to Tom to come over to speak.

"I don't think they are having much luck down there," he said quietly. "I hear a lot of banging and swearing going on, but now it seems the damn engine won't even turn over. The way this is playing out is a bit disturbing. We are stuck here, essentially helpless, incommunicado, while this vessel has gone in an instant from running perfectly to a piece of crap. I need to keep a close eye on these birds so when you go back to the compound, tell Pierre that I think this is a situation twenty-nine. He will understand and act appropriately. Tell the rest to be on alert and be aware of everything going on, OK?"

Tom didn't bother to check with Schmitt on the repair, but hurried back to carry the warning to the others. Pierre didn't seem too surprised when Tom made a beeline to him as he stood leaning in the shade against the house and received Jacque's warning.

He walked over to the others and explained quietly.

"My colleague feels that we are in a dangerous situation and since he is a threat assessment operative, we better listen and be on the lookout. I need to get to the boat and retrieve my weapon, but I shouldn't leave you here alone."

Joseph jumped up and volunteered to go to the vessel and find a way to discretely get the 9mm Glock the Frenchman had hidden in the bait well. As he approached the dock, Jacque signaled for him not to talk and pulled the Glock out of its hiding place and also handed over his compact survival knife, and pointed to Joseph's cowboy boots. The young Indian slipped the knife

275

in between his linen cargo pants and the boot wall and tucked the 9mm in his waistband under his loose fitting tee shirt, a safe and well-concealed spot. Joseph walked back quickly up the grassy lane and saw the others were now up and wandering around the courtyard orientating themselves.

"Here's your Glock," Joseph indicated, discretely palming the gun over to Pierre, "no problem getting it. Schmitt and the others were screwing around in the engine area, including that topside man who had been eyeing Tom when he went down to the boat."

The manservant Ramon returned for the third time and told the group that Dr. Von Braun would greet them in the library and would they please follow him into the house. They entered the large wood-paneled room and were seated on brown leather sofas that faced a massive, dark gray, cut stone fireplace. A bottle of fine port wine sat on a side table with five glasses. Von Braun entered the room with a hearty greeting.

"Welcome, welcome to La Lupa. I am Josef Von Braun, the owner of this humble scientific outpost in the middle of nowhere." He slowly walked over as they stood to greet him.

Expertly disguised in appearance, not one of them knew they were face to face with the man they sought. Berhetzel had taken great care to transform his visage. His head was shaved, he sported a silver gray, closely cropped beard and he had hidden the mole and scar with great care. Deepening his sun wrinkles to make him appear haggard. He also wore a black eye patch over his right eye. He walked slowly, bent severely over a native wooden cane, stepping deliberately with a slight shuffle. He was dressed in a white guayabera shirt, neatly pressed white linen pants and white alligator skin loafers.

"You must forgive me for my bad manners for not personally greeting you immediately on your arrival, but I was at a critical point of my daily work and like your Thomas Edison, I get so involved I lose track of myself. Please, please, sit down and introduce yourselves."

Kate stood first just after sitting on the sofa and started explaining who they were.

"My name is Dr. Kate Venzsky, the leader of this expedition. My background is Veterinary Medicine, but currently I am on loan from the USDA to the CDC in Atlanta because of my expertise in mycology and toxic plants. I never thought my interest in fungi would put me in the middle of the Amazon, but it seems like so many other mysteries in this river basin rainforest, the powers that be feel this area is full of potential treatments and cures yet to be discovered. I was low 'man' on the USDA totem pole so I was selected to lead this eclectic group. To my near right is Dr. Tom O'Dell, my fiancé who wouldn't let me come here without him, but he does have good scientific credentials as a practicing veterinarian and has good survival skill training. The young man on his right is Joseph Blackfeather, a Sioux tribal shaman who has generational knowledge of the type of plants we search and is real good in locating the specimens. We also have two Frenchmen providing general security and protection from any pirates and such. So far, our biggest threat has been the endless bugs."

"Ah, yes, those pesky Arthropoda. Well, I won't bite and am very pleased to meet you. It is a rare treat to have scientists that share my interests in plants and animals. We lead an isolated and lonely existence here on La Lupa, but that solitude has allowed me to work undisturbed and develop my ideas. We have had visitors on occasion, but they were usually missionaries looking to save souls or oil and mineral geologists looking to exploit this Eden, and more recently drug runners or foolish adventurists who run low on supplies or are just plain lost. They end up here by lucky accident, their electronics and GPS gadgets failing them miserably. How many lay dead out there feeding the consuming appetite of this wilderness is anyone's guess. This is a dead zone in more than just the modern definition. We exist here in a permanent battle to maintain our existence. One day La Lupa will be returned to the jungle, happily erased by nature."

"So, Dr. O'Dell, you are engaged to this beautiful woman. You are a lucky man I think!"

"I think so too. It's a pleasure to meet you, but I'm really only an extra set of eyes to help spot plants and, while I do have some training in mycology, Kate is really the brains of the outfit. I do think I could now make a good mushroom omelet without killing anyone. My real job is a practicing dairy veterinarian in northern Wisconsin and, after we return home, Kate and I will decide if I move and change jobs or if she relocates north to raise the family we hope to have. She gets paid the big bucks so it's more likely our children will grow up singing *Dixie*. I do hope that what we are doing here might be viable commercially so we may benefit financially ever so slightly."

Von Braun smiled and offered, "Animal scientists! Both of you! I am so pleased! I will take you on a tour of this facility. I think you will find my life's work interesting. You see, I have been doing selective breeding of domestic farm animals for nearly twenty-five years. I try to create animals that grow efficiently with low feed to weight gain ratios, producing highest quality lean protein muscle, easy breeders with shortened gestation periods, increased offspring numbers per litter, and a docile beast that is easy to handle and ship without stress. Today, this would be called genetic engineering, I call it intelligent selection. My work has been primarily done on chickens, turkeys, goats and pigs because they do very well on this climate, but I have had success with cattle also. It's just they get so big it is difficult to feed them here. Unfortunately, I recently lost a majority of the swine when they found a way out of their containment area and ingested some toxic mushrooms from the pharmacological garden. That's where I experiment with plants for their anti-cancer and general anti-pathogen properties. Those animals went wild and destroyed most of my gardens and nearly obliterated the mushroom nursery. Poor things seized violently, were in a complete stupor and we had to destroy them. The only porcine specimens I have now are the weanlings, which were confined separately. I wish I could have shown you the adults. The sows hit 700 kilos easily and were well muscled, but not fat. I can't keep adult boars because they get even bigger so I collect and freeze semen on the young males prior to being slaughtered. I have semen stored on many species here in my own liquid nitrogen storage tanks and used to fly in the nitrogen, but now since I am basically all solar and don't use the diesel generators so much, I can produce and compress my own liquid nitrogen. I use the excess now to cool the buildings and to back up the refrigerating systems. All this I will give to the world, all my research and discoveries when I am no longer able to think or produce productively. My gift to the world, my opus, will be freedom from hunger through super foods and perhaps some discoveries on genetic diseases.

"Please, pardon me for running on, I don't get visitors often, and never those who could appreciate my work. But enough about me, Joseph, tell me about why you are on this expedition."

Joseph cleared his throat and explained, "There is not too much to tell, I am a full blooded Sioux American Indian shaman, or medicine man, on a reservation on the American Plains. I am the keeper of our history, traditions and native medicines. My great-grandfather, one of the great ones in my tribe, trained me to find medicinal plants through observation. I have no scientific basis for being here chasing fungi, just generational knowledge. I can't really explain it, but I have the ability to heal disease by compounding the mushrooms with herbs and other plants. My native instincts seem to draw me to useful plants so I am like a drug dog in cowboy boots."

"I am so very pleased to have you here," Von Braun lied. "Now I suggest we go on a short walk and I will show you some of my work. Pardon my feeble walking, but I have unfortunately been unable to cure the ravages of aging. Come now, and I will show you La Lupa!"

They walked through the house's rear doors and into the laboratory. There the air smelled of solvents, chemicals and lab animals. The lab was a mixture of very modern microscopes, centrifuges, blood analyzers, incubators and equal amounts of old mechanical equipment of questionable age. Dissection tables, surgery tables for small animals and anesthetic machines sporting oxygen tanks were up against one wall. On the opposite side were racks of suspended plastic cages filled with white mice and rats that paced obsessively back and forth at the front of their lucite cells. No question this was a working lab.

After explaining some of his work, Von Braun took them out through the attached plant-filled solarium and into the fenced fields and animal confinement pens. The genetically modified animals were impressive with their docile attitudes and gigantic size. Tom wondered how huge the economic impact of such beasts could be for struggling farmers and protein-starved populations. These animals were salvation for much of the third world.

Von Braun asked if they could then walk down to the boat barge to see their collected specimens and equipment. They leisurely walked to the dock while the former Nazi pointed out and described interesting birds, insects and plants. The man was virtually an encyclopedia of nature.

At the dock, Schmitt was talking to the mechanic and Jacque, and greeted Von Braun like a long lost friend, being careful not to grease up the doctor's white linen shirt and slacks. Kate then showed off the plant collection and their field equipment and feeding media, of which Von Braun took great interest in. He asked a ton of questions, focusing on the propagation media, its composition and how they used it. His rapid fire questioning exposed his scientific brilliance and showed the value of the work they had done.

The disguised Nazi, excited, near euphoric with what lay before him decided that one way or the other, he would take these plants from them. His life depended on it, their lives were over.

Chapter 80

The mechanic had said the problem on the vessel was a small computer part that regulated the engines fuel-air mixture and that part was only available in Porto Alegre, at least that was Schmitt's fabricated explanation to Kate. It would take nearly three days to get the part and return from the marina supply by speedboat. The next scheduled mail boat delivery was nearly a month away and since Schmitt was La Lupa's supposed supply vendor, he wasn't going anywhere. Kate was told the mechanic would have to retrieve the new part. It was a well-orchestrated and delivered lie intended to keep the Americans under Von Braun's control. They weren't going anywhere.

Kate was distressed by the news as it was another delay in their schedule which meant as soon as the boat was operational they would have to start back without even coming close to finding Berhetzel. At least that's what she thought. She planned to discretely pick Von Braun's brain while they waited for the mechanic's return to see if he knew of anyone that might fit Berhetzel's profile, just a single clue would be better than going back to Paris empty-handed. The question was how to do it without exposing the real reason they were in the Amazon.

Berhetzel was a master at playing the congenial Dr. Von Braun, his staff obeying his strict orders understanding that these Americans and the two Frenchmen were a clear danger to their lives at La Lupa. The ruse of the disguise was accepted as was every order he gave.

He was practically giddy about what he had seen on the boat, but needed a little time to extract more detailed information from Kate on their work including some of the pharmacology properties of their plant collection. He invited them to dinner that evening and then returned to the house to plot their disappearance in the all-consuming rainforest.

Kate assembled her team under a colossal live oak halfway between the dock and house for a private meeting.

"I understand how everyone must be feeling about this delay, but look at it as a chance to recharge before we have to go back. We do need to find a way to tell Brad or Jules what is going on. I imagine they are pretty concerned by now, no contact for over three days. So Brad has had no one around that can fathom his humor. Poor guy!"

"I can try to call them if I can get a small boat and test the limits of this dead zone. Pierre and I are very uncomfortable with our situation here. We need to be on the map again just in case we need emergency extraction. We don't like being in a virtual no man's land. It is a primary faux pas," said Jacque. He excused himself and went down to the dock.

The mechanic and Schmitt set Jacque up with a square-stern canoe with a 12 horsepower motor that puttered loudly down the clear tributary onto the massive Amazon. He started to speed dial every five minutes or so looking for a connection to Paris. He had five gallons of fuel to feed the old noisy engine, and pulled his hat low over his ears as rain poured down from a surprise low-hanging cloudburst. He throttled up, pushing the canoe faster down the river while testing the phone's connection.

He did not notice the quiet runabout moving directly to his rear and never heard the single gunshot that sent him tumbling into the muddy current.

Schmitt idled the runabout, making slow circles stalking the spot where Jacque fell into the carnivore-filled river. He would soon be a fine French meal consumed by piranha, bull sharks, crustaceans and giant turtles. He waited a half hour and then pulled next to the old, wood canoe and hacked large holes in the hull, swamping and sinking the vessel. The Frenchman would now be just another lost soul never to be heard from again. One more Frenchie to go and the rest would be easy. They, too, would soon disappear, presumed victims of the hostile Amazon. Then Von Braun would have their plants and their infinite future would be assured. A future without any interfering Americans.

Chapter 81

Dinner was to be at eight that evening so they had several hours to rest and shower, the first long hot shower they had had in over two and a half weeks. Ramon had laundered and pressed all their clothes and brought the men new white shirts and slacks to wear, and found a beautiful lace-trimmed special occasion dress for Kate that belonged to one of the resident women. Kate put her hair up, put on what little makeup she had brought that hadn't melted and looked stunningly beautiful.

Pierre asked to be excused from dinner because Jacque had yet to return from his search for technology and, although he was concerned, he told the others not to worry—Jacque was a tough mother and a survivor. If in twenty-four hours the soldier hadn't returned, then he would be concerned.

The dining room had been set like royalty was coming. Fine china settings were surrounded by ornate, sterling silver utensils, and each seating had five sparkling crystal glasses that were for water, champagne and each course's wine service.

Von Braun was in true form proposing toast after toast. The meal of freshwater shrimp the size of small lobsters served as a cocktail, the baby greens fresh from the garden and a main course of braised duck and fennel was followed by a delicate coconut sorbet and a final cheese course. The meal was, without a doubt, the best they had since their flight to Paris. Everyone was enjoying themselves, drinking too much and feeling no pain as they retired to the hearth-lit library for after dinner drinks and cigars. Only Joseph was fully functional as he only drank ice tea.

After another toast, Kate decided the time was right to ask Von Braun some probing questions.

"Dr. Von Braun," she asked, "are there any other old settlements, villages or plantations close worth exploring for fungal plants?"

"No, nothing that has been active in the last ten years. That would mean you would have a very difficult time recognizing any of the structures or cultivated areas as the rainforest will have returned most things organic back to the soil. The majority who try to make a go of living under nature's thumb, get squished by it. Constant isolation has a maddening effect on most normal people. To prevent that you must make your existence a pleasant one," he gestured to the glasses of brandy and the beautiful library, "or the jungle will chase you away or eat you alive."

Satisfied with his answer, Kate asked, "We had heard of a man named Berhetzel who worked around here in the fifties and that he had an extensive collection of fungi he studied. We are sure he must be dead by now, but would still love to explore his old plantation to see if any of it still exists or if any of his plants might be growing wild. Have you ever heard of him?"

Von Braun sipped his brandy and smiled.

"I haven't heard that name spoken in many years," he said, not lying. "Yes, I am familiar with the man. He used to pass through here every several years usually coming to beg for some diesel or a tool he didn't have. I heard he died of cancer about fifteen years ago, which was fine with me because I sensed he was evil and I'm sure an old political refugee from Germany after the war, likely a Nazi. His place was about 100 kilometers upriver, but I never visited him, even to get my tools back. It might be worth a visit, but I'm sure it's really overgrown. Schmitt knows the area well as he used to deliver that far upriver. If you like, he could use one of my speedboats and run you up there for a look around tomorrow. No sense sitting here just waiting for an engine part. Ramon could pack you a nice picnic lunch, if you wish."

Joseph was glaring at Kate with an 'Are you nuts?' look. She suddenly realized she had just exposed them to a man they barely knew. Their host now seemed anxious to end the evening.

"I hope you enjoyed the evening, but I must confess, I am not used to entertaining and drinking like this. Must be getting old, but my workday starts at dawn so if you don't mind, I will need to retire for the evening. My old body is saying, 'Go to bed dummkopf'. So, I will bid you good night. See you in the morning."

Joseph waited for a minute after Von Braun exited and leaned over to Kate and said, "Are you crazy? I don't trust that guy to know any more about us than necessary. With Jacque missing and the boat broken down, we are sitting ducks. I say if Schmitt gets that powerboat tomorrow, we highjack him and get the hell out of town. Screw the damn plants! What if Von Braun really is a friend of Berhetzel and he informs on us, we know what Berhetzel is capable of. I say leave and have Jules call in the Marines. I feel bad about leaving Jacque, but he's a big boy and perfectly capable of surviving on his own, or maybe we can pick him up on the way back to Porto Alegre. Maybe Jules should also call in the Army, FBI, CIA, Interpol, the Men in Black or whoever, but we need to leave now! My gut is telling me something is terribly wrong."

Tom was now suddenly alert, "Joseph is right, we just might be in a pickle and I'm in agreement that we abort the search for Berhetzel and have Schmitt get us out of here. He'll do just about anything for money so we just offer him a good bonus to use that speedboat to get back to civilization. He can always return to Von Braun and tell him we forced him at gunpoint. Let's keep the pretense up till after we visit the old plantation and then just go. The current will be in our favor so, screw the damn plants and focus on our own safety."

Kate was looking down at the ground with tears in her eyes. "I'm so very sorry for letting the wine talk for me. As soon as I said the name Berhetzel, I knew it was a bad decision. We better leave tomorrow, but I want to be sure we find a way to take some of the unknown specimens with us. Once we are able to connect with Brad, I will get us some more protection. God help me, I hope I haven't screwed up!"

Chapter 82

Von Braun returned to his room, his brain trying to comprehend why his real name, Berhetzel, suddenly came up in their conversation. The only answer the Nazi could conjure was that these Americans were not really searching for rare or unknown fungi, but rather they were trying to locate him. Thank God he had taken the effort necessary to produce a masterful disguise. Now he knew without a doubt these imposters had to be FBI or CIA agents and likely had some connection with what happened in Europe in the last weeks. He summoned Ramon to his room.

"Please make sure Schmitt receives this immediately," he said handing him a sealed note. The note only consisted of two capitalized words: LAB MIDNIGHT.

Berhetzel sat down in an old oversized calf leather chair that faced out to his laboratory developing his plans for the next twenty-four hours to protect his interests and eliminate this American threat. There had to be a connection to Paris he reasoned, and if that really was the case, he knew his time at La Lupa was limited because these Americans would have to disappear without a trace, something that was actually quite easy in the all-consuming rainforest. The problems would begin with the invasion of search and rescue agencies, bounty hunters seeking location rewards and general good-doers trying to solve the Amelia Earhart-like vanishing of the three Americans and two Frenchies. His undisturbed work time would disappear and he needed that to perfect his modifications and train his army of mercenaries. He also would need more than a year's worth of fungal spore extract available to him if he were to work independent of the plantation. The accelerated growth media on that boat hopefully would speed the replacement of his stores.

He would have to count on support from the hundreds of thousands of secret Nazi sympathizers from around the globe to hide and assist with his plans. When he finally struck the world's major governments, there would be no mercy. The attack had to be swift and complete, emasculating and deactivating each major country's leadership and military within hours. A modern-day Blitzkrieg, stunning the world. The resulting chaos would be his only opportunity to seize control of nuclear arsenals so that he had the ultimate power to vaporize his enemies and not suffer a similar fate. He currently had his scattered mercenaries living under the radar in the nuclear states ready to do his bidding. He only needed the numbers of weaponry to properly arm them. His promises of wealth and power beyond imagination would keep his secret army silent, but ready to do his bidding. Not one life on the planet was safe now, but his own soulless one.

Schmitt arrive precisely at midnight, waited just outside the lab door anxious to hear what Von Braun's plans were, anticipating that he was soon going to be busy tidying up all these American loose ends that were a threat to La Lupa. He was near salivating at the thought of killing, almost as much as he had been at the train stations where he was truly a god deciding life or death. He also had a carnal interest in the woman who acted so high and mighty.

As soon as he saw Schmitt at the lab door, Von Braun exited his bedroom door and made the short trip over to his research building. He unlocked the entry door, felt and found the light switch. The overhead illumination struggled, but finally popped on.

"Schmitt, this evening we have had an interesting development that threatens everything we have built here and our very lives. As it turns out, I believe the Americans are really down here looking for the man I was during the war. This disguise has protected me so far, I think, but it is only a matter of time before they make that connection to me. So, tonight I want the other Frenchman to disappear and then tomorrow you will load up the thirty-six foot Sea Ray and take them upriver about 100-150 kilometers where those damn army ants are working. I think that's very close to the old Jesuit mission. Get them as close to the ants as possible, on the pretense that there is an old plantation belonging to a man called Berhetzel, an old client of yours. A man who died about fifteen years ago. I'll leave the rest up to your ingenuity and imagination, but they are not to return, and there is to be no evidence of trauma to their remains. Do not let them use their phones once you are outside the safety zone, so take the portable jammer along to block any signals or reception. Get there, get it done and get back here. When you return, we will need to disguise our existence here to prepare for the scrutiny that is sure to come. Then we — you and I — will leave for a while so I can complete my work. You will be my most important general in the coming war."

Schmitt seemed taken aback by the mention of "war". It had been some time since he was involved in war, and while he found enjoyment in the idea of war, he was unprepared for the nearness of this impending battle.

"Yes, I said war. You see, I plan to restore the former glory of our Fatherland by bringing forth our future — a Fourth Reich, our new Reich, our New World Order!"

Chapter 83
Paris

The lack of contact over the last 36 hours with his friends was really starting to concern Brad. Their GPS tracking signals had stopped working on four of the five of them, with only Jacque's unit registering a weak signal on the computer. The program had the FFL soldier moving at a slow, but steady rate of about four kilometers an hour following the Amazon's course toward Porto Alegre. It was as if they were on a slow raft drifting with the current. Brad was assuming they had experienced some sort of mechanical failure and since they were unable to call for help, were just drifting with the river's current. He called Jules.

"Bonjour Brad," Jules greeted. "I hope everything is OK with our team."

"Probably, maybe, as far as I can tell it is. I just haven't been able to make voice contact for over three days and only the GPS transponder belonging to Jacque is working, and it is moving slowly toward Porto Alegre, following the river's course. I wasn't sure if the problem was here or at their end so I had your IT man, Philipe, go over the equipment and the software. He feels the problem is originating from South America. He mentioned heavy storms, cloud cover and natural dead zones as a probable reason for the interruption of data and communications. I was told to relax, be patient."

"Philipe is a good man, probably the best in his field in France, and he hasn't been co-opted by some nefarious government agency. I would take him at his word," Jules reasoned.

"OK," Brad replied, "I'll keep watching out for any other data or communications, but if we don't hear soon, someone is going to need to check up on them in person. By the way, how is Jean?"

"Much better. He has gone to live with Susan to recover while his house is being restored. I sat with them at Robert's state funeral. Le Prèsident gave an eloquent and moving eulogy. There was a very large crowd in attendance — families of the death camps, a dozen or so survivors, and leaders of the Jewish community from around the world, including Israel. It was truly moving because they buried Robert with honors as a National Hero of the Republic!"

"How is Jean?" Brad asked.

"He can now speak again clearly, and besides the soreness in his chest from those old Nazi slugs and a persistent soft cough from the smoke, he is doing better than any of his doctors had predicted. It's just that he is very, very angry and wants Berhetzel dead."

"Does he know what's going on? If I were him I'd want to know everything!" Brad was emotional and was as desperate as everyone else to have justice for Jean and Robert.

"I filled him in on all the events that have happened, including Fred Garrett's conclusions and explained to him that our friends are in Argentina right now trying to locate the monster. He hates that decision and feels we should have relied on satellite surveillance and then used a drone strike to take him out. Now we know that the satellites are unreliable or nearly worthless in that wilderness. Besides, I want intact what Berhetzel has in his longevity formula and that device he uses to kill. All that research can be put to use for good and even without the man, my people at the Pasteur can back engineer it. The potential humanitarian and economic benefits of his work, I think, would be incalculable."

"So, for now, we wait?" Brad asked.

"Oui, for now we are to be patient and trust in our team. God help me if I am wrong!"

Chapter 84
Berhetzel's Compound

Schmitt was in predator mode, but stayed clear from the boat barge until 0300 hours. The surrounding jungle was mostly quiet except for the occasional stirring of a nocturnal animal and its cry of death when a jungle hunter captured it. There was a rhythm of the rainforest, the struggle between life and death that Schmitt appreciated the most. Now he was a hunter also, tasked to protect La Lupa from an enemy that threatened her existence. This was the fun part of his job.

The last Frenchman was now in the sights of the night vision scope that was attached to his modern graphite crossbow. The broad head on the bolt had been dipped in fresh venom from a tiny colorful dart frog, so even if the wound were not lethal, the poison would finish the man within seconds. Schmitt was surprised that Pierre was awake, actually on duty, guarding the boat and its booty. He respected disciplined men, and his target was a true soldier and deserved this quick and painless death. Pierre stood at the stern of the boat looking over the water, smoking a distinctive Gauloise, expertly flicking ash into the water. Schmitt activated the scope's red laser dot, which hovered at the base of the man's skull. It would be a swift kill, but disappointing that, in that moment of death, he would not see the face of death, that expression of surprise that came with an unexpected lethal blow. But this man was dangerous and Schmitt would take what he could get. He held steady on target, surging adrenaline pumping up his heart rate. As the Frenchman tapped out the cigarette, he stretched, pulling his arms up in a prolonged reach and the Nazi took his shot. There was a brief pause of time as the arrow walloped his neck, splitting his first cervical vertebrae, severing the spinal cord. In a terminal reflex, the man grabbed at his throat rotating to face his assassin. As Schmitt stood, there was a brief instant of recognition and then a flash of anger on the soldier's face as he fell over backwards into the water, bloodying the clear tributary.

Schmitt boarded the boat and flashed a bright flashlight across the stern and then into the crimson cloud that floated around the corpse. He grabbed the boat hook and snagged the Frenchman's belt and pulled him to the side of the boat until he could reach the man's feet. Schmitt looped a red nylon braided rope around each foot and secured it to a stern cleat so it would not drift away. He then pushed a non-motorized canoe into the water and paddled over to the body. After retying the rope to the end of the canoe, he started up the tributary into the wildness that lay inland. He slowly moved up the waterway paddling silently, dragging his trophy behind him.

He paddled for ninety minutes using the soft amber light from the kerosene lanterns to navigate around tree snags and tangled vined obstacles. The lanterns hissed with a petrol smell and smoked as gigantic moths and other strange insects flew kamikaze into the heated glass, falling to the canoe floor, toasted. Giant bullfrogs protested his intrusion and splashed into the water from their hidden observatories. Owls screeched as he passed by and alligator-like caimans mewed and hissed their protests. Schmitt kept paddling farther into the interior satisfied the indigenous carnivores and scavengers would quickly consume and scatter the man's remains. After ninety minutes of steady paddling, he was secure in an area that no sane person would ever visit.

He pulled the rope, dragging the body back to the stern of the canoe. The 50 cm bolt was covered in aquatic weeds so Schmitt removed a utility knife from his belt and cut away the debris and then cut around the arrow and worked it loose from the man's spine, nearly decapitating the corpse. The projectile pulled away taking some flesh along in two bisected strips. Proud of his kill, Schmitt decided he would mount the arrow with the still-attached human flesh on a nice mahogany board, along with a clever inscription recording his marksmanship. What he failed to notice in the arrow's broad head, clinging to a small tag of flesh and hair, was hidden a fully functional GPS transponder. Pierre was dead, but his shadow would live on as a small silicon chip that, for now, was his beating telltale heart.

Chapter 85

Kate, Tom and Joseph were up early that morning as the soft light of dawn filtered into their rooms and the plantation's oversized roosters loudly announced the new day. Small white cards had been slid under their room doors sometime overnight and invited them to a morning buffet in the courtyard.

Outside the air was refreshingly cool and smelled damp from an overnight rain shower. The roosters were now sporadic in their crowing and were being diluted by the chatter of the monkeys, parrots and peacocks that roamed the formal garden. The small primates would charge up to the buffet's tables to steal a piece of fruit or sweet roll, but run from Ramon and his swinging broom. Kate and Tom made a beeline for the coffee station, pouring large cups of the black stimulant. Joseph, amused, watched the monkeys feint charges as he gulped down several glasses of fresh-squeezed blood orange juice, but respected the broom he now controlled.

Von Braun came out the front door in about twenty minutes, followed by Ramon carrying a large tray of eggs prepared as a simple scramble or in various omelets. He arranged the eggs next to the sausages, ham and smoked salmon between the fruit, strudel and breads.

"Good morning, my friends. I hope you rested well last night after all that fine drink," commented Berhetzel pleasantly. He was very good at playing the part of gracious host.

"Good morning! Yes, I know I slept well," replied Kate as her stomach gave her hunger away.

"I certainly did!" agreed Tom.

"Excellent! Well, I had Ramon set up this buffet for you and with the exception of the coffee, which is from Colombia and the salmon from Scotland, everything else has come from La Lupa. I must excuse myself now and check on some of my timed experiments, but I will return soon with Schmitt to set you on your way to find the old Berhetzel plantation." The Nazi bowed slightly to Kate and walked slowly around the house to the laboratory.

They plated their breakfasts and sat at a white table-clothed, cast iron garden table, Tom and Kate opposite Joseph.

"You know, for a guy your age who didn't drink last night, you look like crap!" Tom teased.

"That's because, unlike the two of you, I didn't sleep well at all. I tried, but dreams kept coming and were persistent and frightened me awake. In one dream army cavalry soldiers were shooting arrows at us, but we couldn't escape because our feet were stuck to the ground. Arrows were darkening the sky casting a black shadow over us. Weirdly, the forest animals lined up to attack us and were led by an evil-looking old, gray wolf. That wolf reminded me of a classic Hollywood werewolf with glowing merciless eyes," remembered Joseph.

"Eh, werewolves are only dangerous on a full moon," joked Tom. Kate nudged him in the ribs, scoffing at his inconsiderate joke. She understood Joseph was really beginning to be afflicted by these visions.

Joseph went on, ignoring Tom, "In another, my grandfather was there speaking in our ancestor's tongue. He had a warning, 'Caution, Joseph, you are very close to the answer you seek, but death and destruction hovers near you and the rest of creation. Remember what I taught you about the men who kill only because they are driven to do so for their insatiable lust for blood. Make yourself invisible to them and when you reappear you must be the white wolf and send their souls to Hell. Do not hesitate as Custer did, but use your gift of life to end the reign of the Destroyer.' I could feel his body heat and he appeared as a young warrior brave in buckskins and war paint. It was him at his youthful best with strong, clear eyes and resolute voice. It was frightening, but at the same time strangely reassuring. I spent the rest of the night rolling over and over in my head his words and warning, trying to connect the dots since all this began and I didn't sleep a wink. I think we better be sure that Schmitt has some weapons on board because I think we are about to find Herr Berhetzel and I don't think he is going to invite us in for a friendly drink."

Kate responded, "Well I've made my decision about this excursion of ours. This is our last day, we check out this supposed Berhetzel plantation site, return and get the heck out of town. We are way out of our league here and we need to turn this investigation over to a three-lettered government agency. Let them find the man. My guess is that Berhetzel has returned to Europe and is based out of there. Today, or at the latest tomorrow, we leave and head home. Any discussion?"

"Yes," Tom said. "Please pass me the hot sauce for my eggs and then find someone to stamp our passports, it's time to go home!"

Von Braun returned with Schmitt who addressed the Americans.

293

"I have loaded everything we need for the excursion today, including some chilled wines, beer and a lunch that Ramon put together. Dr. Von Braun has offered the use of his beautiful powerboat, and even though we will be going 160-180 kilometers, we should be there easily before noon. We will be moving fast so you may want light jackets and rain gear just in case the weather turns bad. I transferred your collection equipment and computer over also. I want to warn you, this area we are going into is experiencing an invasion of army ants this season, but as far as I can tell from the earlier reports, we will be just short of them. But there may be scout ants ahead of the main column so before we leave the boat, I will have you spray your clothing with a local repellent and apply a plant-based lotion to all exposed flesh. These insects will literally eat you alive so no one gets out of my sight or goes off on their own. Just in case we stumble into a column of ants, each of you will have two foggers that act like smoke bombs. If there is a problem, don't panic, they don't move that fast. I haven't been to this place in more than a decade, so it might take twenty minutes to cut our way from the old boat dock, if it still exists, to the main house. The man was a paranoid recluse so don't get ahead of me because there might be booby traps still out there."

"Will Pierre come with us or stay here?" Kate asked.

"Neither," Schmitt answered. "He left this morning to find his partner, but said he would only be gone four or five hours, so he should be back by noon. He seemed confident, though his demeanor displayed a bit of worry, that he could locate him."

"So what do you want us to do now?" Tom said.

"I think you should be sure you have everything you need to document the trip — the jackets, rain gear and a change of clothing in case it rains buckets. At best maybe you will find some unique plants. At worst, you may have the chance to see one of the most destructive armies on earth at work, a rare, once-in-a-lifetime opportunity."

Von Braun warned them, "Follow Schmitt's orders exactly and you will be safe. We went through a similar episode seven years ago and that is when I developed these repellents. They nearly overran us, but the repellents slowed them up until we had dug perimeter ditches and filled them with brush soaked in diesel, and when they started to breach the ditch, we lit the fire barrier. That worked well until the rain came that put out the fires. I thought La Lupa was finished, but the rain started to come down like a hurricane and the ants were drowned or washed into the waterways, which ran like torrents and dispersed them. So, you see, nature has a balance. But in this world it pays to be lucky."

After they collected their gear they boarded the 36-foot Sea Ray and cast off in the smaller waterway. Before long they were at the junction with the

Amazon and its muddy flow. Schmitt opened the throttle and soon they were on plane and moving at 60 kilometers per hour. It felt like traveling on a jet plane in comparison to the boat barge. At that speed, the air was refreshing and the persistent hovering insects were blasted out of the way. Kate stretched out sunning herself, Tom sat with Schmitt in the pilothouse, and Joseph was asleep in the forward cabin recuperating from his restless night.

Kate tried calling Jules, Brad and the two FFL soldiers every half hour to no avail. There just seemed to be no way to reach anyone from this wilderness. She hoped at least the GPS trackers were still signaling as they may have been their only connection to the team in Paris.

The damage from the army ants soon became visible tracking down from the hills toward the river. What looked to be thousands of acres appeared to be under attack with the areas furthest away sporting a flush of new green growth and the jungle closest to the water looking like a forest fire had raged through. They passed floating partially consumed mammals from monkeys to tapirs. The cry of birds trying to protect their nests quickly became a disturbing panicked chorus. This was nature at her worst, the Destroyer of life taking a different path to death.

Soon Schmitt began slowing the boat to carefully hug the north bank of the river.

"I'm looking for landmarks and that old dock. We are very close because I recognize those three massive trees. This has to be the mouth of the feeder waterway, it's just so overgrown. Look, there is a concrete piling with a tie down. That was part of the old dock, I'm sure!"

He carefully pulled up to the piling, which was about eight meters off the shore and Tom tied the forward cleat of the boat securely to the old piling.

"How is that for a piece of luck?" Schmitt said. "The only one left of the six or eight originals and it's still solid. Almost nothing lasts around here. Dr. O'Dell, take that boat hook and extend it fully to check how deep the water is by that piling please."

"Looks to be two meters and a real mucky bottom. How about we tie the stern up to that tree so we are closer from the rear of the boat?" Tom asked. Schmitt agreed and he pulled the stern around to within three meters of the shore and Tom threw a grappling hook and line and snagged the tree limbs pulling the boat in tight.

"Tell the rest of our crew to take only what they absolutely need, the minimum personal items, leave their phones on board because the less we carry the faster we can get the hell out of here, and I'm not going back for a lost phone," Schmitt said.

Tom woke Joseph and saw Kate was putting together the waterproof bag with the computer and sampling equipment. Schmitt called them up to the pilot station for instructions.

"OK, here we are," he started, "I'm not so sure I would have found it because the jungle has reclaimed it very well. If not for that piling, we would still be looking."

"What is that awful smell?" Kate asked.

"I learned all about these little bastards when I stayed after delivering diesel to the Von Braun plantation. These ants ate their way right to his back door. Each colony of army ants has a unique odor, which allows them to recognize each other so they can work together and defend the queen," he explained. "She produces an odor called a pheromone which attracts and maintains the integrity of the colony. The colony produces formic acid, which is probably used to kill or paralyze their prey or enemies and digest the organic matter of those plants and animals into simpler fats, sugars and proteins. That underlying rotten meat odor is the result of that organic destruction. Now had you asked me that question ten years ago, I would have had no answer, but after almost losing the battle at Von Braun's place, I made a point of learning all about them. I believe we should know our enemy and believe me, nothing stands in the way of these tiny soldiers!"

Schmitt lit a cigarette and pulled a bag of fireworks from a plastic bag hanging off the back of the captain's chair.

"Cover your ears," Schmitt ordered.

He lit and tossed ten M-80 mini bombs that exploded with loud repetitions, leaving blue-gray smoke plumes drifting back toward the boat.

"What are you doing?" Tom shouted.

"The ants drive their prey in front of them just like hunters doing a game drive. The ones that won't swim for it stop at the water's edge. They can't retreat so they become very aggressive and territorial. Found that out at Von Braun's. My biggest concern is the pit vipers or adders that are real thick around here. No one has anti-venom out here so depending where you are bitten, you'll be dead or in need of immediate field limb amputation. Otherwise, you should spend your last minutes digging a nice grave. Those fireworks will temporally disperse them, but we will need to do the same when we return, and then check the boat.

Joseph liked this less and less, but then the German handed him an old double barrel shot gun, which instantly made the young Indian feel better. Schmitt took a compass reading and said, "OK, I'm 99% sure we head this way, northwest," pointing his arm to about ten o'clock. The first thing you need to do is spray yourselves with this basil-based repellent — all over — and coat any exposed skin with this lotion. It will neutralize the acids from the ant bites. I can't use it because I'm allergic to it and break out in hives. I'll take my chances with the bloody insects. Also we will drink these bottles of citrus juice and water that will mask your breath's CO_2 smell. The locals think it will keep the spirits of the ants away, it certainly can't hurt."

They slid off the stern's swimming platform and into the waist deep warm muddy water, holding on to the grappling hook's rope, and pulled themselves up the slick river bank. Schmitt had tossed a long machete onto the bank and quickly started cutting through the overgrown jungle toward the northwest.

"You see," he said after about thirty minutes of hacking away the brush, "how fast nature reclaims her birthright? The stones we are walking on, while they are moss covered, are actually manmade bricks that I'm sure were fired on site when the Jesuits first settled here and established their missionary outpost. That was about 1870. They were here till the end of the First World War when malaria and the Great Influenza Pandemic interrupted their supplies because they were, at that time, a low priority. And Porto Alegre was being devastated by the flu. Of the original six priests, only two were still alive and they went to help the poor in Porto Alegre and never returned. Then in 1950 or so, Berhetzel took it over."

"Just ahead are the original gates with the old thick ipe wooden doors and brass hinges still hanging. You can see the carved crosses on each door if you look carefully. All these plantations were heavily defended because of rogue bandits who would steal anything and kill just for fun. Other than the Spanish conquistadors, who were the original terrorists down here, and these bandits were feared nearly as much as the Spaniards for their style of merciless terror. They took what little people had and didn't hesitate to kill. Those doors kept out the evil and the wood they are made from is like iron. It'll last forever. That type of wood is now used for premium docks and decks and I suspect each one of those doors is worth several thousand dollars in today's market. We will rest now over by that old well foundation for a few minutes and rehydrate with that citrus drink. If you listen carefully you can hear the ants working the foliage, chewing and dropping leaves from the canopy and… look, see the advance scout ants on the ground? Notice how they zigzag back and forth in front of us? That means they are marking us for the evening menu. Little creeps!"

Schmitt handed each a bottle of the cold citrus water and they drank it down quickly, seduced by its delicious taste. What they didn't know was it was spiked with a fast acting sedative and voluntary muscle paralytic agent. In less than a minute they fell to the ground unable to speak or move, but conscious of their surroundings.

"My friends," he announced, "I am sorry to inform you that you just drank a combination of a low-dose curare derivative and a mild fast-acting memory killing sedative. I will be leaving you here to experience the wonders of nature firsthand. You know the eternal struggle between life and death. See that large tree over there? Oh, pardon me, you can't move your heads. Well, anyway, I will tie you to that tree so you will be easy for the ants to find, especially since that spray and lotion you applied is really a pheromone attractant, not a repellant. I think I would pray that the vipers find you first. If your scattered bones are ever found, you will be just another lost expedition who was in the wrong place at the wrong time."

He dragged them each to the large tree, sitting them upright after tying their feet and hands with a hemp cord. He placed Kate between the two men.

"This rope is a natural hemp material that has been soaked in sugar cane syrup and organic alcohol. The ants will consume every speck of it, leaving no evidence of your detention here."

"Now, since I have become somewhat fond of you, I think you deserve an explanation of why you find yourself in your current pickle," he said looking directly into their catatonic eyes.

"Dr. Von Braun has creative devices and drugs that he will use at some point to seize world power, but also improve mankind's lot in life. Tremendous wealth comes with that power and that is why I do his dirty work. Your two Frenchmen are dead and when you are gone, things around here will return to normal. We will continue our work and regenerate the mushroom garden, which is our fountain of youth. Your host at La Lupa is actually a man in his later nineties. Remove the disguise he wore for your benefit, and you would see a man who appears and acts to be in his late thirties. We are miracles for sure and he needed your technology and specimens to renew that fungal plot. You see I am also in my late nineties, but the point is we will be immortal with those miracle capsules he has developed. So we lured you here to first take your specimens, but also to be sure no one else could duplicate Von Braun's discovery."

"I really wanted to have some fun with you, my sweet," he said to Kate, "but Von Braun forbade it. Too bad because I have sixty years of unfulfilled passion waiting to be released." He gave her numb lips a soft kiss and pushed her hair away from her staring eyes. "I think you should be able to see the little bastards work."

"So, my American friends, I leave your fate to the whims of Mother Nature. I understand the acid from the ant's bite feels like you are being set on fire. Until they arrive here, relax and enjoy some sleep because the picnic will officially begin as soon as the ants get here. Unfortunately, you will be the main course, served rare. Bon Appetite, my tiny friends."

Chapter 86
Paris

Brad had been awake nearly all night attempting to contact Kate and the boys during their daylight hours in Argentina. He drank two pots of coffee and knew that any sleep today would come only after he became decaffeinated. Most of his day was spent at the computer scanning the GPS program for the location signal alert that had been absent for over three days. Typically, the transponders would be auto-located every six hours and plot their movements on a 3D map. He grabbed some shortbread cookies and a glass of orange juice and walked out to the terrace to check the laptop and watch the city come to life in the predawn hour.

The program came up quickly and he immediately received an alert that said 'Contact confirmed and plotted #1, 2, 3, 5 transponders'. That was the first time there was a location in three days, and Brad almost aspirated his cookie when he gasped with surprise. The data stream showed Pierre stationary at about 165 kilometers north and east of Kate, Tom and Joseph who also had moved to a stationary point starting about two hours previous. They now were clustered together showing the three GPS signals nearly on top of each other. Either they were working or resting in a very tight area. Jacque evidently was still slowly heading toward Porto Alegre. Relieved and grateful, he gave the command for a visual. The World View Satellite alerted with a countdown to positioning of three hours, twenty-three minutes and sixteen seconds before available viewing at ground level. Brad did some time zone conversions and determined that that pass would occur in the dark of night. The next full sun pass would occur in about ten hours so he set a reorder function for each pass after the first in the next thirty-six hours. He then pulled out his phone to call Jules. He answered on the third ring.

"Bonjour, Brad. How are you? Any word on our friends?"

"Bonjour, Jules," Brad said politely, "I'm fine and yes, they are back on radar again, but strangely in three different areas. Your men are far away from them in separate areas. There won't be a prime daylight pass for ten hours for a visual. I don't know what to actually make of all of it."

"I don't like it at all," Jules said, "we need to meet with my friend in national security who enhanced the G8 photos and see if he has access to better equipment that can help us. Maybe he can get us thermals or infrared images. You keep calling their cells. I'm going to set up transport to get down there. I smell a rat because my men would never abandon their responsibility and separate from the group at the same time. We are dealing with a Nazi so I pray they never let on to anyone why they really were there, because if they did they are most likely already dead."

Shaken by Jules' analysis, Brad hung up glad he hadn't brought his family over to France since now it looked like he was heading to South America. God he wished he had acted a couple of days ago. They better be all right!

Chapter 87

Schmitt waited till the sedation had fully put the trio into a deep sleep that would last several hours until a large portion of the ant army was near. The advance scouts would set a trail to the food source and the ants would race frantically to the hot meal and slowly and painfully they would carpet the Americans and pick their bones clean. Eventually, when the jungle was restored, animals and insects of all sizes would scatter and consume the bones as a calcium source. He really wanted to stay and watch the cruel death, but Von Braun had radioed with instructions to return to La Lupa Immediately.

Schmitt started the Sea Ray and cut the grapple rope when he couldn't de-snag it, then tossed all the American's personal items including their cell phones into the middle of the river, only keeping the collection equipment and laptop. Once they downloaded the program and incorporated the data into their own equipment, their computer would also be destroyed.

With the current in his favor, Schmitt made the trip back to the plantation in half the time it had taken to get to the old Jesuit outpost. He pulled up to the dock in less than two hours.

He found Von Braun at the laboratory putting small fungi on the stolen media plates and packing them in Styrofoam coolers. Larger spore laden plants were placed in zippered specimen bags that had small ventilation holes manufactured into them. Seeds from the genetically engineered crops were sealed in small pouches and all his encrypted data and notes on breeding the giant farm animals were also vacuum-sealed in the heavy plastic. It was obvious to Schmitt that they were evacuating the Plantation, and from the pace Von Braun was setting, it was to be soon.

"I really hate the idea of leaving this place with so much work left to do," Von Braun said, "but you know as well as I do that this area will soon be swarming with all sorts of agents from the United States and Argentina. We will need to be well clear before that happens or leave a trail for them to follow. Only the four of us that originally came from Germany will be leaving, the others know nothing of importance and can live here as long as they are able. It will be critical that they believe we are to return in one month or two and that might be possible based on the end result of the investigation for the Americans and what we accomplish while we are gone. Put Ramon in charge with my full authority to enforce the rules and tell the rest that the compound will be under my direct twenty-four hour surveillance. That should keep them honest and diligent indefinitely. They can be our decoy and diversion by telling them we are on our way to South Africa to collect specimens."

"Yes, Herr Doctor," Schmitt replied acknowledging his orders from the man who was now out of the disguise he had used to fool the Americans.

Schmitt went to talk to Ramon, happy at the thought of finally getting out of this rainforest and knew whatever Von Braun was involved in would either deliver great wealth, power or both. He might become very wealthy in his 'old age' and because of the eternal gift he and the others had been given at La Lupa, he had received something few men, except possibly biblical figures had enjoyed — youth in his old age. He had suspected Von Braun was not really a philanthropist, a benefactor for mankind, but that everything he had worked so hard on was a play for ultimate power. Now he was poised to be perhaps the second most powerful man in the world and that would be worth all his selfless servitude over the last sixty-plus years. Everything he had been asked by Von Braun to do had been done without question as did the other men who had sailed on that freighter from Marseille in 1945. Now, it appeared Von Braun was going to take that power and wealth to control some nation, continent or perhaps the entire planet. Schmitt had seen evidence of the death ray weapon with the dead animals that would appear outside the lab and had seen the computer records he had accessed when Von Braun had been in Europe. He understood that whatever happened now, it was very unlikely he would return to La Lupa, despite what Von Braun had said. Perhaps they would also assume new identities and if they did he would go back to his birth name Goebbels, to honor his long dead family and his famous uncle Hermann, whose first name he had already used.

Now his job was to supervise the loading of the boat barge, thankful to be piloting the modern vessel after the time spent with the Americans on the simpler older version. Trunks of equipment, specimens and records were carefully loaded along with weapons, supplies and the best wines and cigars. Three hundred liters of biodiesel were blended into the fuel reserve and each man's personal belongings limited to one duffel bag each. By a little after midnight they were loaded and prepared to go and he did a double check of the manifest with Von Braun. They were to leave at 0200 hours.

Schmitt kept thinking, wondering if the three he had tied to that tree were still alive or if the snakes or other predators had finished them before the ants had chance to torture them. Either way they wouldn't be escaping like he was and would soon be recycled into the earth. Death was always the great equalizer and he had been able to cheat her by feeding others in his place to satisfy death's cravings for flesh. He had kept death in a cage like a hungry lion and fed her like a zookeeper whenever she growled for food. Never in his wildest dreams would he have thought the entire world would sit dreading his decisions on merciful life or death. He had always been Von Braun's mechanic of death and, crazy or sane, it would be his name they would fear and pray to their god for deliverance from. Eventually they all would pray to him — the 'son' — for mercy. To their new deity, Von Braun, they would bring their wealth as offering of worship. It would be a demonstration of power only Hitler could have dreamed of. *Sieg heil, resounded in his mind.*

Chapter 88

Amazon, upriver

167 kilometers northwest

Joseph was the first to regain function of his voluntary muscles as they started firing, testing their own function. His thigh and calf muscles rolled in and out of exaggerated cramping knots as blood-carrying oxygen was pumped in and muscle waste forced out. He was weak and physically disoriented, but had a fairly clear mind. Numerous ants had already traveled up his leg under his plants and he could feel their nettle-like sting as they bit down. He saw fiery red welts on Kate's exposed legs and the large wheals of inflammation that joined the bites like clusters of bright red grapes. He was unsure about Tom who he couldn't see, but was convinced he was taking his share of hits, too.

The acidic putrid odor of the approaching column was burning his throat and tearing up his eyes. The ants were close and getting closer. He could hear the grinding of foliage as they advanced on them but thankfully they were ignored by the panicked retreat of numerous snakes from pythons to slim green racer like reptilians. Mammals — tiny shrews, spotted ocelots and fat tapirs — rushed by nearly running each other over. While these mobile animals willing to swim would survive, the anchored Americans were meals with wheals and doomed to die painfully in a very short time.

The column was minutes away.

Kate finally came around, followed then by Tom shortly after. Kate was scared and crying.

"How are you, Joseph? Are your ropes as tight as mine?" Tom asked hoarsely.

"I am really hog tied," the Indian replied, "but I have a knife in my right boot. There's just no way I can get to it. The ant swarm is real close and I'm getting a lot of bites from the advance column. We might have forty minutes if we are lucky. We need a miracle."

"Pray, Joseph, pray to your ancestors. Tom, you and I will pray to Jesus because I'm sure he'll hear us and maybe hear Joseph also. We will not die like this!"

Tom and Kate prayed, Joseph chanted in Sioux.

"Lord, help keep us safe…"

"I call to the keeper of the sky. Protect us…"

Clouds quickly grew upwards, darkening the sky. Rain fell steadily and soon became a torrential downpour.

Thunder roared and lightning flashed, illuminating the darkened sky. Rain came in blinding sheets, washing them free of ants and cooling the stings. Soon there was two inches of water on the jungle floor and the excess water started to wash in currents toward the river. Suddenly Joseph could feel something gnawing at the hemp binding his hands. He pulled stretching the rope tight until it snapped, freeing his hands. He reached into his boot and pulled out the knife Jacque had given him and cut his hands free. He turned and saw a grizzled old gray-white rat hobbling away, nearly swimming in the water toward the river.

"Thank you, my grandfather," he hoarsely whispered and took the knife to free Kate and Tom. They struggled to stand, unsteady on their feet. Kate immediately hugged Joseph and embraced and kissed Tom.

"There was a very old rat that chewed the ropes on my wrists freeing them. He headed off to the river over there," the Indian explained. "I am sure it was Grandfather!"

"Thank you God and God bless you, Nelson!" Kate exclaimed.

The torrents kept pounding down and many of the ants drowned in the rising water, but a few tried clinging to their legs and some boarded floating leaves and were being washed toward the river. The heavy rain was going to allow them a window of time to get away from this insect army so they made their way carefully down the trail Schmitt had cut, looking out for snakes and other predators. At the river they were not surprised to find the boat gone, but the grapple and line still hung from the tree where they had tied up. Joseph climbed, using the rope and untangled the four-pronged hook and tossed it down to Tom.

"Great," Tom exclaimed, "now we can try to put together a raft and I have an idea about using those old doors hanging from the gate. If those doors really are Ipe then they will be as dense and heavy as steel. They may not float, but if I remember my college physics, floating on water is more about surface area displacement and that is why large steel ships don't sink. There are lots of vines to tie the support logs together and those doors must be at least three by four meters so we need to find some long pieces of finger thickness vines, dried are better and then pull those doors down. Kate, we have to cut those doors free so whatever we cut of those vines you think we can use, bring them back and we will assemble the raft here on the river bank or possibly in the water."

They returned to the old gated entry and Joseph started cutting the vines away as Tom pulled at the large brass door handle rings trying to pop the hinges, which eventually did pull away from the old support column's crumbling mortar. Joseph stuck the tip of the knife in several areas of the doors and repeated "Solid," as the doors appeared in good condition.

"These doors aren't Ipe, they aren't dense enough, but I think will work OK because those vines seemed to have oozed some kind of sap that hardened and protected them from decay and insects. You see, it looks almost like polyurethane. If you polished it, they could look like a ballroom floor!" Tom explained.

They managed to pull the doors loose from the columns, but really struggled to free them from their tangled plant prison. After thirty minutes they had the two doors, a huge pile of vines and twelve old flotsam logs that had washed up on the river bank that they could weave the vines around and then marry the doors to the logs with more strong, fibrous tendrils. In two short hours, they had put together a solid raft.

"Well, it ain't pretty, but I think it will hold together. OK, Joseph, let's slide this baby into the water. Kate, grab those push poles and those pieces of plywood we found and once we are in the water, we'll rig some paddles up."

The two men horsed the heavy door raft slipping and sliding in the rain slick clay mud until it fell down into the water and bobbed up like some great cork.

"Well, I'll be damned," Tom said proudly as Joseph patted him soundly on the back.

Joseph tied the grapple hook rope up, securing the vessel to the riverbank and Kate and Tom used it for support as they boarded the raft. Then Joseph tossed Tom the rope, jumped into the water and pushed the floating deck into the current of the river. The raft tilted as he pulled himself up on the deck, nearly tossing Kate into the bank. She screamed as she fell hard on her bottom, her muddy feet slipping. The rain was still pouring down and washed away the mud, as they cupped their hands to drink the liquid.

"The river is really moving fast, "Tom shouted over the pounding rain, "at this rate we will make good time as long as we get past La Lupa. Joseph, use the poles to keep us close to the near bank, I don't want to be real obvious with all the crap that goes on down here. Our goal needs to be getting to Porto Alegre or locating a military or tour barge to get us out of here. Most importantly, we have to squeeze by Von Braun's undetected and unharmed. I'm sure they think we are dead from the ants, but we can't chance possible detection. We will travel at night when we get close and hug this side of the Amazon."

They all nodded in agreement and the men pushed forward steering the raft from opposite corners while Kate sat balanced in the middle shivering from effects of the relentless downpour, all of them afraid, but determined to survive.

Chapter 89
Paris

Le Department Intelligence Francaise

Jules and Brad sat on either side of the French data analyzer watching him punch GPS coordinates into the computer with incredible speed. Paul Ducane had been friends with Jules and Robert for over twenty years and in typical French fashion, put loyalty to friends ahead of government rules and regulations, a possible hold over attitude from the French Revolution. What they were doing was clearly illegal, but since he was in charge of this intelligence division, he only had to answer to himself. The watched the large LED screen darken and lighten as it cycled from night to daytime periods until they finally arrived at the spy satellite's last location transmission of the American's GPS transponders. Ducane stared at the screen, studying at the distant landscape views and then started progressively zooming closer and closer. He silently shook his head as he focused hard at the screen.

"Here is the approximate area you were looking for," he said, "these scanning satellites do pass rapidly over the location points, but will record and transmit at each data opportunity. When I enlarge and then condense this large panoramic of the area moving from north to the Amazon River, close to your GPS signals, there is an area of deforestation or at least denuding and I can't be sure if it is from fire or some other natural cause. Everything around this area looks normal so it probably wasn't fire. Let's take it to max zoom and resolution to see if we can get a clue. This will place us within 500 meters, more or less, of their last recorded signal."

With a few expert keystrokes the image rotated ninety degrees to true north and with each movement they came in closer and clearer. The bare treetops appeared and only limbs and branches were apparent, all greenery missing. No char suggesting fire or broken branches from wind damage were visible. The scanning increased until they were the max of one meter off the ground. They stared at the screen and could just begin to recognize a thick line of ants.

"Son of a bitch!" Brad yelled. "They're ants, army ants! They are eating their way across the jungle. I saw a movie as a kid starring Charlton Heston where they ate him literally out of house and home. I think it was called 'Naked Jungle' and it scared the crap out of me. Those ants will consume everything organic in their path whether it be plant or animal. That means Kate and the boys are in real danger if they are stuck there!"

Jules stared at the screen, his anger building.

"Paul, is there any way to do what you just did now, but sync it to the exact date and time we recorded their data transmission and look at it in real time?"

"Oui, I can try."

He paged backward through the screen images until he was close to the data intersect. He focused on the images and then typed commands, switching to a weather satellite.

"Unfortunately, there was and still is a massive weather front in that location with heavy rains and cloud cover that will black out ground views for the next forty-eight hours. There are about 2300 satellites in space and over half of those are Russian. Most orbit over the northern hemisphere because the majority are spying on something, but south of the equator, there is less meaningful military, economic and social information. Argentina is considered poor pickings except for natural resource exploration. You are going to have to wait out this weather pattern because I have no way of getting what you need in real time."

"So we know something is going on with the ants, but have no way to precisely determine if our three are there or somewhere safe," Jules said.

"I don't know what you were told when Le Pasteur purchased those mini-transponders, but they don't work well in remote areas, just like cell phones. In America and Europe, they are fine in urban areas, but outside of that, Bon Chance!"

"Then we are going to have to take a little trip and see for ourselves. Brad you get a taxi and return to the apartment, I'm heading to the office to make arrangements and then go home. Pack lightly because we will buy whatever we need once we arrive in Porto Alegre. I want us to be in the air by late afternoon. I don't think they are safe and I really believe they didn't stumble on those ants by accident. They were left there to die or be consumed by the ants. Someone wanted their deaths to look like they were in the wrong place at the wrong time. I think we can be on site at their last location in about 36 hours. God help us if we arrive too late. Allons y!" *Let's go!*

Chapter 90
La Lupa

0200 hours

Schmitt had the boat barge loaded with all the essentials for the trip by midnight just as he had been asked by Von Braun. He had placed all the important equipment, data and specimens that would be directly under his supervision on this vessel and all his and the other two men's personal items were placed on the Sea Ray. He filled both fuel reserves and ported extra petrol and biodiesel just in case they needed it. Schmitt took very little of his own belongings except clothing, old family photos, and his favorite handmade fly fishing rod. He did place the crossbow bolt—his trophy — into the aluminum rod tube and then rolled up his photos and placed them in the same waterproof container. He took two old double barrel shotguns, several 9mm Lugers and six hand grenades just in case bandits or any authority threatened them and Von Braun couldn't buy them off. Schmitt had his men sink the multiple canoes, flat bottom boats, and runabouts in the middle of the Amazon. The remaining residents would be trapped with plenty of supplies, but isolated until someone stumbled upon them. Placebo capsules containing the ground corn and Brewer's yeast and none of the components of the real-life extending capsules, were prepared to keep the residents routine in place. Schmitt wondered how long it would take for their aging process to really accelerate. If they eventually returned, would they find a senior citizen-filled compound or would they remain mostly unchanged?

Precisely at 0200, Von Braun arrived carrying two large duffel bags. He greeted Schmitt, "Is everything I asked accomplished? Are we ready to leave now?"

"Yes, I followed your wishes completely and both vessels are loaded and awaiting your orders, sir!"

"Good man, Hermann, call the men over, please, for a toast."

The four gathered on the dock, the engines of the boats idling. Von Braun pulled four small cut crystal liqueur glasses wrapped in a soft cloth from his khaki vest pocket and a flask of Schnapps from his rear pocket.

"Well, gentlemen," he started. "We are embarking on a new adventure, leaving the place that has been our safe haven for all these years. We may return, but I believe we are destined now to be princes and kings in a new world that I will control. You will be royal generals, loyal only to me. Now, a toast to the future. Prost!"

"Prost!" they shouted in unison, breaking the night's calm.

Von Braun tossed his glass to the dock shattering it and each man followed suit. They shook hands, boarded their vessels and started the trip to the Amazon. A blue cloud of diesel smoke cleared as they pushed into the tributary and soon they were on the great river that ran high, moving fast from the heavy rains upriver. Schmitt had the Sea Ray run point so they could use the boat's strong running lights to navigate the muddy waters. He estimated that by running full throttle in this current, they could be at the Porto Alegre dock well ahead of Von Braun's noon goal when he wanted to address the assembled residents of the plantation in the communication center adjacent to the Lab — an explanation for their departure. Schmitt could smell money and power with every order he followed without question, each earned trust — a small deposit on his account. He also knew the price for incompetence or failure was death.

Von Braun had this escape plan in place long before he sent those drones to test his weapon of death. He knew where to sell these two boats and where to search for a yacht and pilot on the docks of the Brazilian port. He had the money to buy influence and intended to travel wherever he would be accepted for the value he brought to those in charge. Money spoke and they would benefit from the protection and secrecy it provided. Unfortunately, if the Americans were found, there wouldn't be a safe place to hide in all of South America.

He had set up that noon meeting to ostensibly explain their departure from the compound and set the rules and goals to be followed in their absence. That is what everyone thought, but the Nazi had planted incendiary plastic explosives all through the lab, main house, and resident housing in the form of a foam-like insulation he created. It only required a small pencil shaped remote detonator to activate its destructive power. He had placed the detonators the morning Schmitt had left with the Americans. The remote was in his vest, but as a backup, an automatic timer would fire the detonators at 1225 hours just in case they didn't make it in time or were captured.

They focused on the river moving in the Sea Ray's wake. Schmitt chain-smoked almost nervously as he piloted the boat barge at its maximum speed.

"Herr Doctor, please do not think me importunate, but I was wondering about our plans after arriving in Porto Alegre. Only if you wish to share, of course."

"Well, Schmitt, we are going to be nomads for a while until I complete the rest of my work. I will purchase a yacht big enough to travel in comfort so I can work, and when we stop, I will field test in areas all around the world until I am satisfied. Only you and I will receive the spore capsules unless I can propagate those plants on the ship. The other two will receive only placebos. You are my second in command, my right arm, and you will share in my success. We have all worked hard denying our past, but what I have accomplished will validate our youth and correct the corruption of these modern impure societies. Those years we lived with Germany's power were only the internship to what lay ahead for us."

"Will we ever return to La Lupa?" Schmitt asked.

"I need at least sixty days to complete my work in a mobile laboratory, our new yacht. After that, we will settle somewhere in Europe to execute my plans, so, no, La Lupa is our past. For now you must continue to trust the decisions I make, for in the end, we will be all powerful and incredibly wealthy. Is that something you want, Hermann?"

Excited, Schmitt snapped to attention as an autonomic response to authority ingrained in his youth as an SS officer. The only thing missing was the audible click of hard leather boot heels snapping together as his rubber soled boat shoes were mute.

"Jawohl, mein Führer! Danke!"

Chapter 91
On the raft

Amazon River, Northwest

Their escape vessel sat low in the water, almost directly level with the surface of the river, barely able to accommodate the weight of the three tired passengers. They spread out with the two men on diagonal corners and Kate balancing directly in the center. If one person shifted their weight around too rapidly the raft would roll and threaten to dump them onto the river. Soon, they learned the nuances of their homemade rescue pod. The men paddled nearly continuously through the night to keep warm in the steady rain and Kate sat wrapped in a piece of blue tarp that they found floating with the current. Still, she shivered to stay warm. The men had set a good pace with their makeshift paddles and the muddy current pushed them forward at a steady rate. The landscape along the river looked the same from one area to the next and except for an occasional navigational channel marker there was no real way for outsiders to know exactly where they were. The traffic was low on the river during the rainy season, but danger always lurked with drug runners or ransom speaking pirates that patrolled the waters. Fortunately, they still had their wallets with some dollars and their official identification in case they were lucky enough to be rescued by a government agency. Otherwise they would stay out of the main channel and paddle all night just to stay warm.

The rain lightened through the predawn and other than the sounds of the morning animals waking and the persistent buzzing attack of the hungry mosquitoes, they traveled in silence, rhythmically moving forward with each paddle stroke. The night had seemed endless, but eventually vanished with the warming sunrise that broke through the clouds stirring the jungle's birds and primates. The sky cleared and the temperature started to climb, drying and comforting them. Tom checked his watch and saw it was 0700 hours depending which time zone they were currently in. Kate had her head down to her knees and started crying a little, which turned into a stream of tears as all the fear and emotion washed from her in the morning light. Things seemed better even though they really weren't.

A mid-river island appeared and Tom and Joseph started over to it. Once in the shallows, Joseph jumped in and pulled the grappling rope and beached the barge on a gravelly shore. One side of the island was a rookery for storks and other wading birds, but the side they pulled to was relatively free of water birds and feathers. Joseph waded the shallow current and started picking up fresh water mussels and large crayfish folding them into his t-shirt. They found a dry spot next and soon Joseph had a fire going using a dry vine friction bow. Once the fire was a good blaze, he located and filled a rusted gallon-sized tin with water. He boiled and tossed out three rinses of river water before settling on the fourth to cook the mussels and crawdads.

While he cooked, Kate and Tom explored the island looking for salvage and found several clear plastic water bottles, a gallon jug and a real kayak paddle. They returned to find Joseph working on a second batch, the first, cooling on palm leaves.

"That smells incredible!" Tom said, "I hope it tastes as good as it smells!"

"We better take advantage of it now because who knows when we will have another opportunity to eat again," Kate replied. "We'll boil water to rinse and clean these bottles and then fill them up with fresh boiled water. Hopefully that will hold us until tonight so if we are lucky and can find a similar island, we will just do this again, maybe find some bananas or other fruit for carbs."

They ate the mussels and crayfish like they had never eaten before and Joseph smiled as the compliments rolled his way.

"I don't think we should worry too much," Joseph reassured them, "we didn't get away from those ants by chance. That was the work of the Creator and my ancestors and grandfather. I'm pretty sure we are under their protection and will be fine as long as we stay focused on the mission. Just think of this as a little detour. I bet Brad and Jules have already sent help so I don't think we are going to be on the river too awfully long. I remember this island from the rookery and that huge roosting tree so I think we will pass Von Braun's place at around noon this afternoon. That is when we will be at the most risk. We will have to hug this side of the river and set some branches around us for camouflage. Once we are past the compound it will be an easy trip to Porto Alegre to get help. This time tomorrow, we are in Brazil and out of harm's way."

They finished the meal and prepared the water bottles. Joseph added camo to the deck and everyone smeared mud to their faces and clothes to disguise their appearance. They pushed into the current under the now hot sun and stayed close to the riverbank, fighting the snags, but relishing the relatively cool shade. The mud helped with the biting insects and their visibility — they were passed by two motorized canoes unnoticed. They would not expose themselves without knowing whom they were dealing with. Their fears grew worse as noon approached. Would they make it past Von Braun's alive?

Chapter 92
Paris

The Pasteur Institute's jet was in the air from Orly Airport ahead of schedule because the jet was already fueled and the crew all immediately available and on board before Brad and Jules arrived. The flight plan was to fly overnight to Miami, refuel and then continue to Porto Alegre. Jules requested four additional FFL soldiers be assigned to him and they seemed even tougher than Pierre and Jacque. These four were part of an FFL subgroup called 'The Elites' and functioned much as the U.S. Navy Seals, providing stealth-like responses to solve difficult situations whether they be political, military or civilian. For them, this trip was personal since two of their brothers were unaccounted for. Two of the men were experienced pilots capable of flying any type of aircraft including helicopters, one was a field trauma physician and surgeon, and the last was a seaman who could pilot any watercraft that floated. Each person on the plane carried diplomatic passports and the FFL men were armed with automatic weapons and other lethal devices. They brought with them medical equipment and supplies, RTE meals, and cases of electrolyte and plain water. If everything in Miami went smoothly, their ETA for boots on the ground was late morning.

"You had better rest now, Brad, I don't think we are going to have much time to eat or sleep once we land in Brazil. It looks like the weather is starting to clear so hopefully we can get relay transmissions from the satellite on their GPS coordinates because that would save us a ton of search time. Otherwise, we have to go to the last recorded location, by the ant army and work from there. A bit of a needle in the haystack scenario given the vastness of the Amazon basin," Jules said.

"So are we traveling by boat or air?" asked Brad.

"Both. You and I, along with one air pilot and flight surgeon, will be on an air/sea copter that has thermal imaging capabilities, and the other two will be on a very fast boat porting extra aviation fuel so we can stay up in the air as long as necessary. Plus, it will carry food, water and overnight supplies just in case we can't locate them quickly. We land on the river, anchor, refuel, eat, sleep or whatever. You know this search for Berhetzel originally seemed like a good idea, but now, in hindsight, it looks downright stupid."

"Don't blame yourself, Jules, we all knew the risks and accepted them. Those five will turn up just fine and look at those Foreign Legion men. They're looking for their two brothers so I don't suspect they are going home empty-handed," Brad said.

"Yes, but did you see, they brought extra body bags on board."

"I'm sure that is SOP for them. Quit worrying, everything will be OK," Brad said reassuringly.

"Well, hopefully you are right, but remember that this was my idea, any blood will be on my hands."

"No, my friend, the blood would belong on Berhetzel's hands. Remember, he is the man Nelson fingered as the Destroyer. Our friends will be fine, if for no other reason than because Joseph says he is under the protection of his ancestors."

"I pray you are right. I do believe God will also protect them just as he spared Jean, but until they are again with us, I will be afraid for them. We have challenged a devil and I hope he's not leading us directly into the gates of Hell!"

Chapter 93
At the dock

Porto Alegre

Berhetzel watched the close-circuit television signal being beamed to his computer as La Lupa's assembled staff stood patiently in the laboratory's communication area in front of the large hi-def screen. This was where he had often assembled staff to discuss the plantation's needs and to celebrate holidays. These people were never allowed in the main house socially — that was Ramon's domain — but lived their lives working the grounds for the food, shelter and the comforts he provided. They expected little and represented three generations of the three couples who had started in the early 1950s. With the exception of the children, they all appeared to be the same age, young adults. They called La Lupa, 'Milagro Jardin de Dios', God's Miracle Garden, because of their longevity and health and all the oversized animals and plants that grew there. Much of this area was God-forsaken, but they felt truly blessed to live under Von Braun's generosity.

Berhetzel was impressed as they quietly seated themselves on lab benches and he did a quick head count. There needed to be a total of twenty eight, twenty adults and eight children. With everyone accounted for, he started his address.

"I am speaking to you from Porto Alegre and would like to welcome you and wish you a good day. First, I would like to thank you for all your years of loyal service that you have given to the plantation. My work has flourished with your help and for that I am grateful. Now my work is taking me back to Europe where I will collaborate with colleagues to bring my scientific breakthroughs to the masses. You will have a secure home until I return, although I am not sure when that will be. Now, please feel free to fill your glasses with the wine and champagne Ramon opened for you and the children should help themselves to the fruit juices. After my toast back on this screen, please help yourselves to the food he also prepared. Fill your glasses so I can propose that toast."

Berhetzel watched as the happy, simple residents topped their glasses with drink. They stood looking at the monitor and, as he raised his glass of water, smiled widely and said, "To the future and our unfinished business. Salut!"

They replied, "Salut," in unison and started on their drinks, laughing. Berhetzel took his laptop and punched in 07/05/45-May 7, 1945 — the date Germany surrendered to the Allies. The screen flashed 'Execute?' and he pressed Enter. He watched the screen as the residents tumbled dead to the floor in a split second. Not one twitched or moved a muscle—another validation of his work. Next, he held the explosive remote up to the screen and pushed the trigger, which whined and squealed like a fax signal into the computer microphone, a series of screen commands flashed in nanoseconds across the monitor. The screen flashed white and yellow and then went blank.

La Lupa was no more. The buildings, animals and human remains would be cremated to ashes and any connection he had there erased. There would be no going back now. The future lay elsewhere linked to his genius. With his immediate past satisfactorily erased, he closed the laptop and smiled to himself. They will, he thought, find the remains of La Lupa in the intensive search for the Americans. If they were still looking for him, which we was sure they were, they would spend a lot of time sifting through that rubble. They would only accomplish wasting valuable time as he perfected his arsenal and army elsewhere. One day soon, his name would be revealed to the world as the supreme leader of the planet, a man to be feared, honored and possibly worshipped. He only really needs a little more time and since he had also had switched Schmitt's supplement to the placebo, he was the only man on earth with a near infinite amount of years ahead of him. The world would need another Superman to save her now!

Chapter 94

"We are real close now to Von Braun's place," Joseph whispered, "so as soon as I see that huge broken palm tree that hangs down into the mouth of that tributary, we are going to have to hunker down on this raft and drift silently with the current. I think it's just around this next slight curve and then that tree should be visible. So, when I wave my hand downward, we sit and drift. No verbal communication. Kate, fold that tarp up and sit on it. Remember, no movement, no noise!"

The last several hours on the raft had been hellish with the extreme heat building in the late morning and the intense humidity from the heavy rains making the air thick, heavy and stagnant. The insects — that seemed to prefer the shade of the riverbank just as they did — were starving for a meal and clouded around them, eating them literally alive because much of the mud they had smeared on had dispersed in rivulets of perspiration. Tom joked they would need a transfusion when civilization found them, but Kate worried about malaria, yellow fever and all the other serious vector-borne diseases her CDC training had covered. They all would need to start medications after blood tests once they got home to help prevent a possible debilitating disease.

Kate almost jumped off the raft at the first explosion, which was followed by boom, boom, boom, a thirty-second delay and boom, boom. The sky was instantly filled with squawking, colorful birds flying in a frantic escape, looking like firework flack erupting after the deafening explosions and thick black smoke that plumed skyward. Joseph and Tom crouched defensively on the raft and Tom quickly tossed the grapple to the river bank and pulled them as close as they could get into the shadows. The smoke continued to roll skyward and the birds tried flying back toward their roosts and nests only to be repelled by flames, which now shot skyward with the smoke.

"What do you think?" Kate asked the men softly.

"I think we lay low here for a while to see if anyone comes out of that creek. Then if no one comes out, we should head over and check things out," Tom said.

"Agreed," Joseph affirmed, "whatever just happened was no accident, we have to take a look."

They waited one long hour until the smoke was thinner, the birds settled and then started across the river where they pulled up and tied to the opposite shore.

"Just like before," Joseph admonished, "watch out for snakes and remember all communication should be non-verbal. The plan is to work our way as close as we can, watching for any human activity. We don't see life, we move in closer; we do see anyone, we get the hell out of town. This was probably an intentional move by Von Braun to cover his trail and, odds are, no one is still around, but don't take any chances. There may be booby traps set and since I'm the master tracker here, I will cut our trail in. Any questions?"

They both shook their head 'no' and the young Indian started to pick his way forward using his knife to cut small branches and vines away. A light breeze was now blowing smoke toward them and it smelled of burning buildings and cremated flesh. Kate gagged on the odor and had to cover her nose and mouth and breathe through her fingers to decrease the free flow of acrid smells that hung in the air. Slowly they pushed their way forward and soon the manicured dock area appeared. No one was around and the long tree-lined lane appeared clear leading to the house and lab. There was not a sound except an occasional 'pop' as the wood burned intensely, but no human, no animal, no bird moved or acknowledged their intrusion.

Slowly, they crept forward, walking a few steps, stopping to listen much as a hunter stalking his prey would do. Soon they were at the old gates leading to the plantation courtyard. The house and lab were gone, replaced by two large smoking piles of burning wood and debris. La Lupa Plantation was gone and, in the distance, more smoke was evident drifting skyward in the back area of the plantation where the staff cottages had been located. Just to the left of the main house was a small building that still stood intact, the size of a two-car garage. No humans were anywhere to be seen, but the strong odor of burning flesh coming from what had been the lab suggested somebody or some large animals had died in that explosion. They got as close to the burning piles as they could, looking for evidence of human remains, but the intense heat and smoke pushed them back. Tom walked over to the lone still-standing building and reached to pull open the double shed doors.

"Stop," Joseph screamed, "it might be a trap!"

Tom quickly whirled around and retreated away.

"We need to see what's in there," Tom said, trying not to look stupid.

"Right, but no one is going to open those doors directly. Grab the hose from that landscape faucet and we can tie it to the door handles and pull them open from a safer distance. I'll do it, so hand the hose off to me by the door and then you two hide behind a large tree or something."

Joseph nervously tied the right door, retreated, and tugged it open. Nothing happened so he repeated the opening of the left. Nothing. Joseph cautiously looked inside, walked in and then came out and waved them over.

"You aren't going to believe this," he said smiling.

Inside was the plantation's excess food, water, medical and clothing stores, all labeled and arranged neatly in typical German fashion. Bins of construction chains, ropes, work clothing, hats and gloves were stacked to one side. Reel mowers, hand tools, machetes, axes, and other gardening equipment covered one entire wall. The building was literally a packed treasure trove.

"Hey, look at this! A raft!" Tom shouted.

Kate and Joseph looked down into a large wooden crate and saw a large waxed corrugated box marked U.S. ARMY SURPLUS INFLATABLE EIGHT MAN.

"Come on, let's tip the crate over and dump it out!" Tom exclaimed.

He and Joseph pushed the wooden box onto its side and then lifted the bottom up, sliding the raft out of the box along with two folding aluminum paddles.

"Boy, I hope it's not rotted," Joseph said as he carefully split the tape seal around the box.

They dumped the olive green rubber raft that probably weighed close to 100 pounds. The rubber surface was smooth, and appeared new and pliable. The foot pump blew air as Tom pushed down on the diaphragm. It all appeared in perfect condition and could be used to transport them back to Porto Alegre safely and comfortably.

"Joseph, I think your grandfather is still looking out for us!" Kate said joyfully, "we can stock up on supplies, load this raft and let the river wash us down to the ocean, and look at these cans of bug repellent — 100% DEET! Thank you, God!"

"OK, so we hit the jackpot, but before we loot this place we better look around some more for Von Braun," Tom suggested.

They walked back to the burning piles, but again, only saw ash and flames. Then they went back to the animal compounds where Tom opened the gates so the trapped animals could escape. All the males, Von Braun had said, were sterilized, except the roosters, so these giants were doomed to extinction in the predator-filled jungle, but that was better than a slow starvation trapped in a fenced prison. The small staff cottages were almost totally consumed, with only low flames and glowing embers. No smell of burned flesh there.

"Look," Kate exclaimed walking over to the fungal garden, "they dug up his entire precious mushroom planting. That verifies Von Braun has escaped from here. I bet he is in cahoots with Schmitt."

Satisfied the premises were vacated, they headed back to the small storage building, unrolled the raft and chose the food, water, toilet paper and new clean clothes they needed. The raft itself was so big they decided to inflate it right there, throw in their supplies and drag it down to the dock. Thirty minutes later they started to slide the supply laden raft across the manicured lawn down to the dock and then finally shoved it into the water. They stood back, sweat dripping down from the effort, watching the life raft drift smoothly in the light breeze, grinning with satisfaction at their good fortune.

"OK, we have the fresh clothing so let's take turns bathing in the creek since the water here is the cleanest we are going to find. Joseph and I will head up the lane and light up these Cubans we liberated so you can have your privacy Kate," Tom explained, "you need anything, just scream."

"Gee, thanks, I get to test the waters to see if the piranhas are hungry this afternoon. But it's worth it just to get all this mud off and smear on some DEET."

The men retreated up the lane and found a dry leaf-covered spot under an enormous live oak and nearly fell to the ground from exhaustion and relief. Tom and Joseph cut their cigar tips with one of the Swiss Army pocketknives they found and lit up using a small Bic lighter they had also taken. The old cigars burned a little hot, but had a nice relaxing effect on the men. Twenty minutes later, Kate appeared walking up the shaded lane wearing a clean cotton shirt and rolled to the calf white pants that had been stored for the women of La Lupa. She wore a large straw hat over her wet hair and was smiling, looking beautiful.

"This is the best I've felt since we left here with Schmitt to go on our little 'picnic'! Here, I brought one of the Malbec bottles and a corkscrew we borrowed, but even without a glass I think we can sample this fine 2002 vintage. I can't wait to take a swig!"

"Well, while you two enjoy the vino, I'm going to wash up," Joseph said, excusing himself.

"A toast before we drink. Here's to our escape and our revived future, bug free, and to getting the hell out of town!" Tom proposed as each drank from the bottle.

"You know, I think old Von Braun and Berhetzel are connected somehow, but how exactly, I don't know. But I know this, if we find him or Schmitt, I'm going to take the sadistic bastards out. I almost never get mad, but they have stirred up my suppressed Irish temper. Also, I want to get him for keeping such a bad bottle of wine. This stuff is horrible," Tom grumbled.

"You're right about the wine, but obviously it wasn't intended for Von Braun, probably for the staff. And I don't want to find any of them. I'm done, I just want to go home and get married. We got in way over our heads down here thanks to Jules and I'm tired, I just want us to start our life together. Let the experts find them, to Hell with the money and fame."

"The money and fame would be nice, but you are the only real important factor in my life other than Jed!" Tom chuckled.

"Jeez! Story of my life, second banana to a black Lab!"

"Jed will be very happy to be second to you. He loves sexy women!"

"I think I'm really going to like that dog, he's got good taste."

"He'll love you like I love you — limitless and boundless."

"A man after my own heart and a dog doing the same. What more could a girl ask for?" Kate giggled.

"A Lab of her own?"

"No, how about an air-conditioned hotel room with a king-sized bed, crisp linen sheets on a sultry night with the man I love," she purred, leaning in for a kiss.

"What? No Lab?"

"Nope," Kate laughed, "I only need one beast in that room." They embraced, kissing.

When Joseph returned a few minutes later he found Kate sleeping with her head on Tom's shoulder. Tom slowly got up and laid her head down on the straw hat and walked down to the water to bathe. When he returned after fifteen minutes, she was still asleep with Joseph standing quietly on guard.

Tom picked her up like a small child and they walked away from the remains of La Lupa to the waiting rubber raft. Kate woke as Tom lowered her onto the raft and the two men pushed off onto the clear waters of the creek. Soon they were on the Amazon, refreshed, rehydrated and anxious to go home.

Five hours later as the sun set, they pulled up to a small island to call it a day. The next morning they would make a strong push forward to where their final rescue waited in more civilized waters. Odds were now that they would survive their misadventure. Time to go home, if Jules would let them.

Chapter 95
Porto Alegre

With severely discounted prices, the two boats had sold before nightfall for cash, American dollars. Since the buyers were undoubtedly involved in some sort of illegal activity, no questions were asked, and the titles endorsed and signed without question or real names. The next morning Schmitt took the cash and stopped at four different banks converting dollars to cashier checks made out to Von Braun's corporate front, Longevity Laboratories. As usual in South America, no inquiries were made.

After a full day of looking unsuccessfully for a mid-sized yacht and captain, Von Braun called a meeting with Schmitt.

"It seems, Hermann, that there are no vessels for sale that will meet our needs. They all require a high number of refueling stops, and with that, the scrutiny at Port of Call Customs each time we stop to refuel. We would have to file some sort of float plan and would be on everyone's radar. The exact opposite of our requirements, so I decided we are going to split up. I have hired passage on a Shrimper, which won't draw any real attention from authorities and will eventually land somewhere on the Gulf Coast of the United States. From there I will set up work somewhere incognito, in a very remote area. You and your men will fly to Havana once your papers are in order and then take a boat charter to Matamoros, Mexico, which sits directly on the American border. I have a contact you will meet, Stephen Ziegler, who will get you across the border when I summon you. Your job will be to keep the men fit and out of trouble until I make that contact. That could take three to four months. When we reunite, I will have everything we require to become very rich and powerful. I need you and the men so do whatever it requires to be prepared for my call. Our time is near."

"Whatever it requires, Mein Führer," Schmitt affirmed.

"You will have access to this account," Berhetzel said, handing a small black checkbook to his right-hand man. "Use it judiciously. The money is not traceable back to me, but I will monitor the account usage. You will draw in American dollars so use American banks. Ziegler will provide you with everything else you need including new cell phones, computer access and foolproof documents. It is his sole responsibility to get you to where I want you to be."

"Once the authorities start searching for the Americans and visit La Lupa, all bets are off. They will figure out our connection to their disappearance and we will be the subject to an international man hunt. I need to expedite a new plan and narrow the scope of my goals to achieve the result I desire without unnecessary exposure to ourselves. Before I call on you to join me, I will have all that worked out."

Berhetzel knew that to accomplish his goal of decapitation of the world's leading military and nuclear powers, his attack had to be a well-coordinated, modern day blitzkrieg. He needed about thirty to fifty men equipped with his death ray device to throw the world into chaos and then in history's greatest poker bluff, hold them at bay with the threat of greater attacks to come to the general populations, even if at that point he wouldn't have the means to deliver on that threat. In a world full of sheep, you only have to remove the government, the controllers, and then simply fill that void. Instant communications would make the fear of his ultimate power immediate common knowledge to nearly entire populations. Nations and their governments would fall like dominos after Berhetzel gave that initial push. Once he had control of a major nuclear arsenal, like the United States, the rest would be easy. He had done the math over and over again in his head, three of his mercenaries could take out the President, Congress and Pentagon, two or three could take out the Royal Family and British Parliament, two each for France, Germany, Pakistan, India, North Korea, Iran and Israel, and five each for China and Russia. Twenty-six men and fifty-two operating devices at a minimum. Double that number if he had the time for good measure. With trillions or quadrillions of dollars and incalculable power at stake, he would need at least several months to produce the weapons and then two to three months to train and put in place the assassins. That would put his victories and rise to power sometime after the New Year. Out with the old and in with the new. It all seemed so fitting to him.

Chapter 96
Porto Alegre

There was a large land/sea amphibious helicopter, an old, well-worn commercial prototype of a U.S. Coastguard HH-3F Pelican, ready to fly when Brad and Jules arrived. Jules did everything he could to get his pilot to fly them immediately to the GPS referenced area, but the passing storm made the journey too dangerous. They were promised an early-morning start. In the meantime, Brad tried again and again to locate the implanted GPS trackers by pinging each transponder and still there were no usable coordinates detected. The last location was consistently registering at the army ant jungle site, so that was to be their initial search area.

Jules spent the remainder of the day calling home, reassuring his wife that he would be careful and emailing an update to Jean. His doctors had forbidden him from traveling for now and Jules had promised to keep him informed. For Jean, this was personal, and the search for the Nazi Berhetzel had become a life controlling obsession. Whether he be captured dead or alive, it made no difference. Jules was worried that Jean's emotions could also jeopardize his health so he had made a promise to keep his friend supported with real-time details on the mission.

Brad went out that evening with the FFL team because he really needed to blow off some steam after being totally sequestered in Jules' apartment for all those days. Plus, it was the only thing he could do to keep his mind off Tom, Kate and Joseph. They stayed out until the early morning drinking and gambling, returning to the hotel at 0300 hours with a planned 0600 assemble in the lobby. Brad knew he was in trouble, but the Frenchmen had consumed at least twice as much as he had and acted like they had seriously overindulged. He was positive they would not make that travel deadline.

Brad was in the hotel lobby a couple minutes before six, badly hung over. The French soldiers were surprisingly chipper, sober, shaven and looking fit. He was the opposite, looking like a homeless drunk with swollen eyes and a two-day-old beard. He went straight to the coffee service and gulped down two cups of the strong black liquid, which only served to make him more aware on how bad he felt. Jules took one look and started to tease him.

"Mon ami, you look like Merde!"

"And who is Merde?" Brad groaned.

"Not who, my friend, but what," he laughed, "you look like shit."

"And feel like it, too. I can't believe those other four participants over there look like they rested all night! What's with that?" Brad asked.

"They are French, what more can I say?" Jules mused.

"Right, French, I forgot about that."

The six assembled at a corner table, Brad with his black caffeine, the rest with plates full of fruit, eggs, meats and pastries. Jules sipped on a Kir Royale.

"D'accord, I see we are all refreshed and ready to go with the possible exception of our American compatriot. We will have to make the ride upriver as smooth for him as possible, right, Paul?" Jules asked.

"Oui, smooth as Dennis' shiny head. No problem!"

"Bien, then you, Eric, Brad and I will taxi to the airstrip and be on our way. Louis, you will pilot the refueling supplies, water and food upriver on the jet ride airboat with Dennis. That should keep you, at worst, only three or four hours behind us. Hopefully this will be an in and out extraction, but we are prepared, God forbid, if it turns into a recovery mission. We should have enough provisions for eighteen to twenty hours of air travel with the fuel we are porting, and food enough for up to ten days. Questions?"

"Will we have enough air sickness bags on board?" Brad asked. No one laughed.

Dennis interjected, unconcerned about cutting Brad off, "We have discussed the entire scenario and my men and I feel our brothers, based on their training and nature, would have never separated from the Americans. Ils sont mort — they are dead, Docteur Brad. The four of us will stay on after this mission to recover their remains. It's just who we are. D'accord?"

"Yes," Jules offered, "and since I sent them down here, you will have the full financial resources of Le Pasteur to support you. Allons y." *Let's go.*

They split into two groups, one heading to the marina and the other to the private commercial airport. Brad fought nausea and a pounding head as they arrived on the tarmac next to the large beat-up looking helicopter.

"You're kidding, right? We are going to fly THAT thing into the jungle so we can be a twenty-first century version of Amelia Earhart? I can just see those ants smacking their little lips right now."

Paul walked around the chopper doing a meticulous preflight inspection along with the owner's mechanic, checked the maintenance log and gave Jules a thumbs up. Despite how it looked, it had flown for years, logging hundreds of hours flying provisions to outposts all along the Amazon without incident. Jules liked the idea that it was commonly seen flying over the area as it would alert no one and possibly give them a small element of surprise.

They boarded and strapped in, and Paul started the large chopper while talking to the small commercial airstrip's control tower. He lifted up smoothly and pushed the noisy craft forward until they were over the river and then added some speed as they followed its course looking for evidence of their friends. Flying low just over the tree canopy was causing Brad to experience motion sickness on top of his hangover and he looked almost as green as the trees they sped over. Jules was focused on the river and about one hour into the flight, were very near Pierre's last reported GPS signal. They could see a light fog arising over a small cleared area. As they neared, it was apparent that it was light plumes of smoke so Jules tapped Paul on the shoulder and signaled with his rotating hand to circle and where to put the chopper down, pointing to a cultivated area.

They circled and saw no residents, so the pilot set the big bird down. They grabbed their weapons and jumped out, leaving Paul with the idling helicopter.

"Eric, you take point about one hundred meters in front, and Brad and I will investigate as we move forward," Jules ordered.

They walked from one smoldering pile to the next, which now were only metal, ash and small chunks of charcoal that glowed and emitted light gray smoke. Everything had been consumed including evidence of the twenty eight souls killed by Berhetzel. Jules carefully approached the storage garage and peered inside.

"Looks like someone looted this building. Look at the ripped up box and all the other stuff scattered around. It appears something large was dragged that way and from that old box over there, it probably was the raft from the box." Brad said, "Let's follow that trail and see where it ends up."

They found themselves standing on the dock where they discovered discarded dirty clothing of two men and a woman. Jules was hopeful now for the first time since leaving Paris.

"This appears to be evidence they were here at some point, so now let's move upriver to their last mark, the army ant location. If they aren't there, we'll move further upriver for an hour or so till we exhaust that possibility. At that point, we will turn and do a slow, meticulous search at water level till we find them. My gut says they are alive, so let's get moving!"

They headed up the grassy lane and suddenly were face to face with an enormous goat and giant rooster quietly foraging in the destroyed house courtyard.

They stopped short and Jules looked to the astonished Brad.

329

"Now what do you make of that?" he asked, gesturing toward the freakish animals.

"Looks to me that whoever lived here was doing some serious genetic manipulating. Berhetzel would stand out as an obvious evil genius who could pull something like this off. Plus, I personally think this whole area stinks like a Nazi was here and it can't be a coincidence that he resides somewhere in this general vicinity. No, he was here and Kate and the boys made his acquaintance. Hopefully they connected the dots and got out before it was too late. Looks to me he figured it out at some point after meeting them and decided to get the hell out of town. If they are alive, I bet they are on the run. We better hustle and find them before he does. Damn Nazi!"

Chapter 97
Moving up the Amazon

The helicopter had sped past the small island sheltering the khaki green raft and its three occupants, high and fast on its way to where the wisps of smoke rose skyward. The three woke quickly from their deep slumber, the first really bug-free sleep they had enjoyed while warm, clean and dry since their overnight at La Lupa. The old rubber raft had been drifting, tethered on a long rope in the slow current at the far side of the island, out of sight from the main channel. By the time the chopper had been audible enough to wake them, it was gone, speeding away.

"We need to move into the main channel as soon as possible so if that thing returns this way we can signal it. Then we will need to act like crazy people, jumping, shouting, and waving to get their attention. Joseph, you be ready with one of those distress flares to wave around. That bird might be our quick ticket out of here!" Tom said excitedly.

Not willing to be passed by unnoticed, they decided to forgo coffee and just drink the bottled water and eat the hard biscuits they had taken from the storage building and then position themselves in the middle of the main river channel. Risky if they ran into some illegal activity, but worth it if they could escape to safety sooner. It hadn't rained in a little over twenty-four hours, the sun was bright and hot, so there would be very little chance they would be missed and not rescued unless the pilot just didn't want the trouble.

Jules had the helicopter head to 'Ant City', as Brad called those GPS coordinates and in twenty minutes, they were hovering twenty-five meters above the ground, near the tree where the three had been tied. They remained stationary while the FFL Flight Surgeon, Eric, slid down a heavy rope stopping just short of the ground. Seeing no ant activity he jumped to the ground and started searching the area. He found the cut and chewed hemp rope pieces and stuffed them in his pockets, walked around in a larger circle and then ran to the rope that was winched up.

"This is all I saw except for the cut vines and probable missing doors from the old gate, so my guess is someone built a shelter or possibly put together a raft," handing the rope to Jules. "They were most likely tied up here and either escaped, were released by someone, or executed and their bodies hidden. I didn't see any evidence of blood by the tree. I think we should head upriver about 50 kilometers, going slow, just in case they went that way to avoid contact with the burned out plantation. That's about as far as we can go without refueling this bird, then we head back and slowly search till we have to land on the water to refuel. I'm almost 100% sure they would travel with the current, but since we are here with limited petro, it's worth covering our ass by looking upriver, too, so we don't have to double back. This thing sucks down fuel so with just under a half plus reserves, I don't want to cover the same ground twice."

The upriver trip only resulted in spotting three tribal natives wading with seines and setting gill nets. They waved to the helicopter as they slowed while passing over the fishermen.

"Let's go back to the ant site and circle a little to be sure we didn't miss anything and then slowly follow the Amazon downstream to carefully look for them on the water," Jules said, nearly shouting into the headset.

The ant area didn't show any new evidence of the lost trio so they started downriver slowly hovering over the water checking both sides of the river for evidence they had passed or, God forbid, spot a floating body. They continued the meticulous process until they reached the burned out plantation where Brad spotted the original makeshift raft hugging the plantation side just above the tributary entrance to the plantation's dock. Jules had the pilot bring the chopper around and pointed to the field they had set down on earlier that morning. The pilot acknowledged the order and started to move the helicopter over to land. He was talking on his head set in French and Brad could tell it wasn't directed to anyone in the cabin. The pilot looked to Jules, smiled and gave a thumbs up.

"The refueling boat has found our friends alive and well on that rubber raft about 100 kilometers from Porto Alegre. We are going to rendezvous with them on the river, get them onboard, top off our fuel and then go back to the airstrip. Thank God this madness is finally over."

Little did Jules know, the madness was only just beginning.

Chapter 98
Somewhere in the Caribbean

Three weeks later

Berhetzel strained to study himself in a small plate-sized mirror that hung from the poorly lit cabin wall of his chartered shrimper. What he saw staring back at him was unsettling — the unmistakable signs of age — sagging neck skin, purple-black bags under his eyes and heavy creasing around the mouth. He had noticed some signs, but refused to look in that mirror until now. What he saw with his deteriorating eyesight made his achy joints quiver even more and affirmed his fears when he found soldering the delicate assemblies difficult to do. He even experienced some shortness of breath going up just three or four steps, and his right hand trembled like a man with Parkinson's. All of this in just a little over three weeks away from La Lupa. The question was *why*?

He wondered if Schmitt was going through the same thing. If not, then possibly the placebo capsules were somehow switched with the real thing. Or was there some other X factor unique to La Lupa that potentiated with the spore capsules? Maybe it was the crystal clear water that flowed at their doorstep, perhaps the water source was the real Fountain of Youth Ponce de Leon had searched in vain for so many centuries before. Something was definitely wrong.

Berhetzel had not had any contact with Schmitt since leaving Porto Alegre, but had spoken with Stephen Ziegler for a brief "Package arrived safe" coded communication when his men made it to Mexico. At that time, he wasn't ready to recall his men to the States, but now would have to ask Schmitt the difficult question, "Have you looked in a mirror recently?" If Schmitt hadn't changed, then the men would have to rendezvous with him as soon as he landed near Mussel Shoals Alabama. Then he would take the supply of capsules Schmitt controlled one way or another. It could be a messy business.

The ship he had chartered was an old shrimper that sat low in the water, noisy and relatively slow. The boat rocked and rolled in heavy weather and always smelled of rotted fish, diesel and sea salt. They had hugged the east coast of South America for two weeks and were now moving due north, skirting Cuba heading to his drop zone. When he landed, Berhetzel would sequester to a secluded farm in the rural interior of Alabama where he would put the final touches on his death ray using the parts and equipment he had removed from La Lupa, and an amazing new 3D printer he had acquired to produce the cosmetic camera mimicking exterior.

His updated device was now specifically DNA programmed to kill only humans, but with an extended range of 250 meters. All people in the broad shot kill zone would suffer an instant, painless death. With that extended range, he could take out the entire Congress with one firing pulse. It wouldn't take much effort to decapitate entire governments given enough devices. Berhetzel, unfortunately, had only so far been able to produce twelve reengineered devices, not near the number he would need to pull off his grand plan to overwhelm the entire world in one attack day.

Berhetzel called and ordered Schmitt and the men back and within three days of that call to Ziegler, he had gotten them safely across the border where they moved east to New Orleans. Berhetzel had purchased the old farm house near Tuscaloosa, sight unseen, through one of his sham corporations, and after offloading his equipment, had one of his U.S. contacts transport him to the farm. He found the house clean, secure and fully stocked with supplies because the man who provided the ride and prepared the farmhouse, Otto Hadasky, was staying on to provide security and function as his mercenary recruiter. Otto was the man who would organize and direct Berhetzel's army of Russian, Eastern Europeans and Balkan war veterans. His mercenaries would follow any order for money and kill without question, even sell their own mothers for the right price.

His plan to use mercenaries was not without risk, as they required a trust-less relationship. Because of the potential risk these men might try to sell a weapon or turn it on Berhetzel, he had built in an automatic self-destruct feature that, if tampered with in anyway, and always immediately after the third pulse firing, the weapon would explode within fifteen seconds, taking out a twenty-meter area. This secret feature would keep the device proprietary so that the user had two safe rounds to fire, but if you screwed with it in any way or had to fire it the third time, you had better be more than twenty meters away from the device in those fifteen seconds. Only Berhetzel had the ability to remotely neutralize that feature and only he could also activate or destroy any number of the devices using his computerized tracking program. The Nazi had to keep his technology proprietary so this was his important secret, his ultimate insurance policy.

Berhetzel met Ziegler, Schmitt, and the other two refugees from La Lupa in a Walmart parking lot in the suburbs of Tuscaloosa on a cool, sunny New

Year's Day. Berhetzel could see Hermann Schmitt and the other two men had, like him, appeared to have aged probably two decades in the last nine weeks. There had to be something wrong with the capsule's potency, or maybe the water was, in fact, the X factor. Or perhaps it was just time for these old men to meet their maker. The more Berhetzel thought about it, the more he felt their longevity had something to do with that pure crystalline water that they used to irrigate the crops, water the animals, cook with and bathe in. Whatever it was that had provided that benefit all these decades, it was now obvious they were in the vortex of an aging storm and that finally falling victim to lurking death was on their horizon. Survival, not world domination, would take precedence, but not before they toppled the United States government, the premiere military power in the world and the real key to world dominance. The power and economy of the United States would, after his coup, provide him with all the resources he would need to solve his immediate problem of accelerating aging. He was the genius who would outsmart death.

With all four of them now physiologically in their fifties, Berhetzel estimated that if the aging was a linear process, then they were aging approximately one year every three days. That only gave him about three weeks to overthrow the American government, establish the terms of surrender and use the virtually unlimited resources of the United States to move water from the old plantation's tributary to his new residence, the White House. He had one shot at this and in seventeen days he would have the perfect opportunity when the entire United States government hierarchy would be present and exposed for the Presidential inauguration in Washington D.C. That meant the outgoing executive branch, the President Elect, Vice President Elect, the old and new cabinets, the majority of the Supreme Court, the Joint Chiefs of Staff and Pentagon brass, and Congressional leaders and members would gather on one large stage, putting aside their political and philosophical differences in a demonstration of a seamless transfer of power. He had thought this out and would send Schmitt and two other men and place them equal distance apart in the large audience. Using the new, more powerful devices, they would decapitate the entire leadership of the country on live television and streaming computers. One shot each to the stage and then the men would rotate 180 degrees and take out the rest of the audience. His instruction would be that each take one broad shot directly to the stage and use that second and third shot to clear their escape route. They then would pocket the devices and within fifteen seconds there would be no residual evidence of them or the weapons. Berhetzel would wait near the White House for the balance of his 'army' with the back-up devices. Once he had control of the Treasury and the nuclear arsenal and launch codes, they could not stop him. Blackmailing the rest of the world into surrender would be relatively easy with his malicious demands. This would be his one and only opportunity to seize power quickly because any delay could mean death from "unnatural" natural causes. If he failed to solve the aging dilemma, he wouldn't be in power for more than four months anyway. In that case, he would be remembered as the genius, the evil destroyer, and as the one man creative enough to topple the most powerful nation on Earth.

Chapter 99
Fort Peck Indian Reservation

Montana

This dream was the first horrible nightmare that Joseph had experienced since returning to Montana after Jules disbanded the group and ceased the search for the fugitive Nazi Berhetzel. Jules had been terribly upset for sending them into harm's way realizing it was his greed and a sense of revenge for Jean and Robert that had him send them looking for an unquestionably dangerous man in an extremely perilous area. The quest for the weapon and life extending formula was on the back burner since they had found the unidentifiable human remains of so many people in the ashes of the former compound. The investigators felt that Von Braun was Berhetzel and that he had organized a Jonestown-like mass suicide and was most likely one of the participants. Unless something radically changed, the book on Berhetzel was closed as far as Jules and the Pasteur Institute were concerned. They never did find out what happened to the FFL soldiers, Jacque and Pierre, but suspected they had been murdered by the Nazi. Joseph had tried to put all those events behind him since returning to Fort Peck and had been concentrating on taking his grandfather's journals and turning them into a historical novel starting with the Battle of the Little Bighorn. Perhaps he could make something good come out of recent events that had so changed his worldview and had given him a new appreciation for his heritage and the simple life he enjoyed. Now, suddenly, he was being visited by the dreams again. At first, he associated the new dream with his work on the novel, but its intensity and his ancestor's warning pleas were clear and unambiguous. The message was the Destroyer was active again and was about to attack in a major way and that he and his three friends still had that commission from the ancestors to stop him. Evidently the end game was near and they still had the job to complete. Perhaps that was why this had evolved as a personal battle and not one waged by governmental forces — it was their commission, their responsibility. He decided to call Kate.

"Hi, Joseph, so good to hear your voice! How are you?"

"I am doing real good. I have been trying to assemble Grandfather's journals as a post-Little Bighorn novel and, you know, because so much of our tribal history is oral, the stories I heard over and over again were always detailed and colorful descriptions of my people and their daily lives, so I have a lot of material to work from. Besides that, the hunting has been real good and no big snows yet. I did ride my horse up to the cattle kill last week and other than a slight change in the color of the prairie grass where we seeded, you would never guess what happened up there. The reason I called was to say hello, but also fill you in on some new dreams that have been disturbing me."

"Wait a minute, I'm going to put you on speaker. Tom is down here for the weekend while I drive him nuts with planning our Paris wedding. You might as well put it on your calendar, July 14, Bastille Day, so we will pretend the big parade down the Champs-Élysées is really just for us," she laughed.

Tom piped in, "Hey, Joseph, thanks for calling. What is up with the dreams?"

"You know, I couldn't really appreciate what Grandfather was going through at the time, but pouring through those journals made me realize how much he held close and hidden all those years. The word I'm getting in this new dream is our search for the 'Destroyer' is not over. Evidently, he is still out there, somewhere, and is still a threat to all of us and all life on Earth. It was a vivid and strong dream. They reiterate that our job will not be finished until he is stopped. That means to me, despite what conclusions came out the investigation in the Amazon, I'd bet Brad's scalp on Berhetzel being alive and well, and planning something evil."

"OK, I'll call Jules and Brad and fill them in, then we should gather on a conference call. Jules got burned on our excursion because of those two unfortunate soldiers, and I doubt he wants to risk anyone or anything again. He received quite a reprimand from the Pasteur," Kate answered.

"Jules doesn't strike me as the kind of man to turn chicken shit on us. We were very, very close to closing the book on this monster and I truly believe it is our destiny. Otherwise, how were we able to escape that army of ants after being drugged, sprayed with pheromones and tied up? We got away because we are the ones destined to end this. These new visions have some real troubling images in them, so we have to do something!" Joseph pleaded.

"Like what?" Kate asked.

"There are images I see of Washington D.C. with zooming rescue helicopters, flashing emergency vehicles and hundreds of bodies stacked like cord wood in long rows, ID tags fluttering in the wind. It is always raining buckets with heavy winds blowing paper and trash. People were wandering the streets, crying and calling out names of loved ones, almost like those end of the world disaster movies. I saw a newspaper headline, 'Government Coup d'Etat'. Grandfather was waving me to look at the paper and says in Sioux 'He still lives'. Then the chanting over and over again 'Stop him, stop him, stop him!' The dreams are driving me nuts because, like Jean, this is personal for me. My ancestors are begging me to get Berhetzel so I *will* get his done with or without the rest of you. I know this bastard is alive and, despite what Jules wants, I will need to get him one way or the other," Joseph vowed.

"I understand, but I have to check in with Jules first, get his opinion. It's dinner time in Paris so I'll call him first and then get ahold of Brad. Did you get a sense of how soon we need to move on this?" Kate asked.

"I think it's urgent. My sense from the dreams is that time is running out. Right now, I'm somewhere between overreacting and going crazy. Even if Jules nixes it, I'm going to D.C. to do some looking around. I feel like that character Richard Dreyfus played in 'Close Encounters of the Third Kind' — this thing with the Destroyer is consuming me alive. I don't want my life revolving around some boogieman out there who's going to haunt me for the rest of my life — like he did to Grandfather. So, I go whether or not it's sanctioned because, for me, it's personal."

The call ended with Kate understanding that they would have to support Joseph because there seemed to be no choice but to get back on the hunt for Berhetzel. She believed Joseph and his visions because she had felt the power of his ancestors the afternoon they had met Nelson on that patio on the night before the old man died. But more than that, she had also felt uneasy about the way things ended in South America. There was no way that the Nazi was going to commit suicide after successfully beating death all those decades. He was a survivor and egomaniac and would see his plans out to the bitter end. Maybe he is insane, but with that insanity comes persistence and determination. She could see no way around the fact that Nelson Blackfeather had laid this at their feet and there wasn't a means to stop Berhetzel's plans beyond them completing the job. The solution was theirs alone to find and execute, a government agency would surely fail because it really was Joseph, Tom, Brad and Kate's responsibility. It was their destiny.

It was 2100 hours in Paris when Kate called Jules' cell.

"Bonsoir, Jules, comment vas-tu?"

"Très bien, ma belle Kate, and how are you?" Jules answered in French and English.

"I am very well. I hope I'm not disturbing anything important."

"Disturbing? No. Important? Yes. I am dining with my new friend Simone who is quite beautiful and very lively. She now lives at my apartment. "

"You will never change, will you, you old devil? Always the women."

"Sadly, I cannot change being French. It is a curse I must bear bravely," Jules answered with a laugh.

"Bien, then since you mentioned a curse, I just heard from Joseph who is receiving messages from his ancestors that Berhetzel is still alive and maybe up to something in Washington. He was convinced that it's urgent and feels we should do something. The dreams indicate an imminent major attack on the government of the United States," Kate explained.

"That's interesting because Jean has also been experiencing similar dreams and calls me nearly every day telling me to do something. He also saw an attack on your government. Somehow he and Joseph are now linked together in this. I thought maybe it was PTSD with Jean, but now with Joseph experiencing the same thing, we cannot ignore the warnings," he said.

"Jean had also dreamt that our two FFL soldiers might somehow still be involved, but in what way, he didn't know. So I had a search done for their GPS transponders and guess what?"

"What?" she questioned.

"The technicians located Pierre's signal in central Alabama. We lost it temporarily, but now it seems he is heading north from there. Perhaps he is working with Berhetzel as a mercenary, or is following him. Or perhaps he is just AWOL. If he is part of Berhetzel's entourage, then we are at a distinct disadvantage. Here's another problem for us, I am being watched by the Nazi sympathizers in the government here and I will need an elaborate plan to leave France unnoticed. You all need to get to Washington and do some investigating understanding that he thinks you dead, but knows your real names and appearance. Use that credit card I gave you for everything and be careful. For God's sakes be careful. I'll put together a team here and meet you in D.C. in a couple days."

Kate ended the call with, "Au Revoir," and dialed Brad thinking, *Here we go again*!

Chapter 100
I-85 Georgia

The same day

The black Mercedes Sedan was so quiet, you could barely hear the hypnotic swish of the wipers as they pushed the steady rain off the windshield. It had been a very long time since Schmitt had driven any vehicle, but the crash course given to him by Ziegler in New Orleans had prepared him to understand the modern technology, navigation systems and U.S. driving regulations. He drove at the speed limit, submissively, trying to prevent the authorities from targeting them.

Schmitt looked over to the passenger's seat and saw that Von Braun was still asleep, his lower jaw dropped, mouth open in a slight sonorous position. The man had not moved in over an hour, sleeping deeply in a way that reflected on how much he had appeared to age since leaving La Lupa. They all had aged. Schmitt knew that and he suspected that was the real reason why Von Braun had rapidly put together this road trip. Hopefully he would reveal his plans soon, including a solution for their accelerating aging problem.

As he drove, Schmitt played with the short shaft of the arrow that had killed the Frenchman Pierre. He had fashioned it into a necklace while they were in Mexico, its clinging piece of flesh encased in a clear Lucite teardrop, the shaft and arrow head encased in ornate silver with a fine silver chain fixed onto the shaft. The clear, shiny prize hung from his neck on the short chain like a crucifix. No one would guess what it was without his explanation and nobody would understand its significance to him. His fear now was he wouldn't enjoy it as the trophy of a vibrant powerful man, but it would only hang from his neck as a reminder to an aging man on what his life had once been about — the consummate angel of death.

So far the only thing Schmitt knew was planned was that they were heading to Washington. Von Braun had promised he would reveal his plan to him and the other two men when they arrived in the capital. They carried with them twelve small bubble wrapped items that were sealed in cardboard boxes. Schmitt knew they were some sort of a weapon or explosive devices, and came with a prepared fake invoice for twelve 'Natsee' digital cameras. He loved that play on words, perhaps Von Braun did have a sense of humor after all. They all possessed new driver's licenses, passports and had general admission passes that Von Braun had somehow acquired for the upcoming Presidential Inauguration. Schmitt guessed they were now destined to be political assassins.

Von Braun startled a little from his own snoring, looked around at the dreary rain and then slipped back to sleep. Schmitt felt himself drifting off and turned down the air conditioning and tuned the radio to a classical XM station, where a heroic Wagner symphony was playing. Beethoven's Ninth was next and suddenly Von Braun was awake, alert and focused on the music. As the 'Ode to Joy' finale commenced, he became animated, shaky hands and arms lovingly conducting the music, eyes closed dreamily. For that moment, he was part of the music, the music part of him.

Schmitt smiled as he drove understanding the pleasure and pride the composition cast on any German Nationalist. The music was, to him, the thematic flesh and blood of Hitler's Aryan purification policy. Purity of blood was Germanic joy. Anyone with a radio from the early thirties to the collapse of the war had heard that Beethoven piece over and over on the Nazi controlled broadcasts and became one with music as their nationalistic pride grew.

Schmitt watched tears come to Von Braun's eyes as the music ended. He seemed to collapse deeper in his seat with almost an orgasmic release.

"That was fantastic! Like being in a Berlin concert hall with kindred spirits hanging onto the melodies. What a wonderful sound system in this automobile! Must be the German components, truly incredible!" Von Braun exclaimed.

"*Ode to Joy* reminds of the best years of our lives when we were invincible during the war, and Beethoven, Wagner, Bach and Brahms played on every radio. It was a wonderful time to be alive and Aryan," Schmitt offered.

"Ya, ya, Hermann, I remember! You and I are very much alike, both of us want the same thing, a return to that singular greatness. Only you sit in this automobile with me because you alone are worthy of my total respect and trust. So now I will explain to you why we head to Washington and how we will be wealthy and revered because we are totally feared. The only real problem we face now is our accelerated aging because either my formula no longer works or something else, perhaps the compound's water, was the real youth preserving agent. Six plus decades at La Lupa of retained youth and now the years falling away in days in the face of my unfinished business. Such a tragedy! So I have moderated my grand plan and narrowed my sights

342

to the United States and its government. We are going to overthrow her leadership within a couple of hours, shock the world and control the largest nuclear arsenal and economy on the planet. It will be a Blitzkrieg from just a handful of old men. I have the technology, but not enough time to control then entire world, so we go for the big prize."

"So we will attack the United States, and check it off our bucket lists," he laughed, "not my complete plan, but we will attack to decapitate all three branches of their government, destroy their top military leaders and then occupy the White House as long as we can with threats of nuclear Armageddon. We will purport a plague of my weapons dispersed worldwide and see how much wealth and power we can extract from that blackmail. It could be a very short journey for us, or perhaps the start of a new Reich. Either way, we need to try it before we start peeing our pants. If we die for our efforts then so be it, because I will make sure, like Adolf Hitler, that they will never forget our names."

The XM radio started to broadcast Beethoven's Third Symphony, the 'Eroica', as if it was a confirmation of the old man's plan. He listened to the melodic endorphins, relaxed back into the comfort of the new car's fine leather seat, closed his eyes and smiled smugly as the music started transporting him from his youthful past toward his future grand finale.

Chapter 101
Paris

That same evening

"Bonjour, mon ami, comment sa va?" Jules asked Jean.

"Bien, Jules, why are you calling so late?" Jean asked switching to English.

"I am calling to tell you that Kate and Joseph agree with you, the old bastard Berhetzel still lives and probably is in the United States or, more specifically, the Washington D.C. area. It seems that Joseph has had visions of a mass attack on the city and I believe that aligns with your nightmares, perhaps just a little more specific. We are going to meet up in Washington tomorrow and I wanted to know if you were up to a trip over there?"

"Absolutely, I'll be ready whenever you want. I need to be a part of this!" Jules confirmed eagerly.

"Good, that's what I suspected. I had to give a general explanation of my plans to my superiors since I'm on a bit of a short leash for now. I'm sure they'll pass the information on to Paris and they will contact their counterparts in the United States, but you know how that works, it could be weeks before some paper pusher actually reads the reports. We have located and been following Pierre's GPS transponder in the U.S. and it looks like he is a few hours from the city."

"What? He is still alive?" Jean questioned.

"We have been tracking his signal now for several days. Perhaps he is working with Berhetzel — frankly I find hard to believe — and they are up to something evil in D.C, or possibly they are going on to New York or Boston. I have friends in the FBI in Washington and, once we get there, I will make some calls and get some direct assistance. The last thing I want is a repeat of the South America fiasco. No wild goose chase this time," Jules affirmed. "I need to continue to firm up plans, but expect my driver picking you up at 0500 tomorrow. D'accord?"

"Yes, that is fine. I will be ready, no problem," Jean confirmed.

Jules ended the call with a smile. His friend was driven by an angry lust for revenge. He hoped he could control that passion and use it to their advantage.

He called the French embassy in D.C. and arranged housing for them, and emailed the contact information to Kate so they could taxi over to the beautiful building after arriving. At the embassy they would be secure, well fed and have access to weapons if necessary.

At the Pasteur he tested and 'borrowed' a small handheld portable GPS receiver so they could track and pinpoint Pierre's satellite signal from hundreds of kilometers to within 100 meters and hopefully that, along with the help of the FFL team he had used to extract Kate, Tom and Joseph in the Amazon, capture him and anyone else traveling with him like Berhetzel. His team would have first crack at interrogating them, then Jules would transport Berhetzel back to France to stand trial for Robert's murder and the murder of the Minister of Finance. Too bad the guillotine was no longer possible thanks to liberal Parisian politicians. Perhaps the Nazi would not make it out of the U.S. alive, something Jules almost hoped for.

The only person in their eclectic group who was familiar with Washington was Kate so she would be in charge of getting them around town since there would be undoubtedly many restricted areas due to preparations for the swearing in ceremony and the elaborate parade planned for the new administration. All the hotels were reportedly filled, public transportation packed and streets busy with politicians and party representatives from every state. Families and school children were in town to be part of the historic event, along with the thousands of government security personnel. They would need Kate's guidance. Jules anticipated there would be near chaos in the streets just from sheer numbers of lost or confused out-of-towners. Kate fortunately had spent the first five years of her career with the USDA in D.C. and knew the streets, the areas to avoid and the all-important shortcuts to get around faster. That knowledge of the city would be a tremendous asset in getting them around when so many streets would be cordoned off. If Berhetzel was planning some sort of attack on an American leader using his device, this seemed to be a perfect opportunity to pull it off and then escape into the chaos.

They would be in the air by 0812 hours on the commercial nonstop Air France A380, the largest airliner in the world with a maximum capacity of 544 passengers. The team, however, would be isolated from the mass of coach passengers, seated in the luxurious first class cabin, where there were often unoccupied seats. Landing in Dulles International was to be at 1052 hours and that meant they would be hopefully at the French Embassy by noon. The embassy was to email or call Jules when Kate and the rest checked in. Their French Diplomatic passports would get them in, fed, and settled.

The next morning, Jules' driver brought Jean to the Diplomatic entrance of Orly Airport where Jules was already waiting with the four FFL men.

"Good morning, my friends," Jean greeted.

"Bonjour," they all greeted in near unison.

"Jean, you remember these four from the debriefing investigation that we held after South America. They will be our own little army although they were prohibited from bringing any serious weaponry with them. So, beyond some knives in their checked bags, we will need to see that the embassy arms them with some basic fire power. Just in case. According to the Head of Security at the Embassy, who called about fifteen minutes ago, Kate and the boys have arrived already and are resting up. It's just after midnight there. Another interesting thing, my contact in Paris who is monitoring Pierre's GPS transponder sent me a new set of coordinates that places him in the Virginia suburbs of D.C. near or in a public park and campsite. If he doesn't move, then this might be resolved by evening. We can only hope. Now, let's get through diplomatic security and board this behemoth."

They secured their seats and soon were in the air watching the jumbo jet's exterior camera view of the takeoff on the private video screen provided for each passenger. It was a staggering bird's eye view of the enormity of the jet and the power of the engine's turbines.

"Now, that was something," Jean said to his friend, "and it has a way of putting things in perspective, too. Thank you for including me in this trip. I promise you I won't let my personal feelings cloud my judgment. I have come to terms with Papa's death, although I still have those nightmares, which I've come to think of, like Joseph, as messages from him. Susan and the grandchildren baby me like some invalid, but I am fine now except for a little memory issue. By the way, to whom am I talking to?"

He laughed.

Jules smiled and chuckled, "I think that is the return of the old Jean I used to sit with and drink to the mysteries of women, politics and life. God spared you, my friend, for a specific purpose and you are linked through Him to that young Indian, and I am positive that when we find Pierre we will find Berhetzel. Perhaps I am wrong about Pierre and he is some sort of self-appointed double agent and still on our side. I'm just not sure because this whole affair has been full of so many strange twists and turns. His colleagues still believe he is dead or undercover and I would like to believe them, but that transponder keeps sending coordinates."

"I overheard them talking and they feel that if he didn't want to be found, he would have hacked the transponder out himself. I believe them that he still is on our side and intentionally helping keep track of Berhetzel," Jean said.

"I hope you're right, my friend. I just don't want any of us in danger again so if any of that is correct, Pierre could be our ace in the hole!" Jules responded.

"And don't forget Nelson and Papa are also watching over us."

"Yes, and that is why we will get the bastard," Jules confirmed.

Jules was happy that Jean was handling his admitted PTSD so well. For weeks after the attack, he had been consumed with rage over the murder of his father, made even worse because it was at the hands of a Nazi. His inbred hate of these purveyors of evil made him obsess on revenge. He ate little and didn't sleep, but eventually his therapist found a medication that returned him back to realm of the living. Still, Jules wouldn't risk giving Jean a weapon.

After landing in Dulles, they recovered their luggage and took two Embassy Limos into the city. It was Jean's first trip to Washington even though his father had come to the Capitol several times a year.

"Mon Dieu! This is a crazy busy place. How far is the embassy?" he asked.

"Not too far, it is in Georgetown just northwest of the center of town in a very nice area. Close enough so we can taxi anywhere easily," Jules said.

When they arrived at the sovereign French soil, Kate was just returning from a late morning run in the cool January air.

"Bonjour! Bienvenue á Washington!" She greeted the six men with cheek to cheek greetings and gave a special embrace for Jean who she had not seen since Berhetzel's murder of Robert and his near death.

"Jean, you look well. How are you?" she asked.

"Physically I am recovered, but I still harbor a lot of emotional baggage. Hopefully I can put it to rest after this trip," he replied.

"Something all of us would like," Jules added.

After everyone had settled in they met in the dining room for a royally prepared lunch buffet. The kitchen chefs had prepared a fantastic meal including champagne, French omelets, fantastic French ham, and pastries served up on elegant china with a sterling silver service that had been a gift to the French from George Washington in thanks for their help in the Revolutionary War. Brad and Joseph beat a quick path to the food. Tom ate heartily having food flashbacks to their time in Paris. France was in his heart again because of his stomach.

"After we eat, Kate will go over what we know and divide us up into teams to initiate our search. My last reading on Pierre was that he was still at the last approximate location and if that holds, we will head there after our meal. I pray that we are blessed with a quick and safe resolution," Jules said.

Fifteen minutes after they started eating, a security officer brought a man into the room and introduced him as Special Agent Rick Sullivan, a man who looked like he should have retired a decade earlier.

After all the introductions, Jules gave Sullivan an overview of why they were there, and provided copies of a brief dossier he had prepared on Pierre and Berhetzel. No mention of Nelson's diaries, the longevity drug or Jean's attack was made. Jules did suggest a possible death ray weapon and gave Pierre's transponder frequency and asked for help narrowing the search. Sullivan listened while typing notes into a small notebook, one finger push at a time.

"So," the agent said, pushing is half readers back up his nose, "if I understand correctly, these men you feel may be a threat to the President or President-Elect would likely use a stealth-like weapon that is some sort of death ray that would kill without a sound or leave a wound. That has to top our current list of crazy things I've heard in the last three weeks of prep work for this political extravaganza. Just so you know, we are vetting about thirty threats a day so that is why you got my sorry old butt. If everything you gave me is accurate, we will post photos of these men at every security check point and scan them into our facial recon program. Plus, we will watch out for any unusual camera-like devices. We only allow cell phones and cameras within the secure perimeters. Also, if this device emits any radiation, it will be picked up at the checkpoints. Other than that, our manpower is stretched as thin as it can be. I will, however, get all of you passes into the secure areas so you can do a walk through. That's the best I can do. If you can think of any way to stop the 'ray' from injuring the Presidents, please call me on this direct number." He handed each of them an official business card.

Jules looked at the card and then to Agent Sullivan.

"Here is what you should do: cancel or move the ceremony until we can get a handle on these men," he responded anxiously.

"That is not going to happen based on what you just gave me. We just don't have the manpower or authority to do that. I'll pass along what you gave me to the Secret Service, but they have their hands full of muck, too. Look, you have my number, I'll get you the passes and see about improving your transponder surveillance, but you will have only about twenty-four hours to find these men before the show starts. Once the curtain is up on that stage, there will be no way to preempt the process, so get everything done before eleven tomorrow," Sullivan said as he turned and left the room.

They kind of looked around at each other and Kate spoke first.

"Interesting man. I feel sorry for them, they have an impossible job to do, but we do also. I think we should split into four groups to see if we can get more accomplished today, find where Pierre is through the GPS data and get orientated with some general surveillance. There are ten of us so let's try this: Brad you work the GPS and stay in touch with Sullivan and pair up with Jean. Joseph, you work with Jules. Tom, you with Captain Berthoude. I'll work with Commander Forêt, and LTs Gaulette and Uhl. We should start after we get to the inaugural site by doing general observing and maybe we will get lucky. If you spot Pierre, don't show your hand. Call in and then discreetly follow him. You see Berhetzel, call in to the group and then Sullivan. No matter what, you check with Brad every thirty minutes until we find where these bastards are. Questions?"

Brad laughed sarcastically, "Just like finding a needle in a haystack and we are the thread. Just how do you suggest we protect ourselves from Berhetzel's death ray?"

Kate reached into a plastic shopping bag and pulled out a pair of polarized professional fisherman sunglasses.

"Tom and I have a theory that the weapon possibly delivers its signal or energy through the eyes. The optic nerve travels through the skull directly to the brain. The shortest and least resistant path to the brain. Anyway, the glasses will help disguise our appearance since Berhetzel, Pierre and Schmitt — if he is also here — know all of us. Don't bunch up together. It could increase the odds of being spotted. So let's go out and make a fashion statement with these shades!"

Brad slipped on a pair of the shiny reflective glasses and exclaimed, "Don't mess with the man with no eyes!" — A reference to the famous scene from the movie *Cool Hand Luke*.

Jules laughed and said, "George Kennedy and Paul Newman, non?"

"One of the best movies ever!" Tom said. "There have been days in the last months I've felt like we were trapped in some kind of a weird science fiction flick. Our 'Destroyer' is still out there looking to kill someone or something and, in reality, we aren't much closer than we were in South America. So far, good is not triumphing over evil! Had Nelson not personally given us this specific task, I would have said a long time ago to Hell with this and turn it over to the authorities."

"Such a wimp!" Brad scuffed.

"Hey, Kemosabe, you weren't almost the main course on an Amazonian picnic," Joseph teased, "I just know we are closer now to ending this than any time since we started the hunt because my dreams are about the end of the evil one. I don't know how, where or when, but I can feel it in my soul."

349

Brad was fiddling with the GPS device and said "Looks like Pierre's on the move again and heading toward the Capital. Joseph, why don't you get our ancestors to send down a couple of small lightning bolts to incapacitate them or slip some scorpions into their beds this evening? Just make sure we spare Pierre. As for the others, I'm fine with just identifying the bodies."

Kate could see that the comment had hit a nerve with Jean. She looked to Brad and gave him a 'knock it off' look and motioned with her head over to Jean.

Brad realized he might have offended Jean and offered an apology.

"No problem," Jean said, "except let me fill that order for at least one body and then you can identify anyone else you want!"

Jules texted Sullivan with the update that Pierre was in the general area of the inauguration, which they were heading to. They would search and orientate themselves so that tomorrow they could be best positioned to identify Pierre or Berhetzel, if they showed up. It was a crapshoot, but there didn't seem to be any other way but to catch them in the act. It was going to be a long twenty-four hours.

Chapter 102

Berhetzel was anxious to get the whole thing over and return to the water source where La Lupa once stood. It would be easy enough to rebuild a smaller version of the plantation for just him and a couple attendants. It would be his final place to live or die as the anonymous author of 'Decapitation Day'. He would now have to be satisfied selling his technology to the highest bidder through an intermediary. His dreams to control the world and birth a Fourth Reich, with him as the immortal Führer, was simply not going to happen when he spent nearly half his time peeing. His new reality was that he was now rapidly deteriorating and personal survival had to be his main focus. In the last hours, he had given up his idea of occupying the White House and blackmailing a leaderless nation into giving him control of their arsenals and treasury. His team still believed that was his plan, so Schmitt and the men would still fire their devices toward the platform stage taking out everyone in front of them within 250 meters, wheel around 180 degrees and take out those behind them. They then would fire toward the exits clearing an escape path. They thought they then had three minutes to escape after tossing their devices before the self-destructive explosion and they would walk away only faking injury. What they did not know was that in reality the device would actually explode in fifteen seconds after that third attempted burst so they also would be victims of the weapon. No evidence, no one to interrogate. Berhetzel would position himself at the White House gates to observe the ensuing panic. But he would not have the pleasure of firing his weapons enough times to walk in untouched. For now, he would observe the chaos and then work his way back on foot to where he would have parked the Mercedes in a parking garage near the Smithsonian Museum complex. He would then drive back to the Alabama farm and prepare to escape back into the jungled Amazon. Ziegler would get him back to Mexico and then Cuba for a flight to Porto Alegre. Ziegler would then replace Schmitt as his right hand man, at least until he wasn't needed anymore. For now, Berhetzel had less than twenty-four hours to wait before he would usurp Adolf Hitler and be crowned the most evil genius in history. Too bad it would have to be an anonymous coronation.

Berhetzel was tired, showing his physical decline. He was having difficulty passing urine and his muscle tone was becoming weaker each day. He now had an obsession with mirrors checking his appearance several times a day. The progressively sagging wrinkled skin, growing age spots and sunken hollow eyes would be enough of a disguise to protect him as he didn't even recognize himself in the mirror. He had tripled the spore capsules, but the only result was bloody diarrhea.

He sent the men out to scout the area so they would feel prepared for the next day's attack. He stayed in the small boutique hotel he had been fortunate to secure rooms at a super-premium price when he offered the owners a bonus of five times the already inflated price to be close to the main event. The three rooms had cost over fifteen thousand dollars for the two nights, but would allow him a good place to rest and easy access to the highway when he needed to get away.

The television was full of news of the scheduled events and was focusing on the changing weather. What had started as a mild sunny day was deteriorating into a gray, cold afternoon with light rain starting early then becoming heavier by nightfall. The all-important next day's weather was predicted to become a Nor'easter with a storm coming off the Chesapeake turning the increasing rain and wind into blizzard conditions about the time the President Elect would be sworn in. By the parade's scheduled start there was the possibility of 6-8 inches accumulated of heavy wet snowfall blowing and drifting around the streets effectively cancelling the grand parade.

Berhetzel planned on treating his men to a great meal this evening to make sure they were back to the hotel at a decent time. He had collected all their personal belongings from the car and placed them into their rooms. They had conservative clothing to wear, all new, and would appear as the rest of the audience with suits and ties under heavy trench coats. They would carry only personal identification, their event passes and the lookalike camera weapons. Hats would help them blend into the crowd. The game plan was for the men to be in their seats as soon as possible after the screening started, in seats that had them placed in near equal distance apart, well within range of the stage. That perfect placement had cost the Nazi thousands of dollars, but in the age of the Internet, you could purchase anything for the right price. He had purchased three sets of two and donated the three unused seats to a local Priest, Rabbi and a Baptist minister. Sounded like a joke, but Schmitt would not be laughing seated next to a Jew.

He would rest his weary body the balance of the afternoon in preparation for his triumphant day tomorrow. Dinner with the men would be his farewell to his associates. Then he would sleep and awake a young man in an old man's body, eager to fulfill his lifelong destiny. He was about to become the destroyer of the greatest nation on Earth.

Chapter 103

By the time Kate and the men arrived in the general area around the secured audience seating for the next day's inauguration, the temperature had dropped ten degrees and a cold, light drizzle of rain was falling. Kate had everyone break into their assigned groups and they split off and went in different directions. They mainly concentrated on the west facade of the Capital Building where the ceremony was to take place, and Brad surveyed the area over and over using the small GPS computer tablet, trying to locate Pierre's transponder signal. The wind and rain continued to intensify and most people were moving quickly to their destinations with collars up, hats pulled down and umbrellas leaning into the strong driving rain. Soon it became apparent, that unless they ran directly into Pierre or Berhetzel, it would be next to impossible to pick them out of the buttoned down pedestrians. Jules called Kate.

"I think this is a waste of time," he said, the wind buffeting his voice. "We can't even tell if most of these people are male or female. In fact, we can barely stay in visual contact with each other. Why don't you contact Joseph and Tom and I'll call Jean and we'll meet at the taxi stand and go back to the embassy before we all get pneumonia."

"It does seem rather pointless, let's do that and brainstorm with some brandy by the Embassy's fireplace," she suggested.

When they arrived back in Georgetown, the wind nearly ripped the taxi's doors off as they exited. They ran to the building's foyer and through security.

They immediately went to the conference room where a roaring fire was crackling.

"The fire smells like the cherry wood I burn at home," Tom said.

One of the embassy staff carrying a tray with coffee, brandy and cognac overheard him and said, "Non, Monsieur, that is French Oak that we bring from home. The same fine wood we age these liqueurs and wine in. The wood burns to warm your body, the liqueurs will warm your soul."

He left the drinks and removed their coats to dry. They each grabbed a small crystal glass of the golden liquids, Joseph pouring a fresh pressed coffee.

"Alors," Jean proposed raising his glass, "to our friendship, our mission and to our enemies being stupid or careless. Santé!" *To health.*

"Santé!" they all affirmed.

"Bernard, the chief of security, gave me this package from Agent Sullivan when we arrived and it looks like we have this new small GPS tracker and ten two-way earpieces for communication that will link up to the tracker. His note says the units are linked with an intensity signal feature so that if we are closer to the target, the signal will be louder and more frequent. He said only use the handheld if the object of our search becomes stationary, then push the green button to zoom in on the locator map. He says that can place us within twenty meters of the signal source. Also, here are barcoded security badges with our photos. How did he do that?" Jules asked.

Kate looked at her badge.

"They pulled our passport photos. I recognize mine."

"Spooky," Brad said incredulously, "your tax dollars at work."

"He even gave us a secure password to use if asked," Jules said. "Are you ready for this? Brave Warrior!"

All eyes went to Joseph who let out a broad smile as he shouted, "Hoka hey!" a Plains' Indian war cry.

Tom felt the hair on the back of his neck stiffen as the shout hung in the air for a prolonged second. He imagined hundreds of warriors screaming their hatred at a surrounded Custer as they extracted their price for years of abuse and genocide. Joseph's cry had startled most of them, with the only ones fully understanding his response, the FFL men. They felt that raw emotion and immediately were patting him on the back in comradeship.

Brad looked at the GPS unit when it started to vibrate silently in his hands. He logged on with his thumbprint.

"Pierre is on the move again and is heading away from that earlier spot we were searching. He now is reaching this unit's max accuracy range. I will have to expand to a general location setting, which won't help us much better than the Pasteur receiver. It appears he is tracking south on Interstate 64 toward Richmond. Maybe he was just visiting the sites as a tourist," Brad joked.

"Tourist my ass," Joseph said. "He didn't chicken out and he wasn't turned off by the weather. Maybe he was a scout or courier bringing someone like Schmitt or Berhetzel in to do their thing, but my gut is telling me nothing has changed. We are still involved in something very dangerous and tomorrow is the logical culmination. Trust mine and my ancestor's warnings, we are on the verge of an American Armageddon. It scares me shitless."

"He is right, tomorrow is the day. I feel it also," Jean added. "I survived for one reason and that was to avenge Papa's murder and genocide of God knows how many souls during the war. There is no way I am leaving this town until this evil is permanently eliminated."

"D'accord, then we will be on task tomorrow to stop Berhetzel and anyone who works with him. We will need to rest well this evening. That means that I will give security the order that no one leaves this Embassy until we leave as a group in the morning. We need to be at our assigned posts at the security stations about three hours prior to when security begins screening pass holders. Hundreds are going to move through screening at a very rapid pace and with the weather looking marginal at best, I bet there will be a mad rush close to the start because no one will want to wait in the cold rain any longer than necessary. Here's how I will assign our teams. Brad and Jean will be in a tent using the GPS, and Jean you can recognize Berhetzel so you two will be Team One. Joseph and I will be Team Two since we both know Pierre, and my young friend has seen Schmitt and a disguised Berhetzel. Tom and Kate will roam outside, sorry, with our muscle scanning visually for any off them. Unfortunately, the weather will apparently be deteriorating from rain and wind to a mixed snow and at near show time, very heavy snow and wind. So, dress warmly and say your prayers. Bonsoir mes amies."

There had been talk of delaying the public inauguration for two days, but the President Elect did not want to be sworn in with a private ceremony to only do it again in public two days later. He was from Minnesota and the new Vice President was from Maine. Her moniker was 'the toughest woman in America' because she came from a family of tough commercial lobsterman. Neither one was going to concede their public moment because they had built their campaign around the slogan 'A Leaner, Tougher America'. They couldn't have imagined their first day in office would test their personal toughness.

Tomorrow it appeared the world would be freed from the 'Destroyer' if he failed or fall with the death wave of his hand as the United States collapsed at his feet.

Chapter 104

As the day transitioned from afternoon to evening, Berhetzel was becoming very worried the deteriorating weather could interfere with the power delivery of his device. He closely monitored the weather forecast and the televised news stories postulating an historic cancelling of the public ceremony. The only good news was that the arrogant President Elect was promising that a "little bad weather" would not interfere with the business of State. They would not "wimp out." Satisfied that the new world leader would stand on that stage with his hand on a Bible, he called for the limousine he hired to take his attack force to a special restaurant for dinner.

The German Eagle was listed as one of the top five ethnic restaurants in the Washington D.C. area. The staff spoke German and dressed in traditional server's attire and would likely be the closest the men would be to their culture since escaping Germany over six decades ago. Little did they know that this would be their last meal unless the ceremony was cancelled.

The owner heartily greeted them at the entrance and took them to a small private dining room. The restaurant had a distinct Bavarian feel with dark half-timbered stucco walls, heavy ebony wood hand-hewn tables and the lingering smell of good German beer. The female severs were dressed in the Dirndl dress and lederhosen and their hair was braided back with tiny wild flowers woven in. If the men hadn't known better, they would have believed they were home, in Munich.

The first steins of Bitburger arrived to happy exclamations as the men thanked Von Braun.

Schmitt proposed a toast, "I think I speak for the men in wishing you success for your coming endeavors and to thank you for supporting us all these years since the war. You have provided us enduring youth and health, cared and fed us, and for all that and more, we truly thank you. Men, raise your glasses to salute our benefactor, Dr. Josef Von Braun. Prost!"

"Prost!" they heartily shouted.

They each downed the large steins in one long swallow and wiped the frothy beer foam from their newly grown beards. This particular beer had been a favorite for the troops during war and they tasted the flavor of their youth in the amber liquid. This was to be a special banquet meal and soon the wait staff delivered plate after plate of delicious meats, cheese and heavy dark bread. The beer flowed and the men felt the nostalgic urge to sing joyfully as the plates of delicacies long forgotten became resurrected memories. They sang the old beer hall verses to reincarnate the voice of a nation when Germany had the world at her feet and they all had felt invincible. Now their voices rang out, a melodic warning to the world to prepare to be dominated by their new Reich.

"Danke, men, I really wish to show my appreciation for your loyalty and support with my promise the best is yet to come! Hermann will go over my detailed instructions for tomorrow's celebration. Again, after we leave tonight, be absolutely sure you understand and do not deviate from your orders. But for now, let us celebrate in comradeship to our past and glorious future. Prost!" Berhetzel commanded as the men took down their second large stein of Bitburger.

Berhetzel had made sure that Schmitt completely understood what was to be done the next day. Each man was to enter security screening from a different portal. Their seats were assigned and they were not to change that seat location. They had been trained by Schmitt on use of the weapon and they understood they were to trigger it three times—the first forward toward the President, the next to the rear to eliminate a large portion of the audience and create a panic, and the final burst directed at the security stations to clear an escape . They believed they had three full minutes, to place the devices under a nearby victim so that when the self-destruct mechanism occurred, that victim would be considered a suicide suspect, misdirecting the authorities. What they didn't know, including Schmitt, was they actually only had fifteen brief seconds to escape so they, too, would be victims. Their orders were to befriend the person seated adjacent to them, those second tickets belonging to the rabbi, priest and pastor, and assist them out in the ensuing panic and bad weather. Most importantly, timing of the assassination was specific — they were to stand at the handshake after the oath of office when the crowd would be giving a standing ovation with the traditional trumpet fanfare followed by 'Hail to the Chief'. At the cannon salute, they were to fire their volleys. The plan was easy enough once they got past security. The new modified weapon, they were warned, would heat up as they ramped up to fire, but as long as the so-called lens was pointed away from them, they were safe. The men were well trained and confident of success and looking forward to returning anonymously to South America and resuming their lives while waiting for the spoils of their actions. They hoped returning would also reverse their rapid aging.

They left the restaurant at ten p.m. full of hope and pride in their cause. The heavy driving rain was colder yet, but the limo was warm and inviting as they climbed in happy, full of beer and new hope. Tomorrow was to be D-Day for America, when the Destroyer fulfilled his destiny.

Chapter 105

Kate looked out the bedroom's window and silently shook her head. Tom came over and wrapped his arms around her from behind.

"Thanks for that," she said, "that might be the high point of my day. Look at that mess out there. The weather forecast is predicting the worst of it to hit almost on cue when the oath is being administered. The news reports did say the President will keep his speech at a minimum and might possibly delay the parade till tomorrow. They also said it would be a real-time decision."

"I'll just be glad to get this over. It's going to be hell out there and, frankly, I don't know how we are going to spot anyone in this mess. I'm going to get dressed, it's almost time to meet down stairs," Tom said.

Kate lingered, staring out at the driving rain, frustrated, closed her eyes and said a silent prayer and whispered, "Your will be done," as she turned from the leaded glass window. It was time to go.

Downstairs, Jules gathered the group for final instruction.

"D'accord, mes amies, you all look dressed not to impress, but to stay warm. This weather is supposed to only get worse so with our twenty-five-minute walk down to the capital, you might want to double layer just to be safe. No sunglasses because you will just stand out like a sore thumb. Today, the less obvious we are, the better our odds. These people are pure evil so take nothing for granted."

"Alors, here are your two-way ear pieces to communicate with each other and to receive Pierre's GPS intensity signal. And here is a small laminated flip book containing computer-aged renditions of Berhetzel, Schmitt, as taken from Kate's cell camera, and Pierre's service ID photo. Watch for the subtle nuances of men trying to hide from the security cameras or screeners. The most common one is face to the floor to avoid eye contact. They will be running facial recognition programming outside from the queue so you will have a small level of backup. After they get in the tent, there will a TSA-style screening going on by the best agents the TSA has in the Metro D.C. area. My understanding is that no umbrellas will go in, and the only electronic devices would be cell phones and simple cameras. No food, thermoses of coffee or hot chocolate, or flasks of liquor will make it through. Any questions?"

"I bet there will be enough coffee and booze confiscated to open an Irish pub. Maybe I can be assigned the job of screening the liquids for content. Might be a good way to stay warm!" Tom exclaimed.

Kate and Jules flashed Tom a quick smile before Brad quickly jumped in and said, "I have the latest on Pierre's location. Looks like he's not moved since about eleven last night," Brad said, "so if our theory is correct, he should start soon to move toward the Capital and, with him, Berhetzel. What if he doesn't move?"

"Then we go get him, "Kate said. "Remember, he isn't the primary target here, just hopefully our ace in the hole to get Berhetzel. If the ceremony goes off without a hitch, we can send the Feds out to get him and then find out if we postulated correctly or are just a bunch of idiots."

"So that means at least one more idiot than me. Good because I really hate being the only one!" Brad joked.

"Why? You always play the part of the Village Idiot so well," Tom laughed.

"That's because I'm married and have had a lot of experience at it," Brad replied.

They broke into teams and started the long walk down to the Capital, their heads down, leaning into the driving rain. The driving wind allowed the cold to cut right through them and Brad indicated his unhappiness verbally, "Christ Almighty," he grumbled.

They fought the wind and finally arrived at the large clear-sided security tent that was rattling in the heavy wind and rain, and introduced themselves to the FBI and Secret Service personnel at the entrance before being admitted. There appeared to be about two dozen Marines working security with automatic weapons at each entrance. It appeared no one could pass through this virtual security rectal exam with any sort of lethal device. Sullivan saw them and came over to talk.

"Welcome to my world," he started, "what you see here is just the tip of the security iceberg. What you can't see is all the electronic, nuclear, radar-based, and God knows what else that probably has all the molecules in our bodies doing the Twist. Just so you know, someone is taking your information pretty seriously because they have doubled the roving agents working the inside perimeters and slowed the screening process on an as-needed basis. You should also know we have narrowed Level A threats down to only four and you're number two, and we all know what number two is!"

"Pardon, what is number two?" Jean asked.

"Merde, number two is merde!" Kate replied.

"What is merde?" Tom questioned.

"Think back to your potty training, Tom. Number one is pee pee, and number two is…" Kate laughed.

"Wow, that was like Abbott and Costello, except no one was at the plate. And we are supposed to save the world?" Joseph mused.

"D'accord, that is enough. We better get going to our assigned areas. Monsieur Sullivan, here is a flip book of who we are searching for. I would assume extremely dangerous," Jules said.

"Thanks. Riley, take this and copy and distribute it to every agent," Sullivan said, handing the photos off to his assistant. "Now before you leave, I want you to step outside into the seating area for some quick orientation."

He led them out through the heavily guarded side exit.

"It is difficult to see, but there are thirty armed snipers on the roof tops of every building and at several levels of each building. They won't help us much today because of the wind they can't see to shoot at that distance. Look up. See any helicopters? Nope, they can't see to fly. We are about in the middle of the audience seating and we can't see the stage either. If the President is in danger, it will have to be a RPG or SAM missile or an up-close-and-personal attack. If your man does have a so-called death ray, then I would put him at the number one threat. Please don't let me down. This is enough of cluster already. Be smart and be safe, and if you need me or any help, press your earpiece control two times. I got to go," Sullivan said. He quickly pivoted and returned to the tent.

People started to filter through security and look for their seats. Jules gave a thumbs up and they went to their stations.

Jean had the appearance of a hungry wolf on the hunt, about to attack. Jules also saw that hatred and wondered if Jean would have the strength to control himself if he got to Berhetzel before anyone else.

Chapter 106

All four of the former Nazis met for the final time to review their plan, escape protocols and discuss "what if" scenarios that might occur. There were to be no deviations. These men were from a time where authority was absolute and a promise of great power and wealth meant they would blindly follow that authority. They were soldiers, Nazis, but beyond on that, they would eagerly obey these orders because they believed in Von Braun.

"Men, I want you to remove all ID except your passports and only take one hundred dollars in case you need it. Remove all rings and jewelry and place them for safe keeping in my brief case. Cover your old tattoos with that spray-on body make up. We don't want anyone getting the right idea about us."

They all laughed and joked as they placed old SS rings with their worn death skulls in the case, and Schmitt reluctantly removed his arrowhead necklace and laid it gently in the case.

"Don't worry, Hermann, I will be careful with it," Von Braun assured.

"Here are your weapons for the party. There is one more feature you don't know about. If you double press the small red button that looks like a tiny LED, you will activate an independent self-destruct mechanism. For this feature, you will only have five seconds to toss it like a grenade, but definitely get rid of it. One of the two auxiliary batteries has enough explosive power when activated to clear 10 square meters. Under no circumstances return here, go to the safe house you were shown, and in seventy-two hours call me on the number you all memorized. I will arrange your extraction. Once we are secure in Argentina, I will make the necessary arrangements to reap our rewards. Remember not to call that number until the seventy-two hours are up."

Only Berhetzel knew that all of it was an elaborate ruse. The phone number was actually for a Mr. Chicken in Arlington. These men wouldn't make it out of the audience seating alive. They would be the sacrificial lambs, he the Judas goat.

The men saluted him as they departed to walk down to the security screening area. Schmitt was going to enter by the North entrance and the other two by the South. They fought the wind that seemed to be testing their resolve, but their adrenaline was pumping and their hearts raced in excited anticipation. By the time they reached their respective entry ports, the lines were actively moving, full of people anxious to get into the shelter and warmth of the tents. The mood was festive with members of both political parties jokingly blaming the other for the horrible weather. As Tom had predicted, the thermos, umbrellas and liquor flasks were piling up rapidly in large green trash carts on both sides of the lines. Some grumbled as they 'hat checked' expensive sterling flasks, but most understood the need to protect the public from drunks and flying debris.

Schmitt entered the North tent a visibly different looking man than he had been in Argentina. His hair had gone from close cropped to long, silver and tied in a short ponytail. He sported a full, well-trimmed, salt-and-pepper beard and wore black wire rimmed bifocal glasses that assisted his failing eyesight. Kate, who roved outside the tent, didn't recognize him and since she was in heavy outerwear with a thick knit hat pulled down and coat hood over that, even Tom might have missed her. Schmitt looked right at her from the side, but never made the connection because, in his mind, Dr. Kate Vensky was dead, forgotten, consumed by an army of tiny foragers. Inside the tent, Brad and Jean were close enough to touch him, but his aged appearance disguised him well, as he looked nothing like their laminated photo ID. He breezed through security and exited into the seating arena. At the South entrance, the other two men who were unknown also entered without difficulty. They had their positions, their newly modified, more powerful weapons and now only had to wait for the triggering event.

The thick driving rain was morphing into heavy crystalline precipitation, the wind sticking multiple white flakes together that fell in heavy clusters. The heads and backs of the audience were coated thickly giving the appearance of row after row of seated snowmen.

The Rabbi finally took his seat next to Schmitt who groaned softly his disgust. The Jew started a conversation about the conditions and Schmitt was polite as he pondered whether he would push the man forward before he took that first shot. No, that was not in his orders, but this Jew was like a personal bonus so he would find a way to eliminate the man.

Schmitt looked around for security, but only could recognize the uniformed Metro Police. He was positive plain-clothed security was circulating, but he could barely see the stage at about 100 meters in front of him. He could hear the military bands playing festive and patriotic tunes over the loud speakers, but really couldn't tell where they were playing from. The temperature had continued dropping and the wind was starting to howl as it pushed the stinging ice crystals. About fifteen minutes before the actual start time, he could hear the crowd in the first rows cheering as dignitaries filed in. The cheers rose like a wave from front to back as the snow-blinded audience, not to be left out, joined in the enthusiasm, just happy to be part of the historic event. Schmitt wondered if anyone would question his taking a 'picture' of really nothing but a snowy curtain.

The announcement came that the ceremony was about to begin and then exactly on schedule, the Armed Service band's fanfare *Hail to the Chief* announced the entrance of the Chief Executives. The blinded audience rose, grumbling about their intermittent view, and cheered their old and new leaders on. A prayer of thanksgiving for the nation was offered by an eloquent Doctor of Divinity and the exiting President was introduced and took the podium. He gave his brief farewell speech, joking about the extreme conditions and Snow-mageddon. Again, Schmitt could only try to listen to the speech as the stage view was nothing but a curtain of white, with the howl of the punishing wind even seeming to force the chief executive words away from the audience. Next, the Chief Justice of the Supreme Court asked the President Elect to stand to affirm the oath of office. With a firm, "So help me God," the new President was empowered and the near-frozen audience rose from front to back like a human snow tsunami, cheering wildly to support their new leader and to thaw their frozen bodies. Trumpets sounded and 'Hail to the Chief' played proudly.

Schmitt firmly held and positioned the weapon, pointing it forward not even pretending to be taking a photo, leaning forward to steady himself against the wind that was now manically howling like a pack of wolves. When cannons sounded, he fired the first burst and smiled as the forward rows of audience toppled like snowy white dominos. He immediately wheeled and released the energy burst on those seated behind him. The weapon was now so hot he could barely hold it as he fired the third burst to his exit path, and immediately dropped the device into the rabbi's heavy woolen coat pocket. He then rushed to the exit dodging the fallen and smiling as the three weapons detonated in near unison. Unsuspecting that he had escaped his own death by milliseconds, he heard survivors yelling to take cover from the 'lightning strikes' as they rushed screaming to the now unprotected exits in a stampede of humanity. He flashed back to his SS Bolts that had been worn proudly on his black Nazi uniform. Lightning, indeed. Schmitt slowed and let the crowd push past him, chuckled at their obvious lack of self-discipline. As he passed the near exit, he made mutual eye contact with Kate, both instantly recognizing the other and he bolted, pushing his way out to the street in a panic, having suddenly lost his own self-discipline. Kate had no weapon nor did Schmitt, but she grabbed the FFL soldier and ran after the fleeing Nazi.

They spotted Schmitt about half a block ahead running and sliding on the slippery surface and they ran after him shouting his name. The air was filled with now with the horns and sirens of multitudes of rescue vehicles that sped to the venue. Schmitt heard his name shouted and he made a mad dash to cross the busy boulevard, just up from the security tents. The snow concealed an approaching ambulance that hit Schmitt broadside, crushing and then dragging him as it slid, unable to brake on the icy pavement, leaving a trail of crimson on the pure white snow.

Kate and the French soldier ran over to the stopped ambulance to find Schmitt's mangled body twisted, with his head laying sideways, nearly severed, attached only by slivers of skin and flesh. He laid crushed, a literal dead end in the search for Berhetzel. Kate stood back and watched grimly as Ambulance 1946 from The Holocaust Survivors Hospital of Greater D.C., slowly pulled off and away from Schmitt.

Chapter 107

The historic extreme weather conditions were forcing Berhetzel to revise his personal plans. No longer would he position himself at the White House because he was rapidly bleeding his vital energy and feared not getting out of Washington and back to his water source. He decided to stay in his room and watch the unfolding events on Fox News Network, which seemed to have the best images of the stage through the blinding snow. The reporters constantly apologized for the poor quality of their transmission and kept returning to their weather personnel who described a virtual shutdown of the entire Metro D.C. area from a snow that had greatly intensified without warning in the minutes just before the swearing in ceremony. There was no meteorological precedent to compare to the conditions on 'Snow-guration Day'.

He watch the television screen intently, anticipating the unfolding of his plan as the President Elect took the oath of office, shook hands and received hugs from his family. As he turned to face the audience, the combined bands played the trumpet flourishes and then 'Hail to the Chief'. As they played, he saluted the former Presidents and then turned to face the flag at attention. When the band finished, he rotated back to face the audience, the canon fire commenced. On the edge of his seat, Berhetzel strained to watch the screen to see the people on the stage, really a world stage, collapse as his weapon found its mark. No one fell or even blinked, but suddenly the stage was flooded with security personnel and the new President announced that due to the rapidly deteriorating weather conditions, he was concluding the ceremony and would address the nation later in the day. The obvious anxious security personnel then hustled the Presidential party off the stage. He turned up the television's volume.

"There appears to be some problem at the Inauguration, it appears to be cancelled due to the extreme weather," the anchorman postulated, "Peter, you're close to the stage, do you have a sense of what has just happened?"

"Yes, we are receiving multiple reports of three or more lightning strikes to the venue seating areas with multiple casualties numbering in the dozens.

The President, as you just saw, is fine and safe, but it appears in the audience we have injured and dead. That is all I have at this point."

Berhetzel angrily turned from the television set with the realization that his plan had failed. The weapon's potency had been limited by the heavy snow, which undoubtedly absorbed the energy bursts and limited their kill zone. He glanced back to the television picture that was attempting to focus on the audience seating, but appeared like a 1950s black and white, rabbit-eared hazy screen picture.

He started to clean up in preparation for his trip back to Argentina and dumped the men's personal belongings into double plastic bags, and laid them next to the bathroom trash. He was leaving with only the clothing on his back and the three remaining weapons as he needed to move fast to get to his contact point to leave town while the focus was on the disaster at the Capital. The world would be closing in on him and, without a true moment of luck or genius, even if he made it back to what was left of La Lupa, he was done for anyway. He would have find a way to survive, he always did.

The television started reporting more stories of survivors from the supposed lightning strikes describing at least one hundred dead including congressmen, senators and celebrities. That was all he needed to hear, pulling on his heavy overcoat, he closed his briefcase containing his passport, extra cash and the two spare weapons. One other was easily reached inside his coat pocket. He walked down the single flight of stairs of the small hotel into the tiny lobby and out the front with his head down to avoid the stinging wind and pushed by two men shooting them a quick sideways glance. He instinctively looked again just as the Frenchman did. Jean's eyes signaled instant recognition as he grabbed the big man looking at a small computer screen and made him look.

"Berhetzel!" he screamed.

The aging Nazi, with panic rising through him, dodged them with incredible speed to his right through some tall, dense evergreen hedges and disappeared from sight into the blinding snowstorm.

Chapter 108

"Kate, we saw him! We spotted Berhetzel at the Spencer Boutique Hotel, he was just leaving and when he recognized Jean, he ran off like a scared rabbit. We lost sight of him immediately in this damned snow. What do you want us to do? We have no weapon," Brad said excitedly, holding down the transmit button on the two-way.

"Wait for us. Everyone on this earpiece system has just heard your call. Jules, Tom, Joseph, you copy that?" she asked.

"Yes," Tom acknowledged.

"Oui, we will get everyone over there. He can't go far in this mess, so wait until we check out the room and then we'll split up to search for him," Jules said.

"I'm sure I can track him no matter what the conditions. These earpieces will be our lifeline. Keep the Legion men there to prevent him from slipping back into that chaos at the Capital, which would really hide him well from us," Joseph suggested.

"Vite! Vite! He is getting away. You must hurry! Please, hurry!" Jean pleaded.

"We all should be there within fifteen minutes. Wait for us!" Kate ordered.

Brad and Jean talked to the desk clerk while they waited for the others. The clerk recognized Berhetzel from the computer-aged graphic, but thought Schmitt may have been there though much older looking. Pierre, he said, was never there, despite what the computer was reading. The four men who were staying were older, "significantly older gentlemen."

The others arrived in less than fifteen minutes, flushed and out of breath from trying to run against the wind and snow. The clerk took them to the rooms.

"There is a very strong signal coming from this room," Brad said, "but where is Pierre?"

"Here in the bathroom trash are some Nazi SS rings and jewelry," Jules said. He walked over to Brad and their earpieces began to screech wildly. They desperately grabbed at their ears to pull out the devices.

"What the hell?" Brad asked.

Jules held Schmitt's necklace, examining it. He then took it over to a desk lamp, rotating it back and forth in the light, examining the Lucite-encased broad head.

"Mon Dieu!" he exclaimed, "Look at this," as he rotated the crystalline teardrop around in the light.

Each looked, but only saw the arrowhead.

"Here, at the base of the arrow, near that remaining bit of shaft," he indicated, "in the teardrop is a piece of dried flesh with Pierre's transponder buried in it. Here is what is left of our friend who even in death was able to show us the way to Berhetzel."

"I need to get going," Joseph said. "I want Jean with me since he also is invested personally in this and has seen the man. I suggest you all listen for our transmissions. We will keep our channels open. Nine times out of ten wounded animals head into the sun and this bastard's arrogant pride, I'm sure, is damaged, so work to the west and north and I'll steer you from my tracking. Let's go!"

"Allons-y!" Jean shouted.

Chapter 109

Berhetzel had slipped through the dense hedge and ran into an adjacent Metro Park to collect his thoughts and his breath. That small burst of adrenaline had his heart in near palpitations, his brain foggy with a light-headed throbbing. He checked his briefcase for damage and pulled the unit from his coat pocket to examine it. His health and vitality was collapsing by the hour and it was obvious he wasn't going to outrun anyone now with the deep snow covering a sheet of ice. He needed to get to a train station, but really had no idea where to head. He looked around trying to orient himself, looking confused. A park police officer silently came up behind him, an apparition slipping out of the snow curtain.

"Sir, can I help you? Are you lost? This park actually is closed due to the storm."

Surprised by the police officer, Berhetzel rotated to face him and said, "Yes, Officer, I'm from out of town and this storm has me disoriented and I can't find a taxi to get me to the train station. My sister is very ill and I need to get to Philadelphia by this evening."

The large Black officer gave him easy to follow instructions and pulled out his notebook to draw a small map to the taxi station. He repeated twice, "After you pass the museum, take the next right, you can't miss the signs."

"Danke," Berhetzel smiled, slipping into his congenial persona. "Would you mind standing by that sign so I can take a photo of my 'Angel of Mercy' against that huge snow drift?"

The big man dropped like a ton of bricks, clueless of what had just happened. The Nazi searched for and removed the man's 9mm Smith and Wesson service pistol, hiding it in the same coat pocket with his weapon. He now had a back-up weapon that wouldn't finger him directly. He knew he was being pursued but between the weather and inauguration chaos, he felt relatively safe. If the U.S. government was already involved, he would already be dead. He decided to draw his pursuers into a lethal trap to take them out as a group. That would be fast, neat and clean. The museum just above the park looked to be a perfect spot to lure them to. He started the climb up from the ravine leaving obvious sign to be followed from the dead cop to the front door of the museum. He entered the deserted lobby and came face to face with a security system that included bag X-ray and an armed guard. He knew his pursuers couldn't be too far behind so he needed a way to get in to lay his trap.

He sent the briefcase through as the guard said, "You will need to check these, sir, they are not allowed in the exhibit area. You might consider returning tomorrow because we are closing in thirty minutes due to the weather as you are the only one visiting now. There will be no one inside to answer your questions, we are the only two that made it in to work today. Now, please come through the body scanner."

Berhetzel didn't see an option, he pulled the gun from his coat and executed the guard and then shot the fleeing, screaming teenage ticket taker. He grabbed his briefcase and ran to the exhibit area. The stress was making it difficult to breath and his chest was tightening into a fist of hard pain. He scanned a large wall map and kept moving deeper to the right to get out of sight. Soon, near what he estimated to be at the far end of the museum he found a convenient emergency exit. Here was where he would make his stand — either taking them out one at a time, or as one larger group and then exiting to the train station and eventually back to La Lupa. He vowed not to fall without taking down these damned pursuers first. He was born for this and he was always victorious, no matter the odds. He WAS the superior being.

Chapter 110

Joseph was hot on the trail and it was leading him and Jean to a park ravine. There they found the dead cop and reported to the rest to head in their direction. There was a trail leading out of the ravine and Joseph studied the snow tracks.

"See these tracks, Jean? They are made by a wolf, and he is leading us to that building just beyond. By the way, wolves have been extinct from this part of the country for over two hundred years! Berhetzel is in there, I know he is."

It was as if a hand was on Joseph's back guiding his hunt. As they got closer, Joseph read the carved granite sign naming the museum.

"National Museum of the American Indians," Joseph nearly shouted, "well, I'll be damned!"

At that moment they heard two shots from inside the museum.

"Come quick," Joseph pleaded on the open mic, "we're just outside the National Indian Museum, the sign says 4th Street and Independence Ave. Two gunshots just came from inside. Get everyone up here including Sullivan right now. I'm afraid the wolf is cornered and is now going to fight to the death!"

Chapter 111

Joseph and Jean didn't wait on the others, they ran up to the entrance and carefully entered where they were greeted by the young woman with a bullet through her neck and the security guard with a hole to his forehead and chest. Jean ran to the entrance to the exhibits and Joseph yelled, "Stop!"

He pointed to the banks of security camera screens next to the dead guard's body and watched as they automatically scrolled through each exhibit area. Berhetzel was moving rapidly toward the rear end of the building. Joseph gave his orders.

"I'll go in on the left, you take the right side and grab some sort of weapon. He's got at least one firearm, but has no idea what we might have. Maybe we can buff him to surrender or at least pin him down until the others get here. Move in carefully and be quiet."

Jean nodded his understanding, started down his side of the circular exhibit's path. Joseph turned away and headed the opposite way searching for a weapon as he passed the elaborate Native American exhibits. He found what he needed and held the old bow as an odd sense of energy surged from his hands and to his heart. He now was the warrior, but hadn't moved on to the next exhibit when he heard angry shouting in French and German tainted English.

The enemies had found each other.

Joseph crept up on the German, whose back was turned away from him, facing Jean, who held a primate stone-tipped spear. He was shouting at Berhetzel to keep attention on himself.

"You are done, bastard!" Jean cursed. "The Indian has gone for help and soon you will be trapped here. Give up now and perhaps you will live long enough to hang. Otherwise, I will kill you!"

"Let me think about that! I have at least two guns and my death ray, and you are going to kill me?" he laughed. "This time I will be sure you are dead along with the others before I escape once more. You see, you are my hostage and bait for the others. If they don't come to your rescue in a couple of minutes, I will simply finish what I started in Paris and be on my way. But I am sure the heroes will try to rescue you."

Jean's eyes found Joseph and glanced over at him. Berhetzel sensing something was wrong, turned to see Joseph with the bow at full draw just as he released the arrow that flew at incredible speed, striking the Nazi in the throat, slicing through his carotids as cleanly as a razor-sharp knife. The museum silence broke to the deafening war cries of generations of Lakota Sioux and the frantic howling of hungry wolves after a fresh kill. Jean ran forward when Berhetzel grabbed his neck and thrust the spear up under his sternum, forcing it with a twist into that black heart. The Destroyer fell, groaning toward the floor as he grabbed the ancient pike that had punctured his heart. He staggered two short steps and collapsed dead onto a museum's exhibit, spilling his blood on the staged battlefield depicting George Armstrong Custer and the Seventh Army's defeat at the hands of the Sioux and Cheyenne at the Little Bighorn.

Epilogue

It was very warm in Paris for mid-July, but Jean's garden courtyard was shaded and the perfect place for Kate and Tom's wedding. The perennials were in full bloom and bees from the rooftop apiaries made it seem like you were in the French countryside. The perfect place for a romantic ceremony. This was the first time they had gathered together since the events in Washington.

July 14th was Bastille Day, a celebration day of French independence from the Monarchy. A special day in Kate's beloved France for her special day.

Brad and his family, Jean, his daughter and grandchildren, Jules with his latest mistress, the four FFL soldiers, their wives and dates, and Joseph all stood up for the couple in a ceremony performed both in French and English ,with a beauty and style that was pure French. There were happy tears all around and even Brad the jokester didn't try to hide his emotions with wisecracks.

After the vows, Jules had prepared an elegant brunch served with lots of fine champagne. Many toasts were offered followed by the traditional 'Santé'. Even Joseph raised his glass although he only sipped a drop or two at each toast.

After the meal they all relaxed and Brad started to pick on Joseph as usual.

"Doesn't it seem a little weird to everyone the way this all played out?" he asked. "I mean, we start looking for the cause of the mass animal die-offs, which turned out to be the work of this 'Destroyer' as envisioned by Joseph's great-grandfather decades ago, end up in Europe chasing a supposed dead Nazi who in reality is an evil genius. We smoke him out in South America, follow him to D.C. where the storm of the century just happens to foil his plan to overthrow the government of the United States. But it doesn't stop there. We topped that by chasing him to the Indian Museum where he is killed by that great grandson of the man who originally dreamt about his plague on the earth. Also he is killed with a piece of crap bow and arrow artifact from the early 18th century, and speared by a Frenchman with another artifact from 15th century Ohio Valley Mound Builders. And I think that shot by Joseph was pure luck. I mean, I would like to see him shoot a shiny red apple off the top of Jules' head, just to see if he really is that good."

Joseph, who was used to the big man's ribbing answered, "Any time, any place. I just need a little time to contact my ancestors because that shot came from them, not me. I had only shot a crossbow hunting so that was the first longbow I ever held, other than the rubber-tipped child's version. It was the Creator with the help of the Ancestors that made that arrow true. The museum director said it was a miracle that ancient dried-out bow could even be drawn back without breaking in half. So it really wasn't me but if you really want to test my marksmanship, I will need a warm up. I think that apple will sit nicely on Brad's fat head."

They all laughed and another toast was offered as the newlywed couple kissed. Jules then gave his take on the recent events.

"Today we gather in Jean's beautiful garden to celebrate Kate and Tom's nuptials. I would like, however, to remember and toast those who started this journey, but are not here to celebrate its completion—Nelson Blackfeather; Jean's father and hero of the Republic, Robert; and Pierre and Jacque who died on this mission in South America. Salute! And to all the others who died at the hands of monsters over the years, rest in peace. Your enemy is dead and in the darkness of Hell. We all need to remember what I told Kate when this first was unfolding — our Lord is always with us and protecting us when He is truly in our hearts. Goodness will prevail over evil, if we are true to Him."

With tears in their eyes, they stood and applauded those who had died. Jules smiled as they responded because he knew his research team had just unlocked the secret of Berhetzel's device. The evil of one man could now be turned to help all of mankind, and it wouldn't be a problem making some money on the side, n'est-ce pas?

CPSIA information can be obtained
at www.ICGtesting.com
Printed in the USA
LVHW082035150422
716311LV00010B/594